DARKNESS HIDES

May 12, 2021

Angelique,
Congratulations on winning the GoodReads contest. I hope you enjoy my new mystery. Let me know if you figure out who the murderer is before its revealed in the end!
All the Best
JC Gatlin

JC GATLIN

MILFORD HOUSE

Milford House Press

Mechanicsburg, Pennsylvania

MILFORD HOUSE
an imprint of Sunbury Press, Inc.
Mechanicsburg, PA USA

FIRST MILFORD HOUSE PRESS EDITION: April 2021

Set in Garamond. Interior design by Chris Fenwick | Cover by Ivan Zanchetta | Edited by Chris Fenwick.

Publisher's Cataloging-in-Publication Data
Names: Gatlin, JC, author.
Title: Darkness Hides / JC Gatlin.
Description: Revised trade paperback edition. | Mechanicsburg, Pennsylvania : Milford House Press, 2021.
Summary: A former Fish and Wildlife Officer finds a string of corpses that appear to have a connection to her estranged sister just as her little beach prepares for an approaching hurricane.
Identifiers: ISBN 978-1-62006-540-2 (softcover).
Subjects: BISAC: FICTION / Mystery & Detective / Amateur Sleuths | FICTION / Mystery & Detective / Women Sleuths | FICTION / Thrillers / Suspense

Continue the Enlightenment!

For James Rouse–

–and all the Taco Tuesdays, old jobs and new homes, classic car shows, live radio DJs, the Outback Pro-Am, Randy Wayne White books, Gulfside Charters, Widespread Panic, and a few crazy stories that can't be repeated here.

CHAPTER ONE

Sunday
August 31

An hour before dawn on an unusually warm Sunday morning, Jasper Wade reversed his truck and trailer toward the concrete ramp at Corman's Launch and guided his boat into the dark waters of Tampa Bay. He really couldn't see much more than a grey curling mist in the pre-dawn light, settling over the bank and cloaking the water's surface. In the distance, the twin smokestacks of the power plant lit-up with yellow lights. They twinkled like stars but didn't provide much light.

He didn't need them anyway. He maneuvered by way of instinct and muscle memory. How many times had he repeated this early morning ritual? Too many to count. In a minute and a half, he'd backed onto the sloping ramp and edged his boat into the water, coming to a stop at just the right point. After forty-five years, he could've done it blindfolded. And in that time, as far as he could remember, he'd never had the jitters.

Until now.

This morning.

For some reason, his hand trembled as if some sixth sense deep in his psyche transmitted a Morse code warning. Maybe it was that hurricane churning in the Gulf. The morning news warned it could hit the area. Still, it was days away--provided it didn't turn northwest and hit the panhandle or the Alabama coast instead, which most of the models predicted. Besides, the Bay looked calm now. Not so much as a breeze. He laughed the thought away and shook his hand.

He'd probably just worked too hard this week. Put in too many billable hours. Taken on too many cases. He needed to cut back. He'd be retiring in a couple of years anyway. He chuckled at the thought. Could he give up his practice and simply fish and golf seven days a week? He loved the courtroom and the cases and picking apart the finer points of the law. That wasn't stressful.

Maybe he felt guilty for ditching church. He'd hear about it later from his wife, for sure. "The Lord may not need a good lawyer," she'd said a million times over. "But there isn't a lawyer on this Earth who doesn't need the good Lord." What could he say? A morning listening to the pastor's continuing sermon on Ruth and the other women in Jesus's family tree couldn't compare to the lure of large redfish and plenty of good-size trout on the flats. Resident tarpon schooled around the bridges. It'd be a good day to fish Weedon Island or Snug Harbor, away from the heavy Labor Day traffic in the open Bay. Today would be relaxing and re-energizing, he knew. So, the shaking had to be something else.

Low blood sugar. That's what he felt. Low blood sugar. He really should've run through the McDonald's drive-through rather than just down a quick cup of coffee at home.

He'd woken at three and dressed as quietly as possible not to wake Liz, the old battle-ax. She tossed in bed when he flipped on the bathroom light but didn't wake. She hated when he chose fishing over church and had no qualms about expressing her displeasure. Determined to prevent any such arguments this morning, he tiptoed out the bedroom and into the kitchen in the dark. The coffee maker gurgled, having come to life with an automatic timer. He grabbed his tackle box and four different rods from the hall closet and carried them into the garage, where his beauty waited.

Olivia.

A Yellowfin 23.

Fast, solid, smooth-riding, and ostentatiously expensive, this boat was the Pride of the Bay with twin Yamaha 200-hp HPDI outboards, built-in transom tackle boxes, a freshwater washdown system, and a console outfitted with a 75-gallon forward coffin-box cooler. A black T-top covered the helm and a tilting stainless-steel destroyer wheel power knob with a lighted switch panel and four-rod rocket launcher. A lockable electronics station boasted a high-end sound system. And his GPS clocked a top speed of twenty-eight mph.

Fast. Solid. And smooth-riding.

He named the boat "*Olivia*" after his daughter, and it centered his whole world. He kept it under a protective tarp in the garage while his truck remained parked in the drive. He talked to it daily, kept it clean and waxed, and well-maintained. Even his phone had more pictures of *Olivia*, the boat, than Olivia, his daughter, if that said anything about his priorities. He loved that Yellowfin 23, if possible, more than life itself.

The boat dominated the garage. And it was a beaut. He ran a hand along the gleaming two-tone hull, caressing it, then picked up a fishing rod like he was offering a gift to the boat gods. Carefully threading a ten-pound braid through the guides, he tied a three-foot, 20-pound fluorocarbon leader using a double uni knot. Once he tipped the leader with a silver Zara spook, he took a moment to admire his work. He couldn't wait to hit the redfish boiling underneath the topwater bait as he *walked the dog.*

He thought about grabbing his .45, but that seemed silly.

Why would he need a gun on the Bay?

The coffee maker beeped, and he filled a thermos. He'd drained the container dry by the time he reached the boat ramp. So, of course, his jittering hand had to be a symptom of too much caffeine–not a concern for the storm circulating in the Gulf or a fear of what his wife will say when he returned home later that afternoon. He smiled, pleased with his diagnosis, and hopped out of the cab. Still, some faint nagging voice inside him just wouldn't quit. And noise in the darkness beyond the white headlight beams made him pause.

The snap of a dead branch. A stirring of leaves in the shadowy brush. The vague feeling of something's presence. A heron screeched, causing him to lift his head toward the cry, then he turned as a pair of intensely bright headlights pulled past the wooden sign welcoming visitors to "Corman's Launch." The tires crunched over the crushed shell and white gravel in the parking area.

He wondered if he'd recognize the approaching truck as he often ran into the same flannel shirts and scruffy faces on the water, especially at this hour. And even if he didn't know their names, he'd know their boat. The headlights nearly blinded him, though, but it looked like they belonged to an old Chevy Hatchback. Ugly as sin. Its body painted an offensive pea-green with chipped and peeling paint. No boat attached.

He chuckled, knowing the driver was probably a lost Weekender—an irritating, pigheaded party animal that usually rose from hibernation during Memorial Day weekend and spent the summer racing jet skis and leaving trash behind for the locals to pick-up. This idiot didn't know Corman's Launch didn't have anything to offer Weekenders. There were no picnic areas or sandy beaches. Just rocky shores and thick mangroves—great for fishing but poor for partying.

Shaking his head, he trotted down the concrete slope and splashed into the shallow water. It came up to his ankles, then his shins, and felt surprisingly cold. He hopped up onto *Olivia.* Muddy boots, four fishing rods, and two tackle boxes covered the floor. Half a beef jerky bag lay crumpled beneath the console, and the meaty smell made his stomach growl. He thought about his low blood sugar again but ignored the pangs and started the motor.

It took three minutes to reverse the *Olivia* off the trailer and release it into the water. He gently beached the boat, nose first, into the sandy shore to the right of the ramp. Hopping off the bow onto the rocky beach, he hastened toward his truck. The hatchback was still there, its engine idling, blaring headlights pointed toward the concrete ramp and onto his idling truck. He wondered now if a pair of teens were looking for a private hidey-hole—though it seemed either too late in the night or too early in the morning for such activities.

Shaking his head, he ignored the stupid teens and hurried across the beach. Another brittle crunch disturbed the dark mangroves. He flinched and searched the shadows--nothing but the idling hatchback, its windshield fogged over.

"Hello?" he yelled. Dumb kids. He continued toward his truck.

Something rustled in the surrounding trees, stirring in the underbrush. The heron flew away.

"Hello?" he yelled again, raising a hand to his brow and squinting into the incandescent headlights.

A black silhouette stood in the white blinding beams.

The sight brought him to a sudden halt, and he almost slipped. His breath caught in his throat.

The figure wore a black sweatshirt, black jeans, and a gray—was it a hat? Some kind of mask? It looked so unreal, so unnatural, so out of place—like a giant stuffed animal. An elephant head with plush grey fur and a comically long trunk, huge floppy ears, and two round button eyes.

Jasper blinked and rubbed his eyes. Opened them.

The figure was gone, no longer standing within the bright headlights of the idling hatchback.

Jasper scanned the woods. He couldn't see much more than fog rising through an impenetrable wall of mangrove trees and underbrush. The towering twin smokestacks of the power plant loomed in the distance. But the beach was quiet. Did he see what he thought he saw? Did he imagine it? No, of course not. He was just getting worked up over nothing. It was probably some pot-smoking teens.

Weekenders. That's all it was. Weekenders. But what could he do?

He rushed forward, moving between the headlight beams of his truck. He hated leaving it parked here with those teens lurking around. They could break in or vandalize it. For now, he needed to move the trailer out of the water. Get to the *Olivia* resting on the beach. He opened the driver's side door and glanced at the running car again.

The pea-green hatchback just sat there. Its engine revved.

"Hey, you guys want something?" he yelled.

No response.

Now there could be no doubt; those kids were up to no good. The underbrush crunched with slow, deliberate footsteps. Branches moved in the darkness. Then came an odd sucking sound, like rubber boots squishing through a muddy puddle, followed by deep, raspy breathing.

"I know you're out there. You're not scaring me." He lunged forward. Froze. The dark turned utterly quiet. Even the insects seemed frightened into silence.

Just feet away, silhouetted in the intense headlight beams, stood that crazy kid. A plush elephant mask obscured his face, pulled down so far over his head that it appeared to rest on his shoulders. His arms were behind him as if hiding something behind his back.

"Who are you?" Jasper stepped back against the door frame of his truck. His voice quivered. "What do you want?"

A muffled voice came from the mask, saying, "His little body looked battered and bloody as if someone picked up a baseball bat and beat the life out of him." Strained, wet wheezing followed. A drooping trunk slapped the figure's chest as two round, black button-eyes stared, unblinking. Gloved hands gripped a wooden club. No, a baseball bat. It cut the air in a sudden blur.

With a crack, Jasper Wade's world went dark.

CHAPTER TWO

Monday
September 1

Kate Parks maneuvered *The Kendell* through the blue waters of the Intracoastal waterway. Her old boat had seen better days, but it remained afloat. Widespread Panic's "*Can't Get High*" blared through the small boat's speakers, announcing her presence to the beachgoers to the east and the island residents to the west. As she slowed, the wind quieted, and the music volume increased. A brown squirrel with a white and black bushy tail and missing its left arm hopped from her left shoulder to her right, hiding in her dark hair as it whipped around her face. It disappeared in the grey hoodie behind her neck, and the wind puffed up her sweatshirt like some kind of windsock. She turned off the music.

"Hold on, Doc," she said, gritting her teeth not so much against the rushing wind but in response to the thumping, rap beats coming from the boat ahead. She slowed the boat. Her sweatshirt deflated while Doc scampered back onto her shoulder. Coming up alongside the party craft, she saw five shirtless boys and three bikini-clad girls standing port-side, all in their mid-teens. They looked down at her as her boat came to a halt.

"There's no drinking on the water," she yelled with her hands on her hips.

A lanky teenage boy with shaggy, sun-bleached hair and wearing swim trunks and sunglasses held a long neck bottle in one hand as he lifted his other to his ear. "What?"

"There's no drinking on the boat," she yelled. Doc stood on his hind legs, perched on her shoulder. He curled a single right arm close to his body and chirped.

"I can't hear you," the teen yelled back. Piercings adorned his nose, cheeks, and lip, and rings hung down from both nipples.

"Chillax, Kate!" One of the girls waved as she turned down the music. "We're not hurting nobody."

"It's not negotiable," Kate screamed, then realized she no longer needed to raise her voice. The rap music had stopped. "You're violating Florida Statute 327.65-2A. No person shall operate any vessel on the waters in such a manner as to exceed a maximum sound level of 90 dB A."

The teens laughed. The boy with the piercings slapped his buddies' shoulders, then waved to Kate. He slid his sunglasses low on his nose. "We turned off the tunes. What more do you want?"

Kate stared at them for several seconds. She self-consciously rubbed her left shoulder, the one with a metal rod and screws holding it together, the result of a nine-month-old gunshot wound that ended her career with Florida Fish and Wildlife. She shook her head and moved her hand away. "It is a violation of Florida law to operate a vessel while impaired by alcohol or other drugs."

"Who says we're impaired?" He pushed the sunglasses back up the bridge of his nose, over a stud glinting in the sunlight, and folded his arms across his bare chest. "And even if we were, what could you do about it?"

His friends laughed.

Kate stepped closer to the edge of her boat. "Do you want to find out?"

He threw up his arms. "Ah, c'mon. You're bluffing."

"I'm not bluffing."

He nodded at his friends then back at her. "We took your boat safety classes and know you're not a real cop. You can't arrest us. You can't even write a ticket."

"I'm a Florida Fish and Wildlife Officer on inactive duty status and currently temporarily working with the Sienna Key law enforcement," Kate said.

The kid shrugged. "So?"

"So, *Allen Snead*..." Kate emphasized his name as Doc jumped from her shoulder to the console, next to her iPhone. She grabbed the phone and held it up for the teenagers to see. "Sienna Key is a small town, and I know your father. You want me to give him a call?"

Her iPhone beeped as she held it in the air. She glanced at the screen. The name "Fun Size" appeared next to a smiling, red-headed male face, along with the text message: "Question: where's the extra paper plates?" Ignoring it, she raised her phone again. Doc chattered on the console, whipping his bushy tail and chirping.

She regarded him a moment, then focused on the teens in the boat. "So, Allen Snead, what's it gonna be? Get rid of the alcohol or explain this party to your father—this party on his three-hundred-thousand-dollar boat?"

He stared at her for several moments as if considering her bluff. "What're you gonna do? Call all our parents?"

"No, Allen," she said. "Just yours."

Allen let out a defiant huff and flipped his bottle upside down over the side of the boat, pouring the beer into the water. His friends followed, dumping their bottles. Kate yelled at them as Doc twirled and squealed, landing back on her shoulder. The blonde girl on the boat waved at her.

"Miss Parks, I know you're not with Fish and Wildlife anymore, but..." She hesitated, looking at her friends. "We saw something weird."

Kate watched the girl a moment. "What'd you see?"

"There's a pontoon boat just floating out there. It has a little dog in it."

Allen shouted at her, telling her to hush. She pushed him away.

"No one on it or nothin," she continued. "Just the little dog."

Kate watched Allen a moment, then the other kids. She stared at the blonde girl. "Did you call the police?"

"No," she said. "We'd been drinking and, well, you know---"

"We thought we might get busted." Her girlfriend came up beside her, holding the empty beer bottle.

"Maybe you could call it in or go check it out or something," the blonde continued.

"Where'd you see it?"

"Out by Widow Rock." The girl pointed north. "You know, the old lighthouse on the other side of the island."

Kate glanced at Doc. The squirrel chirped and bounced down the back of her neck, leaning slightly to the right with his single front paw. He disappeared into the pouch of her hoodie. Waving at the kids, she whipped her boat around and hit the throttle. *The Kendell* sped through the blue waters, picking up speed. Running alongside the island, she maneuvered out of the Intercoastal and looped back north. Five minutes later, Widow Rock loomed in the distance.

The lighthouse stood like a relic now, outdated and rotting in the salty winds and sun. Sunlight glinted off the panes in the tower, and for a moment, she thought it lit-up. Just an illusion, though. The lantern in that old structure hadn't shined in decades.

Beyond it, on the horizon, red and blue flags flapped wildly atop an olive-green pontoon boat floating aimlessly like a ghost ship in the choppy waves. She slowed *The Kendell* and pulled up alongside the derelict craft. Doc came out of the pouch in her hoodie to peek over her shoulder. The squirrel chattered at something, and then she saw it too. A white English bulldog stood at the helm, barking, and ran to Kate's position as she grasped the handrails.

"Hello there," she said to the dog, holding out a hand, palm up. It couldn't have been more than a year old. Watching her with large chocolate eyes highlighting a wrinkled, sagging face, it sniffed her fingers. Satisfied, he snorted and sneezed and wagged a stubby tail. She laughed. "Where's your owners?"

Doc stretched his furry body from her shoulder toward the boat, curling his single tiny hand and sniffing the air. The dog barked, and Doc stiffened, then scuttled down her shoulder and returned to her hoodie's pouch. Kate felt the squirrel's weight on the back of her neck as she secured the tie line to the cleat. A moment later, she climbed aboard the empty pontoon boat. The bulldog approached and sniffed her leg. Content, he snorted and looked up, wagging his stubby tail.

Kate looked around. No keys in the ignition. No fishing tackle. No sign anyone had been driving. Doc snuck out from her hoodie and peeked over her shoulder. He chattered as she bent down and petted the fat bulldog. Tags jangled from his collar, and he snorted and licked her hand. She read the engraved info and found the name "Tug" printed on the front. The back displayed an address and phone number. "Well, hello, Tug," she said. "Good to meet you."

The bulldog wagged its tail and seemed to respond to hearing his name.

When her iPhone buzzed, she straightened and glanced at the screen. Again, the name "Fun Size" appeared next to the smiling, red-headed male face. The message read:

"PAPER PLATES????"

Glancing at Tug, she typed back: "Why?" and hit send.

A response came right back.

"Chips and queso for the group."

Kate didn't reply and instead ran her thumb over the contact list and found "Chief Trace Guerra." When he answered, she could hear the irritation.

"Why are you calling me?" His loud voice crackled through her phone's speakers. "You better not be on the clock."

"Trace, I've got a derelict vessel with a lone bulldog in it," she said.

"And you found this derelict vessel while having fun on the water?" he asked. "Cause you know, it's Labor Day, and you're not on active duty."

"I know. I know," she said. "You don't have to keep telling me that."

"Well, obviously, I do."

"Look, I'm calling as a concerned citizen. I've got an abandoned pontoon boat with somebody's pet in it. There's no sign of the owners."

"You think someone fell overboard?"

"I don't think so." She scanned from bow to stern again. No fishing equipment. No cooler. No radio. No sign of anyone. There weren't even keys in the ignition. "It looks like it might have broken free from dock somewhere. I can tow it in. You want to meet me at the pier?"

"You don't have to do that," he said as if losing his patience. "It's not your job any—"

She didn't let him finish. "The dog's name is Tug, and he's got tags with the owner's address."

"Kate—"

"I'm just being neighborly," she added. "Just a concerned citizen reporting a derelict vessel as defined in s.327.02 of Florida Statutes. See you at the pier."

She slipped her phone back in her pocket as she progressed to the boat's console. It took a few minutes for her to look up the owner—a Jerry and

Maxine Flagg of 4848 Sunset Ave.—and another half hour to tow their boat back to the marina at Sienna Key.

Chief Trace Guerra stood waiting for her. A broad man with a thick body and a large head made even larger by a shaggy black beard and hair to match, he wore a tan uniform with short sleeves and a black cowboy hat.

"You know it's Labor Day," he called out to her.

"All day long."

"You're not even supposed to be working, and you're certainly not supposed to be patrolling the waterways."

"I wasn't doing either." Kate avoided eye contact with him as she tied off *The Kendell* and leaped onto the dock. The bulldog followed, sniffing the planks of the boardwalk. "I don't have to tell you that we don't have the luxury of days off. We're servants of the people."

"You're a—"

She raised a hand and stopped him. "No sign of the owners or anyone else on the boat." Doc vaulted onto her shoulder and chirped at the Chief. Kate nudged the one-armed squirrel with her cheek.

Trace regarded her a moment, then said, "I called the Coast Guard. They're searching the area, just in case." He stood close to six feet, maybe a little taller in his boots. He was forty-five years old and looked it, with grey streaks along the edges of his temples, running through his black hair and framing deep-set brown eyes. He removed his black cowboy hat to wipe sweat from his forehead.

Doc hopped from Kate's shoulder to his. He jumped, startled when the squirrel landed on him, and he shook his head at Kate. "I don't want your rodent."

The bulldog cocked its head, watching the commotion with great interest.

"His name is Doc, and just hold him a minute." She stripped out of the sweatshirt and stood in the warm sun, wearing a dark blue T-shirt. "No keys. No fishing gear. Not even as much as a lure," she continued. "I don't think there's anyone out there."

His head turned to the water. "You found the boat out by Widow Rock?"

"Abandoned and adrift."

The bulldog stepped beside Kate and lifted his head. His eyes followed the squirrel's movement.

The Chief reached for the squirrel, but it deftly avoided his hand, launching itself up his chest and onto his shoulder. "And the owner's address is in Palma Sola," he said, grazing his index finger through its tail. The squirrel leaped from his right shoulder around to his left.

"That's what it says," Kate said, not paying attention.

"If the boat just broke loose, how'd it get all the way from Palma Sola to Widow Rock?"

"You got me."

He wiped his forehead. "I'm sending a car to the Flagg's address to check it out."

"You don't have to. It's just twenty minutes from here. I can go check on the residence." She looked down at Tug. "You ready to go home?"

The dog watched her, panting. Doc leaped from Trace's shoulder onto Kate and chirped. She gave it a quick pat atop the head. Tug wagged his tail, running around Kate's legs as the squirrel climbed from her shoulders onto her back.

The Chief shook his head. "Kate, c'mon. You don't have to do this."

"I want to. I really do."

"Would you just go home?"

"*You* go home." She ascended the dock then stopped. The bulldog cut short with her. "How's Nellie?"

The Chief smiled. "Nellie's eight months and seven days. How do you think she is?"

"Did she get the book of baby names?"

"She did." His lips curled into a thin smile. "We've already chosen a name, though."

Kate continued. "I highlighted the ones that work well with your last name. Guerra isn't an easy name to pair with. And it had to be a strong name with character and definition."

"You highlighted girl names," he said flatly as if they'd had this conversation a dozen times before.

Kate continued anyway. "Repeating sounds in a first and last name are more pleasing, so I only highlighted names with one or more of the following letters: G, U, E, R, A." She spoke fast before his attention span could waver. "But I eliminated names ending with the letters G and A to create better rhythm and flow."

Trace raised a hand, stopping her. "You highlighted girl names."

"You're having a girl." Her voice was firm, final.

He shook his head. "No, Kate, We're not."

"All the signs say otherwise."

He shook his head. "Kate . . . go home. Catch ya' in the Bear's Den mañana."

"I am, I mean, I will." She waved goodbye and shuffled across the boardwalk. Glancing over her shoulder, she yelled back, "But, first, I'm stopping at the Flaggs. I have their dog."

Trace let out a loud breath and called to her. "Hey, Kate."

She stopped and turned. "Hey, what?"

"Stack them eights!"

She shot him a quick smile. "Stack them eights," she repeated.

As the authorities impounded the pontoon boat, Kate led the bulldog from the pier to the parking lot where her white Tahoe waited.

"C'mon, fat boy." She was sure he understood. "Let's get you home."

* * *

An old Chevy hatchback with a faded, peeling green paint job rolled off the Causeway into Sienna Key and pulled into the Starlight Motel parking lot. A pretty girl in jeans and a light blue cotton blouse got out of the hatchback and hesitated beside the side mirror. She could see the Causeway bridge from there and the makeshift memorial of black balloons and white cross along the exit ramp. A salty breeze came off the Bay and jostled the balloons. The wind tousled her hair, and she pushed a strand from her face. After a moment, she looked away from the sad little memorial and carried her suitcases into the front office.

"One room, please."

A man behind the front desk looked down at her. "Single or a double?"

"Single." She handed her credit card and driver's license to him across the counter. "And I'd like a room with a view of the Causeway off-ramp."

"A view of the ramp?" His eyes narrowed, puzzled.

"Yes." She looked back out the window and at the black balloons swaying in the breeze. "Yes, I'd like a room that looks out at the Causeway."

"Very well." He glanced at her driver's license, looked at her, then back at the card.

"Is there a problem?" she asked.

He shook his head and ran the card. "Thank you, Miss Wade."

He handed it back to her.

She took it and smiled at him. "It's Olivia. Olivia Wade."

CHAPTER THREE

Kate left the marina with Tug sitting in the passenger seat and Doc in a squirrel crate buckled in the back. She drove onto the narrow streets of Sienna Key. Located on a barrier island off the coast of Manatee County, it snuggled between the southern mouth of Tampa Bay and the northern tip of Anna Maria.

Downtown Sienna Key on Labor Day looked the same as any summer day. The tourist invasion was on, and the out-of-state license plates outnumbered the Florida plates three to one. Along Main Street, with its colorful shops promoting beach supplies, swimsuits, souvenirs, and restaurants, people window-shopped along the sidewalks. Around them, sleek BMWs and rental cars competed with golf carts for parking spots.

Kate flipped on the radio as a newscaster finished the latest update on the hurricane.

If there was any tension about the impending hurricane, there wasn't much evidence of it. False alarms inundated the community over the years. Most times, storms in the Gulf blew farther west, plaguing Galveston and the Texas coast. Sometimes their force was exaggerated by newscasters taking advantage of a ratings boost. The long holiday weekend gave little attention to the storm and instead focused on exciting Labor Day festivities. The parade went by without a hitch, even though Mayor Bentwood slipped in the rear viewing stand under the influence of too much Fireball Whiskey. The Palma Sola Bay Yacht Club held its annual Labor Day Eve gala. The evening was marred only by developer Forrest Frazier slipping his hand under Abigale Anders' braless evening gown in the middle of the dance floor, where he landed on his butt after Willie Anders unceremoniously decked him.

The only outward sign of concern on Main Street was the card table set up outside the town hall building, where a group of college protesters handed out flyers. They competed with the annual outdoor art show. The easels and displays of local artists and their vivid paintings of sailboats and seascapes crowded the sidewalks along Main Street. The students were vocal and determined, despite the competition from the artists.

As Kate paused at a red light, a young woman left the card table and approached her vehicle. She tapped on the glass. Considering it an invitation, the bulldog barked and climbed across the center console into Kate's lap. She pushed him back into the passenger seat and rolled down the window. The woman thrust a red sheet of paper into the car. Kate took the flyer and glanced at the headline pleading to save the old Widow Rock Lighthouse.

"Will you sign a petition to make the lighthouse a historic landmark?" the girl asked, leaning into the window. "When we get enough signatures, we're going to take it to city council."

Below the headline, details of food, games, and live music at the Tiki Hut–a little seafood bar and grille downtown–were listed in bright bullet points. And, printed in large block letters was "Darren Riggler and the Repeaters: live all afternoon." She smiled and whispered the name Darren Riggler.

Talk about a blast from the past. As noble as it would be to save the old lighthouse, it would be nice to see Darren again too…

The girl continued. "We're having a benefit for the lighthouse tomorrow at the Tiki Hut if you'd like to join us."

Kate thanked her and promised to try. She rolled forward when the light flashed green.

She sympathized with their cause. She had a history with the old Widow Rock Lighthouse. Growing up near it, she and her sister would sneak inside and play on its long spiral staircase and around the old lantern at the top. Now a development company wanted to knock it down and build condos or something in its place.

Kate cruised toward the Causeway, the umbilical bridge connecting the island to the mainland. Its lanes were crowded with heavy vacation traffic, cars returning home with sleepy kids, lawn furniture, ice chests, and inflatable water toys. She slowed, waiting in a line of traffic for the bridge.

In the grass to the side at the exit ramp, she noticed the wreath of flowers and a white cross planted near the curb. Three black balloons were tied to the cross and swayed in the breeze. She'd promised herself she wouldn't look at it, but she just couldn't help it. Just as quickly, she looked away.

Her iPhone buzzed, and she expected to see Fun Size's grinning face appear on the screen. She'd forgotten to respond to his question about paper plates. It was her brother-in-law, though.

"Redd?" she asked, answering the call. The timing was almost eerie, and she glanced at the swaying black balloons above the cross again. "H-How you been?"

"Holding up." His voice was quiet through her car speakers, and she turned up the volume as he cleared his throat. He sounded nervous. "Your sister needs you."

"I seriously doubt that."

"She's not doing well. She hasn't been well since . . ." His voice fell quiet. "Since, you know…it happened."

She stared at the memorial. The wreath and three black balloons looked new, even though the white cross appeared weathered and dirty. It'd been standing there for a solid year now. She diverted her eyes and focused on the call. "Elise made it pretty clear that she never wanted to speak to me again."

"You're family. She's your sister. No matter what was said or done, that will never change."

"She blames me. I mean, she didn't even visit me in the hospital."

"I know. That wasn't right. We should've been there for you." He cleared his throat. "How's your recovery going? Are you okay?"

"Look, Redd. If things have changed, just tell her to call me, I'll pick up." A police scanner affixed to the center console crackled with a request from dispatch with the Florida Fish & Wildlife Commission, interrupting her. The noise startled the bulldog, and he sniffed the small, black device. Her old partner's familiar voice responded. It sounded like a busy day at Fish and Wildlife. Labor Day weekend always was. She glanced at the scanner and killed the volume. The bulldog licked it, and she gently pushed his head away. Strictly speaking, she wasn't even supposed to have a police scanner, but she found it online for $129, and it made her feel connected to her old job. Her old life. She realized Redd was still talking as his voice came through the car speakers. She'd almost forgotten about him. "Listen, I'm working, and I've got to go," she said, interrupting him. "Tell Elise to call me."

"You know she won't," he said, almost as somber as he began. "You need to call her. If you want to fix this, you need to just come over."

"I'll try." She disconnected the call with her brother-in-law as her old partner's voice came through the scanner again. She cranked the volume and listened to their conversation: Florida Fish and Wildlife business.

Traffic finally moved, and she rolled forward, leaving the call and the memorial and the horrible memory behind. Crossing over the Causeway to the mainland, she drove into Bradenton, a city of just under 60,000 people between Tampa and Sarasota. She pulled onto Manatee Avenue and proceeded to the Palma Sola Club, a luxury community of estate homes that dotted the shoreline of a cozy inlet off the Intracoastal Waterway. Some featured in architecture magazines and television programs detailing the glamourous life. Others served as winter retreats for CEOs, baseball players, and rumor had it, the father of a teenage pop star.

Tug seemed to recognize the area and stood up on his hind legs in the passenger seat. He planted his front paws on the window.

Kate came to a small, gated community and waited at the front gates. A security guard waved to her.

"Officer Parks, what brings you out here?" he asked.

Kate pet the bulldog's head. "I'm looking for Jerry and Maxine Flagg of 4848 Sunset Avenue. I've got their dog."

"I think they left town," he said. "Gosh, Kate, it's good to see you. How long has it been? What're you doin' since—well, since, you know…you left."

"I haven't left the Fish and Wildlife Commission," she said and rubbed her left shoulder. It constantly ached, reminding her of the screws and metal rod holding it together. "I'm just on leave while I recuperate, but I'll be back."

"Of course. Course you will," he said. It was a pity platitude, and she recognized it in his voice immediately as he continued. "We're pull'n for ya, Kate. We're all pull'n for ya."

He waved her through, and Kate drove along the heavily landscaped streets lined with palm trees. Tug's stubby tail wagged faster, and drool spilled from his mouth. He licked the glass, leaving behind a slurpy trail of saliva.

She wound through the neighborhood and found the address, a greyish blue two-story with an empty driveway and storm shutters covering the windows. She parked and climbed out of her Tahoe. With Tug following close behind, she approached the front door and rang the bell. No answer. After a moment, she knocked.

Clearly, Jerry and Maxine Flagg of 4848 Sunset Ave. had already left town, probably to a home up north. Walking around back, she found a dock where the boat had perhaps broken free. She looked out at the water when her iPhone buzzed with another incoming text. She glanced at the screen and saw the name "Fun Size" next to that grinning goofy male face. She read the message.

"Found paper plates.

New question: Any mayo?"

Glancing at the fat dog watching her every move, she typed back, "NO!!!" and hit send.

When no reply came back, she slipped her phone in her pocket as she walked to the front of the property. She returned to the Tahoe, with the bulldog following, and radioed Trace.

"The house is locked up," she said into the handset. "Hurricane shutters are up. No one appears to be home. Front gate security says they left town. Looks like they just left their dog behind."

"People do weird things when the media starts hyping up a storm." Trave's voice came through loud over the car's speakers.

She nodded and looked up at the sky. There was no sign of the hurricane yet, but the media coverage started days earlier. And the storm had a name: Sebastian.

Satellite photos revealed Sebastian as an imposing Category 4 filling much of the Gulf of Mexico, spanning more than 420 miles with spiraling winds of 130 miles-per-hour. And it was deadly. The storm already ripped across Cuba, leaving behind a wreck of buildings and homes in its wake. Now, churning over the warm Gulf waters, Sebastian grew stronger with each passing day. Forecasters feared Alabama and the Florida panhandle were in its path.

"So far, it looks like it's heading north," Kate said, noticing the birds in the sky. "Still with hurricanes, you never know."

"You never know," Trace repeated.

"Panama Beach has got a bullseye on it, and maybe Destin. I doubt we have anything to worry about." Kate looked down at Tug and then back up overhead. Dozens of birds filled the sky, all headed south, and she wondered if the wildlife knew something the weatherman didn't.

"What are you gonna do with the dog?" Trace's voice crackled over the radio.

"Take him home for the night, I guess," she said. "The vet won't be open today."

"Then will you just go home already?" he asked.

"I am," she said, then thought of something that just had to be said. "But Chief, I want you to take a serious look at that baby name book."

"We've already named the baby," he said. "It's Thomas. After Nellie's father."

"Are you two familiar with assonance?" She didn't wait for him to answer. "Assonance takes place when two or more words close to one another repeat the same vowel sound. It's common in poetry and song lyrics. By repeating vowel sounds in a first and last name, you can create a name with rhythm."

"Again, we've already named the baby."

"I created a separate assonance chart matching vowel sounds in Guerra," she said, not listening. "It's a loose sheet of paper I just slipped into the book, so be careful. It might fall out."

"Kate," he said. "I'm hanging up now."

"Okay, I get it." Maybe she was overstepping some stupid line, but she had to do something for him. He'd always been there for her—like a surrogate Dad when her own father up and left. He even pulled some strings to get her on the Sienna Key police team after her injury. Helping him plan for their first child was the least she could do. "I guess we'll see," she said, but the line had already disconnected.

Climbing into her white Tahoe, she waited in the driveway for a moment. Tug sat in the passenger seat, trembling. Jumping up, he put his paws on the passenger window. Doc chirped in the back seat and rattled the water bottle in his cage, and the bulldog's head turned sharply toward the noise.

In all the commotion, Kate had forgotten about the earlier text message. She took out her phone and pulled up the contacts. Finding "Fun

Size," she typed, "You know I don't allow mayo in the house." She shook her head and hit send. She waited for a reply. When none came, she added, "What's going on at my house?"

Still, no reply.

Tug stared at her. She stared at the screen, waiting for Ian's answer.

A minute later, she tossed the phone on the console and started the engine. The bulldog whined as they backed out of the driveway, and he jumped into the back seat, pawing at the rear window.

Calling the dog, she left Palma Sola and returned to Manatee Avenue, headed for home. Fun Size was up to something, and it was time to find out what.

* * *

Olivia Wade parked the old Chevy hatchback in downtown Sienna Key and walked along the crowded Main Street. A college girl approached her with a flyer, and Olivia took it with little interest.

"We're having a fundraiser to save the old Widow Rock Lighthouse," the girl said. "It'll be at the Tiki Hut."

"The Tiki Hut?' Olivia glanced at the flyer. "Where is that?"

The girl pointed and said, "Just a couple of blocks."

"I'll be there." Olivia paused and studied the girl with the armful of colorful flyers. She removed a photograph from her purse and held it up. "Have you seen this woman? Do you know her?"

The girl studied it for a second. "Oh, yeah. I've seen her before, but I don't know her."

Olivia thanked her and headed the couple of blocks to the Tiki Hut. She found a table in the crowded restaurant. A few minutes later, a waitress arrived and handed her a menu.

"I'm looking for someone," Olivia told her and fished the photograph from her purse. "Have you seen this woman before? I understand she works for the Florida Fish and Wildlife Commission."

The waitress glanced at the photo and smiled. "Oh, yeah," she said. "That's Kate Parks, but she doesn't work for Fish and Wildlife anymore."

CHAPTER FOUR

Kate drove to Palmetto Gardens, a mobile home park situated where the Manatee River flowed into the wide-open Gulf of Mexico at the southern tip of Tampa Bay. She parked at a narrow pier with twenty houseboats tied up along either side. Hers was the last one on the end, a floating white houseboat that rose and fell with the river.

She let Doc out of his cage in the backseat, and he scampered over the headrest, tipping to his right as he moved. An unusual number of minivans filled the parking lot, along with a light blue Vespa scooter. Fun Size was here, and she wondered what he was up to. She glanced at the flyer on the passenger seat and picked it up. Carrying it one hand, she tried to lift the bulldog with the other, which proved impossible. Even without a nagging shoulder injury, Tug would've been too heavy for her carry. He plopped to the pavement in a flurry of white fur, stubby legs, and slobber. Jumping to his feet, he looked up at her. She whistled, and he followed as she walked up the dock, her footsteps sounding hard against the wooden planks. Doc chirped on her shoulder as if tattling on the dog, and Kate found Tug sniffing the posts. She whistled again, and he waddled behind her to the houseboat.

As big as an average apartment, Kate's houseboat rose two stories high, with a sliding glass door along the upper bedroom that opened onto a spacious deck, decorated with chairs and a table, and a large umbrella. Directly beneath it, the front door opened into a living room, kitchen, and dining area.

Kate brought Tug aboard and entered the floating home.

"Fun Size, you here? I got your---" She stopped, surprised to find a crowd of women crammed in her small living space. Four ladies were seated on her sofa, others on chairs, and even more sat on the floor among scattered posterboards and markers. Fun Size stood in the center of the room as if holding court. Kate wasn't sure to make of it. "What's going on here?"

"I told you not to call me that!" Fun Size, aka Ian Biggs, placed his hands on his hips and glared at her. A year younger, fifteen pounds lighter, and a full inch shorter than Kate, he wore shorts and a vertically striped shirt. His fair skin looked even whiter contrasted with his bright red hair. He shot her a puzzled glance as if her question was absurd. "Whaddya mean, what's going on?"

Kate studied the twelve women invading her space, many holding babies in their arms. That at least explained the succession of minivans in the parking lot.

"Fun Size," she said.

He cringed and glared at her. "Don't call me that."

"Who are these people?" she asked, ignoring him.

"Meet the Mommy Warriors." He waved an arm toward his army of mothers sitting on the couch, chairs, and even standing by the sliding glass doors to the patio. "We're planning a rally to save the Widow Rock Lighthouse," he said.

Of course, the lighthouse. Kate glanced at the flyer and set it on the end table by the couch. The bulldog huddled behind her legs and let out a bark.

The commotion ruffled the feathers of an owl seated on a perch above a large cage in the corner. A curved head spun around, revealing a bird with only one large round eye. She winked at it, and it winked back. Tug cautiously approached the perch and sniffed the base.

One of the ladies held a finger sandwich in one hand and motioned to Kate with the other. "Is this your place? And, if so, do you have any mayonnaise?"

Kate stared at her, wide-eyed. "What do you want to do with it?"

"I want to put it on these sandwiches," she said. "I looked for a jar in your fridge but couldn't find any."

"I don't allow mayonnaise in this house." Kate snatched the sandwich from the woman's hand and gave it to the bulldog. The woman gasped as Kate turned to Ian. "Why are you having your meeting here?"

"Simple. My Smother won't let me have our meeting at her house," he said. He handed her a sign with the phrase "Save Our Lighthouse" painted in large red letters.

"C'mon! Work with me." Kate took the sign and placed it on the end table. "My place isn't big enough for a meeting either."

"But there's no mother hoovering over us here." He held up another hand-painted sign. "Look...we're running out of time before bulldozers knock down the lighthouse and condos go up, and we lose a valuable piece of this island's history."

Kate glanced at the flyer on the table. "I saw that you're having some benefit at the Tiki Hut to get people to sign a petition."

A woman rose from the couch. "If we can get enough signatures, we can present it to the city council, and they can designate Widow Rock, a historic landmark."

Ian nodded. "Fact. We're running out of time. We've got to act fast."

"We who?"

"These twelve concerned mothers." Ian gestured toward his team.

"And every concerned citizen of Sienna Key." A woman rose from the sofa and shook Kate's hand. "My name is Diana," she said. "Princess of the Amazons. Protector of the Weak. Defender of the Downtrodden."

"Isn't that Wonder Woman?" Kate stepped back from her.

Diana smiled. "If the tiara fits…"

Kate shook her head slowly and wondered what she'd gotten herself into. "Look, I think everything you're doing is great, and I'll try to show up to the benefit tomorrow and sign the petition, but, come on… don't you think it's too little, too late?"

"Forrest Frazier is a Kingpin." Ian pounded his right fist into his left hand as his voice rose with excitement. "We stopped his development before. We'll do it again," he added as the women around him cheered. "As long as the lighthouse is standing, we can save it." He handed her another sign.

Kate took it, glanced at it, then handed it back to him. "As I said, I'll come by if I have time, but I'm not making any promises. I have to work."

"That's an excuse."

"That's life." Kate picked up several signs lying on the floor. "The Kingpin won. His development plans are happening whether we like it or not."

Diana stepped beside Kate and helped pick up the signs. "Can't you do something?" she asked. "Don't you know someone? You used to work for the Fish and Wildlife Commission."

Kate rose and stiffened. "I *still* work for Florida Fish and Wildlife," she said, emphasizing 'still.' "I'm just on inactive duty status and currently temporarily working with the Sienna Key law enforcement."

"Join us." Ian placed a hand on her shoulder. "Tomorrow morning. We'll make a difference, just like old times."

Kate glanced down at him, still holding several protest signs in her arms. "I can't," she said.

"We stopped him from mowing down 130 acres of Florida panther habitat for a housing development. We can stop him from tearing down the lighthouse too."

She looked away. She knew she was disappointing him, but what could she do?

He fired back at her. "Fine. Have it your way." His brows drew downward in a frown, and he snatched the signs from her arms. He motioned to the women in the room and marched to the door.

Kate looked after him. "Wait. Where are you going?"

"Home," he said. "I'd rather deal with my Smother than all the negative vibes you're putting out."

"I'm not putting out any vibes. I just can't make any promises for tomorrow," she said. She stopped him, and her voice softened. "C'mon, you don't have to go. It's Labor Day. Let's grill some hamburgers. Watch a movie. We'll find something to binge on Netflix."

"I have work to do."

"Fun Size . . ."

"Don't call me that!"

"Okay, Ian . . ." She tried to disguise her annoyance in front of the others. "Please . . ."

"What?"

"You can stay. All of you," she said, looking at the group of women crowding the doorway. "I can ask one of the neighbors if they have some . . ." She cringed as the word came from her mouth. ". . . mayonnaise."

"It's going to take more than mayonnaise to save the lighthouse." He held the door open as the women filed out. He looked back at her. "And when did you get a dog?"

Kate looked over at Tug. "He's a rescue. His family abandoned him," she said. "I'll take him to the kennel tomorrow."

His head turned from the bulldog to the one-eyed owl to the one-armed squirrel perched on her shoulder. "Another animal? And I thought my place was crowded."

Kate watched him leave. Exhaling, she wondered what to do with the plate of finger sandwiches then placed it on the floor for Tug.

"We don't need him anyway," she said as the bulldog wolfed down the sandwiches.

When he finished, she picked up the plate and meandered into the kitchenette. Tug snorted and raced behind her, followed by the limping squirrel. The owl screeched and flew into the kitchen, where it crashed into the wall and tumbled to the floor.

Kate picked the bird up and perched him on the back of a chair. "You gotta be careful, Bert. You only got one eye," she said as she walked to the fridge cluttered with drawings held in place by magnets. All depicted a stick figure woman with a gun protecting a stick-figure child. A stick figure man in black spewed scribbles of deep red. The whole scene made her shoulder ache, and she caught herself rubbing her upper arm again. She stopped and opened the fridge door.

"Mayonnaise—uggh," she muttered under her breath and recoiled at the thought.

Tuesday
September 2

Early the following day, Kate rushed out her boathouse as she slipped on her shoes and buttoned her blouse. Tug followed, and she loaded him into her Tahoe and flew out the parking lot without even buckling her seatbelt.

Sitting on top of the yellow book in the passenger seat, the bulldog looked up at her as if trying to figure out where she was taking him.

She intended to drop him at the kennel on her way into Bradenton. She was out of time, though, and instead drove straight to the Coastal Care Medical Center. Ten minutes past her appointment, she parked, grabbed her purse, and whistled for Tug to follow her into the building. Once inside, she told him to "sit" as she stepped to the front desk. A receptionist looked up from her computer. Kate nodded.

"I'm Kate Parks, Florida Fish and Wildlife Officer on inactive duty status and currently temporarily working for the Sienna Key law enforcement," she said, reciting the words like a mantra. She didn't need to provide all that information, as it wasn't relevant, and they already knew who she was and why she was there. She'd been attending physical therapy there for the last nine months. But stating and restating that she still worked for the FWC and that her position with the Sienna Key law enforcement was temporary had become a habit, if not a reminder.

The receptionist stared glassy-eyed at her.

Kate let her purse fall from her shoulder. "I have an eight o'clock appointment," she added.

"You're late," came a booming female voice to the left, and Kate turned to see a large woman with curly hair and dressed in blue scrubs standing in the doorway to the back offices. The woman pointed at the dog. "You can't be bringin' no rottweiler in her."

Tug looked up at the woman and spun in a circle, inviting her to pet his rear.

"Wilhelmina," Kate said. "I'm sorry I'm late."

"Late or not, you can't be bringin' no rottweiler in here." Wilhelmina pointed at the dog with her clipboard. "You take him and leave him in the car."

"It's too hot to leave him in the car," Kate said. "His name is Tug. And besides, he's not a rottweiler. He's a bulldog." She whistled for Tug to follow.

Wilhelmina talked as they wound through the building, holding her clipboard like a weapon, and never took her eyes off the bulldog. "Lawd, oh' Lawd! As if running late isn't bad enough, you bring a vicious rottweiler in her with you," she said, walking swiftly ahead of them. "There oughtta be a law."

She led them into a locker room, where Kate changed into shorts and a tank top. She dropped her purse in the cubby and shut it. The locker room opened into an even larger area in the back that looked like a small gymnasium. Dozens of patients walked between parallel bars and rode stationary bikes. Others sat or lay on mats with a physical therapist assisting with leg stretches and bending exercises. Wilhelmina led Kate to a reach 'n range overhead pulley system. Kate sat in the chair as her physical therapist put down her clipboard and adjusted the machine's controls.

"Have you been doing your daily exercises?" she asked, still eyeing Tug and keeping her distance. Tug sniffed her leg, and she jumped, backing away from him.

Kate nodded. "Three times a day," she lied, watching the woman grab the clipboard and use it to push the dog away.

Tug looked hurt by the woman's reaction and shuffled over to an elliptical and sniffed a metal leg. Kate called him, and he returned to her side. She looked at Wilhelmina. "When is the doctor gonna let me go back to work?"

Wilhelmina glanced up from her clipboard. "Your doctor released you for work two months ago…at the police station."

"I mean my job with Florida Fish and Wildlife."

"Raise your right arm," Wilhelmina instructed. Kate complied and stretched her right arm high above her head. Tug watched intently. The therapist then nodded to Kate's left. "Now, your other arm."

Kate raised her left arm, but it didn't go as high. She brought it about even with her ear, then winced. She dropped it back down.

"Exactly," Wilhelmina said, shaking her head and making a note on the chart on her clipboard. She then adjusted the weights. "Mmmm-hhhmmm! Now less talk and more stretch'n."

Kate sat back, grabbed the pulleys with both hands, and pulled with her left. Her left arm came toward her as her right arm extended. She pulled with her right, and her left arm extended. The weights rose and fell in rhythm with her breathing, and Wilhelmina smiled.

Tug sat on the floor, mesmerized.

"Good girl," Wilhelmina said, still eyeing the dog. "I'll be back in fifteen."

She left, and Kate continued with the arm pulls. It had become a morning ritual ever since she was shot in the line of duty nine months ago. The bullet shattered her shoulder, and after two surgeries and a solid nine-months of physical therapy, she still wasn't a hundred percent. She was getting better, though slowly.

Tug watched her, his head rising and falling with the weights. Ten minutes into it, a young lady with blonde curly hair approached. Wearing jeans and a light blue blouse with a floral pattern, she didn't look like a patient or a therapist.

"Ms. Parks?" she asked, standing over her.

Kate looked up but continued pulling the weight. "Yes?"

"I went to the police department, and they told me I might be able to find you here." She knelt beside Kate, and Tug sniffed her leg. She brushed him away.

"I'm Olivia Wade," she said. "And my father is missing."

CHAPTER FIVE

Kate released the handles and cords on the elliptical, letting them snap back. The weights fell with a loud bang. She thought she might have misheard the woman standing beside her in the noisy, crowded physical therapy gym. "Excuse me?"

"I'm Olivia Wade. My daddy went fishing and hasn't come home yet." Worry lines creased her face, and she ran a hand through her blonde curls. Her eyes were red and puffy, as if she'd lost sleep.

Kate straightened and faced her. "Your father's missing? How long has he been gone?"

Olivia shook her head. "Since yesterday. He never came home last night."

"Have you talked to the police?"

"Yes. I just left the police department to file a missing person's report, but they won't get involved until he's been missing for at least forty-eight hours. I know something's wrong. Can you help me?"

"I can try. What's his name?"

"Jasper Wade."

A chill raced down Kate's spine.

"Jasper Wade?" She thought she misheard the woman over clanks and clangs of the noisy equipment around them. For some reason, the name struck a nerve. An extremely sensitive, painful nerve.

"He's a very famous attorney. You've probably heard of him." Olivia opened her purse and pulled out a photograph. She handed it to Kate. "He's a criminal defense attorney, and his firm runs TV commercials all the time."

Kate examined the photo. Jasper Wade looked to be in his fifties. Balding. Slightly overweight. Maybe she had seen him on TV. Still, there was something about him she didn't like. The sight of his face made her stomach turn. She didn't know why.

Olivia continued. "I think Daddy went fishing in Tampa Bay, but I'm not sure. It could be one of the lakes around here."

Kate put down the photo and scrutinized Olivia. She looked like a farmer's daughter, young and innocent somehow. Nothing like she imagined the daughter of some wealthy, powerful attorney would look. She wasn't sure if that was a good thing or a bad.

Olivia reached for Kate's hand. "I just know that something's wrong. His truck's gone, his boat's gone, and he's not answering his cell phone."

"Can I keep this?" Kate held up the photograph.

Olivia nodded.

"I'll see what I can do," Kate said. "I'll follow-up with Chief Guerra, and we can send some boats out to check the area. Do you know where your dad fishes?"

Olivia shook her head. "Again, I don't even know for sure he was on the bay, but I feel like he mentioned he was taking the boat out into the Gulf this weekend," she said. "Sometimes he goes fishing in a lake, and there's a place up in Georgia where he goes sometimes."

"Do you know where he launches?"

Olivia looked puzzled. "Launches? You mean like a rocket launch?"

"Does he use a local boat ramp?" Kate asked quickly, growing impatient. "Where does he normally park and launch his boat?"

Olivia stared blankly at her. "I'm sure it's at the same place everyone does."

"Does he have any friends he fishes with?"

"Daddy has many, many friends, and I've called everyone I could think of. No one's seen him."

"Well, what kind of boat does he have?"

"A red one."

"Do you know that type or model?"

"A very expensive one."

This was getting her nowhere, and Kate studied the young woman, looking for some sign that this was all a joke. "You're not giving me much to work with," she finally said.

Olivia let out a flurry of tears and shook her head. "What is the most expensive kind of boat you can buy?" she said, wringing her hands together. "Look for that."

"I'll see what he has registered. Maybe I can get some people out looking for him." Kate stood and placed a hand on Olivia's shoulder, comforting her. "What's your contact info?"

Olivia stopped crying and sniffled.

"Here's my number." She said, pulling a card out of her purse. "I'm staying at the Starlight Motel in Sienna Key. It's my private number, so please don't share it with anyone."

Kate scanned the motel card, then looked back up at Olivia. "Wait…you live in Lakewood Ranch. Why are you staying at a motel in Sienna Key?'

"I'm visiting all my daddy's friends, and I want to stay close."

"Okay." She looked at the card. A phone number was scribbled on the back. "Give me some time, and let me see what I can find."

"Ms. Parks," Olivia whispered. "I'm worried that time is the one thing Daddy doesn't have."

When Olivia left, Kate returned to the locker room and stared at the photo. Something about it—she wasn't sure what—alarmed her. Again, a wave of nausea hit as she dropped the picture in her purse. She couldn't stand to look at it again. When she finished her therapy session, she changed and made her way to the white Tahoe in the parking lot. Tug climbed into the passenger seat, and she moved the yellow book before he could plop his butt down. The worn "Sign Language for Dummies" cover now smelled a little ripe, thanks to Tug sitting on it, but she didn't care. It'd been a while since she last studied it.

Driving, she left Bradenton and headed toward Sienna Key over the Causeway. At the end of the bridge, fresh flowers lay beside the white cross placed along the exit ramp. The wreath still hung there, too, along with the black balloons. She tried not to look at it but couldn't help herself.

A few minutes later, she made her way downtown and turned onto Main Street. Shops were lowering their awnings, preparing for what the weatherman on the radio termed another "end of summer scorcher."

Downtown Sienna Key prized its beach stores. There were four of them within a dozen storefronts of each other, all vying for trade with outdoor racks crowding the sidewalk. Even the sandwich shops boasted a beach theme, where white wicker tables and chairs sat shaded under colorful umbrellas. The town's beach didn't look different from any other beach, other than the old Widow Rock Lighthouse looming on the horizon.

The town seemed a little sleepy after the long holiday weekend. However, the coffee shop looked especially busy, with an overflow of latte-sipping patrons seated at the outside tables.

Kate parked in front of the police department, or the "Bear's Den," as Chief Guerra liked to call it. She helped Tug out of the passenger seat then grabbed her purse. The double glass entrance doors welcomed her into an empty lobby. Tug followed. The receptionist, a thin woman in her late sixties with brightly dyed orange hair and equally dark rouge on her cheeks, looked up from her computer and stopped typing.

"Morn'n, Travel Agent," Kate said as she held the door open for Tug. The bulldog waddled inside.

"Who do we have here?" Travel Agent bounced up from her reception desk. Wearing jeans and a T-shirt encouraging everyone to "*SMILE! It increases your face value*," she bent at the knees to pat Tug's head. She'd been answering phones and handling dispatch and earned the nickname "Travel Agent" long before Kate or even Chief Guerra were born.

Tug sniffed and snorted and spun around, inviting the woman to pat his rear.

"This is Tug," Kate said. "I rescued him from a derelict vessel yesterday."

"How exciting." Travel Agent scratched Tug's ears, and he turned again, wagging his butt at her. "Are you going to keep him?"

"I'm taking him to the kennel," she said. Travel Agent straightened and stretched. Tug huffed at the discourtesy of stopping the scratches and again wiggled his butt at her.

Kate fished the photo of Jasper Wade from her purse. "A woman named Olivia Wade approached me saying that she tried to file an MPR on her missing father and was told to come back in forty-eight hours."

Travel Agent scrunched her face and rubbed her chin. She wore a headset and flipped a small black mic away from her mouth. "I'm not aware of anyone coming in about a missing person, but I've only been here for the last thirty minutes."

Kate thanked her and led Tug through the police department. A narrow hallway branched into a locked area with the cells and another corridor with the offices. She walked past the offices to a breakroom in the back with an exterior door that opened to a patio and a nice view of the channel that led to the Gulf. Two police boats, moored to the posts on a long dock, bobbed up and down in the salt waters. A teenager, with thick, black, horn-rim glasses and a raging case of acne marring his cheeks and forehead, unfolded metal chairs and set them up in rows facing the water. He straightened as Kate approached.

"I've got your safety packets set up," he said, pointing to a box of red folders. Orange life vests filled a large bin beside it. "You should have enough life jackets for the demonstration. I think there's twelve people registered, but I set up fifteen chairs, just in case some people bring friends."

"Thanks, Ernie." Kate nodded but had other things on her mind. She took the photo of Jasper Wade from her purse. Again, she felt chills run down her spine. "Did you talk to a woman about her missing father this morning?"

Ernie looked puzzled. "Who's missing?"

"Jasper Wade." She handed him the photo.

A pelican flew overhead and landed on a post, watching them. Tug looked up at the bird and barked.

The teen studied the photo. His eyes looked like large saucers, magnified in the lenses of his glasses. "I think he's an attorney."

"He is," she said. "And I have the strangest feeling like I know him from somewhere."

He handed the photo back to her. "He advertises on TV. Maybe you've seen his commercials."

She glanced at the photo again. The sight of that man made her feel dizzy, and a sickening wave washed over her. "There's something else," she said, wondering why this man was causing such an extreme reaction from her. "I can't put my finger on it, but I know we've crossed paths before."

Ernie shrugged. "Nobody's come in looking for him, as far as I know."

"His daughter approached me at PT. She said he never came home after a fishing trip."

He shook his head. "She hasn't been here."

Kate slipped the photo in her purse and looked back at the door into the building. "What about Jared and Jensen? Could they have talked to her?"

He shrugged. "Haven't seen them all morn'n. They're probably out on patrol."

"And Trace?"

He shrugged again and returned to sorting the red folders.

"Okay, thanks," she said and headed back up the dock toward the building. Tug ran after her.

Behind her, Ernie yelled, "Hey, people are gonna start arriving soon."

"Chill," she said. "I'll be right back."

She opened the back door and held it for Tug. Inside, she rushed through the breakroom and into the corridor of empty offices. Chief Trace Guerra's office appeared on her left. The room was lit, but no one was in it. At this time of the morning, Trace normally sat at his desk, drinking coffee and flipping through a worn copy of *Golf Digest.* Jensen and Jared's offices across the hall were unoccupied too, and she entered Trace's cluttered office.

Boxes of files surrounded his desk and lined the walls. A set of golf clubs stood in the corner. Framed photos and certificates decorated the walls, along with an old Bulls Eye putter with flecks of white paint along the flange that hung displayed right smack in the center of it all. Directly below the golf club, piled up like presents under a Christmas Tree, where every one of her recent gifts: a rocking horse, a bassinet, and dozens of frilly, pink baby clothes. He hadn't taken them home yet. Her book of baby names still lay on the desk. She reached for it, and a Hallmark card dropped out, landing on the desktop.

She picked up the card and stared at it a moment. *First comes loves, then comes marriage…* She opened it and read the inscription inside. "*Trace and Nellie, Hope you're ready for the most perfect little girl in the world. May she bring you both a lifetime of happiness. –Your friend, Kate.*"

Ernie entered the office, interrupting her. He pushed his glasses up further along his nose.

Tug waddled over to him.

She put down the book and Hallmark card. "You find Trace?" she asked.

He nodded. "They're breaking up a protest at the lighthouse."

Kate inhaled deeply. Had she heard him correctly? "A protest?"

"Yeah, it's a bunch of women calling themselves The Mommy Warriors, and they're launching dirty diapers at the bulldozers."

"The Mommy Warriors?" Kate cursed under her breath. "Ian."

"Ian," he repeated. "Looks like he's the ringleader."

"Instigator is more like it." Kate tore past him out the door. She stopped in the hallway, looked back at the desk, then returned to grab the book of baby names. She rushed back out of the office.

"Wait," the teen yelled. "You got people showing up for your safety training."

"Life vests, Ernie. Life vests," she said. "That's all they really need to know."

Carrying the book, she sprinted down the hall and into the lobby. Tug raced after her, barking.

CHAPTER SIX

Kate drove to the northern, rocky tip of Sienna Key with Tug in the passenger seat. As she approached, the old lighthouse became visible in the distance. Beneath it, a collection of pickup trucks and minivans surrounded Ian's light blue Vespa scooter, and she pulled up alongside Chief Guerra's squad car. Jared and Jensen's vehicles were there too. She gave Tug a quick pat between his ears and told him to sit tight.

The book of baby names lay on the passenger seat next to the yellow "Sign Language for Dummies" book. Tug sat on both of them and stared at Kate as she slipped out of the Tahoe.

Ahead of her, a crane and two bulldozers, along with several men wearing hard hats, yelled obscenities and made hand gestures to a crowd of women across from them. The women all raised signs with one hand and held babies in the other as they chanted, "Save our history! Save Widow Rock!" A news helicopter buzzed overhead, circling the lighthouse. Tampa SEBC-TV News vans outlined the perimeter as an on-location investigative reporter, Simone Adams, faced her camera crew and addressed her viewers. Kate wasn't particularly fond of the woman, and the PD had a policy of never talking to the media—Simone Adams, in particular.

Of course, Ian stood in the center of the Mommy Warriors with a bull horn in hand, orchestrating the war.

Trace and his officers, Jared and Jensen, stood behind a squad car, parked near construction workers. The three policemen knelt near the front tire.

"What are you doing here?" Trace yelled as Kate approached. He looked like a big bear squatting in his tan uniform and clutching his black cowboy hat in front of his face like a shield.

"I heard Ian is leading a protest." She crouched beside him.

"He's doing more than that," he said and pointed toward Ian and the Mommy Warriors. A volley of wadded diapers launched into the construction equipment, leaving behind runny trails of brown and yellow. The men in hardhats scrambled in the opposite direction. Trace continued. "He's leading an excrement assault against the demolition crew."

Kate stared at Ian, his red hair beneath a "Green Living, Blue World" ballcap and wearing dozens of buttons with environmental slogans over his vertical striped shirt. Behind him, his rowdy Mommy Warriors cheered and chanted. "Oh, my God," she said. "It's a poop fight."

Ian screamed into his bullhorn. "We stopped the Kingpin before. We can stop him now!"

Diana, standing beside him, screamed in agreement, "Flush Forrest Frazier!" The other women chanted with her, "Flush Forrest Frazier! Flush Forrest Frazier! Flush Forrest Frazier!" Ian yelled into the bullhorn. "Mommy Warriors, unite!"

Another volley of soiled diapers split the air and exploded in splotches of brown and yellow stew against the crane and bulldozers. More diapers came raining down on the remaining construction workers. The men scooped diapers from the ground and hurled them back at the women. Solid and semi-solid waste matter sprayed the area, and one large diaper splattered on the hood of the Chief's squad car.

Officer Jensen scrunched his face in disgust. "When I get my hands on these protesters, I'm gonna rub their noses in those diapers. Every last one of them."

Jared pushed him. "Now why you gotta say that? You know you can't say things like that."

Another diaper blasted the windshield. Jensen rose and hurried back to his squad car. "I'm outta here!"

"I'm not dealing with this either." Officer Jared chased after him and scrambled into the car beside his partner.

Trace's head veered from his officers to Kate. "This needs to end. Now."

"Good Lord! This smells so bad." Kate looked around. A sheet of plywood lay on the ground beside her. A diaper settled on top of it. Picking up a stick, she used it to fling the diaper from the plywood, then lifted the board by its edges as protection. She glanced at Trace.

He put on his hat. "Brush your teeth and comb your hair. We're going in."

With marginal protection, they gripped the edges of the plywood and inched forward onto the battlefield.

"Hey!" she yelled from behind the board. "I'm Kate Parks, Florida Fish and Wildlife Officer, on inactive duty status and currently temporarily working for the Sienna Key law enforcement."

They advanced blindly in Ian's direction, deflecting diapers with the plywood. As Kate and Trace moved, the women focused their barrage on them. Fecal matter battered their wood shield, and Kate screamed at Ian.

Ian hollered for his Mommy Warriors to hold back, and the torrent of raining diapers came to an end.

"Kate!" His face lit up with an excited grin. "You decided to join us."

"No!" She let go of her edge of the plywood and straightened her back to confront him. "I'm trying to keep you from getting arrested."

He stepped toward her, avoiding splattered diapers on the ground like land mines. He pointed to the construction workers as he spoke. "We're keeping those troglodytes from destroying the lighthouse."

"What happened to the signatures and the petition?" She stood over him, looking down. "I thought you guys were holding a benefit at the Tiki Hut."

"They moved up the demolition to today!" He grabbed a dirty diaper at his feet and slung it at the billboard advertising Forrest Frazier and his planned Widow Rock condo project. Excrement splattered across the developer's face and toothy white smile. Ian smirked. "The island doesn't need another condo nor the likes of that greedy pillager."

Kate gripped his arm. "You're not getting anywhere throwing dirty diapers at the demolition crew."

"If the Kingpin's goons are going to shit on this town, then we're gonna throw it right back at him." He raised the bullhorn and addressed the crowd. "Flush Forrest Frazier! Flush Forrest Frazier!"

The women chanted with him and threw another volley of diapers at the equipment.

"Okay, that's enough." Trace grabbed Ian and brought him to the ground. His thin body squashed a juicy diaper, and poop squished out from underneath his sides. "You're under arrest," Trace said.

The Mommy Warriors booed and launched a volley of diapers at the Chief. Kate raised the plywood to protect them. Behind her, a man wearing a yellow hardhat jumped out of the bulldozer and waved his arms.

"Cease fire! We're leaving!" he screamed at the crowd of women. "We're leaving! Cease fire!"

Diana cheered and thrust a fist in the air. "Yes! We won!"

The women cheered with her.

The news cameras filming along the perimeter at a safe distance from the excrement assault rushed to the superintendent, and reporter, Simone Adams, thrust her microphone in his face. "Can you tell us why Forrest Frazier Development is halting demolition of the Widow Rock Lighthouse today?"

"We're not buckling under the pressure if that's what you're asking," the superintendent said, removing his yellow hardhat and smoothing a hand over his thinning hair. He looked straight at the cameras. "With that storm out in the Gulf, we're just delaying things till after it passes."

Kate watched Simone interview the demolition crew as Trace placed Ian in handcuffs and lifted him to his feet. A mashed diaper dropped from his chest, leaving a running smear of black and yellow through the vertical stripes on his shirt. Trace walked him to the squad car, and Kate caught up.

"What are you doing?" she said, checking her clothes for any remnants of feces. "The protest is ending. You're still detaining him?"

"I'm not detaining him. I'm arresting him." Trace opened the back door to his squad car.

"Wait! Wait! Wait!" Ian said. "I have something I need to say."

Trace paused, and Kate thought Ian was about to tell her something. She watched him closely.

He winked at her then called out to Simone Adams.

The newscaster glanced his way, then snapped her fingers, motioning for her entourage of cameramen to follow her to the squad car. There, she held her mic to Ian's face.

"Ian Biggs," she said standing beside him, then taking a step back, she noticed the smear running down the front of his shirt. Extending her arm, she continued, "As the leader of this protest, do you feel you accomplished your goal today?"

"We've stopped vile, polluting big business today," Ian said into the mic. "This is a win for the underdog and the citizens of Sienna Key who are sick and tired of seeing our small town disappear in the crushing Tsunami of urban development."

"But is the Widow Rock Lighthouse worth being arrested for?"

Ian smiled and looked directly into the camera. "Question. That lighthouse is over a hundred years old, and we're just going to knock it down for what? To put up more condos?"

"That's enough time in the spotlight," Trace said, pulling Ian away from the cameras and positioning him into the backseat of his squad car.

Simone Adams thrust her microphone at the chief's face as he slammed the car door shut, locking Ian in the backseat. "Do you have anything to say about this protest today?"

"No comment," he said, pushing the cameras from his face.

Simone snapped her fingers, and her cameraman swung toward her. "There you have it," she said, looking directly at the camera. "And what started as a peaceful protest and devolved into a diaper-slinging free-for-all has now ended with one arrest and a smelly halt to the demolition. I'm Simone Adams for SEBC-TV Tampa. And wherever there's news, you'll find my shoes."

Kate watched from her Tahoe as the news crew departed. The protesting mothers and soiled demolition crew dispersed as well, and Tug let out an impatient huff in the passenger seat beside her.

She patted his head, then noticed the book of baby names beneath him. She pulled it out from under his butt and brushed away the dog hair. She'd almost forgotten about it. She opened her car door and rushed to Trace's squad car.

"You forgot something," she said, handing him the book.

He took the book from her. "You never give up, do you?"

"Not until you listen," she said. "Thomas is going to be a girl."

He laughed and tossed the book into the front seat. Turning back around, he faced her. "Aren't you supposed to be giving a boat safety demonstration right about now?"

"Intern Ernie's got it covered." She looked over at Ian in the backseat.

"I had to pull some strings to get you here after your accident," Trace said. "Don't make me regret it."

Kate shot him a sly smile. "Stack them eights," she said.

He shook his head and climbed in behind the wheel. "Just get back to your class, okay? We're paying *you* to lead boat safety class, not Intern Ernie."

"Just read the book," she said. "I highlighted the perfect girl names."

"You told me," he said, starting the ignition.

Ian leaned forward in the backseat and pressed his head beside Trace's headrest. "You should listen to her, Chief," he said. His hands were cuffed behind his back. "She's never wrong about this."

Trace shook his head and put the car in drive.

"I'll bail you out," Kate yelled to Ian as they pulled away. The squad car disappeared, and she looked up at the old lighthouse. Seagulls circled along the cupola like vultures. She could almost hear them warning her of something and jumped when her cell rang. She answered the call as more gulls landed in the field around her and picked at the scattered diapers.

A feminine voice addressed her on the other end. "Hello, Kate. I'm Dr. Yvette Cross. I've been treating your sister for depression."

"Dr. Cross, what can I do for you?" Kate asked as she returned to her Tahoe.

"I'm calling about Elise," Dr. Cross said.

"Okay . . ." Kate glanced at Tug. He watched her with utter fascination as she spoke on the phone. She noticed her purse on the floorboard. The photo of Jasper Wade poked out from the top and also seemed to watch her. She shivered and moved the picture so she couldn't see the man's eyes.

The woman continued. "I know Redd called you."

Kate cleared her throat. She didn't know why she suddenly felt hoarse. "He did. He wanted me to come over and see Elise."

"Did he tell you that she's locked herself in Noah's room and hasn't come out in three days?"

Kate shuddered. She hated hearing that. "I'm sorry she's having such a rough time."

"If we don't get her out, get her back out interacting with the world, I'm going to have to commit her—for her own safety and wellbeing."

Kate took a deep breath. "I don't know what you want me to do."

"Just talk to her. Invite her to go out to lunch with you. Get her out of the house for a little bit."

"I'm the last person she wants to see."

"I understand you feel that way---"

Kate cut her off. "She blames me for Noah's death."

"You're right, she does. But she also blames that intoxicated driver. She blames her husband. And above all, she blames herself."

"So how would I help? If she blames me, it's just going to upset her to see me."

"Maybe at first. Maybe for a minute. But if she can repair and re-establish her relationship with you, then the healing process can begin. You're the first step in bringing her out of this depression."

"Why isn't she repairing and re-establishing her relationship with Redd? He's her husband. She's closer to him than anyone else."

"You're her sister. Her big sister. She had a bond with you long before anyone else, before her husband. She loves you in a way that cannot compare to anyone else." The doctor paused. "Kate," she finally continued, "she needs you."

"Okay." Kate glanced at her watch. "I'm actually at the old lighthouse, ten minutes from the house."

"Perfect. You can be right over."

"Maybe…" Kate bit her lower lip as she spoke. She thought about the flyer advertising the benefit at the Tiki Hut. Darren Riggler was printed in bold, block letters. *Darren…* "Maybe I could take her to lunch … Maybe we could go to the Tiki Hut downtown."

"I love the Tiki Hut," the doctor said. "You're doing the right thing… And, Kate, I don't think this is just the first step toward Elise forgiving you; it's also the first step toward you forgiving yourself."

Forgiving.

Kate wasn't sure that was even possible.

She hadn't seen or spoken to her sister in over a year. That last time was at the cemetery. It had been a large funeral, with a tremendous outpouring of support from the community. When it was over, Kate found Elise standing over the open grave where her son's body had just been lowered. Kate put an arm around her sister and whispered, "He's in a better place."

"He didn't deserve this!" Elise shrugged Kate's arm away. "He deserved to grow up and have birthday parties and ride bikes and just be a kid. He didn't deserve this."

"I know…" Kate was at a loss for words.

Elise slapped her. Hard. Kate almost lost her balance.

Elise stood there, her face flushed, her hands forming fists, ready to strike again. "This is your fault," she said through clenched teeth. "You did this. Because of you, Noah is dead. He's dead, Kate, and it's your fault."

Kate brought a hand to her face and rubbed her burning cheek. She waited, staring wide-eyed, but Elise made no effort to continue her assault.

Instead, she turned on her heel and rushed away toward the cars parked along the curb. She disappeared inside a waiting black limo.

Kate hadn't seen her sister since.

She could still feel Elise's handprint on her cheek to this very day. The memory faded, and she looked over at Tug in the seat beside her. He barked and swayed his head. She glanced at the flyer again, then started the engine and rolled out from the shadow of the old lighthouse.

Elise was waiting.

CHAPTER SEVEN

Kate drove a couple of blocks west along streets lined with palm trees and manicured lawns. A dolphin mailbox planted at the edge of a winding driveway identified the Needleman's residence, a large corner lot that welcomed her back to the neighborhood. The novelty mailbox marked the boundary where, as kids riding bikes, she and her sister were to never venture beyond. She turned onto the familiar street.

Ahead of her, at the end of the cul-de-sac, stood a white three-story home. A wooden sign at the curb welcomed guests to "The Bluegill Beach Hideaway." Behind it, the Gulf shimmered a deep blue with fast-moving red and white splotches, sailboats racing in the late morning sun. To the east, the lighthouse rose tall against a cloudless sky.

The Bluegill looked like a classic Florida retreat—a sanctuary where Hemingway or Rawlings might've stayed and drawn inspiration. Square pillars secured the front elevation, and an expansive porch stretched along the perimeter. A double front door must have been fifteen feet high.

Kate passed the wooden welcome sign and pulled into the circular drive. She parked between an old Ford pickup with flaking blue paint on the hood and top of the cab and a yellow rental car. Turning off the engine, she looked over at Tug. The bulldog stared back intently and jumped out the driver's side door when she whistled. Together, they stepped to the porch. Rocking chairs sat empty on either side of the doors, and music chimed when she rang the doorbell. No one answered, so she knocked then let herself in.

A parlor welcomed her with large, picturesque windows framing a scenic view of the beach. Every chair in the room was positioned for maximum exposure. To the left, a staircase wound up to the second and third floors. To the right, Redd Tyler stood behind the front desk, across from a young man in his early twenties wearing Bermuda shorts and a Hawaiian print shirt.

Redd turned as Kate entered, and he approached the front door.

"You came," he said and gave her an awkward hug. "I heard the door chimes, but I was with a paying guest." He motioned toward the young man still standing at the desk.

Kate nodded at the man in Bermuda shorts, then turned to Redd. "I got a call from a Dr. Cross," she said.

"I hope you don't mind. I gave her your number." He returned to the desk and removed several sheets of paper from a printer. Setting them on the desktop in front of his guest, he handed the man a pen while speaking to Kate. "It cost me fifteen dollars in billable hours, but I don't mind." His voice trailed off, and he looked down at the bulldog. "Who's the pooch?"

"Long story." She avoided the question and looked toward the staircase. "Where's Elise?"

"She's in Noah's room. She hasn't left it in three days." His face darkened. "She's getting worse, Kate. Much worse."

"Did something else happen?"

Redd took the paper and pen from his guest and thanked him. The young man turned toward the staircase and called up to his father. An older gentleman, dressed in Bermuda shorts and a matching Hawaiian print shirt, appeared at the top of the steps with three suitcases in his arms.

"Dad!" the man yelled, running to his father on the stairs and taking the suitcases from him. "I told you to let me get those. You should be conserving your strength."

"I can manage," the older man said as he descended the steps. He wore black dress-socks and leather sandals. On the ground floor, he raised an old-fashioned Polaroid camera hanging from a strap around his neck and snapped a picture of Kate and Redd. The flash was blinding.

"Please, Mr. Vaughn. No more pictures," Redd yelled, holding up his arms to cover his face.

"I want to take pictures of every second of this trip," he said as the camera flashed again. "It's been the greatest time of my life, and I want to document every moment."

His son came up beside them and dropped the suitcases. "Dad, they don't want you taking pictures of them."

The old man turned toward Tug. "Look," he said and shot another pic. "She has the cutest bulldog ever. I have to take a picture of that face."

Tug huffed and blinked and turned his head as the man took more photos. Redd reached across the desk and blocked the camera lens with the palm of his hand.

"I charge five-ninety-nine per picture," he said. "Do you want me to add it to your bill?"

The old gentleman lowered his camera. He smiled at Kate.

"Nice to meet you," she said, extending her hand.

"Linus Vaughn, hailing from Decatur, Georgia." He took her hand. "And this is my son, Zachery, also hailing from Decatur, Georgia. Nice to meet you too . . . and your puppy. What's his name?"

"Tug. But he doesn't belong to me," she said, glancing down at the bulldog as he blinked rapidly and shook his head. Slobber flung from his mouth.

Behind the desk, Redd folder his arms across his chest. "Do you know how much dogs cost?" he said. "There's food and collars and vet bills and—"

"He's a rescue dog, and he's going to the shelter tomorrow," Kate answered.

Redd shook his head and wagged a finger at her. "Don't let them charge you for boarding it."

Kate ignored him and focused on Vaughn's luggage on the floor. She nodded at Zachary. "Welcome to Sienna Key. I'm sorry you have to cut your trip short."

"Me too," Linus said. "Sienna Key is a beautiful town. Clean air. Sandy beaches. Friendly people."

Zach put a hand on his father's shoulder. "Why don't you wait outside while I check out of our room."

"Okay, but first . . ." He raised the camera and snapped one last picture of Kate and the bulldog, then meandered to the front door. He opened it but paused at the threshold, and Kate expected him to take another photo. Instead, he addressed his son. "Would you rather live in a sailboat or an RV?"

Zach let out an annoyed chuckle. "C'mon, Dad. Not another one."

"Just answer the question." Linus looked impatient standing in the doorway.

Zach rubbed his chin, seeming to think about the question. "Okay… The waves, the sun, the smell of salt air. Or the open road before you, sunsets, roadside diners. Either one sounds pretty good about now."

"That's not an answer."

"It's the best I got. Now go wait in the car." Zach laughed as his father stepped out and shut the door behind him. He shrugged his shoulders. "Ladies and gentlemen, that's my dad."

Kate laughed. "What was with the question?"

"He's been playing 'Would You Rather?' all week," Zach said as he placed a room key on the desktop. "He thinks it'll help us get to know each other."

"Best of luck on your trip back to Georgia," Kate said, then to Redd, "So, Elise? Upstairs?"

Redd didn't answer. He picked up the room key and examined it.

Waiting, Kate stared out that large, picturesque window. She could see the Widow Rock Lighthouse in the distance. Maybe it was being in her childhood home. Or maybe it was the lighthouse on the horizon. Either way, a memory of her father flashed through her mind—back to when she was five or six. Her dog had run off, and she sat crying on the rocks by the beach, looking up at the old lighthouse. Her father sat down beside her and put a comforting hand on her shoulder.

"Now, stop with all the hysterics," he said. "It's not that bad."

"Yes, it is," she told him. "Corky ran away. I can't find him anywhere, and he ran away."

"Of course he left," her father said. "You didn't take care of him, and he ran away."

Kate pushed the thought away and looked around the room. Truth be told, she never liked this place. Pain and sadness permeated every corner. A darkness spread through the rooms and had only deepened since…

She noticed the framed photograph of a child. A black-and-white print of a little boy, all smiles and dimples, on a boat, wearing a life jacket that was a size too big.

Noah Tyler—her nephew.

Like a blow to the head, she suddenly made the connection: the missing attorney. *Jasper Wade.* She realized how she knew him—*that son of a bitch!* He represented the drunk driver who hit Noah. Her negative reaction to hearing his name when Olivia approached her in the gym suddenly made sense.

She turned toward Redd. "I need to tell you something," she said.

He raised a finger, signaling her to give him a minute.

"It's important," she said. Jasper Wade represented the drunk driver and got him off manslaughter charges, she thought. The whole trial was a travesty, and they knew the attorney pulled strings. Probably paid off the judge. He was a crooked attorney, and now he was missing.

Redd finished running a credit card and handed it back to Zach, saying, "I hope you and your dad come back after the storm passes."

"I hope we get the chance," Zach said, sighing. "Somehow, I don't think we will."

"Don't let the hurricane scare you. It's the third one to blow through here this season," Redd said. "I'm sure we'll still be here when it passes."

"I hope so," Zach said, heading out the door. Kate watched the young man join his father at the yellow rental car in the drive. She looked back at Redd. "That was your last guest?"

"Yeah. They were supposed to stay for the week but are leaving after only three nights. I'm losing $480 on them," Redd said. He walked past her and left the parlor. She followed him, and Tug followed her. He entered the kitchen and fished a keyring from his pocket, saying, "With this hurricane cutting everyone's vacations short, I stand to lose $3,360 in room rentals."

Kate leaned against the center island and noticed an assortment of copper pots and pans hanging above her.

Redd paused. "Hey, thanks for stopping by to see Elise. She's upstairs."

"I don't know what I can do," Kate said. She wondered if she should even mention the missing attorney as Redd inserted the key into a deadbolt on a door on the far kitchen wall. Tug sat at her feet and looked up with intense interest. She decided to go for it. "Do you remember Jasper Wade?" she asked.

He dropped the keys. They clinked loudly, hitting the tile.

"Yes." He picked the keys up from the floor and unlocked the door. He said nothing more about it.

"His daughter approached me this morning," she continued. "She said he's missing."

Redd lingered at the door. He shut his eyes, inhaled deeply then let it out. Still, he said nothing and simply opened the door. Kate trailed him into the dark garage with Tug waddling behind them.

Redd flipped on the lights.

"Do you think that's a coincidence?" Her voice echoed as she spoke.

The lights brightened, highlighting a large table in the center of the garage where their vehicles should have been. Instead, an elaborate multi-level model trainset took the space, with miniature houses, buildings, streets, and landscapes. She was quite familiar with the display, but it looked like Redd had added extensively to it in the last year. She noticed every plastic tree lay on its side as if they'd been tumbled by a storm, and Redd set to turning them right side up as she continued. "Doesn't that seem strange, you know, that she approached *me* about her father?"

"I don't know how they keep falling," he said, focused on his task. "I think Elise is messing with me." Once every tree stood straight again, he flipped a switch on a control box. Houses lit up. Cars rolled forward along the narrow streets. Tiny painted people came to life, mechanically turning and bending. The flurry of activity caught Kate by surprise.

It caught Tug by surprise, too, as he raised on his hind legs to see what was on the table. She gently pushed his front paws to the floor. He sneezed in frustration and sniffed the table leg. She continued explaining her case to Redd.

"His daughter told me she tried to submit a missing person report," she said, glancing around the garage. A small dirt bike leaned against the wall. A blue and orange helmet hung from handlebars. She turned back to Redd. "I didn't even put it together until just now. Do you think she approached me because of . . . because of Noah?"

Redd squeezed his eyes shut. His fists clenched. Kate instantly regretted bringing it up.

"I keep the garage door locked," he said, slowly opening his eyes again. "I don't know how she'd be getting in here. Still, every day I find all the trees knocked over."

Kate shook her head, studying him.

"You said Elise is upstairs?" Her voice choked, and she stepped away from the table. Tug barked, and Redd sat on a stool beside the table with the controls in his hands. The engine and cars sped up on the tracks.

Kate returned through the entry into the kitchen.

"Hey! Your dog!" he called out, never looking up from his trainset.

She whistled for the bulldog, but he didn't follow as she left the garage and trudged through the kitchen back to the parlor. Dragging her heels, she took her time up the staircase, passed the second floor, and made her way to the third. The top of the stairs opened to a dark hallway with five doors—four bedrooms—all shut. A bathroom loomed at the end of the hall.

When Elise was little, she used to be scared to death of their large house at night and, whenever she woke in the middle of the night and had to pee, she would creep into Kate's room and shake her awake. Kate always complained, but she also always went with Elise down the hall to the bathroom and talked to her through the door so Elise wouldn't be scared. She smiled at the memory.

Noah's bedroom stood waiting to her left. A "NO ADMITTANCE" sign hung on the door. She came to it and knocked. A voice from inside told her to go away.

"Hey, Kid," Kate said. "It's me, Kate Parks, Florida Fish and Wildlife Officer on inactive duty status and currently temporarily working for—"

"I know who you are. Now go away." Elise's voice sounded muffled behind the locked door.

"Everyone's worried about you." Kate pressed a cheek against the door, listening. "What are you doing?"

"I'm guarding a bridge and asking people riddles before they cross." Elise's voice had a sharp, angry edge. "What do you think I'm doing? Now go away."

Kate pounded on the door. "Either open this door, or I'm going to find an ax and break it down." She waited for an answer. "Okay…I don't even know where to begin to find an ax, so that was kind of a hollow threat."

She paused again. The door remained locked. She pounded on it.

"Open up, or I'll do something else. Something you'll regret." She thought about it a moment. "I'll sing, Elise. I'll stand out here for hours if I have to, singing every single song I can think of that we listened to growing up. You know I'll do it."

The lock clicked, and the knob jiggled. The door opened.

Taking a deep breath, Kate entered the room.

CHAPTER EIGHT

Kate stepped into Noah's bedroom and found Elise sitting in a rocking chair.

"Hey, Kid," she said. The room seemed frozen in time, with blue-painted walls, puffy white clouds along the crown molding, and a brilliant, yellow-orange sun with long rays of light proudly displayed over the bed. A toy chest sat in the corner, waiting to be opened. Shorts, underwear, and a T-shirt lay spread-out on top of the dresser, waiting for a little boy to put them on. A bookcase filled with Dr. Seuss books anchored the far wall beneath the window. A baby monitor rested on the top shelf, next to a framed photo of a child holding a stuffed elephant.

Elise sat in a rocking chair with a large children's picture book in her lap. Her face was thin and pale from months locked in her sealed prison. She looked strained with fatigue but still lighted from within. Her disheveled black hair flowed to her shoulders, uncombed and knotted. She didn't respond as Kate came up beside her. "How're you doing?"

"Fine. Go away." Elise turned away in the chair.

"You don't seem fine. Redd said you haven't left this room in days." Kate waited for a response. When none came, she added, "Your therapist called me."

Elise still didn't answer.

Kate knelt beside her. "I haven't seen you in a while."

"I heard you were shot." Elise opened the large picture book in her lap. "I guess you survived."

"I was in the hospital for a while," Kate said, rubbing her shoulder. "I'm still in physical therapy and temporarily on inactive duty status with the---"

Elise interrupted her and began reading her book out loud.

"Every night, Charley follows the same routine.
And slips into his favorite PJs, brushes his teeth, and says his prayers.
He climbs into bed
And waits for his mother to tuck him in and kiss him goodnight.
"Don't forget to turn on the nightlight," he would say.
"You're a big boy now," his mother would always answer. "You don't need a light."
Still, she always flips on the light, and tells him, "Don't let the bedbugs bite," before shutting his bedroom door.
"And Charley would lay in his bed

In his dark, quiet bedroom
Peeking out from under the covers
At the pale, yellow glow coming from the night light
And at all the eerie blackness around it…"

Kate put a hand on Elise's shoulder, and she stopped reading. She didn't look up.

"*Where the Darkness Hides*," Kate said. "I remember that book."

"It's Noah's favorite," she whispered as if she finally let her guard down. "I like reading it like I used to do."

Kate watched her sister for several seconds. Finally, she stood and picked up the framed photo from the bookshelf along the wall. The image of Elise and Noah together holding a giant stuffed animal made her smile. Mr. Belvedere, a colossal plush elephant, looked bigger than little Noah, with a head of shiny grey fur and a comically long trunk, huge floppy ears, and two round button eyes. She returned the picture to the bookshelf. She looked around the room, realizing it had been well over a year since she'd been in here, and nothing had changed in that time.

"I remember when we painted this room. Do you remember that? Redd wanted to paint dinosaurs on the walls, and you wanted trains."

Elise didn't respond.

Kate continued anyway. "We compromised and just painted the walls this sky blue with white clouds and sun. We spent the whole afternoon---"

Elise let out a long and irritated sigh. "What are you doing here?"

Kate looked back at her. "Why don't you come downstairs, get out of this room, get out of this house."

"I can't. I'm waiting."

"Kid . . . Noah isn't here."

"Stop calling me Kid." Elise folded her arms together and sat back in the rocker.

Kate backed off. She knew her sister hated being called 'Kid,' but it was something their father called them when they were young. When he left them, she assumed the role of parent, as their mother was never in any shape to do the job. Calling Elise 'Kid' just seemed natural.

Elise continued rocking. "Besides," she said. "I'm not waiting for Noah. I'm waiting for Doogie."

"Who's Doogie?"

"My friend. He talks to me." She pointed to the baby monitor on the dresser.

Kate picked it up. It didn't even look like it was turned on. She set it back down on the dresser. She noticed the line of stuffed animals sitting atop a shelf overlooking the bed, next to the yellow sun. The baby monitor sat quietly on the bookcase. "There's no one there."

"He will be. He likes it when I read to him."

"You know this isn't healthy," Kate said. "You need to leave this room."

"No. *You* need to leave this room." Elise's voice remained firm but emotionless.

Kate continued. "You're scaring us. You're scaring me."

Elise looked down at the book in her lap.

Kate stepped to her and knelt, putting a hand on the open page. "You can't stay here alone, in isolation."

"I like isolation." Elise turned her head. "It means there's no people. I hate people."

Kate stood and let out a long breath. She stepped to the window, thinking. After a moment, she turned back around. "Remember . . . remember when we were kids, and you built that giant sandcastle on the beach with the towers and used shells for flags? You spent hours building it, and then the tide rushed in and washed it away. You sat and cried and cried. Do you remember what we did?"

"We yelled cuss words at the ocean," Elise whispered.

"You did that. I brought my pail and shovel over, and we rebuilt the whole crazy sandcastle with even more towers and more shells. But we did something else too."

Elise crossed her arms, and the book dropped off her lap onto the carpet.

Kate continued. "We dug a mote. You and I dug a mote, so when the tide came rushing back, the mote diverted the water and protected the new sandcastle."

"It was pointless. We shoulda just let the waves wash it away."

Elise was baiting her, but Kate didn't bite. She looked over at the bookcase again and stared at the photo of Noah and her sister. Noah loved that giant plush elephant, and she wondered whatever happened to it. It wouldn't have fit on the shelf over the bed with the other stuffed animals. It wasn't on the bed. She pushed the thought out of her mind and focused on Elise. "The sandcastle wasn't pointless back then. It was important." She held up her left hand and hooked her pinky finger with Elise's pinky finger. "We're sisters. We always will be."

Elise flinched and pulled her hand away. "Don't touch me."

Kate stood and changed her tactic. The tone of her voice shifted. "What if I tell you that there's a man downstairs wearing socks and sandals and Bermuda shorts."

Elise looked up. "Is he old?"

"Of course."

Elise seemed to think about it a moment. "I like making fun of stupid old people."

"I know. And if you don't hurry, you're going to miss the opportunity."

After a moment, Elise nodded. She didn't smile but rose to her feet. Together, they left the bedroom and walked into the hall, leaving the door open behind them.

"Redd?" Kate shouted as she walked down the staircase into the front parlor.

"Where's the old man wearing socks and sandals?" Elise asked, coming down a few steps behind Kate.

Kate called for Redd again.

Tug came scrambling from the kitchen, responding to her voice, and raised his front paws on the first step. She pet his head as she moved off the staircase.

"You got a cat?" Elise asked, inching past the dog. His tail wagged, and a stream of slobber stretched from his mouth. "I hate cats."

"It's a bulldog, and his name's Tug," Kate said.

"He looks like a fat cat," Elise said. Standing in the parlor, she turned her head from left to right. "Where's the old man wearing socks and sandals?"

"Go sit in the living room, and I'll see if I can find him." Kate left Elise in the parlor and made her way into the kitchen.

Redd was coming out of the garage and shut the door behind him. He turned the deadbolt and removed the key from the lock. He looked over at Kate.

"Any luck waking the living dead?" he asked, his eyes narrowing.

Kate smiled. "She's awake and out of Noah's room. In fact, she's in the living room."

She motioned for him to follow, and they made their way out of the kitchen, through the parlor, and into the adjoining living room.

Elise sat on the couch with the bulldog at her feet, sniffing her ankles. She lightly kicked his face, slinging a wad of slobber from his mouth. He looked up at her, as if in shock, and sneezed.

"It's good to see you out of that room," Redd said, but Elise didn't acknowledge him.

Kate sat on the couch beside her and flipped on the TV. The weather channel appeared, and a meteorologist motioned toward a satellite view of Florida, tracking the hurricane in the Gulf.

"Turn it up," Redd said, taking a seat in a recliner in front of the TV.

Ignoring him, Elise turned to Kate. "Where's the old man wearing socks and sandals?"

Redd picked up the remote and flipped the channel. Investigative Reporter Simone Adams appeared on screen along with images of the picketing at the lighthouse. Next, the reporter stood next to the developer with a mic in her hand. Forrest Frazier's smug face filled the screen as the camera zoomed in for a closeup.

"The Widow Rock Lighthouse is an eyesore and a safety hazard," he said into the mic. "It's time to knock it down, despite what some sentimentalist protesters chant."

Redd jumped from the recliner. "Murderer!" he screamed at the set.

Kate rose from the couch. Tug barked at the sudden excitement.

Redd brushed past them and stormed out of the living room. She could hear him stomp up the staircase so violently, it shook the house. She looked at Elise, who appeared unfazed.

A minute later, the house shook from Redd's heavy footsteps marching down the steps, and he roared into the living room gripping a baseball bat. He whipped past Kate, making a beeline for the TV set. Forrest Frazier's face still filled the screen. Redd swung. His bat smashed the glass. The TV shattered, sparked, and went black. Kate rushed to him.

"The man shouldn't be breathing," he yelled, slamming the TV with another swing. "He has no right. He should be rotting in prison. He should burn in hell!"

Elise remained on the couch, watching stoically. Redd dropped the bat and cried out. He paced the room as Kate unplugged the television.

"You need to calm down," she said to him. "This isn't helping anything."

"That pile of human waste should be six feet under the ground for what he did."

"I know," she said quietly. "I know."

"Payback is coming. He can't escape karma." Redd kicked the shattered television, knocking it over. "He needs to pay for what he did!"

Kate placed her hands on his chest and pushed him out the room and into the parlor. "You're not helping anything. Now go cool off."

Redd grunted at her. With bat in hand, he lumbered to the front door and slammed it shut behind him.

Kate heard him scream and kick something outside. She returned to the living room and looked over at Elise.

Elise remained sitting on the couch, unblinking. She stared at the smashed TV set on the floor. "I wanted to make fun of the old man in socks and sandals," she said.

Kate sat down beside her again and put an arm around her. "Let's go to lunch. We can eat downtown."

Elise shook off Kate's arm. "I don't like eating. I only like throwing up the things I eat."

"Remember the Tiki Hut?"

Elise remained focused on the wrecked television. "I remember it was shut down for health code violations."

"It wasn't shut down for health code violations."

"Well, it shoulda been. Then maybe the roaches would starve to death."

"It doesn't have roaches," Kate said, her patience thinning. "They're having a benefit for the lighthouse."

"Why?"

"That—Mr. Frazier—plans to knock it down and build a condo."

"Not interested. I don't like benefits, and I don't like eating. I only—"

Kate didn't let her finish. "I know, you only like throwing up the things you eat. But that lighthouse was a big part of our childhood, and in a few days, it could be gone."

Elise didn't respond.

"So . . . whaddya say? Let's go have lunch at the Tiki Hut." She started to put her arm around her sister again, then thought better of it. She folded her hands in her lap.

"If I go, will you promise not to talk about Forrest Frazier or anything?" Elise asked flatly, without looking up.

"Yes," Kate answered. She knew what "*anything*" meant. "In fact, we don't even have to talk at all."

"Okay, then I'll consider it." Elise sat back with her arms folded. "When the food comes, can we send it back and tell the waiter it wasn't what we ordered?"

"No," Kate said. "We aren't doing that."

"Can we set something on fire?"

"No. We aren't doing that either." Kate clenched her mouth tight. The bulldog sneezed, catching her attention for a second.

"You're not giving me very many reasons to go, but . . ." Elise paused then muttered a quick, "I'll need to change first."

"Perfect," Kate said, a little more cheerful than intended. "It's sister time."

Elise cringed. "Stop it. You sound like a tampon commercial." She rose from the couch and marched out of the living room.

"I love you, Kid," Kate yelled, following her sister into the parlor.

"I hate you," Elise yelled back, heading up the staircase.

Giving her some space, Kate stepped outside onto the front porch. Redd sat in a rocking chair beneath a hanging fern and puffed on a cigarette. The baseball bat rested in his lap.

"I thought you quit smoking," she said, taking a rocker beside him.

"Only when I'm stressed." He nodded at her. "Forrest Frazier brings out the worst in me."

"Guess you'll be getting a new TV?"

"I've spent $3,600 on TVs in the last twelve months." He took another drag on the cigarette.

She watched him inhale and exhale a cloud of smoke. "I understand why you hate him, but—"

His eyes turned red, angry, and he interrupted her. "That man is living, and my son is not. My son is dead because of him, and there is no justice in that. And you know, his attorney, the guy who got him out of murder charges--"

"Jasper Wade," Kate said.

"Jasper Wade," he repeated. "I'm glad he's missing. In fact, I'm hoping something terrible happened to him. He doesn't deserve to breathe either."

"Okay." Kate shrank back. "I should've never told you his daughter approached me."

"That attorney is just as corrupt as his client, and they can both go to hell." Redd jumped to his feet, and the bat dropped to the floorboards. It rolled across the porch as he stepped to the edge and tossed his cigarette butt onto the lawn. He swung around and yelled at her. "Forrest Frazier gave us an offer on The Bluegill. After everything that happened, after everything he did to us, he had the balls to step right up on this porch and ring the doorbell."

"What?" Kate couldn't believe what she was hearing. "When?"

"About six months ago." He turned his back to her again. "Showed up like we were old friends or something and said he'd write us a check right here on the spot."

Kate stood and stepped next to him. "What'd you do?"

"Told him I'd kill him if he ever stepped foot on my property again." He laughed quietly as if the memory brought some perverse pleasure.

Kate reached out to touch his arm, to comfort him, then thought better of it. She withdrew her hand. She noticed the baseball bat on the floor. His rocker still swayed forward and backward, despite no one sitting on it.

"Can I ask you something?" she said, studying the back of his head, wondering if he was even listening. She needed to change the subject. "Who is Doogie?" she asked.

He shrugged his shoulders. "I think he's imaginary. Elise talks to him in Noah's room."

Kate looked up. The window into Noah's room was directly above them, and she could hear Elise's muffled voice as if she was talking to someone. She looked over at Redd. "The name sounds familiar."

"I don't know about that," he continued. "He's just in her warped head."

Kate didn't respond as they stood next to each other on the front porch in silence for several minutes. She noticed his old pickup in the drive next to her white Tahoe. The blue paint was flaking on the hood and top of the cab, and the tires were bald. She looked back at Redd as he lit another cigarette. Surely Elise had more than enough time to change, she thought and returned inside the house.

Upstairs, in the dark third-floor hallway, she heard Elise's voice coming from Noah's room. The door was shut. And it sounded like she was talking to someone. Kate opened the bedroom door.

Elise stood over the dresser with the baby monitor in hand. "I'll be back, Doogie. I promise," she said into the hand-sized receiver.

Kate stepped into the room and took the baby monitor from her. She glanced at it, but nothing was coming from the speaker—no other voice. No companion. Just static. She stared at her sister, puzzled.

CHAPTER NINE

Kate drove into downtown Sienna Key with Elise riding silently in the passenger seat. Tug sat in Elise's lap, straining to lick her cheek as she held his head away from her. She'd only said one thing since she got in the Tahoe: "I'm glad Redd smashed the TV. I wish I'd done it myself."

Kate looked over at her. "Why?"

"It makes him happy," she said with no emotion. The sign language book lay on the floorboard at her feet. "I like to smash things that make him happy."

Kate didn't respond and turned on the music. Widespread Panic's "*Climb to Safety*" rocked the speakers, and she cranked up the volume. A friend once told her that Widespread transcended the stifling categorization of a band. They were more than blues or soul or rock; they were a way of life. She knew the lyrics to every song and couldn't help but sing right along. She hoped it would have a therapeutic effect on Elise and her deep depression, which nothing seemed to relieve. She encouraged Elise to join in.

"You promised you wouldn't sing if I let you in the bedroom," Elise said and killed the music.

Kate focused on the road. "What do you want to listen to?"

"The only music I tolerate is Russian funeral dirges, wolverine mating calls, or Vanilla Ice. For obvious reasons." She sat back in her seat, folded her arms across her chest, and stared straight ahead, unblinking.

Kate puckered her lips with annoyance. She didn't turn the music back on.

It was hard to imagine when Elise was a carefree girl playing at the beach and singing aloud. It seemed she always fought anxiety and fears. She remembered when they were kids hiding in that old lighthouse. Their parents were continually fighting—their dad yelling about their mother's tendency to sleep all day, not clean the house, not have dinner ready. She'd had it with his drinking. Whenever their parents would start to fight, Kate and Elise would escape to the lighthouse and play.

Then one night, their father left and never returned.

Elise sat at the bottom of the spiraling staircase in the lighthouse. Kate sat beside her.

"It's no wonder he left," Kate said. "Mother didn't take care of him, and he ran away."

It seemed like a lifetime ago.

Kate pulled into the Tikki Hut parking lot as the DJ interrupted the music with a news bulletin on the hurricane. She switched off the radio and parked.

"Just so we're clear," Elise said. "I'm not going to eat anything. I'm just going to sit there and count roaches."

Kate turned off the engine. "You haven't been out of the house in, what, months?"

"So?" Elise said. "You haven't minded your own business in, what, months?"

Elise was baiting her again, and again Kate refused to bite. Instead, she said, "You're in a depression, and you have every reason to be. I get it. Any mother would be despondent after going through your loss."

"I'm not depressed. I'm not sad. I'm not anything. I feel nothing."

"Everyone's just concerned."

"Well, call everyone and tell them to go to hell." Elise opened the car door and shifted out of her seat, then stopped. Without looking at Kate, she said, "The only good thing to happen to me in the last year was you not showing up and asking a lot of dumb questions."

"That's harsh." Kate paused, and the silence stretched between them. Neither moved. Sitting on the center console, Tug turned his head toward Elise, then Kate, then back to Elise. Finally, Kate climbed out of her vehicle.

Trucks, cars, and golf carts filled the parking lot. People were coming and going, some in groups, chattering away about the hurricane turning east and hitting somewhere along the Florida peninsula.

Tug leaped onto the ground, and Kate hooked a leash to his collar. Together, they trotted to the restaurant. When she noticed Elise still sitting in the Tahoe, she called out to her sister. Elise climbed out and slammed the car door shut behind her.

As they entered the restaurant, a college girl handed them flyers. "You want to sign our petition to designate the Widow Rock Lighthouse a historic landmark?"

Kate took it and thanked her. She signed the petition then handed the pen to Elise. Elise scribbled something on the paper. Kate glanced at her signature and saw that she signed her name as *"Adolph Hitler."*

The girl at the table didn't seem to notice and bent down to greet Tug. "He's just the cutest dog ever," she said. "What's his name?"

Elise took the leash from Kate's hand and gave it to the college girl. "He's not a dog; he's a cat," she said. "Hold him. We can't bring him inside anyway."

The college girl looked surprised but took the leash as Kate and Elise stepped inside.

It was a theme restaurant built in what looked, felt, and sounded like a rickety crab boat. The Tiki Hut's windows overlooked the Intercoastal, and the Bradenton city skyscape outlined the shore a good mile across the water. Fish netting with shells, crabs, and boat wheels decorated the walls. A hammerhead shark was mounted over the front entry. Four saltwater aquariums with exotic fish separated different restaurant sections, but the place also served great food. The room was crowded with couples and families from every neighboring county, eating with both hands. A live band played in the corner, just like the flyer had promised.

Kate noticed the band as soon as she walked in and couldn't take her eyes off the lead singer: Darren Riggler. Tall with shaggy brown hair, he wore jeans, cowboy boots, and a blue Gators ballcap turned backward on top of his head.

"Oh, my God," Elise said. "Is this why we're here? Because your old boyfriend is playing?"

"Oh, look at that," Kate said rather unconvincingly. "You're right. That's Darren up there, isn't it?"

"That's why we're here, isn't it?" Elise said. "Your old boyfriend blows into town, and you're arranging a run into."

Kate shook her head. "This isn't a run into."

"That's exactly what it is," Elise persisted. It was the most energetic she'd sounded since leaving the locked bedroom. "You're trying to arrange a run into."

"Of course not," Kate said. "I'm here to support the lighthouse."

Elise threw up her hands in disgust. "I'm so outta here."

Kate grabbed her arm and pulled her back. "You're not going anywhere. C'mon. Let's find a table."

Sitting down at one of the window tables, Kate glanced out at the water and saw jet skiers rush past, trailing a wall of white water behind them.

Elise slouched in her chair and folded her arms, pouting. "This place really sucks butt," she said.

A waitress came over to the table and glanced down at them. "Kate!" Her voice rose with excitement. "It's good to see you."

Kate immediately recognized the woman. "Lenna," she said. "How are you? How's Heather?"

"She's better," Lenna said, smacking her gum. She moved her fingers near her lips and brought her hand down toward Kate. "We're still staying with my Monster-in-Law. And Heather drew you another picture," she said as she signed the words with her hands.

Kate returned the thank you sign, keeping her right hand flat and moving it from her lips toward the waitress. "Tell her I saved all her artwork. They're hanging on my fridge," Kate said, pausing with her hands in mid-air. "You know, I'm sorry. I can't remember how to sign that."

Lenna laughed. "That's all right."

"I have a *Sign Language for Dummies* book in my car," Kate said. "But I don't have a lot of occasions to use it."

"I'll grab the new picture from my locker." Lenna put a hand on Kate's shoulder. "I promised her I'd give it to you next time you came into the restaurant."

Kate introduced her sister, and Lenna looked over at Elise. "Pleased to meet you. Your lunch is on the house, both of you."

"We can't let you do that," Kate said.

"I want to," Lenna said quickly. "It's the least I can do after what you did. And what happened." Lenna's eyes looked toward Kate's shoulder.

Kate self-consciously rose a hand to her arm and touched it. She looked over at Elise. "How does a grilled chicken sandwich and the house salad sound?"

Elise didn't respond. She kept her head down and stared at the open menu.

Lenna, smiling, nodded and scribbled across her order pad.

Kate continued. "And, please, no mayonnaise."

"Got it, no mayonnaise," Lenna said and turned to Elise. "And for you?"

Elise looked up from the menu. "I want something with your best rat parts."

"Come again?" Lenna lowered her notepad.

"Are you still serving horse meat?" Elise asked, unblinking.

Lenna opened her mouth, stuttering.

"Okay, just give me anything that's fallen on the floor," Elise continued, her eyes becoming intense. "And make sure the undocumented workers in the back spit a good loogie in the tea. I like mine extra thick and slimy with added nose snot. Maybe you can find someone with a cold."

"Elise, stop it," Kate said. She turned to Lenna. "She'll have a grilled chicken sandwich too and the house salad. No mayonnaise."

Lenna flipped her notebook shut. A flash of patience crossed her face as if she understood the dynamic and made allowances for a difficult customer.

As she left the table, a thin woman with hair pulled back in a tight bun strode into the restaurant. Wearing a grey pantsuit and a strand of white pearls, she pushed through the crowd and approached Kate's table.

"Good afternoon," she said.

Kate looked up, surprised.

Elise shook her head and placed her face in her palms. "What are you doing here?"

"I thought I might find you here," she stated. "I asked your sister to take you to lunch to get you out of the house, and she suggested this restaurant."

"To get *me* out of the house?" Elise asked, then nodded toward the band playing onstage. "We're here because of *him*."

Kate ignored her and extended her hand to their guest, introducing herself.

The woman took it and smiled. "Good to finally meet you. I'm Elise's psychotherapist, Dr. Yvette Cross."

Elise let out an irritated sigh. "Kate, meet my therapist who clearly has no respect for my boundaries," she said. "Doctor Cross, meet my nosy sister who has no respect for everyone else's boundaries."

CHAPTER TEN

Kate pulled out a chair for Dr. Cross in the noisy restaurant. "Would you like to join us?" she asked.

"Oh, I don't know if that'd be appropriate," the Doctor said, taking a seat anyway and turning to Elise. "But I am impressed to see you out of the house. That's a big step. Doesn't this feel good?"

Elise crossed her arms. "Aren't you violating some kind of ethics law?"

Dr. Cross turned to Kate. "I didn't know Elise had a sister. She said her whole family died in a California wildfire during a road trip to Disneyland."

Kate shook her head. "I think that was just her childhood fantasy."

"Please, don't let me interrupt your lunch," Dr. Cross said.

"Good. Go away," Elise said quickly.

The Doctor ignored her. "I ran into an investment group with an expressed interested in buying your bed and breakfast." She took out an envelope. "They're called the Friends of Historic Restoration, and they gave me a proposal to give to you and Redd."

Now the expression on Elise's face changed from irritated to surprise. "What?"

"We discussed this, remember? It'd be good for you, you know, and Redd to sell that old rundown house and move." The Doctor handed the envelope to Elise. "You two could start over."

Elise glanced at the envelope in her Doctor's hand but didn't take it. "Redd would rather I stake him through the heart with a wooden spoon than sell The Bluegill."

"Just look at their offer." The Doctor set the envelope on the table. "Read it and talk it over with Redd. The Friends of Historic Restoration is a charitable group that restores old homes and preserves the beauty and integrity of the past."

"We're not interested," Elise said.

"I already spoke to Redd, and he seemed very interested." The Doctor pressed her lips together and glanced at Kate as if looking for a vote of support. "I'm sure your sister would agree. The Bluegill holds too many unhappy memories. You could sell it and move to another city or another state. It would be healthy to start over."

"No." Elise looked down at her empty plate.

Dr. Cross persisted. "This investment group is willing to pay cash and is offering double what that old place is worth."

Kate picked the envelope up from the table and opened it. "Are you a Realtor or something?"

"No, I'm just a psychotherapist." The woman smiled, then added, "And of course, a friend. I have Redd and Elise's best interest at heart."

Kate took the folded paper from the envelope and glanced at the offer. It looked like the Friends of Historic Restoration was a land trust offering a whopping seven figures for the old Bluegill. She whistled as she folded the paper and returned it to the envelope. "Elise and I grew up in that house," she said. "It's hard to let go of it."

The Doctor smiled thinly. "What would be best for your sister's mental health? Remaining there or selling it and moving on with her life?"

Kate returned the paper to the envelope and set it on the table. "Elise said she isn't interested. What more do you want?" Kate was ready to change the subject and sounded a little offended.

"Well, like I said, I already spoke to Redd about it," the Doctor continued, taking the envelope and slipping it into her purse. "And he is, in fact, very interested. He's ready to move on. He's ready to put this behind him."

Waitress Lenna returned and set plates of sandwiches and a large sheet of paper on the table. Kate glanced at the drawing. Another stick figure woman with a gun, protecting the stick figure child. The stick figure man in black, with the abundance of red crayon splattering from his chest. A gray box hovered in the sky with yellow ray beams around it. The scene brought back painful thoughts, and Kate grasped her shoulder. Still, she thanked Lenna for giving it to her.

"Don't mention it. My little girl draws this same picture over and over. I got a million of these." Lenna set a pitcher of iced water on the table. As she filled their glasses, she glanced at the Doctor. "You want anything?"

Kate removed the top bun on her sandwich and found it smeared with mayo. It covered the bread, the lettuce, the tomato, and the grilled chicken breast. "I'm sorry," Kate said. "I ordered no mayo."

Lenna looked flustered. She formed an 'A' with her right hand and rotated it across her chest in a clockwise motion. Kate nodded and smiled, giving her the 'okay' sign by forming an 'O' with her thumb and index finger. Lenna took the plate away.

Elise placed an elbow on the table and picked at her salad. The Doctor watched her as the three women sat there in uncomfortable silence.

Ten minutes later, the band stopped playing, and Darren stepped off the stage to the delight of a group of teenage girls demanding he pose with them for pictures. Kate watched him for several moments, wondering if he even noticed her. He looked good, wearing boots, tight jeans, and a t-shirt with an American flag printed on it. She looked away, feeling the scrutiny of Elise's eyes.

She was about to say something when a shadow fell across the table. Kate looked up to find a tall guy with a mop of shaggy brown hair spilling out from under a backward ballcap. He flashed a crooked smile and held up his hands as if in surrender. "Nine to five, babe."

"Darren!" Kate shrieked with excitement. She'd forgotten how good-looking he was. No, she decided. He was more than just merely good-looking, though his features were classically handsome. The almost sullen set of his mouth, the thick, untamed, wavy brown hair that looked as if he'd just rolled out of bed, the way his green eyes looked lazily out from under heavy lids. All worked together to create an air of boyish charm and mature sex appeal. He was a strikingly attractive man who made her feel giddy as if she'd had one too many drinks. He had a way with women, and that made her uncomfortable.

He leaned down and kissed her on the cheek. A white light flashed, and Kate didn't know if she was more surprised by the public display of affection or the surprise photographer. Before she could say anything, Darren called the woman over and asked to be left alone. He turned to Kate and flashed a seductive smile. "You look terrific," he whispered.

Kate blushed. "Thank you. When did you get in town?"

"On Sunday. We played a beach bash in Clearwater, and we're playing here this afternoon for the fundraiser. They're raising money to restore that old lighthouse." He waved back toward the stage.

Kate grinned. "I know. I heard. You guys sound great." She gestured toward Elise. "Darren, you remember my kid sister."

He flashed Elise a brilliant smile, revealing a chipped front tooth. She'd forgotten about that little chip, and it was the perfect imperfection.

"Yeah," he said. "I remember. How ya been, Raw Meat?"

"Ugghh," Elise said without looking up at him. "I figured that was you singing when my ears started bleeding."

Kate continued, speaking over her sister. "And this is Elise's, um, her friend, Dr. Yvette Cross."

The Doctor stretched an arm across the table to shake his hand. "Pleased to meet you. I'm sorry. I didn't catch your name."

"It's Darren, your honor. Darren Riggler."

Dr. Cross laughed. "I'm not a judge; I'm a doctor. And you and your band sound terrific."

"Thank you. We just released a new CD, if you want to get one. Ten dollars each or two for twenty-five."

The Doctor scrunched her face. "That can't be right."

He looked back at Kate. "It's got a song I wrote for you."

"For me?"

"Yeah, I hope you don't mind."

"Mind? I'm sure I'll love it."

"I'll play it during our next set. You're going to stay for the next set, right? You're not leaving, are you?" He stretched out a hand, and she took it.

"No, we'll stay," she said, feeling the tight grip of his hand around hers. "I want to hear my song."

"Okay. This is so awesome," he said, still holding her hand. He squeezed tighter. "I can't believe you're finally going to hear it. I hope you like it. If you do, you can buy a CD, and I'll autograph it for you."

Kate giggled. "That'd be great. I can't wait to hear it."

"I can't wait for you to hear it." He finally let go of her hand. "Maybe we can get together tonight?"

Kate paused and shrank back in her seat. "Oh, I don't know, Darren." She thought about Ian and suddenly tasted something sour. "I've got a lot on my plate."

"Well, I'll be here through Thursday. We're playing in a bar in Pembroke Pines on Friday night, and then we'll be in Fort Lauderdale on Saturday. So maybe we could get together before we head out."

"Maybe…" Kate said slowly. The warmth of his hand lingered on her palm and fingers. "We'll see."

"Good. I'm going to hold you to that maybe." He smiled. "Okay? I'll call you later. You still have a phone, right?"

"Yes." Kate laughed. "I still have a phone."

"Awesome. I gotta get back to the band, but…" He grinned at Elise. "Raw Meat, it was really good to see you." He shook Dr. Cross's hand. "And it was a pleasure meeting you, counselor."

The Doctor took his hand. "Wait, Darren… I have to ask. Why do you call Elise Raw Meat?"

He laughed. "That's a long story."

"Back when we were dating," Kate explained. "Redd and Elise invited us to dinner at their place, and she served him raw meat."

Darren turned to a bandmate calling him from the stage. He turned back to Kate. "Looks like I gotta get back. Break's over. But don't forget, you said, maybe."

She shot him a warm smile. "Nine to five, Darren. Nine to five."

He grinned and winked at her. Pointing a finger, he said, "Nine to five." Never taking his eyes off her, he stumbled back to the stage.

As Kate, Elise, and Yvette continued their lunch, Darren and his band resumed playing.

"This next song goes out to a chick who holds a special place in my heart." Darren's deep voice echoed through the restaurant. The band launched into a ballad, and Kate rose from her chair and jumped to the dance floor. She swayed and clapped as Darren sang.

"I bend the ear of anyone who listens
Tell them our story and how it ends
We shoulda run away, we coulda been happy
If we got away, I coulda made you love me

"So I find another bar, sit beside a new friend
Buy him a beer and tell our story again
What else can I say?
What else can I do?
It still hurts, it still hurts,
It still hurts to think about you."

Elise joined Kate on the dance floor and pushed several people out of her way. She grabbed Kate's hand and laughed. "This is your song? It's a breakup song!"

Kate shook her head. "Maybe."

"It totally is," Elise said, pointing. "You broke his heart, and he wrote a song about it."

Kate stopped dancing. It *was* a breakup song. And she broke his heart. She totally broke his heart. The Doctor came up beside them and tapped her shoulder.

"I'm taking Elise home," she said in Kate's ear.

Kate flipped around. "Oh, no. Don't go."

"Elise wants to go," the Doctor said, struggling to be heard over the music. "I'm going to take her home."

Kate rushed back to their table for her purse and the drawing the waitress's daughter had made for her, then followed Elise and the Doctor outside. Tug barked and ran to her, dragging the college girl holding the other end of his leash. Kate took the strap from the girl and rushed to the parking lot, where Elise and the Doctor were headed for a rose-colored Mercedes.

"Kid, wait," Kate said. She hugged her sister. Elise stiffened. Kate stared at her a moment, then whispered. "It was good seeing you. I'm going to check on you later in the week."

"You don't need to." Elise turned away and opened the passenger door. "And stop calling me 'Kid.'"

"I want to check on you in a few days." Despite holding onto Tug's leash in one hand and the drawing in the other, she managed to extend her pinky finger in their traditional sign of sisterhood. Elise didn't take it.

"Don't be afraid to make it longer," Elise said as she plopped down into the passenger seat and shut the door.

Kate watched the rose-colored Mercedes reverse out of the parking slot. The college girl came up next to her and tapped her shoulder.

"Your sister signed the petition," she said. "But did your parents really name her Adolf Hitler?"

Kate ignored the girl and watched the Mercedes drive away.

If there was one thing she learned today, it was Elise was turning into their mother. She saw it in her demeanor and mood. Every facial tick and sarcastic comment. When their father left them, their mother fell into a deep depression, worse than anything she'd ever seen before. The Doctor prescribed meds, but their mother wouldn't take them.

Things seemed at their worst when Kate was going to Prom. Elise asked Kate not to leave.

"She didn't take her meds," Elise had said.

"Mother is a grown woman," Kate said. "If she doesn't want to take her meds, there's nothing they can do about it."

Kate made it back home late that night. She slipped out of her heels and tiptoed upstairs in her beautiful dress. Mother's bedroom door was open. Kate peeked into the room; Mother wasn't in bed. Kate switched on the light and went to the bathroom. Empty. She crossed the hall and looked in Elise's room. Her sister was fast asleep. Kate returned downstairs, looked in the kitchen, the living room, the library.

She found Mother outside on the lanai, lying on a deck chair, arm dangling over the side. A broken wineglass lay shattered on the flagstones and an empty bottle beside her.

Kate dialed 911, but she was too late. When the EMTs arrived, they pronounced her mother dead.

Elise and Kate watched from the staircase as the coroner removed the body.

"What happened?" Elise whispered.

Kate shook her head, watching. "We didn't take care of her."

Now, so many years later, Kate was watching it all happen again. She needed to take care of Elise. She just didn't know how.

CHAPTER ELEVEN

Kate and Tug left the Tiki Hut and walked six blocks through downtown to the Bear's Den. She called the bail bondsman from her iPhone and arranged Ian's bond before she reached the station.

Entering the building, she asked Travel Agent about Ian's status.

"Ask the chief," Travel Agent said quickly from her reception desk and continued her conversation with a voice coming through her headset. She waved at the dog as he followed Kate into the back.

She poked her head into Trace's office. He wasn't there. She led Tug through the breakroom and out the back door to the dock. Intern Ernie had a hose in hand, washing the police boats.

"Finally," he said, turning off the water. He pushed his glasses up farther on his nose. "Your afternoon class has, like, twenty people signed up, and I'll have to print-up some extra safety packets."

"Thanks for covering the morning class for me," she said. "It's been a crazy day. How'd it go?"

"Okay, I guess." He took a clipboard out of the box of red folders. "There were a lot of questions about how to prepare for Hurricane Sebastian."

"Yeah, the storm's got everyone worked up." She took the clipboard from him and gave it a once over when Officers Jensen and Jared stepped onto the dock, interrupting them. Tug rushed over to them, wagging his stubby tail.

"You posted bail for one Ian Biggs?" Jared asked.

Kate nodded and laughed. "Guess someone had to, right?"

Jensen shook his head in disgust. "If you ask me, he should have to sit that cell for a couple of days with a truckload of stinky diapers in there with him."

Jared shot him a disapproving glare. "Be nice."

"Why?" Jensen asked. "In fact, I wouldn't stop there. The only thing he gets to eat is just plates of runny baby shit."

Jared pushed him. "Now why you gotta say that? That's her boyfriend."

Jensen pushed him back. "He threw dirty diapers at us!"

"Okay, the guys a local terrorist," Jared said. "But he's Kate's local terrorist."

Jensen shook his head at Kate. "I'll never get what you see in him," he said, waving for her to follow. "The shithead's ready for release."

"And just so you know," Jared said to Kate as they walked to the back door. "We made him wash the squad cars."

* * *

Elise remained silent as Dr. Cross drove along the island back to the Bluegill.

The Doctor prattled on about something, but Elise wasn't listening. All she could think about was getting home, retreating into Noah's dark room, and sleeping. Dreaming. Noah visited her in her dreams.

"You told me that you always wanted to live somewhere with seasons and snow in the winter," the Doctor said as she finessed the steering wheel. "You and Redd could buy a little farm in the Midwest or some land in Georgia. They have peach trees, you know, and you love peaches."

Elise stared out the window. The Mercedes turned onto her neighborhood street, and they passed the large corner lot where the Needleman's dolphin mailbox stood vigil. A boy riding a bicycle whizzed past it. Not long ago, Noah rode his bike up and down the same street. He would pedal as fast as he could, yelling to her that he had to be going a hundred miles an hour. Sometimes he'd swerve into a flock of white ibis grouped in the street, disturbing them and laughing as they took flight around him. She wanted to go back to those days. If she closed her eyes, would she just drift asleep? Maybe never wake up.

She realized, for some reason, Dr. Cross was still talking, and she sort of listened to her voice and noticed the woman's hair was pulled back so tight in a bun that it didn't even move in the wind.

"It would do you both good to get away together, spend some time on each other and focus on your marriage," the Doctor said. "And when you're both ready, you can take in another child."

Elise glared at her. Had she really heard what she just thought she heard? "We could take in another child?" she asked, nearly choking on the words.

"I'm not saying you're going to replace Noah," the Doctor said quickly. "I'm not saying that at all. But, Elise, if you stay where you are, you're not going to get any better. What's worse, you and Redd are moving further apart."

"The only place I'd ever want to move to is the Grand Canyon," Elise said. "Just so I can push Redd into it."

"Okay . . ." The Doctor slowed and turned the steering wheel. "When we get back to your bed and breakfast, I'll give Redd the proposal. You don't have to worry about it."

Elise wasn't listening and mumbled under her breath, "Or maybe Mount St. Helen."

They came to the end of the street and pulled onto the circular drive. A wooden sign welcomed them to The Bluegill. The Doctor parked next to

Redd's pickup. Elise hated that old truck and wished Redd would sell it. The Doctor grasped her hand, surprising her and slipping an envelope into it.

"Please take it and just read it," she said. "Give it some serious thought before making any decision one way or the other."

"I don't have to think about it," Elise said. "We're not selling."

"Do you think Noah would want you to live like this? Do you think this would make him happy?"

Elise glared at the Doctor, ready to push her into Mount St. Helens, then closed her fist around the envelope, crumpling it. "Look, don't take it personally," she said. "I have a general contempt for all of humanity."

Leaving the car door open behind her, she rushed to the front porch. Inside the parlor, she called for Redd. He didn't answer. She turned toward the kitchen. Model train whistles and chugging sounds came from the garage. Angrily, she rushed up the stairs into Noah's room and slammed the door shut behind her.

She couldn't concentrate. Her depression seemed to be spiraling, and she was losing control. She tried everything she could to heal the gaping hole in her heart, focusing on happy memories with Noah. That's why she loved reading his book. The last time she read it, she noticed her hands trembling.

Picking up the large picture book from the floor, she fell into the rocker and flipped it open on her lap. Noah was near, she could feel his warmth, and it made her smile. Turning a page, she began reading.

"Because every night in Charley's room
The shadows grow
And the corners deepen
And the floorboards creak
As hushed footsteps creep
But Charley hides under his covers
And shuts his eyes
And closes his ears
Because he doesn't want to see, and he doesn't want to hear
What waits in the spooky places
Where the darkness hides."

Elise put down the book. Around her, the stuffed animals on the bed watched as if they were listening. She glanced at the baby monitor atop the bookcase.

"Doogie," she said. "Would you like me to continue?"

CHAPTER TWELVE

Kate and Tug followed Officers Jared and Jensen through the back door and down a narrow corridor to the holding cells. Ian sat behind bars and stood when they entered. He looked oddly out of place, wearing grey sweatshirt and sweatpants. She couldn't help thinking that maybe he did look shorter out of his regular vertical striped shirts.

"Looks like your bond is posted," Jared said.

Jensen unlocked the cell door and opened it. "C'mon, troublemaker. Let's go get you signed out."

In the lobby, Travel Agent, now wearing a bright red T-shirt urging people to "*Commit a random act of kindness*," placed a stack of forms on the counter for Ian to sign. Tug approached her, and she cuddled him at her desk.

Ian glanced up at Kate as he signed the release paperwork. "Question. What took so long? Where've you been?"

For a long second, Kate stared at him, debating whether or not to say what she was thinking. Not necessarily that he looked shorter out of vertical stripes, but that his passionate causes weren't as cute as they'd seem nine months ago when they'd first met. The height difference between them appeared more significant now. And maybe she was only a year older, but somehow, he seemed extraordinarily juvenile and immature. She wanted to say all that and more but settled for, "I think you mean, thank you."

"You're right. Thank you." He took a brown paper sack from Travel Agent and opened it. The putrid stench of his shirt, pants, and ballcap from the protest site assaulted their noses. Kate took a step back. Travel Agent turned her head while Ian crumpled the sack closed.

Jensen cringed. "Don't open that bag till you're outside!"

"In fact, let's just burn it." Kate pinched her nose and sidestepped to the door. "C'mon, jailbird. I'll drive you home." She turned back to Travel Agent and whistled for Tug. "Tell Intern Ernie I'll be back in time for the afternoon class."

They left the police station and walked downtown. She held Tug's leash and jerked it a couple of times to keep him from sniffing park benches, trees, and fire hydrants.

Ian followed along the sidewalk. "Look, I know you're mad, but don't take it out on the dog," he said.

She nodded, acknowledging they needed to slow down, but she didn't want to. They walked for several minutes in silence.

"You know they made me wash the squad cars," he finally said, carrying his paper sack of soiled clothing.

She glanced down at him. "Sounds like you deserved it."

"I deserved it for doing what's right? For following my conscience?" He caught up with her and tried to hold her hand. Tug pulled on the leash, yanking her forward. Ian called after her. "Where'd you park?"

"At the Tiki Hut. I took Elise to lunch," she yelled back to him.

"Impressive," he said. "How'd you manage to get her out of the house?"

"I'm not sure." She slowed and brought Tug to a patient trot. "It's been a crazy day," she continued. "Do you remember attorney Jasper Wade? His daughter approached me at the physical therapists' and told me her father was missing."

Ian stopped walking. "Jasper Wade? Wasn't he the attorney that represented--"

"Yes." Kate nodded. She stopped, and Tug pulled on the leash. She fought to keep him still. "He represented Frazier and got him off on charges for killing my nephew in a drunk driving accident."

"The man is scum, and his attorney is too." He seemed to think about it a moment. "That's why you shoulda been out there protesting with me. We need to take the Kingpin down."

Kate didn't even let him finish the thought. "Don't start with me again," she said. "I've had enough of your protesting, and when I told Redd about Wade missing, it set him off all over again too."

"He has every right to be mad. Forrest Frazier murdered his son, and he got off scot-free because of that scum-sucking attorney. Frazier and everyone associated with him needs to pay for what they're doing."

She took a deep breath and adjusted her smile. "Are you talking about my nephew or the lighthouse?"

"Both. And everyone they screw. The environment they burn. The mom-and-pop shops they run out of business. The history they obliterate." Ian shook his head, looking up at her. "You just don't get it."

"I do get it. I totally get it, and I get why you're fighting so passionately . . . but I'm not discussing the lighthouse with you."

"This isn't just about the lighthouse." He stopped walking. "But since you brought it up, there's something I need to tell you. I met somebody."

She turned to him. "Come again?"

"In jail," he said. "I met Reverend Shipp. And he knows how to stop the demolition of the lighthouse."

"You met a reverend in jail. What was he in there for?"

"Indecent exposure, but that's not the point." He talked fast, as if the faster he spoke, the more likely he could convince her. "The reverend says that the town founder was born in that lighthouse."

"That's an urban legend."

"Possibly. Still, the founder's great, great-grandson is out there somewhere. We find him, and he can confirm it really happened."

She considered what he was saying and wondered if she heard him correctly. "Wait—Reverend Shipp? Are you talking about the nudist cult?"

"Correct. They may be nudists, but they're not a cult, per se." He shrugged as he spoke. "The Reverend knows the great, great-grandson of the founder. He's going to help me track him down and get before the city council so they can declare the Widow Rock Lighthouse a historic landmark. We wouldn't even need the petition, and Frazier wouldn't be able to touch it."

"Good lord, Ian—" she said. "You're dragging me into another discussion about the lighthouse."

"It's critical."

"I'm done talking about it!"

"Fine. If you don't care, then I won't bother you with it anymore." He walked past her, throwing his hands up. "If you think the Kingpin can violate the law and get away with it, and there's no problem there…"

She caught up with him, pulling Tug along with her. "You got arrested today for trespassing, possibly terrorism."

"At least I'm standing for something," he said, his eyes set on her and blazing.

"Is the lighthouse something worth standing for? It's old. It's unsafe. It's an eyesore, and even worse—it's a deathtrap. Me and my sister were lucky we didn't get hurt playing in that old building as kids."

"Question. If not the lighthouse, then how about your nephew? Isn't he worth fighting for?"

"That's not fair." She watched his eyes turn dark.

He took a deep breath. "Thanks for bailing me out, but I need some space."

"Oh, come on. One has nothing to do with the other." She watched him head to the curb, looking both ways as traffic passed. "Where are you going?"

"My Vespa is in impound."

"Are you coming back to my place?"

"I'm going to crash at my Smother's." Carrying his crinkled paper sack, he crossed the street. From the other side, he called to her. "I've got work to do. I need to track down the founder's great, great-grandson."

"You can do that at my place."

"I need to go check on my mom anyway."

"Ian, listen, I admire your passion, but it's misguided."

"Maybe it is…but you know if you're the only one left with any passion, you gotta use it. You gotta use the hell out of it." A truck passed in front of him and blew his red hair as it sped by. "I can't live any other way. I'd rather be out in the trenches getting my teeth kicked in than standing on the sidelines playing it safe."

Playing it safe, she thought. Truth be told, maybe that's what she was doing with him.

They'd met in the hospital as she was recuperating from the gunshot wound. He was supposed to deliver a pizza to her room but got lost somewhere between reception and the maternity ward. She waited for him at the elevators, wearing an open gown and lugging an IV drip behind her. He was a cute, sweet-looking, short guy, and they struck up a conversation.

"I moved to Florida to save the manatees," he told her, wearing a vertically striped shirt and a green Little Nero Pizza visor. "Did you know there are barely twelve hundred left in the wild?"

She told him that she worked for the Florida Fish and Wildlife Commission and was intimately familiar with the manatee's plight. "That's a figure from a few decades ago," she explained. "Now, there are closer to seven thousand due to the efforts of the FWC."

He seemed taken back by this. "Still… you know, uh, they need our help."

"I'm sure they do." She smiled at him, and he gave her his phone number.

When she hobbled back to her room and told the nurses about the cute pizza guy, they insisted she call him. So, she did.

She and Ian were talking daily by the time she got out of the hospital.

He'd just moved to town. His mother, whom he referred to as his "Smother," had retired to Florida, and finding himself down on his luck, he moved in with her while trying to get back on his feet. Or as he put it, while he saved the manatees. Kate liked him and enjoyed helping him with his causes, especially since her sister had stopped speaking to her.

She found his quirks cute, such as his closet filled with vertically striped shirts. He only wore vertical stripes, as a rule, never horizontal. Vertical lines made him look taller. However, his height didn't concern her.

She liked everything about him—from his physical insecurities to his environmental passions to the vertically striped wardrobe and even the tattoo on his upper back of a black Polynesian elephant. "Elephants embody power, strength, dignity, and longevity," he told her. "They're protectors of nature." She realized it was how he wanted the world to see him, and she swore never to call him "Fun Size" again. Though it was a promise, she struggled to keep.

Before long, he seemed to stay at her boathouse more and more, and she found herself joining his causes. The manatees. The Florida panther. Protesting any housing development or commercial construction project by local real estate tycoon, Forrest Frazier. All his causes were a convenient distraction ...from the tragedy of her nephew's death and her sister's anger and silent treatment ...from Darren taking off with his band when she needed him most ...from her injury and her time off from the FWC ... from the darkness closing in around her as her world came to an abrupt halt.

So, yes, truth be told, she was playing it safe.

She watched him disappear down the sidewalk across the street, then looked at Tug. He looked up at her and snorted.

CHAPTER THIRTEEN

Kate returned to the Bear's Den and instructed the afternoon class on the do's and don'ts of boat safety. Just as Intern Ernie had forewarned, the majority of questions centered on the coming hurricane and the best ways to protect their boats and property. When it was over, she escaped to her office and tossed her purse on the desk. The photo of Jasper Wade fell out. She picked it up and studied the face.

How could he have defended that, as Redd put it, 'pile of human waste?'

Noah's death was still incomprehensible. Senseless. Unbearably painful. She wished she hadn't said anything about Wade's disappearance to Redd. She should've known better.

Wade's disappearance, she thought.

Turning to her computer, she typed "*Jasper Wade Noah Tyler trial*" in the search and brought up a dozen or so hits. She clicked an article from the Tampa Bay Times, and it opened on the screen.

She read the headline: "Five-year-old dies in car accident with drunk driver." Noah's innocent smile, with missing front tooth and freckled cheeks, appeared below it, along with a mug shot of the drunk driver, real estate tycoon Forrest Frazier.

There were more articles, including several about the trial. Kate noticed one that showed Frazier with his attorney, Jasper Wade. The headline read: "Frazier acquitted of manslaughter in death of five-year-old."

She scanned the article and found a reference to Jasper Wade's law firm: Wade & Flagg, Attorneys at Law, PC.

Flagg?

Kate sat back in her chair and glanced down at Tug. She thought of the pontoon boat adrift in the Bay and the boarded-up house in Palma Sola. Leaning forward, she typed "Jerry and Maxine Flagg" in the search and found a number of hits, including Wade & Flagg, Attorneys at Law, PC. He was Jasper Wade's partner in the firm.

She searched for an alternate address for the Flaggs and found a phone number with a Connecticut area code.

She picked up her iPhone and dialed the number. The phone rang, and a woman answered.

"Flagg residence …"

Kate looked down at the dog. He cocked his head, curious. She focused on the woman who answered the phone.

"Is this Maxine?" she asked.

"This is housekeeping," the woman answered.

"Is Maxine or Jerry Flagg there?"

The woman sounded impatient. "They're at their Florida home. They won't be back here until spring."

Kate paused, thinking. "Do they have another residence?"

"Just the two, ma'am. The one here in Connecticut and the one down in Florida."

She hung up and crossed the hall into Trace's office. He was putting golf balls into an overturned red solo cup, and she stopped the ball with her foot before it made it into the cup.

"Jerry Flagg," she said.

He positioned another ball and swung. "Come again?"

"Jerry Flagg," she said again. "The derelict craft. The abandoned bulldog."

"Yes?" he asked with little interest as the ball rolled into the cup.

"He's Jerry Flagg of Wade and Flagg, Attorneys at Law, PC."

"And?" He stepped to the solo cup and fished out the ball.

"And…" she said as he returned to his spot and positioned the golf ball on the floor. She stared at him a moment and continued. "He's Jasper Wade's partner in the firm. You know, Jasper Wade. His daughter Olivia reported him missing yesterday."

He hit the golf ball into the cup again. She bent down and turned the cup right side up, trapping the ball inside.

"That means," she said, rising. "They're *both* missing."

Trace cleared his throat. "That girl that approached you—"

"Olivia."

"Olivia," he repeated. He approached the cup and picked up the ball. "Olivia, who didn't report him missing…who didn't come into the department…who didn't submit an MPR. Do you see where I'm going with this?"

Kate shook her head.

He returned to his spot and positioned the ball. "Jasper Wade's a high-profile attorney. Wouldn't his staff be out looking for him if he suddenly didn't show up in the office? And what about his wife? We don't know for a fact that Wade is even missing."

"But isn't it odd that we're questioning the whereabouts of *both* partners in that law firm?" She approached him and placed her foot on the ball again, preventing him from putting.

He shrugged, aggravated, and placed the putter back on the wall. "Kate, c'mon. You checked the Flagg residence yourself. They boarded up the windows and left town ahead of the storm."

"Do we know that for a fact?" She turned away from him and focused on the rocking horse and bassinet she'd bought for the baby. They remained stashed in the corner. Frilly, pink baby clothes lay scattered on various boxes beneath his stupid old putter hanging proudly on the wall.

Trace returned to his desk. “Maybe it’s worth making a few calls. I’ll ask Jensen and Jared to reach out to the families and the office to do a wellness check.”

Kate wasn’t listening and stared at the dusty Bulls Eye golf club on the wall. Flecks of white paint dotted the flange. She flipped around when he called her name. “I’m sorry?” she asked.

“Jensen and Jared can contact the families and the office,” he said again. “Maybe they’ll dig something up.”

The thought of Jasper Wade and Jerry Flagg weighed heavy on Kate’s mind as she left the Bear’s Den for the day and headed out of Sienna Keys. Tug sat in the passenger seat, and she had to pull the drawing the waitress’s daughter had made for her and the *Sign Language for Dummies* book out from under him. Approaching the Causeway, she noticed the Starlight Motel—where Olivia was staying. She turned into the parking lot.

In the passenger seat, Tug raised up on his hind legs and placed his paws on the glass. He looked back at her as if questioning where they were going.

Kate hopped out of the Tahoe and looked at the motel building. The late afternoon sun dominated the sky behind it, and she cupped a hand over her brow to shade her eyes from the light. Her purse hung over her shoulder, and it took her a minute to find the card Olivia had given her. When she found it, she noted the room number.

The room was toward the front of the motel building, looking out over the Causeway Bridge. She knocked on the door. No answer. She knocked again.

Turning the card over, she found the phone number Olivia had scribbled on the back. She entered it into her iPhone. Listened to it ring.

No one answered.

A red sun hung low on the horizon by the time Kate made it home. She grabbed the drawing and crossed the dock toward her houseboat with Tug in tow, and ran the connections in her mind.

Jerry Flagg and Jasper Wade were partners in a law firm. They both defended some shady characters who’d committed heinous crimes. Theft. Drugs. Murder. Had they lost any cases? Could they have defended a criminal who now had a bone to pick? She’d have to talk to Trace about it tomorrow and look into their cases. Of course, that was assuming the two men were even missing at all.

She took in a deep breath. The air seemed alive, heavy with moisture in the warm evening. The wooden slats creaked beneath her feet as the water slapped softly against the wooden pilings. The faint sound of a sitcom’s laugh track drifted out from one of the other houseboats, and Tug seemed interested in investigating the noise. He trotted toward the boat. She called for him and whistled. He came running.

Inside her houseboat, Doc chattered excitedly in his cage, and Bert hooted and blinked his one large eye. They followed her into the kitchenette, where she added the new artwork to the fridge, right along with the many other drawings. She fed the animals then fixed a grilled cheese and a glass of wine for herself. The animals followed her onto the deck, where she sat among the potted plants and watched the sunset. Seagulls circled above them.

She still had Darren's CD and popped it into a player sitting atop the table. His deep voice filled the speakers.

"I bend the ear of anyone who listens
Tell them our story and how it ends
We shoulda run away; we coulda been happy
If we got away, I coulda made you love me

"What else can I say?
What else can I do?
It still hurts, it still hurts,
It still hurts to think about you."

Kate only half-listened to the song as her brain focused on Jerry Flagg and Jasper Wade. They had a reputation for defending some dangerous people. If they'd lost a case, it'd make sense for one of those criminals to look for some payback. She'd have to check if any of their defendants were recently released from prison.

She rubbed her aching shoulder and flipped her laptop open. With a couple of keystrokes, she looked up release records then stopped.

What if there was a victim who wanted payback? Could there be a sufferer who didn't see justice served because Wade and Flagg, Attorneys at Law, PC got the offender off on a technicality? A thought flashed through her head, one that she didn't want to think.

Her brother-in-law, Redd. He was a sufferer who didn't see justice served because of Wade and Flagg, Attorneys at Law, PC. Because of Jasper Wade.

Darren's song ended, and she considered playing it again. She got up from her chair and changed the CD. From the corner of her eye, she noticed a man standing on the dock, watching her boat. Watching *her*. She gasped. He stepped out of the shadows and into the lamplight.

She rushed to the edge of her deck. "Hello?"

"That's your song," he called out, waving to her. She recognized the deep, masculine voice.

Darren Riggler.

She couldn't believe he was here, standing on the dock. And the bigger question was why.

CHAPTER FOURTEEN

"Darren?" Kate asked. He stood under the warm glow of a dock lamp, looking up at her. He was honestly the last person she expected to see. "What are you doing here?"

"I wanted to see how you liked the show this afternoon." The planks creaked beneath his boots as he stepped toward her boat and climbed up onto the deck. When he was standing in front of her, she raised her head and looked up at him. He was so tall. Even taller in his boots.

"It was good," she said slowly. "I'm just surprised to see you . . . here."

"I remembered you live on a houseboat, and I wanted to make sure it didn't go all Titanic with you in it?"

"What are you talking about?"

He moved closer to her, his voice whispering. His fingers grazed her hand. "There's a storm coming."

"Among other things."

"Other things." He grinned, revealing the chip in his front tooth. "I think about other things sometimes." The smile faded. "I thought maybe we could talk. Catch up, you know. I wanna talk to you about something before we head out."

"Talk?"

"Yeah, talk. You know . . ." His breath felt hot on her face. "It's all the rage today. Kids everywhere, it's all they ever do anymore . . . talk."

"Among other things." She let out a nervous laugh. "I know how your mind works."

He shook his head as if trying to determine if she was teasing him. "You know they say that storm is going to be pretty bad."

"Category Four."

"It's gonna be bad, Katie. Real bad, and the weather reports are predicting it'll make landfall around here. So, why don't you pack up and hit the road with us? You could meet us in Fort Lauderdale. Watch the band. Have a good time."

She moved away from him, putting space between their bodies. "I can't go to Fort Lauderdale."

"Why not?"

"Because there's a storm coming." She repeated his words with his exact inflection.

"I know," he said. "So, get out of town. If that hurricane is headed northeast, then you should go south."

"I can't. I've got to help the town get prepared." She turned away from him, then whipped back around. "People depend on me."

When he looked down at his feet, she touched his chin, lifting his head.

"I was just listening to the song you wrote for me," she said, changing the subject.

He smiled. "Do you like it?"

She nodded. Was he really here, standing in front of her again? He disappeared on her just when she needed him most. If she was honest, though, he was never far from her mind. She'd been infatuated with him since the night they met some six-plus years ago. Had it really been that long?

She, Elise, and Redd celebrated at a crowded New Year's Eve party at Brewsky Bill's in Bradenton. They were talking and laughing and waiting for the countdown to begin.

On stage, a band performed classic southern rock songs from Lynyrd Skynyrd, The Black Crowes, and The Eagles. The lead singer was tall, with long, dark hair swept back from his face and striking green eyes. He worked the crowd, and she enjoyed his music. She enjoyed the eye contact they were making even more. Every time she looked up, he seemed to be staring directly at her, as if he was singing just to her. And she'd look away.

"Any requests?" he finally yelled down from the stage.

She waved to him from their table and grinned mischievously. She wasn't going to make this easy. "Do you know *Nine to Five*?" she yelled.

He scratched his head. "The Dolly Parton song?"

"That's the one."

"That's a, um…" He looked confused standing up there on the stage, behind the mic.

Her voice rose with excitement. "A girl's song?"

"A pop song," he answered.

She laughed. "If it's beyond your vocal range, then…"

He interrupted her. "No, I can do it."

The crowd cheered, and he beamed at his bandmates. He pulled the song up on his Smartphone, and a few minutes later, the band was struggling their way through Dolly Parton's classic about working women getting ahead. Toward the middle of the song, the crowd joined in. Darren pointed at Kate and wiggled his index finger, inviting her up on stage.

She didn't realize how tall he was until she stood next to him. He had to be at least six-four, if not six-five. Maybe it was the cowboy boots. They could add an inch or two.

He handed her the mic, and with a squeak, she sang the refrain. When they finished, the crowd cheered, and he smirked at her. "You happy now?"

"I'll admit, I'm surprised," she said.

By one, the new year began, and the band wrapped. Darren hopped off the stage and approached her. "You're a Dolly fan, I take it?"

She looked up at him and shot him a coy smile. "Well, I've never been to Dollywood."

"You wanna go someday? With me?"

She chuckled. "Oh, you're a bad boy, aren't you?"

"No." He nodded as he said it. "Why do you say that?"

"Because you're in a band," she looked behind her at the bass player and the drummer loading equipment into their van. "And bands have a reputation."

"Well, let me tell you, my only reputation is for being a very talented performer. And I write my own songs."

"You're modest and talented. The total package." She laughed and couldn't believe she was so shamelessly flirting with him. "What's your name?"

"Darren," he said. "Darren Riggler and the Repeaters. What's yours?"

"Kathryn Parks with the Florida Fish and Wildlife Commission, but my friends just call me Kate."

"Nice to meet you, Katie." He added the "ie" to her name, which she normally detested. But coming from him, the extra syllable sounded cute. A little chip in his front tooth somehow made him even more appealing. He looked sheepishly down at his boots. "I'm going to do something I never do and ask you for your phone number."

"You *never* do that?" She emphasized the word "never," not believing it for a second.

"No," he said defensively. "I'm actually kind of shy."

A girl wearing a halter top, Daisy Duke shorts, and red cowboy boots approached and pushed Kate out of the way. She wrapped her arms around Darren and pouted.

"C'mon, babe, you haven't called me," she said.

He took a step back and looked over at Kate.

Kate wasn't sure what to make of it. A fan? A girlfriend? A random stalker? She didn't really care for any of those prospects. She shook her head and walked. "Good night, Darren Babe."

He called after her, but Kate left that night and didn't see or think of him again. Or at least, not until Valentine's Day rolled around.

She sat solo at the bar at the Tiki Hut. Elise and Redd were parents now and had abandoned her. She didn't have a boyfriend or even a date for Valentine's. It didn't matter. She had a drink to nurse, not really paying attention to the band… until the lead singer began a familiar song.

He was singing "*Nine to Five.*"

She glanced up from her drink. There was Darren Riggler, tall and dark hair sweeping back off his face, wearing black boots, and belting out the Dolly Parton classic. She turned away. He finished the song without her ever acknowledging him.

To her surprise, he started singing it again, a capella. The band behind him looked puzzled, then caught up with the verse. He finished and waited as if expecting her to get up or say something or climb on stage with him. When she didn't, he started the song over. The band played it five more times before the restaurant owner commandeered the mic and urged them to move on to a Bon Jovi staple.

Kate watched them perform the rest of the night. A few hours later, a little after one in the morning, she approached him in the parking lot. He and the band members were loading amps and large black speakers into the van, and he greeted her.

"I take it you're a big Dolly fan," she said to him.

"Well, I've never been to Dollywood," he said.

She rushed to him and kissed him. When their lips parted, his stare drilled into her.

"What was that for?" he asked.

"That's for playing '*Nine to Five*' a hundred times tonight," she whispered.

"It was seven, but who's counting?" He kissed her this time. Holding her, he whispered, "You know we're never getting booked here again, right? It's your fault, and now my band hates you."

"That's okay," she whispered. "I was planning to break up the band anyway."

He stepped back, his eyes wide with shock.

"I'm kidding," she said, drawing him close again. "It's a joke."

She kissed him again.

She smiled at the memory.

The song he wrote for her reverberated from the speakers in her boathouse, surrounding them. The music faded and silenced stretched between them as they stared at each other in the dark. She'd forgotten how green his eyes were.

"We shoulda run away; we coulda been happy," he whispered. His arms closed around her, holding her in a way she hadn't felt in a long time. "If we got away, I coulda made you love me. What else can I say? What else can I do? It still hurts . . . it still hurts to think about you."

His lips brushed hers.

"You know." She could barely get the words out. "It should hurt. You're the one that took off with the band and left me behind."

"I was an idiot," he said. "We shoulda never gone out on the road."

He didn't mean it, though, and she knew it.

For several years, they saw each other off and on whenever his band played in town. But was it a relationship? Darren was a player, with a girl in every city. She never owned his heart. But maybe they meant something to each other after all?

Impossible. She was one of many. She knew that, and she knew him. A girl in every city. One of many, many girls who wanted to possess him, make him hers. She remembered a very uncomfortable call from one such crazy psycho fangirl.

"He's mine," she'd threatened Kate over the phone. "You don't back off, and I'll beat your ass till hell won't have it." She sounded unstable and obsessed, and Kate realized then that a relationship with a musician would never work out.

And it didn't. They broke up. Moved on. She ended up with Ian Biggs in a stable, adult relationship. Stable or stale? Was there a difference? Darren probably ended up with that crazy chick. Or maybe Kate was the crazy one.

Darren broke the embrace and stepped away from her. His eyes glistened as he stood there in the night air on her deck. Moonlight illuminated his face, and he looked wildly handsome. She'd almost forgotten how attractive he was. How electrifying his touch could be.

His voice took a serious tone. "I want you to reconsider. Meet me in Fort Lauderdale…"

Her iPhone rang, interrupting them.

She stepped back, moving away from him. Answered the call. "This is Kate Parks, Florida Fish and Wildlife Officer on inactive duty status and currently temporarily working for the Sienna Key law enforcement."

"Ms. Parks." A high-pitched female voice crackled through her phone's speakers. "I was wondering if you had any news on Daddy." It was Olivia Wade.

"Where have you been?" Kate answered, looking at Darren as she spoke. He winked at her. She looked away, concentrating on the call. "I've been calling you all afternoon and stopped by the motel. You need to fill out a missing person's report."

"I just remembered something." Olivia sounded urgent. "On Saturday, he mentioned something about fishing at Corman's Launch."

"Corman's Launch? That's a pretty remote area."

"So that means something?"

"I can check it out . . . and Olivia?" She clenched her mouth tight as she considered just how to ask the question. "Are you familiar with Jerry Flagg?"

"Who?" she asked.

"Jerry Flagg, your father's partner in the firm," Kate said. She thought it was odd she had to explain that.

"I don't care about anyone but Daddy," Olivia screamed. "Please. Find him."

"You need to file a Missing Person's Report," Kate said. "I spoke to Chief Guerra. He doesn't have any record of you coming into the station to—"

"They wouldn't let me file it." Olivia's tone had a sharp edge to it. Impatient. Irritated. "They told me to wait forty-eight hours."

"Who are they? Who'd you speak with?"

"I don't know. It was whoever was at the police station." Olivia spoke louder, her voice trembling. "Look, Ms. Parks, Daddy is missing, and I'm terrified that something is wrong. I don't care about paperwork and reports. I just want you to find my daddy."

"We're doing the best we can. But, one more question . . . if you don't mind." Kate took a breath. She looked back at Darren, into his eyes, then turned away just as quickly. She focused on the call. "Did you know your father represented Forrest Frazier, the man who killed my nephew?"

Olivia went silent. "No," she finally said. "I didn't know that."

"Forrest Frazier was intoxicated and operating a moving vehicle. He hit my sister and killed my nephew in the crash. Your father got Frazier out of the manslaughter charges."

"I'm sorry to hear that," Olivia said. "I'm sorry that happened to you and your family. But Daddy represented a lot of people. I'm sure it wasn't personal."

"No," Kate said. "I'm sure it wasn't."

"Now, please, let me know as soon as you find him." Olivia disconnected.

Kate put her phone away and glanced at Darren. Some little part of her was tempted to tell him, yes, to drop everything and meet him in Fort Lauderdale. They could run away together. But she knew better. He was a player. An illusion. And she had real responsibilities and people depending on her. She had a job to do.

She had to find Jasper Wade.

And she prayed Redd hadn't found him first.

***

Chief Trace Guerra pulled his squad car into the empty Sienna Key Island Shops parking lot. He talked to Nellie on his phone as he drove.

"Thomas is kicking." Nellie's voice sounded positively radiant through the phone. "The doctor said he's developing right on schedule. He's about eighteen inches now."

"That's great." Trace smiled as he talked to her. To be honest, it scared him. Forty-five was too old to start a family.

"My mom scheduled her flight for next month right before the due date. She's going to stay with us for the first month."

"A whole month?" The smile disappeared from his face as he scanned the parking lot. The retail anchor, a Publix Supermarket and Pharmacy, closed promptly at 10 PM. A sign was posted under several light posts warning "No overnight parking," but one truck and trailer parked diagonally across a good eight or nine slanted parking slots still remained. Trace pulled alongside it.

He listened to his wife's voice as he studied at the truck and empty boat trailer. "She's offered to stay up with the baby to help us get some sleep. Do you know how exhausted we're going to be? We're lucky to have her."

"Honey, I'm gonna have to call you back."

He ended the call.

The vehicle didn't look abandoned. In fact, it seemed well cared for. He called dispatch to send out a tow truck, then ran the plates.

His laptop returned the name: JASPER WADE.

CHAPTER FIFTEEN

Wednesday
September 3

With the sunrise, Kate felt Doc's weight in the hoodie behind her neck. She steered *The Kendell* toward the shoreline along Apollo Beach, nearing Corman's Launch. The photo of Jasper Wade, taped to the glass above the steering wheel, flapped in the wind. She stared at his picture and asked under her breath, "Where could you be?"

An hour earlier, she'd picked up her old boat from the pier instead of attending her scheduled physical therapy session. She'd heard Trace report the truck abandoned in the Publix parking lot, and there were several crews out looking for the man. She didn't know why she didn't tell him that Olivia suspected her father was at Corman's Launch.

Scratch that. She knew exactly why she hadn't said anything. She was stuck on desk duty. The gunshot wound nine-months ago left her with a metal rod and screws holding her shoulder together and shook her to her core. She needed to prove to herself that she was field-ready. This was a test to determine if she could return to her position with Florida Fish and Wildlife.

Or was she out here because of Redd?

Some nagging feeling in the back of her head just wouldn't go away. A little voice warned her of—*what?* She noticed she was rubbing her shoulder and stopped.

So far, she'd seen no sign of Jasper Wade's boat. She took a bearing toward the south-eastern neck and could see the power plant's smokestacks in the distance and the Sunshine Skyway Bridge behind her.

She brought *The Kendell* to rest along the shore of Corman's Launch. Doc chirped and scampered onto her shoulder, hanging on to her sweatshirt with his single arm, as she splashed into the shallow water. A fisherman tied down his Anglerfish skiff to a trailer on the ramp. When he pulled out of the water, she waded toward the concrete incline.

She looked around at the water, the woods, the ramp. A dark stain tarnished the concrete above the waterline. It looked like blood. It could've been anything. Doc chirped as if he noticed something odd too and scrambled down her arm to the ground. He sniffed the dark stain on the concrete.

Standing, Kate scanned the trees when her iPhone rang. Ian's smiling face appeared above the name "Fun Size" on the screen. She really needed to change that.

"How's your mom?" she asked, answering his call.

"Smothering," he said. He sounded a little harsh, then his voice relaxed. "Truce? I'm sorry about our fight yesterday."

"It was hardly a fight."

"Still, you bailed me out of jail, and I should've been more appreciative."

"Did you track down the founder's grandson?"

"Great, great-grandson, and no, I didn't." His voice crackled over the phone's speakers. "All I've got is a name."

"At least it's a start, right?" As she spoke into the phone, she lifted Doc off the ground and placed him back on her shoulder. He stood on his hind legs and leaned toward the iPhone held to the side of her face. She rubbed his head with her index finger and concentrated on Ian. "Just no more throwing dirty diapers at demolition workers."

"Agreed," he answered.

"And you're not going to rile up the Mommy Warriors again or any other Mother's Day Out organizations."

"Agreed," he repeated as if memorizing a lesson for school.

"And you're going to leave Forrest Frazier alone?"

His coolness was evidence that he was not amused. "Listen, Kate. I gotta go . . .

* * *

. . . but I'll see you tonight." Ian stood on the curb outside the Mayfair Plaza Building in Bradenton, wearing his call-to-action buttons over a freshly washed vertical striped shirt and a "Green Living, Blue World" ball-cap. He spoke to Kate on his iPhone. "Again, I apologize for yesterday. I appreciate everything you do."

He looked up at the twelve-story Mayfair Plaza building with mirrored windows that reflected blue sky and white clouds. The ground floor contained a bank and investment center, with other stories dedicated to an insurance company, a call center, and the headquarters for a grocery store chain. The entire twelfth floor housed the offices for Forrest Frazier Development.

"Don't mention it." Kate's voice came through his iPhone as he stepped from the sidewalk into the parking garage. The attendant booth and extended barrier gate arm weren't keeping him out, and he approached a crowd already assembling in the garage. He tapped the arm of a sixty-something man dressed in a conspicuous tan trench coat. The man turned to reveal a bullhorn in one hand and a protest sign in the other. Ian gave him an energetic thumbs-up. Behind the man, a crowd huddled just outside the elevators, all wearing trench coats and holding hand-painted picket signs.

A red 1961 Ferrari 250 GT turned into the garage and paused at the attendant booth.

Ian snapped and pointed at the man in the trench coat as he told Kate, "Listen, I gotta go. Talk to you tonight."

"Okay, sounds g—" Kate's voice clipped as he ended the call and faced his colleague.

"Okay, Reverend Shipp," he said. "Are you ready?"

Reverend Shipp gave him a concerned look. "There's no media here. Where's the news vans?"

"Inconsequential," Ian said. "The Kingpin just pulled in."

"Okay then. Let's do this." Reverend Shipp lifted a bullhorn to his mouth. He addressed his congregation. "The devil's arrived."

The crowd cheered.

As the barrier gate arm lifted and the Ferrari rolled forward, the Reverend dropped his bullhorn and sign and discarded his trench coat, revealing a wrinkled, hairy body—stark-naked and bare as the day God made him. His congregation followed suit, with fifteen men and women removing their trench coats and exposing all their glory. They raised signs and chanted, "Save Widow Rock! Save Widow Rock!" as the Ferrari parked.

Forrest Frazier got out of the car, chewing a cigar and wearing a Brunello Cucinelli suit with Ray-Ban Aviator sunglasses. He hesitated in front of the mass of naked protesters. "Go home, people!" he said. "I've already paid-off the news. You're not making any headlines today."

He raised a fob and aimed it at the Ferrari. The car beeped.

Ian grabbed the bullhorn from the Reverend and shouted, "You can't demolish the Widow Rock Lighthouse. We won't let you."

Chewing his cigar, Forrest pushed past the nude men and women and entered the elevator carriage. Ian ran after him.

"Question," Ian called out. "Do you even care that the lighthouse is a historic landmark in Sienna Key?"

Forrest pressed the elevator button. "I thought you were in jail for yesterday's temper tantrum," he said.

"I got out on bail." Ian held the doors, preventing them from closing. "And I'm going to stop you, no matter what."

"Is that a fact?" Forrest removed the cigar from his mouth, glaring at him. He pressed the buttons again, but Ian kept his hand on the doors.

"You can bank on it," he said.

Forrest returned the cigar to his mouth and spoke with it between his teeth. "With what? A petition of lunatic nudists and a few soccer moms?"

"Newsflash," Ian said. "I have over three-hundred signatures."

"My condo plans will add five hundred new residents and create jobs and bring millions into Sienna Key. You should be thanking me, not fighting me."

Reverend Shipp stepped beside Ian and rammed a bare arm into the elevator carriage, waving his fist at Forrest. "We're going to stop you. The town founder was born in that lighthouse, and you can't tear it down. It's a historic landmark."

Forrest spit as he laughed. "That's an urban legend."

Ian shook his head. "We're going to find his great, great-grandson and confirm it."

An alarm buzzed in the elevator. Forrest glanced at the panel then glared at Ian.

"Listen, you loud-mouthed Leprechaun. I'm doing this town a favor." He raised his voice over the alarm. "I know who you are, and my attorneys are filing a restraining order against you as we speak. If you come within a thousand yards of my properties, including the Widow Rock Lighthouse, I'm going to see to it that you're locked inside that old building when the demolition starts."

"You don't scare me." Ian removed his hand. The alarm stopped, and the doors started moving together.

"No?" Forrest plucked the cigar from his mouth and held it between his fingers. "Then you're as stupid as you look. If you or anyone else in the Florida Taliban cross the line again, I'll teach you what fear means." The doors closed, and the gears grumbled as the elevator rose.

Ian watched the floor indicator light up along with the upwards directional arrow. He wrung his hands together and said, under his breath, "Have you ever heard of karma, Mr. Frazier? 'Cause it's coming for you."

* * *

Forrest Frazier took the elevator up to the twelfth floor, chewing his cigar. That redheaded pumpkin pounder grated his last nerve, but he couldn't let anyone see that. With his stress level this high, he knew he should've hit the gym. But a persistent hangover pained him too much to think about working out. The elevator came to a halt, and the doors opened.

The Forrest Frazier Development offices were large, expansive, and modern, with picturesque windows overlooking downtown Bradenton. Every corner showed-off the firm's success, from luxurious hardwood floors to posh artwork decorating the walls to ceiling-mounted suspended light fixtures. The furniture, even the office cubicles, was high quality and comfortable. Forrest wouldn't have it any other way. His name stood for something. The public knew he was a self-made millionaire, for success bred success.

The elevator doors shut behind him. Without so much as a hello, he tore past his staff, ignoring every "good morning, sir." He entered his private corner office, slamming the door behind him, and made his way to the dry bar. Two ibuprofens with a shot of bourbon would dull his headache—maybe. It would be his third pair of tablets that morning. He glanced at the clock and berated himself for having scheduled an investor meeting so early in the day.

As he slipped out of his suit jacket and tossed it on a visitor chair, the office door creaked open. A buxom, young blonde poked her head in and said, "Good morning."

He waved her in.

"Shelly, I want you to call the police and have those protestors arrested." He tossed his chewed cigar in the trash and found a fresh one from a cigar box on his desk. "And get those nudists clothed. No one needs to be seeing that this early in the morning."

Shelly stood in the office doorway, summer fresh in a light blue miniskirt, white belt, and heels that looked more appropriate for a night of clubbing than a professional office setting. When Forrest saw her, he almost forgot about Ian. Her blonde hair flowed to her shoulders, framing a heart-shaped face, feminine and attractive. She closed the door behind her.

"The police are already down there breaking it up," she said, calmly placing a list of phone messages on his desk. "The bank called the police as soon as the first protest sign appeared."

"It took them long enough to get here." Forrest chewed the new cigar and watched her walk across the office.

Despite the demands of his real estate empire, he always found time to treat himself with gorgeous babes. As far back as his college years at Florida State, he and his drinking buddies kept score of their conquests and even developed a point system to rank the women on a hotness scale.

Shelley was a definite eight. Maybe even an eight-point-five. He made a mental note to invite Shelly up to his suite at the Ritz.

"What were they protesting about this time?" she asked, stepping next to him and disrupting his fantasy.

"What else? The Widow Rock Towers project." He turned to her with the cigar dangling from his mouth and holding his glass. "That Leprechaun has been causing trouble since day one."

"He won't bother you anymore."

He stepped to a model of the condo resting atop a table along the wall. "If he had his way, there would be no contemporary development, and people would just be vegetarians and live in huts powered by solar energy."

"Well, it doesn't matter." She massaged his shoulders as she spoke in a quiet, soothing voice. "Interest in Widow Rock has been pouring in, despite the protests." She released his neck and sauntered to his desk. She picked up a stack of papers. "We've got over two hundred and seventy-five RFI's," she said. "Your commercials have been very successful."

"Of course, they are. This new condo will be the hottest spot in Florida." He flipped through the papers and suddenly stopped. "Noah Tyler" appeared as the first lead. It was listed on the following page, too, then the next. He looked up from the papers. The cigar fell from his mouth. "Is this some kind of joke?"

Shelly shrugged. "What do you mean?"

"Noah Tyler?" He threw the papers at her. "It has Noah Tyler's name on it, every page, over and over!"

"Who's Noah Tyler?" She picked the papers up from the floor, along with the chewed cigar, and set them on the desk. "It must be some kind of computer error or something. Maybe this Noah guy hit the submit button on the website over and over."

"Noah didn't hit any submit buttons. *Noah* didn't submit this." He emphasized.

She looked flustered. "Why? Who is Noah?"

He ripped the page from her hand and crumbled it up. He threw it at the model of the Widow Rock Towers. It bounced off the plastic building and knocked over a couple of green-painted palm trees on the base.

Shelly looked confused. "I don't understand. Who is Noah?"

"It doesn't matter," he said, huffing. "Shred any pages with his name on it and delete him from the database." He stormed into his private bathroom and slammed the door shut. Turning on the faucet, he glanced at his reflection in the mirror. The red veins on each side of his nose were more prominent than usual. A sign of stress. Of high blood pressure. He placed his hands on the vanity and inhaled, calming himself.

When he came out of the bathroom, he noticed Shelley had left. He stepped to the dry bar. The bottle of brandy was still open, and he poured himself another drink. Sinking into his desk chair, he opened the cigar box and picked up a fresh cigar. He faced the condo model.

"Noah Tyler," he whispered. "Are *you* haunting me? Or your parents?"

***

Elise didn't know if it was morning or night, sitting in the rocking chair in Noah's room, wrapped in an afghan. The blinds were drawn, drowning the room in darkness. She held a flashlight that shined on the children's book in her lap, *Where the Darkness Hides*. Flipping the page, she stared at the images of a little boy in his pajamas and read the prose.

"And out of the shadows
from the corners of the bedroom

from behind the closet door
from under the bed
the monsters emerge."

The bedroom door opened, and Dr. Yvette Cross entered the room.

"Knock. Knock," she said, sounding sickening cheerful. Her navy-blue pants suit contrasted sharply against her white skin, and her black hair was swept back and tied in a severe bun. She stepped to the window and opened the blinds. Sunlight invaded the room.

Elise groaned and covered her eyes. "The sun," she said, "it's melting my brain."

The doctor turned toward her, silhouetted by the bright morning light behind her. "It's good for you. Besides, Redd asked me over. He said you've been locked up in here all night."

"I didn't want to be around him." Elise remained focused on the book, never looking up. "Or anyone else. I hate people."

"That's an unhealthy attitude." The doctor reached for the book in Elise's lap.

Elise gripped the book tighter. "You're an unhealthy attitude," she said, clutching the book to her chest.

The doctor took a step back. Her eyes narrowed. "Elise…Noah isn't here."

"I know," Elise said. "I've been reading to Doogie—as if it was any of your business." She pointed at the baby monitor on top of the bookcase.

The small speaker crackled. The doctor walked to it and picked it up. She stared at it for several seconds.

Elise watched her, then said, "Why don't you just turn into a bat and fly away."

"You and I both know there is no Doogie." The doctor's voice was gentle but condescending. "He's all in your mind." She turned a dial. The static increased.

A raspy voice came from the speaker. "Hello?"

The doctor nearly dropped the monitor and turned to Elise. "Who was that? Who were you talking to?"

Elise didn't look up. "Maybe if I wear garlic cloves, I can keep you away from me."

"Who is Doogie?" The doctor sounded panicked, almost frightened. "Who are—"

An angry male voice interrupted her. "Doogie doesn't exist."

Elise turned to see her husband standing in the door frame. He entered the bedroom with a scowl on his face, and his hands balled into fists.

CHAPTER SIXTEEN

Kate steered *The Kendell* through Tampa Bay, hugging the shoreline past Corman's Launch, and followed the coastline. The late morning sun lit the Gulf water with shimmering sparklers as the breeze picked up, twisting her hair. She talked to Trace on her iPhone.

"I'm just running late," she said. Doc stirred on her shoulder, wagging his bushy tail and chattering as if responding.

Trace's voice came through the phone's speakers. "Your physical therapy is running long?"

"Something like that." She studied the tangle of mangrove trees along the coast and changed the subject. "So, Chief, the perfect baby name is Dakota. Dakota Guerra."

"We're not naming our son Dakota."

"You're not having a son."

"You're just going to have to come to terms with this," he said with a frank, matter-of-fact tone. "Little Dakota is going to be Little Thomas."

"I think you're going to be surprised," she said, tooling along the shoreline and noticing an inlet ahead. "Look, Chief, I gotta run. I'll be in the office before lunch."

She ended the call and steered her boat toward the firth, rimmed by mangroves, tangled and nearly impossible to enter at low tide. Mosquito Cove. Its entrance between two sand bars was narrow and treacherous, so very few boats ventured into it. Kate maneuvered slowly through the sand bars. There, the greenish-blue water was dead calm, sheltered from the Gulf winds, and the stillness provided a sense of isolation. Surprisingly, two fishing boats anchored at the far end of the cove.

One of the fishermen waved toward her, flagging her down. She skimmed toward him.

"There's an abandoned boat back there," the man yelled, pointing toward the mangroves. That snarl of the shore was more brackish swamp than land and looked impossible to maneuver a boat into—even during high tide.

Still, the fisherman was right. She could see it too. Barely.

The edge of a discarded boat.

* * *

Elise watched her husband storm into Noah's bedroom. He stepped beside her as she sat in the rocking chair.

"I'm paying you a hundred and fifty dollars an hour to pry her out of here," Redd said, stepping beside her and shaking a fist at Dr. Cross. "Not to encourage her fantasy."

The doctor, still standing by the bookcase under the window, held up the baby monitor. "There was a voice. Someone just spoke."

Redd looked back at Elise, then over at the speaker in the doctor's hand. "It's your imagination. My wife's got you spooked."

Elise ignored them and rocked in her chair. She opened *Where the Darkness Hides*. "What if I stake you through the heart?" she asked, ignoring them and turning the pages in the book. "That would kill you for sure . . . but I guess that would kill anyone."

Redd gripped her arm tight and pulled, nearly ejecting her from the rocker.

The afront surprised her, and she slapped his hand away. "Don't touch me," she said, glaring up at him. Dr. Cross approached her too, and she threw the children's book. It hit the bookcase and knocked the baby monitor to the floor."Leave me alone," she screamed. "I'm not leaving. You can't make me."

They crowded around her.

"She's hysterical," the doctor said.

"C'mon." He grasped Elise's wrist, held it tight. "You need to get out of this room."

Elise shrieked, flailing her arms and kicking at them. She wasn't going without a fight. Dr. Cross grabbed her ankles, restraining her legs. Redd got his arms around her core and lifted her from the rocking chair. She cried and squirmed and smacked him.

Redd carried Elise out of Noah's room. Her sobs echoed through the hallway, but her struggle was pointless. She was locked in Redd's arms, and she wasn't breaking free. He carried her across the hall into the master bedroom.

Dr. Cross followed with a small medical bag in her hands. As Redd dropped Elise onto the bed, the doctor prepared an injection. Redd held Elise down as she thrashed against his powerful hold. The sheets twisted around her legs. The doctor stepped to them and gave Elise a shot in the arm.

Almost instantly, Elise felt a wave of calm move through her. Her body relaxed, and she exhaled. Redd's control loosened as the doctor pulled the sheets over her.

"She's getting worse," Dr. Cross said, stepping away from the bed.

Redd rose, and Elise felt the movement in the mattress. "I know," he said. "But I'm paying for the best meds, and the best treatment money can buy. I'm spending thousands per month. What else can I do?"

Elise shut her eyes and listened to their voices, talking about her as if she wasn't even there. She stifled a yawn.

"You need to get her out of this house," the doctor said. "Did you even look at that offer?"

Their voices grew faint, and Elise knew they were either whispering or had moved several feet away from her. Still, she heard every word and wanted to tell Dr. Cross to take her offer and shove it up her butt. She hoped Redd would set it on fire. Maybe he'd set the doctor on fire while he was at it.

"I looked at it," he said.

Elise cringed. She fought against the drowsiness. What were they saying? Were they plotting against her? She *had* to know and tried even harder to stay awake.

"And?" The doctor's hushed voice was barely perceptible.

"I don't trust it. Who are the Friends of Historic Restoration?" Redd asked. They sounded several feet away now, probably by the window. She had to concentrate to hear him. "Why are they offering so much money?"

"They're a group of investors looking for properties to restore," the doctor said. "They like this old beach house, and they're willing to pay you twice the amount this place is worth."

"Who are *they*?" Redd asked. His voice sounded so far away. Had he left the room? Was he in the hallway? Or had he fallen down some deep well? "When'd they see our home?"

"Redd, you're asking the wrong questions." Now the doctor's voice echoed up from that deep well.

"What does that mean?"

"It means you should be asking if Elise is getting better? What will her condition be if she stays here, if you both stay here—"

The doctor's voice trailed off. Both were too far away now. Maybe they'd left the room. Maybe they'd tumbled down that well. Or maybe Elise fell down the black well. She could make out an unintelligible tone but no distinct words. With the silence, a warmth washed over her. The characters from her children's book appeared—*little Charlie and the monsters emerging from the closet and from under the bed*—and she succumbed to that place where the darkness hides.

* * *

Kate could barely make out the edges of a boat trapped in the mangroves. Approaching with extreme caution, she steered *The Kendell* into the thicket.

Gnarled branches obstructed her view, so she held them out of her way. A boat was, in fact, bobbing in the shallows. Abandoned. Derelict, but not old or weathered. It looked new and very expensive.

She moved more branches and got a closer look. The name "Olivia" appeared on the hull, scrawled in red cursive lettering.

Doc chattered on her shoulder. She lifted a hand to him, and he scampered onto her arm. He jumped onto the console and raised up on his hind legs, looking at the boat.

Kate leaped onto the abandoned craft. It shifted and wobbled with her weight, but she kept her balance. Doc babbled loudly at her from the console on *The Kendell*, as if warning her of some lurking danger. She ignored him and stepped along the deck.

Nothing looked out of the ordinary. A pair of muddy boots lay discarded on the floor. Four fishing rods leaned across the back bench-seat beside two tackle boxes. A crumpled bag of beef jerky settled beneath the console. A polaroid sat atop the driver's seat below the steering wheel.

She picked up the photograph.

A giant stuffed elephant stared back at her. Plush grey fur. A comically long trunk. Huge floppy ears. Two round button eyes. The thought of Mister Belvedere flashed through her mind. She dropped it.

Stumbling backward, she slipped but caught herself.

Mister Belvedere. That was a silly thought. A coincidence. Noah was on her mind, and she jumped to a conclusion. She experienced apophenia—where the mind makes connections to unrelated phenomena. That's all it was. Apophenia.

Overhead, four vultures flew in a lazy circle in the sky. She feared what they might be homing in on.

Hopping out of the boat, she splashed into the shallow water. Doc squeaked and hopped onto her shoulder. She felt his tiny hand tug the hoodie of her sweatshirt as she waded in the direction of the vultures. The mangrove branches tangled around her. Thick creepers stretched from branch to branch. The dense growth looked untouched for a hundred years, covering the muddy pools she sloshed through. A frog croaked somewhere near her feet, and swarms of gnats clouded the air. She swatted at them and stopped.

A putrid odor assaulted her. Her eyes watered. Looking up, she saw the vultures were directly overhead now. Her heartbeat hastened as she forced herself forward. Whatever was out there was close now.

She waded through the underbrush. The odor intensified, and she covered her nostrils with her hand. A low buzz grew louder. Doc squealed and ducked into the hoodie. Stepping forward, she pushed back the brush and craned her neck to find black flies swarming above some contorted mass. A body rotting in the mud and heat.

Jasper Wade.

She was certain of it, though the face, contorted in pain and frozen in death, no longer looked like the man in the photograph back on *The Kendell.*

Floating, his decomposing remains stretched out like a fallen mannequin. His eye sockets were empty black holes beneath ash-colored cheeks. His mouth remained slightly open, leaking a viscous green fluid that dribbled into a congealed pool beneath his chin. Flies landed on his ear. A small crab emerged from his right nostril, raising a single claw, and scurried into the open mouth.

Kate's legs went slack, threatening to collapse beneath her, as she backed away from the corpse in silent, mindless horror. Careening, she tore back through the mangroves. She rushed to the abandoned *Olivia.* Jumping up into the boat, she stumbled to the console. The Polaroid still lay there, waiting.

The photo of the giant stuffed elephant wasn't apophenia. Her mind *wasn't* making meaningful connections to meaningless coincidences. The giant elephant–with plush grey fur, a comically long trunk, huge floppy ears, two round button eyes—*was* Mister Belvedere.

She squeezed her eyes shut.

"Oh, Redd," she whispered. "What have you done?"

CHAPTER SEVENTEEN

Kate watched the Manatee County Sheriff's Department swarm Mosquito Cove. Police boats lined the shore, and officers taped-off the area around the body while a crime scene unit searched the *Olivia* and sifted through the mangroves. She watched them for several moments then looked down at the Polaroid in her hands.

Doc, sitting on her shoulder, let out a series of judgmental clicks, and she told him to hush.

That giant stuffed elephant stared up at her, and the image spooked her.

She couldn't believe she swiped it. It happened so quickly; she didn't even think about it. It was in her pocket before she realized what she'd done. She just grabbed it from the boat, snatching it before anyone could tie it back to her brother-in-law. Connect it to her sister. Link it to their grief. But what was done was done. She couldn't return it to the corpse. Now she'd just have to deal with it. Deal with the consequences. Find the truth, wherever that may lead.

First, she'd talk to Redd. Confront him, if necessary. They'd go to Chief Guerra together.

She'd find a way out of this. She had to protect him. It was up to her to shield her sister from any more pain. Elise wouldn't be able to take another heartache. Kate did what she had to do to save her sister.

"I heard you found the body." A male voice came from behind her.

She returned the photograph to her pocket and turned to see her old partner—correction, her partner; she was just on leave—approaching.

"Trim," she said. Her fingers grazed the Polaroid in her pocket. "I wasn't expecting you."

A tall man with dark hair wearing a tan Florida Fish and Wildlife uniform stepped next to her. Doc raised up on his haunches and chirped at him. He chuckled and gave the squirrel a light scratch on top of his head. "You still have the rodent."

"He's the best partner I ever had," she said. Doc squeaked his approval.

"Nice," Trim said. He motioned toward the boat. "That's some craft."

"It's a Yellowfin 23," she said.

"Looks expensive. Figures it would belong to an attorney."

"Jasper Wade." The name left a foul taste in her mouth.

"Yeah." He nodded, then continued. "Jasper Wade." They stared at each other for several moments. "How'd you find him? I mean, what were you doing out here?"

"Following up on a lead," Kate said. "Wade's daughter approached me about finding her missing father. She said she thought he might have been fishing at Corman's Launch."

Trim shot her a concerned glance. "Why didn't you call us---call me?"

"I guess I wasn't sure." She looked away. Boats filled the Bay waters. Most were police, but a crowd of curious onlookers was growing too. People stood gawking on their boats, pointing and snapping photos with their phones. News helicopters circled above.

Trim stepped beside her. "You weren't sure about what?"

She whipped around and faced him. "Look, Trim, I can still do my job."

"I know."

"I'll be back," she continued. "Once the doctor releases me from desk duty."

"That's what I don't get." He shrugged his shoulders as he spoke. "Why'd you transfer out of the FWC? Why are you working for Sienna Key?"

"Chief Guerra needed me to head up his boat safety initiative. He asked for me specifically," she said. "I couldn't tell him no. We go way back."

He nodded and said, "You and I go way back too."

"It's not just that . . ." She searched for the right words. Truth was, she didn't know why she left the FWC. When Trace offered to pull some strings to bring her into his department, she jumped at the chance. Maybe it was Sienna Key. Perhaps it was a sense of protection for the deaf girl she rescued. That incident resulted in her taking a bullet that brought her to a crossroads. "I . . ." she finally said. "I don't want the guys seeing me like this. It's bad enough being down and out. I don't want to go through this with everyone monitoring everything I do and feeling sorry for me."

She started to say more when Doc squealed and rose up on her shoulder. She turned her head toward him and then noticed Trace pulling-up in a boat. Wearing his tan uniform, he held his cowboy hat in one hand and steered with the other. His black beard rippled in the breeze. She waved to him, and his boat turned and headed in her direction.

"I thought you were in physical therapy this morning," he called out to her as he pulled up onto the shore.

"Olivia Wade contacted me." She looked back at the crime scene unit, busy around the body. "She thought her father's boat might be at Corman's Launch. I just wanted to check it out."

"You shoulda reported it." Trace flipped his hat on top of his head and stepped out of his boat. "It's not your job anymore."

Kate shrugged. "I can still handle following up on a lead. I'm not a cripple."

Trim nodded at her. "He's right. You shoulda called it in." He shook Trace's hand as Kate cleared her throat.

"Chief, you remember my partner with Fish and Wildlife," she said. "Agent Trimble."

"Call me Trim," he said. "Hope you're treating my partner right while she's on leave."

"We're not gonna want to give her up," Trace said. "You know . . . when she heals."

"And, I am healing," she said, absent-mindedly touching her shoulder. "I'll be back at Fish and Wildlife soon."

"I know you will," Trim said. "We're expecting it."

An agent near the boat called out, and Trim responded.

"I think they found something," he said to Kate and Trace as he took off for the group huddled around *The Olivia.*

Kate watched him a moment, then turned to Trace. "I know what you're gonna say, so don't even bother. Olivia called me, and I just wanted to check it out first."

"Kate, you've been acting strange lately," he said, removing his cowboy hat and wiping his forehead. "You know this is out of our jurisdiction, and on top of that, it isn't your job. What's wrong with you?"

"I'll be back—"

"I know." His expression grew hard and determined as he returned his hat to his head. "You'll be back at Fish and Wildlife. But until then, it's not your job."

She gritted her teeth. "It's Jasper Wade," she said. Again a foul taste lingered in her mouth. "He was the attorney that represented . . ."

"I know," he said quietly. "I know who he represented."

* * *

Elise woke when Redd nudged her. She was lying in bed, not sure what time it was or how long she'd slept. He set a plate of waffles and a glass of milk on the nightstand. The waffles smelled of hot batter, melting butter, and syrup—her favorite.

He sat on the edge of the bed, next to her, and gestured to the breakfast he brought her. His smile looked forced and uncomfortable.

"I thought you might like an early dinner," he said, holding the plate in front of her face. She inhaled deeply with surprise, then pushed it away.

"Don't try to bond with me," she said. She stretched her arms and yawned. The baseball bat leaning in the corner of the room near the door caught her eye.

Redd stood, holding the plate, and the mattress shifted with the weight distribution. "I'm not trying to bond with you . . .The power will probably be out for a while when the hurricane hits, and I wanted to use up the eggs and milk," he said, stepping to the foot of the bed. He walked to the window and opened the curtains. Sunlight filtered into the room. "I ran to the hardware store and got hurricane supplies too," he added. "They jacked up the prices on everything. Spent a hundred and fifty-two dollars on seventy-five dollars-worth of supplies."

She sat up in bed and glanced at the window. Warm sunlight filtered into the room.

"What time is it?" she asked as she rubbed her eyes.

"A little after four," he said.

She flipped back the covers. "Four o'clock?"

"Dr. Cross gave you something to let you rest," he said. He picked up the glass of milk and handed it to her. She refused it.

"You didn't fix dinner," she said, yawning and shaking the drowsiness from her head. "You made breakfast."

"You need to eat something," he said.

"I'm not hungry."

"At least you sound coherent for a change." He returned the glass to the nightstand. "The hardware store was out of plywood. I'm going to swing by some construction sites and see if there's any plywood lying around I can borrow," he said. "You want to go? Get out of the house for a bit?"

"I just want to sleep." She laid her head down on the pillow. He grasped her hand and pulled her back up.

"It will do you good to get up," he insisted as she pulled away from him. "To get out of bed."

"I can't."

"Well, at least eat something. You haven't eaten or drank anything all day."

She shut her eyes, scrunched her face, and covered her ears with her hands. "Everything you're saying to me just makes me hate you more."

Redd stood and grabbed the plate from the nightstand. "Fine. There's ten dollars and thirty cents I'll never get back."

He left the room and slammed the door. She could hear him stomp down the two levels of stairs. The vibrations rattled the walls. The baseball bat fell to the floor with a loud thwap, startling her. She looked back at the door. Downstairs, the front door slammed shut. The bang echoed loudly, followed by an unsettling silence. Elise sat up, alone in the empty house.

She climbed out of bed and crossed the hallway into Noah's room. Afternoon sunlight streamed in through the window and hurt her eyes. She closed the curtains. The children's book and the baby monitor still lay on the floor, and she picked them up. Her little boy's presence enveloped her, and she considered sitting in the rocking chair and reading *Where the Darkness Hides* again. However, her head ached, and her eyes were still blurry from the sleep medication. She needed to find something to dull the pain.

She set the baby monitor on top of the bookshelf, next to the framed photograph of her and Noah with the giant stuffed elephant. She stared at the monitor, sitting silently there until she turned it on.

"Hello?" she asked into the speaker. "Doogie, are you there?"

There was no answer, and she stepped away.

Noah's clothes still lay spread out on the dresser. Blue shorts. White underwear. A red Spiderman t-shirt. He was supposed to wear them to Kindergarten the following Monday. Now he would've been starting the first grade. The thought brought tears to her eyes, and she knew she needed to find something to dull the pain.

She left Noah's room and tiptoed downstairs like she was sneaking through the house just as she'd done growing up. She didn't want her parents to hear her—even though they were long gone. She wondered if her mother could still see her from some nether world. She was certain Noah could. She felt him near her so many times over the last year.

She took a breath and prayed that it wasn't true. He shouldn't see her like this.

In the kitchen, a box sat on the counter. She looked inside. Batteries, charcoal, peanut butter, jelly, paper plates, plastic utensils, baby wipes. A battery-operated Coleman lantern lay next to two cases of bottled water. Redd's hurricane supplies—all one hundred and fifty-two dollars-worth. However, she was more interested in what was hidden in the cabinet above the refrigerator. A bottle of Jack. She poured herself a glass. Swallowed it down. Poured another.

The locked garage door mocked her on her right, and she threw her drink at it. The glass shattered, spilling Tennessee whiskey down the front of the door. She smiled at what she'd done and pulled open a cabinet drawer. A key lay hidden beneath the silverware tray, and she used it to unlock the door.

In the garage, she flipped on the lights. The model trainset with all its black railroad tracks and plastic houses spread out on a large table in the center of the room, right where her car should've been. She stepped to the table and flicked every single tree, knocking them down.

***

Kate tied *The Kendell* to the dock behind the Bear's Den. Trace was already off his boat and extended a hand to assist her.

"You shouldn't have even been out there," he said as she stepped onto the dock. Doc jumped from the boat to the planks and hopped around her feet.

"Olivia Wade asked me to look for her father, personally." Her hand reached into her pocket and grazed the Polaroid.

"Still...it wasn't your job," he said. Their feet tapped on the planks as they crossed the dock. Doc hopped after them, wagging his bushy tail. The area where chairs had been set up for her safety seminar now stood empty. Trace continued. "Your job is boat safety instructor."

"For now," she said quietly. She appreciated his getting that job for her and letting her hideout at the Bear's Den. Still, she couldn't hide forever. "For the foreseeable future," she added.

He glanced at her as if he knew something she didn't. Or at least something she wasn't ready to admit. He took a breath and asked, "How's your shoulder?"

She didn't answer. Instead, she focused on the blue water in the channel. A sportfishing yacht passed them, headed for the open Gulf. She didn't notice as her fingers brushed the Polaroid in her pocket. Was it really Mr. Belevedere? She had to confirm it?

She bent down, allowing Doc to hop up on her arm and scamper up to her shoulder. She then headed off the dock and up the sidewalk to the back patio.

Trace called after her. "Where you goin'?"

"To see my sister," she said, opening the door. "There's something I need to check."

"You've got a safety class at six," he said, throwing up his hands.

"I'll be back in plenty of time." She slipped through the doorway and entered the building. Behind her, Trace yelled, "Stack them eights!"

She waved to him as the door shut and made her way through the building. Her Tahoe was parked in front. A few minutes later, she drove across the island to the Bluegill.

The Polaroid in her pocket weighed her down. She couldn't believe she took the picture. She'd snatched it on impulse. It was a split-second decision. An action that went against every fiber in her body, morally, ethically, legally—but she had to know. She had to see if it was the same elephant. Mr. Belvedere. And, if it was, then she'd know: Redd was involved.

She parked in front of the Bluegill and noticed Redd's old pickup wasn't there. She approached the house anyway. The front door was unlocked and creaked when she opened it. "Hello?" she called out. "Elise? You here?"

Her voice echoed as she stepped into the parlor. "Elise?"

Doc moved from her left shoulder to her right and let out a series of chirps and squeals.

She made her way upstairs to the third-floor landing and checked the master bedroom. Empty. She crossed the hall into Noah's room. Elise wasn't there either.

A collection of stuffed animals sat haphazardly on a shelf, as well as scattered on the bed. A yellow and brown giraffe. A Kermit the Frog.

Several teddy bears. A sock monkey. A Spider-man doll. But no stuffed elephant.

Noah's clothes lay on top of the dresser. The framed photograph of her sister and nephew sat on the bookcase. Elise looked so healthy and vibrant in it. Happy. Noah's smile was larger than life, hugging the giant stuffed elephant. No hint of the fate that awaited him. The last thirteen months had left such a deep wound, and not just on Elise, but on them all.

She removed the Polaroid from her pocket and compared it with the framed photograph. The stuffed elephants looked identical: same grey plush fur, same comically long trunk, same large floppy ears.

"Mister Belvedere," she whispered. Doc squealed on her shoulder, and she told him to hush. "I know. I know," she said. "I feel guilty enough. You don't have to rub it in."

Elise entered the bedroom, startling her.

"What are you doing here?" Elise asked. "In my son's room … with your rabbit?"

Kate swung around, still holding both pictures. "Where's Redd?"

"I don't know. I'm not his warden."

"It's important that I talk to him."

"I told you, I don't know." She rushed toward Kate and snatched the framed picture from her hands. She checked for any damage then returned it to the top of the bookcase. "What are you doing in my baby's room?" she said. "I don't like for people to come in here and touch his things."

"A man was murdered," Kate said. "I found his body."

"So?"

"It was the attorney who represented Forrest Frazier. His name was Jasper Wade."

Elise didn't respond.

"Did you hear me? Jasper Wade was murdered."

"Yeah, I heard you the first time."

Kate touched her sister's shoulder. She cringed, and Kate withdrew her hand. "Would you stop fighting me at every turn? C'mon, Kid, we're sisters. We're all we have, and I'm trying to protect you."

"Will you ever stop calling me that?"

"Of course. My bad." Kate took in a deep breath and turned away from her. She ran her hands through her hair. Elise could be so irritating, and she couldn't take it another second. Regardless, she needed Elise to listen. "Where is Mister Belvedere?" she asked.

"Why?" Elise sounded as flippant as ever.

Kate's tone held a note of impatience. "What happened to Mister Belvedere? Where is he?"

"Why?" Fatigue had settled in the pockets under Elise's eyes, and her voice softened. "I threw Mr. Belvedere out a long time ago. Noah got sick and threw-up all over the thing, and I couldn't wash the stain out, so I tossed it in the trash."

Kate glanced at the Polaroid. The grey fur on the stuffed elephant's body had a discolored patch, just like Elise described.

An hour later, Kate and Doc returned to the Bear's Den and found Intern Ernie on the dock out back, his arms ladened with orange life vests. A crowd of people sat in folding chairs, waiting.

"Where have you been?" Ernie's voice singed with a not-so-subtle hint of aggravation as Kate dropped her purse beside a box of red file folders. He dumped the life jackets onto the planks and said, "You've got a safety class starting."

"Sorry, it's been a busy day."

"Doesn't matter." He grabbed a jacket and handed it to her. Doc stretched from Kate's shoulder to investigate the odd orange vest. He scratched the squirrel's little head and smiled at Kate. "I'm just glad you're back," he said. "I can't take another minute of this."

Trace called to them from the back door. "Kate, you're back. You think Olivia Wade is still at the Starlight Motel by the Causeway?"

Kate turned and yelled back to him. "As far as I know."

"The Sheriff's Department has asked us to notify her." He waved to Kate to follow him and disappeared inside. The door shut behind him. Kate handed the life jacket to Ernie and then lifted Doc from her shoulder and handed the squirrel to him as well.

"Can you watch him for a few hours?" she asked him.

"Wait." He took the squirrel. His head turned from her to the crowd of students sitting across from them and back to her. "You've got a safety class."

"Life vests, Ernie. Life vests," she said. "That's all they need to know."

She raced up the sidewalk and into the building. Trace was waiting for her in the lobby with keys in hand.

As they drove out of downtown, she noticed the Causeway leading off the island was unusually crowded. All the tourists were leaving ahead of the storm. Along the off-ramp, the balloons at Noah's curbside memorial bounced in the wind. She avoided looking at it as Redd turned into the Starlight Motel. He parked, and she brushed a finger over the Polaroid in her pocket.

She wondered where Redd was. The Manatee County Sheriff's Department would figure out his involvement at some point, and she needed to get to him first. But once she found him, then what? Confront him?

Trace said her name, and she glanced at him, surprised. Shaking it off, she followed him to Olivia Wade's motel room and knocked on the door. He removed his hat and held it in both hands, waiting.

When the door opened, a young woman with curly blonde hair stared at them for several seconds, then broke down crying.

CHAPTER EIGHTEEN

Bile rose into Kate's throat. From the moment Olivia agreed to go to the morgue to identify her father's body, Kate had alarm warnings going off deep in her psyche. She feared Jasper Wade would turn up dead, and now she feared Redd's involvement even more. But the thought of seeing that corpse again made her shudder. As she followed the medical examiner along a narrow corridor in the morgue, she couldn't stop trembling.

Trace, walking close behind her, looked professional as ever. This was just a typical Wednesday afternoon, for all she could tell.

Olivia, however, surprised her. After an initial breakdown at the motel, the young woman composed herself quite quickly and changed into a floral print dress. She pulled her blonde curls back and became almost . . . Kate didn't want to say stoic. Maybe, detached? Perhaps Olivia simply hadn't processed her father's death yet. Perhaps she was distancing herself from the grief. Or maybe she was wearing the camouflage of self-defense, protecting herself from the shock and horror to come in the next few moments when she'd be identifying her father's remains on some cold metal table.

Those little warnings screamed loud in Kate's head. Something was off. She couldn't put her finger on it, but there was something wrong about Olivia. She could sense it. Or was she just projecting another fear onto this young woman? Truthfully, Redd's anger scared her. It terrified her. And it would be easier to blame this woman than imagine Redd being capable of murder.

She self-consciously touched the Polaroid in her pocket. It felt slick and smooth, and the edge cut her fingertip. She removed her hand and poked her finger in her mouth.

They took a flight of stairs, then made their way down another corridor. Finally, a medical examiner greeted them and opened a door. He stood aside, motioning them to enter. "This is the viewing room," he said.

Trace guided Olivia inside. Kate followed. The small room was lightly decorated with two chairs and a plastic palm tree. The space felt uncomfortably small. A heavy curtain covered a window on the wall to their right.

Kate noticed Trace's grip tighten on Olivia's arm.

Olivia ran a hand over her floral print dress as if smoothing out the wrinkles, then nodded. The examiner stepped to the side of the window and pulled a cord. The curtains parted.

Kate tensed. On the other side of the glass appeared a small, dimly lit room, empty except for a stainless-steel cart bearing a body covered by a thin white sheet. An attendant wearing teal scrubs stood to the side of the cart. She noticed the examiners signal to each other; then the attendant slowly pulled back the sheet to reveal Jasper Wade's balding head. The face was as severely beaten as she remembered. His eyelids sunk into empty sockets.

Olivia gasped, barely suppressing a cry of horror. "That's . . . that's him. That's Daddy."

Kate pulled up a chair, and Olivia fell into the seat as the examiner told them a restroom was available down the hall.

"That's Jasper Wade?" Trace asked.

Olivia nodded and looked away. "Y-Yes," she stuttered, her voice choking. "Who could've done this to him?"

Kate's hand slipped back into her pocket, and her finger with the papercut touched the Polaroid again.

The medical examiner went to the window and pulled the cord. The curtains came together.

They exited the narrow room and returned to the corridor. The journey out the building went much faster, it seemed, and Kate noticed how bright the evening sun had become when they stepped out of the morgue onto the parking lot.

Trace put on his cowboy hat. He ran a hand over his chin, smoothing his beard as if thinking deeply about something. "Miss Wade, I need to ask you a question."

Olivia nodded and dabbed a scarf at her watery eyes.

Trace took a breath. "Kate stated that you reported your father missing with our police department but were told you had to wait forty-eight hours before we would look into it."

"Yes," Olivia said.

"There is no policy to wait forty-eight hours before investigating a missing person."

"Are you serious?" Olivia's eyes narrowed as she glared at Trace. "I don't care about policy. My daddy is dead."

He raised a hand. "And I don't believe you reported him missing. We have no record of—"

Olivia cut him off. "You're just trying to cover your ass. I came into your police station to report my daddy missing, and your staff told me to come back later."

Trace leaned forward, closer to her. "Who told you that? Who told you to come back later?"

"I don't know. Clearly, now that you know who my daddy is, you're taking this very seriously. It's just too bad that you didn't show the same concern when I first came in."

"There's no record of you coming into the station at all," he said. "There's no report. There's no---"

Olivia spoke over him. "I was told to come back after he'd been missing for forty-eight hours. If you have a problem with your staff, you take it up with them. But I can assure you, Chief Guerra, this isn't the last you're going to hear of it. My family is very powerful, and we'll sue you and your team of apathetic deputies till hell won't have you. Expect a call from the governor very soon."

She turned and hurried toward the street.

"Wait. Olivia, where are you going?" Trace yelled.

"I'll call for Mother's town car," she yelled as she crossed the street. "And believe me when I tell you, Mother will hear all about this!"

Kate watched her storm away, disappearing down the block.

It had been a long day. The night would be even longer.

* * *

At a quarter past ten, Forrest Frazier sat behind his desk, chewing a cigar and staring at his computer screen. The monitor cast a pale glow across his face, highlighting the desk around him in the dark room. The office door opened, allowing in a rush of light from the hallway.

"You're late," he said. He looked back down at his keyboard. "So, how'd it go?"

Heels clicked on the tile floor as a woman stepped into the office. She flipped on the lights.

Forrest looked up at the thin woman with jet-black hair pulled back in a severe bun and wearing a grey pantsuit.

Dr. Yvette Cross cocked her head and shot him an irritated look. "Redd's on board, but we've still got to convince Elise." She walked to his desk and leaned against the corner.

He stared at her with the cigar pointing upwards from his lips. "What's it going to take to convince her?"

"Time." She smiled and licked her lips.

"How much time?"

"They lost their little boy." The doctor shook her head and spoke slowly, deliberately.

Forrest removed the cigar from his mouth and let out a long, exaggerated sigh. "A year ago. It's been a whole year. How long are they going to milk this?"

"You're not dealing with some investor here. This is a grieving, broken family who is being asked to give up their home. It's going to take time."

He gave it a fleeting thought, despite despising her liberal, bleeding heart viewpoint. She needed to toughen up if this was ever going to succeed. "I'll give you another week," he said, returning the chewed cigar to his mouth. "Then I'm rescinding the offer. I'll find other ways to persuade them to vacate the land."

She slinked around the desk and leaned against the edge of it, across from him. "That hurricane in the Gulf will be here in a few days, and nothing's going to happen till it passes. Let me handle everything, and the Tylers will fall inline." She snatched the cigar from his mouth and tossed it in the trashcan. "Besides," she continued, "you're not the only investor in Friends of Historic Restoration. You can't rescind anything without my consent."

"Don't push me, Yvette." He watched her and shifted in his chair. "We both stand to lose millions if this falls through."

"Is that all you ever think about? Money?" She laughed and reached behind her head to remove the pin holding her bun in place. She shook her head, letting her black hair fall to her shoulders.

He placed his hands firmly on her waist. "No, I think about you too," he said. "Once in a while."

She bent forward, leaned closer to him, and whispered, "Do you ever think about losing me?"

One corner of his mouth twisted upwards. "That was a mistake I'll never make again."

"Good boy." She kissed him, square on the mouth. When their lips parted, she straightened and looked down at him. "Now, let me work on the Tylers, and you keep working on the other little projects you got going on around town."

A steady series of knocks interrupted them, and he cocked his head to find Shelley standing in the open doorway. She rapped her knuckles on the door casing.

"I—I didn't know you were with a client," she said, sounding angered.

The doctor's body stiffened as she took a quick, sharp breath. "I thought we were alone."

"I thought Forrest was alone," Shelley said, entering the office. She made a beeline for the desk.

The doctor's eyes narrowed. "Forrest?"

"Um, Mr. Frazier," Shelley said.

"It's all right." Forrest raised his hands. "Shelly, this is Dr. Yvette Cross, one of my colleagues."

"Colleague?" The doctor tilted her head and scrunched her face as if she smelled something rotten.

"I just wanted to let you know, he's doing it again," Shelley dropped a stack of papers on the desk.

Forrest took the top sheet. Then he flipped through the subsequent pages. The name "Noah Tyler" appeared over and over.

"There must be at least a hundred of them," Shelley said.

"What is it?" The doctor took a page from Forrest's hands. "Dear God," she whispered.

"And they're filled out with that dead kid's name," Forrest yelled and swept the stack of paper off his desk with one clean swipe of his arm. Paper scattered across his desk and onto the floor.

The doctor bent at the knees, picked up a sheet of paper, glanced at it, and then picked up another. "Who's doing this?"

"The protestors. The environmentalists. Redd Tyler. Take your pick. They're running the whole Widow Rock condo project over budget."

Shelly knelt and picked up the remaining paper from the floor. Forrest yelled for her to stop. "Leave them," he said.

She stood and smoothed her skirt, then fluffed her hair. "Then…if that'll be all."

He nodded and waved, signaling for her to scram. "Thank you, Shelly. That'll be all."

"Mr. Frazier," she said, heading for the door.

"Thank you, Shelly." He raised his voice.

Shelly's eyes shot daggers at the doctor, then at Forrest. She shut the door behind her as she left.

Dr. Cross locked it. She turned, putting her back to the door, and glared at Forrest. "Your assistant is working late."

"I don't have time to play Jealous Janice with you." His voice was hoarse with frustration. "I have a lot on my mind. Those tree-huggers have pushed construction costs way past the budget, and these idiots keep blocking us at every turn."

The doctor twisted a hand through her hair and fixed it back into the bun. Her eyes filled with tears. "Why do I get the feeling your assistant is helping you ease those troubles?"

"Lemme stop you right there." He interrupted her. "You're jumping to conclusions."

"Am I? We've been down this road before. Now here we are, speeding right down it again."

"I don't have time for this." He picked up one of the paper leads left on his desk and stared at it. The printed name "Noah Tyler" mocked him.

She shook her head, giving him a pitiful look.

Forrest never took his eyes from the paper in his hands. "You know how I feel about you. Nothing else matters."

"Except for the Tylers selling their home to the trust," she said. He crumpled the paper into a wad and rose from his desk. She raised her hands, blocking him as he approached. "I don't see Redd or Elise filling out web leads with Noah's name."

He took a step back, giving her space. "Then who would?"

"I don't know." She took a breath. "You're a powerful man. Powerful men have enemies."

"You're right. And I'm not playing any more games."

She looked away. He huffed and opened the door.

"Where are you going?" she yelled after him as he rushed through the hallway. Shelly looked up from her desk as he shuffled past.

"I'm done playing their games." He punched the down arrow to call the elevator and stepped into the carriage.

* * *

Elise stood in the kitchen and poured herself a drink. The box of hurricane supplies remained untouched. The bottle of Jack still sat on the counter, waiting. She downed the glass. Poured another.

She'd carried the framed photo of her and Noah hugging the stuffed elephant downstairs when Kate left and had been staring at it ever since. His little face was the first thing she saw when she woke up in the morning and the last thing she saw before going to sleep. It made her both happy and sad at the same time, and she was determined to shake off her grief and hollowness. But she was slowly losing the battle. She downed the glass and poured another.

The window shade was open, and she could see out into the night. Redd's old pickup wasn't in the drive. She had no idea where he was, when he'd get home, or if he was ever coming home.

She didn't care.

The streetlights shining through the window hurt her eyes, and she shut the drapes. Her hands were trembling.

Ignoring the shakes, she returned upstairs and found herself in Noah's room. She sat in the rocking chair and shut her eyes and rocked. Back and forth. Back and forth. She could almost feel Noah beside her. When her eyes opened, she half expected him to be sitting on the bed, flipping the pages in his favorite book.

A wadded-up envelope lay on the floor, and she rose from the rocking chair. It looked like the offer Dr. Cross wanted her to read. When did that get in here, she wondered and picked it up. Sitting on the bed, she opened the envelope and slipped out the letter. She unfolded it and smoothed out the crinkles.

The Friends of Historic Restoration were offering seven figures for the Bluegill, but she didn't care. She wadded it up again and threw it at the wall.

Where the Darkness Hides lay on the floor by the bookcase, as if Noah had just been reading it. Opening the cover, she licked her index finger and turned the page. Noah's presence embraced her, and she smiled and started reading aloud.

"When morning arrives, and Charley's mother enters his bedroom,
She asks, "What have you done? Who made this mess?"
And Charley answers, "It wasn't me. Honest, it wasn't.
It was the monsters that emerge from all the spooky places where the darkness hides."
"There's nothing to be scared of in the dark," his mother says,
sitting beside him on the bed.
"If monsters appear and if they snarl and spit,
you just shout at them, 'I'm not scared of you! Not a single bit!'"
And Charley says he plans to do just that.
"So, at the end of the day, when nighttime arrives
Charley performs his nightly routine,
he slips into his favorite PJs, and brushes his teeth, and says his prayers
And when his mother turns on the nightlight and shuts the door
He sits up in his bed and watches the spooky places where the darkness hides.
And he waits.
And he repeats his mother's words,
"If monsters appear and if they snarl and spit,
you just shout at them, 'I'm not scared of you! Not a single bit!'"

Her eyes teared and the words blurred. She lowered the book.

She concentrated on relaxing, but she could not stop the flood of images racing through her mind, a montage of memories. Some people suffer memory loss after a car accident. She was afforded no such mercy; she remembered every detail about that night.

About that night thirteen months ago.

About that crash.

She was driving home, upset. She'd just had a fight with Kate. A bad fight. Noah was crying in the back seat. It was late. Her iPhone vibrated, and she looked down to read the text. Redd had sent a message. At that instant, she was coming off the Causeway. Blinding headlights headed straight for her. A car was going the wrong way on the exit ramp.

Her foot felt unnaturally heavy, preventing her from moving from the accelerator to the brake. But the brake was mashed to the floor, and she wondered why she wasn't decelerating. Or maybe the other driver was speeding up.

The collision was instant. Time froze. A water bottle spun slowly in the air under the sunroof. She remembered thinking, "That's odd." Then time sped up faster than she could witness, and everything happened at once: The sound of screeching tires. The tightness of the seat belt constricting against her chest. The glass exploding upward out of the windshield and raining back down on her.

Funny. Amid that carnage, she remembered dreaming. A detailed, intricate dream. She was swimming in the depths of the Gulf. Struggling. Fighting to rise to the surface. Kicking her feet. Frantically waving her arms. But she kept slipping, falling deeper into a black watery grave. Falling into the sharp coral arms spiraling up from the ocean floor. The coral reached for her. Grasped hold of her. Cut her. Encircled her. Entombed her. She was drowning.

The blare of a faraway horn woke her.

She opened her eyes. The smell of gunpowder assaulted her, probably from the airbags. Her head leaned against the steering wheel. The horn shrieked in her ear. She tried to lift her head. Pain ripped through her neck.

She ignored it and craned her head to look in the backseat.

The car seat was empty.

The backseat window to her left was cracked like a spider's web and smeared with blood.

Noah's broken body lay on the floorboard behind the passenger seat. His neck snapped, his little head lying at an unnatural angle against his shoulder. Blood covered his forehead.

That horrific image burned into her eyes. She saw it every time she closed them. She needed another drink.

"I'm so sorry, Noah," she whispered and returned his book to the bookcase. She looked around the room at his toys, his stuffed animals, his clothes laid out on the dresser. "I'm so, so sorry."

A voice crackled over the baby monitor.

Elise stared at the device. Maybe it was just her imagination like Dr. Cross told her. Like Redd kept saying. Her nerves were frazzled. So, it was possible. When she heard it again, she jumped.

"Elise?" A male voice from the baby monitor pierced her depression. "Are you okay?" he asked.

CHAPTER NINETEEN

Elise walked to the bookcase and picked up the baby monitor. A man's voice addressed her over the speaker. "Are you okay?"

"Doogie?" Elise smiled for the first time that day. "Oh, dear God, Doogie."

"Are you okay?" he asked again.

She pointed toward the stuffed animals on the bed, though she knew he couldn't see her. "I'm missing my baby."

"I know." His voice sounded empathetic and comforting.

"It's my fault." She was on the verge of tears. "I blame my husband, and I blame my sister, but it wasn't their fault. It was mine."

"It was the drunk driver's fault." The man's tone turned adamant yet consoling. "The man who hit you. It's his fault, not yours."

She wiped her eyes. "Do you think--" She hesitated, afraid to say what she was thinking. "Do you think Noah can forgive me?"

A knock from downstairs echoed through the house. She turned her head. The rap grew louder, then turned to a frenzied pounding. She picked up the monitor. Took a breath, held it. Her heart stopped.

"Someone's here," she whispered.

* * *

Kate stood at the driving range and watched Trace swing his club. He struck the golf ball and sent it soaring into the dark sky beyond the lights. His head turned upward, following the ball. He whistled, clearly impressed with himself.

"Look at it go," he said. After it landed on the fairway, he grabbed another golf ball and placed it on the tee.

Kate watched him swing. "Why are we here?" she asked as the second ball soared into the night. He turned to her.

"What better place to hang out than a driving range," he said.

"At ten-thirty at night?" she asked.

"It's open till midnight" He handed her the driver. "Your turn."

She rubbed her shoulder and took the club. He positioned a new golf ball on the tee. She stepped into position and gripped the club.

"How's the physical therapy going?" he asked.

"Fine." She concentrated on her grip.

"And your shoulder?"

"Better." She swung. Searing pain ripped through her shoulder. Had she really had nine months of therapy? She dropped the club.

"I thought so." He stepped toward her and hit the ball. It climbed upward and disappeared somewhere in the black sky. When it landed on the fairway, he stepped back and placed another ball on the tee. "Try again."

Kate started to swing but stopped. The pain shot through her. She turned to him. "Are you going to tell me what we're doing here or not?"

He scratched his beard. "I thought we could talk."

"About?"

"About this morning."

"There's nothing left to say. Olivia approached me about finding her father, and that's what I did."

He stared at her without saying a word. After several seconds, he cleared his throat. "You know that old putter in my office?"

She nodded. "The one hanging on the wall."

"Exactly," he said. "It's called White Fang, and it belonged to Jack Nicklaus."

"I figured there was a story behind it."

"I bought it at an auction." He knelt and set another ball on the tee. "Jack Nicklaus used that putter when he set a scoring record in the 1967 U.S. Open." Rising, he swung and struck the ball. It landed on the fairway. He whistled again and turned to Kate, picking up where he left off. "Nicklaus borrowed the putter from a friend during a practice round, and his wife painted the blade white to reduce the glare from the sun."

"Spare me the metaphor," she said. "I get it. Life is like golf. Sometimes you get bad breaks from a perfect swing. Sometimes you get lucky even when the swing sucks. But whatever happens, you have to play the ball wherever it lands. Blah. Blah. Blah."

"That's not my point at all."

She raised an eyebrow. "Okay then. Your point?"

"My point is Jack and his wife were a team. He may have been the one on the green, but she contributed in a huge way to his success that day. They were both playing the game, but in different ways."

"If I'm going to play the game," she said. "I want to be on the green." She rubbed her shoulder, then stopped.

He didn't respond and picked up another golf ball to hit. He looked disappointed, more than angry. That bothered her even more.

"Look, I know you're upset about this morning, but I don't have to tell you." She swallowed before adding, "Jasper Wade was the attorney who represented Forrest Frazier and got him out of manslaughter charges."

He placed the ball on the tee, then raised the club. He lowered it again and looked directly at her. "I know who he is. But he represented a lot of guilty people. He got a lot of people out of DUI charges and worse."

"His client was drunk, behind the wheel, and murdered my nephew."

"I know." He looked down, away from her, and swung. They watched the ball launch over the fairway. Without making eye contact, he said, "You gonna hit the ball, or are you just gonna stand there rubbing your shoulder?"

Kate was done with this demonstration. She didn't want or need a golf lesson, and she certainly didn't need a life lesson. Turning, she walked out of the tee area and left the driving range. Trace's squad car was the only vehicle in the parking lot. She slipped into the passenger seat. A moment later, the driver's side door opened, and Trace climbed in behind the wheel.

"I guess we're done talking," he said. She didn't answer. He started the engine. "Whether you like it or not, I need you to focus on your job and leave the investigating to us," he said and backed out of the parking slot. "If you can't do that, then there's no place for you on our team."

Kate stared out the window as he drove through Bradenton. He turned on the radio, and an announcer provided an update on the approaching hurricane. Kate didn't listen. She just sat there, with her purse in her lap. The bag felt unnaturally heavy with the Polaroid in it.

They approached the lighted Causeway taking them back to Sienna Key. When they crossed the bridge, she wished for a way to avoid the off-ramp. *The off-ramp.* Where it happened. Where the white cross and flowers now stood, and the balloons bounced.

"Stop," she yelled.

Trace looked over at her. "What?"

"Stop the car."

He pulled off onto the side of the ramp and rolled to a park. Kate jumped out of the squad car. A white cross with a wreath made of faded plastic leaves was planted in the grass by the curb. The name "Noah Tyler" was painted along the center beam in black block letters.

She took the Polaroid from her purse. Trace stood next to her.

"Kate?" he asked. "What's going on?"

She didn't answer. A car whizzed past, coming off the Causeway, and kicked-up small whirlwinds of dust and gravel, leaving a coat of dirt on her lips. She held the photo and questioned how to tell him.

"You're upset about finding the body," he said, placing a hand on her shoulder. "And it's bringing up a lot of pain from the past."

"It's not just the body," Kate said. "I saw something else."

"What?"

"There was a photo in the boat."

"A photo?" he asked. "A photo of what?"

"A polaroid of a stuffed elephant." She couldn't look at him and focused on the wreath. "It looks exactly like the one Noah had."

Trace took a deep breath. "Let it go. The Sheriff's Department will handle it from here." He paused as if waiting for her to argue. When she didn't, he knelt beside her. "Right? You told them about the possible connection. They'll take it from here."

She slipped the Polaroid into his hand.

He looked down at it. His eyes widened. "Tell me this isn't from the victim's boat?"

She nodded.

He stood, holding the Polaroid. He seemed to be at a loss for words. "Y-You took this from the crime scene?"

Again, she nodded but said nothing.

He stepped away, turned, and stepped back. "This is evidence. It could've had fingerprints. You've destroyed evidence."

"I know. That's why I took it." She remained kneeling, staring at the white cross. "It's Noah's stuffed elephant, Mister Belvedere. This murder is connected to Noah. That means this is connected to my little sister and her husband."

"You're jumping to conclusions."

"That's Mr. Belvedere." She pointed at the photo in his hands. "There's no question about it."

"Kate." He placed a hand on her shoulder. "We need to give this to the Sheriff's Department."

"No, not yet." She closed her eyes, tight. Her mind burned with the memory of that night.

That night thirteen months ago.

The night she babysat Noah. The night he died.

Elise and Redd had gone out to dinner and left Noah with her at the Bluegill. She watched him ride his bike up and down the street and even let him ride past the Neederman's mailbox. He told her about how he wanted to make a bike ramp and jump it like a rocket. She told him stories about how she and Elise grew up in the Bluegill and rode their bikes way past the Neederman mailbox to the old Widow Rock Lighthouse. She promised to take him there one day.

He'd just finished his bath and was getting into his PJs when her iPhone rang. A familiar female voice was on the other end, saying, "I know who you are, Kate Parks."

"Who is this?" Kate asked.

"Darren's girlfriend. And if you don't stay away from him, I'll beat your ass till hell won't have it."

Kate hung up and called Darren. "I got a threatening phone call from that girl again," she told him. "She warned me to stay away from you."

"Who?" He sounded puzzled.

"I thought maybe you could tell me. The crazy woman said if I don't back off, she'll beat my ass till hell won't have it."

He laughed. "That's Samantha."

"And?" she asked. She waited for an answer. "Who is Samantha?"

"Some crazed, obsessed fan." He chuckled, making light of it.

But it only confirmed what she already suspected; Darren had girlfriends in other cities. It was practically a prerequisite for a band that travels the country. Still, she was tired of the threats.

"I'm playing at Brewsky Bill's Brewhouse tonight," he said, "Why don't you come over and watch the show? We'll eat some dinner. I'll even sing '*Nine to Five*.'"

"I can't," Kate said. "I'm babysitting my nephew."

"Bring him along. He's got to eat too, doesn't he?"

Kate looked over at Noah. She knew she shouldn't.

Darren continued. "We're leaving for a three-week tour, and it'll be a while till we see each other again."

She thought about it. She wanted to see him before he left with the band. And Noah did have to eat. "I guess it would be okay," she finally said.

She picked up her nephew and buckled him into the car seat. Brewsky Bill's Brewhouse was a little beach bar along the Tampa Bay shoreline, just on the other side of the Causeway. As usual, the place was filling up. Darren and his band were on stage, playing so loud it was impossible to carry on a conversation unless you were within a few inches of each other. She found a booth, and she and Noah sang along.

After a few songs, Darren took a break and scooted into the booth with them.

"Hey, young man," he said, looking at the five-year-old.

"You remember my nephew, Noah," Kate said. "From the night we had steaks at my sister's place." She looked over at him, watching the shadows on his face.

"And your sister served me raw meat." He leaned over the table and kissed her.

Noah squealed. "Ooohhh, yuck!" he cried.

Her iPhone rang, and she saw it was Elise. "Right on time to spoil our fun," she said and stepped outside to answer the call.

"Where are you?" Elise's voice exploded through Kate's phone. "Is that the TV in the background?"

"No, I took Noah out for a bite to eat."

"A bite to eat?" Elise's anger increased. "It's way past his bedtime."

"It's Saturday night," Kate said. "Noah doesn't have to work tomorrow."

"You're not funny," Elise said. "I knew I couldn't trust you."

"Elise, he's fine. I'll take him home in a few minutes."

"Just stay there. We're coming to get him."

Kate hung up and returned inside.

When she got to the table, she found it empty. Both Darren and Noah were gone. Her heart stopped. A premonition of something terrible—*something* nasty—raced through her head. She called out for them. She yelled Noah's name and searched the crowd. She ran up to the stage and called out to the bass player.

"Have you seen my nephew?" she yelled.

He shrugged his shoulders.

"Where's Darren?"

He shrugged.

People joined her search. The bar manager came over and asked what was wrong. The bass player addressed the crowd over the mic, asking if anyone had seen the child.

"Call Chief Guerra," Kate said, panic rising in her voice. She ran out the back door into the alley.

Darren was there, holding Noah in his arms. He stared at her, baffled. "What's wrong?" he asked.

Kate ran to Noah and hugged him.

"He had to pee, and the Men's Room was full," Darren said. "So, I took him out here."

Kate laughed and hugged her nephew again. "I was afraid I lost you."

"You lost him?" came an angry female voice behind her. Kate turned to see Elise standing in the alleyway. She froze as Darren said, "Raw Meat!" and laughed.

"Mommy!" Noah yelled and ran to her.

Elise picked him up in her arms. Kate stood.

"Elise, look . . . I'm sorry," she said.

"Save it." Elise turned and rushed out the alley. She rounded the building and disappeared.

Kate followed and met them in the parking lot. "Elise, I'm sorry."

Elise buckled Noah in his car seat. Kate apologized again, and Elise flipped around. "I'm tired of your stupid apologies. I don't want to hear your stupid excuses. In fact, I don't want to hear your stupid voice."

She climbed into the driver's seat and slammed the door shut.

"C'mon, Kid," Kate said. "Nothing happened. He's fine, and I would've had him in his room and tucked in bed long before you and Redd ever got home."

"You're at a bar, drinking." She started the engine. "You could've killed him. And stop calling me Kid. I'm not a kid."

It was the last thing Elise said before storming out of the parking lot. Kate watched the taillights, then returned inside to the brewhouse. She slipped back into the booth, alone. Darren and his band were playing again. At the end of the night, he slid into the booth across from her.

"Sounds like Raw Meat is pretty mad at you," he said.

"Yeah, I'll have to apologize in the morning and kiss her butt for the next six months to make up for it." As if on cue, her iPhone interrupted them.

"Who could be calling me this late?" Kate asked, picking up her phone.

"Is it your sister?" Darren asked.

"It's the chief," she said, answering her phone.

A moment later, she got in her car and screeched out of the parking lot.

She thought she was stuck in a traffic jam over the Causeway headed into Sienna Key, but then she saw a plume of smoke in the air. She climbed out of her running Tahoe and left it in the line of cars. She ran past the idling vehicles to the end of the bridge. Something was on fire ahead of her. She picked up speed. Coming to the exit ramp, she saw it.

A Ferrari had collided with another car. The intoxicated driver staggered in the middle of the off-ramp, rubbing his head. Kate rushed to the other vehicle—Elise's car. It lay overturned and crumpled like a wad of paper. Smoke rose from the engine. The windshield shattered.

Elise lay motionless behind the steering wheel, blood gushing from her head. Kate ran to her sister. Elise looked up at her. She was only inches away, and she still remembered the look in Elise's eyes as she met her gaze. "Noah…" she whispered.

Kate looked in the back seat. Her heart stopped. Bile rose into her throat.

Ambulance sirens grew louder. But it was too late.

It was too late.

Tears flooded Kate's eyes as she stared at the white cross. Noah's memorial was all that remained. But it reminded her every time she passed the intersection. It told her of what she'd done.

"We can't give the Polaroid over to the Sheriff's Department," she said to Trace. "Not yet."

"You know this isn't right." His voice choked.

She stood and took the Polaroid from him. She slipped it back into her purse. "I know. But I did what I had to do, and I'm prepared to accept the consequences."

"Why?"

"My sister needs me." Kate looked back at the white cross and stared at Noah's printed name. Traffic whizzed past them on the off-ramp behind them. Talking over it, she said, "Noah's death broke her, and if Redd has done something--*something unthinkable*--it'll push her over the edge."

"You don't know that your brother-in-law had anything to do with this," Trace said, putting a hand firmly on her shoulder. "Your sister isn't the only one struggling with Noah's death. It's clouded your judgment too."

Kate stepped away and turned her back on him. She watched the traffic and said, "The killer left that photograph in the boat as a message . . . a message from Redd."

***

Standing in Noah's dark room, Elise turned her head toward the incessant pounding echoing through the empty house. Someone at the front door wanted in.

Redd had returned; she knew it. She'd let him pound on the door a little longer.

"Doogie?" She looked over at the baby monitor. "Doogie? Are you still there?"

The baby monitor was quiet in her hands. The pounding grew louder. She left the bedroom and walked down the staircase. Opening the front door, she expected to find Redd on the porch.

Forrest Frazier stood there instead.

CHAPTER TWENTY

Elise opened the front door and stared at the man standing on the porch—Forrest Frazier. The monster who murdered her son. The scum that got off scot-free. The demon that ruined her life. She slammed the door shut. He pushed against it, holding it open.

"Stop submitting your dead son's name on my website," he yelled. "It's not funny."

She struggled to close the door, but he fought to keep it open.

"Was that some kind of joke," he said, clenching his teeth, "entering Noah Tyler over and over on my website?"

"Go away," she screamed. "Leave me alone!"

She forced it shut and turned the deadbolt. Dropping to her knees, she leaned against the door and sobbed. The violent pounding began again. It shook the walls.

"I'm sorry about what happened to your son," he yelled. "But it wasn't my fault. You were speeding and texting on your phone. You hit my car. End of story. Now leave me alone. Leave my companies alone. And I'll leave you alone."

"Leave me alone." She sobbed. Her head jolted with the pounding on the door. "You . . . took . . . him . . . away . . . from . . . me!"

"I'm warning you. You push me too far, and I'll---"

"Go away!" she screamed.

The pounding stopped. The parlor turned quiet and dark. Elise pressed her ear to the door. Another voice yelled something at Forrest. Scuffling noises. A thump on the door. She jumped. Forrest's voice let out a string of expletives. Someone cussed back.

Then nothing.

* * *

Kate rubbed her temples as Trace parked in front of the Bear's Den in downtown Sienna Key. His cowboy hat lay on the dashboard. He'd been uncomfortably silent the entire ride back, and she couldn't blame him. When he parked and shut off the ignition, she ended the silence.

"Look, I know what I did was wrong on every conceivable level," she said. "And I know you're angry—"

"Why are you here?" He cut her off.

His question surprised her. "Come again?"

"Why are you here, in my department?" His eyes bore into her, searching. "Why did you transfer out of the FWC to the Sienna Key PD?"

"You asked me to," she said. "You wanted me to head up your safety initiative."

"No, that's not it." He looked away from her and ran a hand across his chin, smoothing his beard. He looked back at her. "There's a hundred people who could give those boat safety seminars. Hell, lately, Intern Ernie runs more classes than you do."

She flinched at the tone of his voice. She wanted to defend herself, but a thick lump lodged in her throat. She didn't know how to answer, so she said nothing at all.

Finally, he said, "You're here because you came home. And you know, as well as I do, that your shoulder isn't healing. You know you won't be returning to duty. And you came back to Sienna Key. You came home."

Tears welled in Kate's eyes. The lump in her throat enlarged, choking her. "I'm a Florida Fish and Wildlife Officer on inactive duty status and currently temporarily working for the Sienna Key law enforcement."

She barely got the words out.

He stared at her for several seconds, then shook his head. "No, Kate, you're not. Not anymore."

Tears rolled down her cheek. "I'm a Florida Fish and Wildlife Officer on inactive duty."

"It's been a year," he said, interrupting her. "And you couldn't even swing that club at the driving range tonight."

She wiped the back of her hand across her cheek. "I'll get better."

"It's been a year," he said again.

A sudden knock on the driver's side window surprised them. Trace turned his head as Kate looked over him to see Travel Agent outside. He rolled down the glass.

"You need to get out to the Bluegill." Travel Agent's voice rose with excitement. She flipped the mic on her headset away from her mouth. "Elise Tyler called 911 about a disturbance."

"I'm on my way." Kate opened the passenger door.

Trace grabbed her arm. "I'll go."

She looked back at him. "It's my little sister."

His brow furrowed. "I'll handle it."

"It's my little sister," she said, strength building in her voice.

He said nothing, staring at her.

Kate continued. "Trace, please."

He tilted his brow, looking at her with uncertainty, and gripped the steering wheel. "Fine. Brush your teeth and comb your hair. I'm driving."

Ten minutes later, Kate and Trace pulled onto the circular drive of the Bluegill Beach Hideaway. Redd's old pickup was out front, along with Dr.

Cross's rose-colored Mercedes. Trace parked next to them and reached for his cowboy hat on the dashboard. Kate jumped out of the squad car and raced into the house. He followed.

In the front parlor, Dr. Cross sat on the couch next to Elise, calming her. Elise held out her hand as the doctor dropped several pills into her palm and handed her a glass of water. She was saying, "There you go, Elise. Just relax now," as Elise swallowed the pills.

"Are you okay?" Kate rushed to her sister's side. Trace stood by the front door, watching.

Elise glared at Kate. "Oh, I don't know, it's Wednesday night, there' a hurricane coming, and you're in my house. I guess everything is peachy keen."

"She's fine," the doctor said before Kate could respond. "Just a little shaken up."

"It was that ass hat—Forrest Frazier was here." Redd bound down the staircase taking two steps at a time, gripping his baseball bat. "He's not getting away with this. He's not coming here, to my house, and threaten my wife."

He gave Kate a brutal, unfriendly stare.

His eyes burned through her, and she took Elise's hand. "Forrest Frazier? Did he threaten you?"

Elise pulled her hand from Kate's.

Trace moved toward Redd and took the baseball bat from his hands. "There's no need for this. And don't go anywhere. I've got some questions for you."

Trace leaned the baseball bat against the wall in the corner. Redd glared at him.

"Did he threaten you?" Kate asked as Trace set the wooden bat in the corner. She took Elise's hand again.

Elise pulled her hand away again. "I didn't speak to him. Doogie scared him away."

"Doogie?" Redd shook his head and clutched his hands to his temples. "Not this again!"

"Yes," Elise's voice cracked. "He protected me."

A vein enlarged on Redd's forehead. "There is no Doogie."

"There is," Elise insisted. "And he's my friend."

"He's not real, Elise," Redd screamed at her. "He's a figment of your imagination. You lock yourself up in that room and never come out, and it's made you stir crazy."

"I'm not crazy," she cried. "He's there. He talks to me. And he protected me tonight."

"Will you stop it? Please? Just stop it." Redd was yelling now and clenching his fists. He approached the couch, but Trace blocked him and pushed him back.

Dr. Cross stood. "I think it'd be best if Elise got some rest now."

"Come on," Kate said. She helped Elise to her feet and guided her to the stairs. The doctor followed, and Kate stopped her. "I think she needs some sister time."

"Elise is in a fragile state of mind," the doctor said. "It'd be best if—"

"I've got it," Kate insisted. The doctor shrugged and stepped aside. She joined Trace and Redd by the front door.

Kate and Elise ascended the stairs to the third-floor landing. They entered the master bedroom, and Elise sat on the bed. Kate shut the door.

"It's not safe here. Maybe it'd be best if you stayed with me for a while." Kate sat on the bed beside Elise and noticed the framed photograph of Noah hugging the giant stuffed elephant. She slipped her hand in her pocket. Her fingers grazed the Polaroid. "Kid, I need to ask you something," she said. "Where did Mr. Belvedere come from?"

Elise's face closed as if guarding a secret. "I'm…I'm not sure," she said. "I think Redd got it for him," she muttered. "Yes, when Noah fell and hit his head, we took him to the hospital. Redd got it for him."

"Kid…"

"I remember bringing it home from the hospital," Elise continued. "I remember because it was so big. That was a giant elephant, and it barely fit in the back seat."

"Kid," Kate caught her error when Elise shot her an irritated scowl. "Elise…I'm worried that Redd's done something…."

"But Noah loved it." Elise picked up the photo. "He just adored Mr. Belvedere. It was bigger than he was, but he didn't care."

"Listen, please… I need to tell you something."

Elise returned the framed photograph to the nightstand.

Kate continued. "I'm worried that Redd has done something. Something bad."

"What?"

"I found a body…a murder victim."

The door opened, interrupting her, and Trace and Dr. Cross entered the bedroom. The doctor approached Elise on the bed. She pulled back the covers.

Elise resisted lying down. "I'm fine. Really."

"We're just worried about you," Trace said, standing in the doorway. "And we need to ask you a few questions."

"This isn't the time for questions," the doctor said.

"No, wait." Elise raised her arms. "Kate wanted to tell me something."

"It can wait," the doctor said, gently pushing Elise back down on the bed.

Elise put her head on the pillow as Kate rose from the edge of the bed.

"I'll stay here with you tonight," Kate said. "You're safe now."

The doctor shook her head and let out a condescending laugh. "Elise is a big girl. She needs rest, not a nursemaid."

"I'm not leaving my sister," Kate insisted.

"You're upsetting my patient." The doctor stood and confronted her. "Elise needs to get some sleep. I'm going to have to ask you to leave." She looked over at Trace. "Both of you."

Dr. Cross pushed Kate and Trace out of the bedroom. In the hallway, she shut the door and turned to them. Kate raised a hand.

"Look," Kate said. "Elise isn't safe here."

"She's fine," the doctor said. "However, your sister simply isn't strong enough to withstand a bombardment of questions right now. That'll have to wait."

Kate wasn't buying it. "The man who killed her son just tried to break into her home."

The doctor looked bored with the conversation. "You're referring to Forrest Frazier?"

"Yes," Kate said.

"Look, Kate is right," Trace said. "Forrest Frazier has no business here."

"There's no evidence that he was trying to break in. There is even any evidence that anyone was even here," she said. She turned Trace. "You know, in her mental state, Elise tends to imagine things."

"She dialed 911 in a panic," Trace said. "Forrest Frazier was here."

"Then you'll have to take it up with him." The doctor pushed past them and headed for the staircase. She paused on the first step. "Besides, maybe this little incident will give her the push she needs to sell this place and move on with her life. That would be the best thing for her."

The doctor descended the staircase. Kate followed.

"Is that what this was all about?" Kate raised her voice as she moved quickly down the stairs past the second level. "Was this some ploy to get her to sell The Bluegill?"

"There is no ploy," the doctor said. She came off the steps into the parlor. "It would be in Elise's best interest to leave this place. Hers and Redd's."

Redd, Kate thought and looked around. She stepped into the living room. He wasn't there. "Where is he?" she asked.

The doctor followed Kate into the living room. From the front parlor, Trace called out for him. There was no answer. His radio crackled, and Travel Agent's voice rippled through the speaker.

"Chief, there's a 415 coming over the wire at the Mayfair Plaza Building," she said.

Kate heard it as Trace entered the living room.

"That's Forrest Frazier's office building," he said.

She nodded and glanced toward the empty corner where Redd's baseball bat had been.

CHAPTER TWENTY-ONE

Kate sat buckled into the passenger seat as Trace raced his squad car over the Causeway into Bradenton, sirens blaring. They reached the Mayfair Plaza Building within fifteen minutes. Three Manatee County Sheriff's Department cars were already parked outside, their lights flashing. Trace pulled up beside them.

The twelve-story building looked empty, with most of the exterior windows dark. The ground floor, however, was brightly lit as Sheriff's Deputies traipsed in and out. Kate and Trace made their way through a bank and investment center and took the elevator to the Forrest Frazier Development offices on the twelfth floor. They were greeted in the front office by a buxom, young woman in a short skirt and high heels.

"Can I help you?" she asked.

"I'm Chief Trace Guerra with the Sienna Key Police Department," he said, flashing his badge. "This is—"

"Kate Parks, Florida Fish and Wildlife Officer on inactive duty status and currently temporarily working for the Sienna Key law enforcement." She extended a hand.

The young woman didn't take Kate's hand. "The police are already here," she said.

Kate pulled back. "And you are?"

"Shelly Martin," she said, handing them a business card. "Mr. Frazier's executive assistant. He's in his private office talking to the police." She led Kate and Trace to his corner office.

Forrest Frazier's office looked chaotic with over-turned furniture and police officers snapping photos. Forrest himself sat at his desk, nursing a black eye and a stiff drink as he chewed a cigar. Two deputies stood across from him, writing in notepads.

"That psycho barged in here," Forrest said. He removed the cigar from his mouth and held it like a prop as he spoke. "He smashed my office with a baseball bat."

Listening, Kate looked at the room. Trophies and plaques embellished the walls, Framed photographs of Frazier posing with celebrities, sports heroes, and political figures surrounded them. A Widow Rock Towers model lay in pieces on the floor, crushed, along with several photographs dangling askew on the wall.

"Did you recognize the attacker?" one of the deputies asked.

"Redd Tyler." Forrest downed the last of his drink and returned the cigar to his mouth. He rose from his desk. At the dry bar next to the window, he picked up a bottle of bourbon, opened it, and poured himself another glass, spilling some over the side. "That boneheaded dipstick is psychotic."

Kate watched him, critically studying his posture. "I suspect you instigated this."

Forrest grinned at her with the cigar between his teeth.

Trace added, "We heard you paid Elise Tyler a visit earlier tonight."

"Yeah," Forrest said. "What of it?"

"You were harassing her," Kate said. She stepped toward him. Trace gripped her upper arm, holding her back.

Forrest glared at her. "Gomer and Morticia were harassing *me*. I just went over there to tell them to stop it."

"Stop what?" Trace asked.

Forrest returned to his desk and picked up a stack of papers. "To stop *this*. There's hundreds of them," he said and tossed the papers in Trace's direction. They scattered on the floor at his feet.

Trace knelt and grabbed several sheets. He rose and offered a page to Kate. She glanced over it. The text looked like a list of real estate leads, with Noah's name typed repeatedly.

"What is this?" she asked, looking over at Forrest. He removed the cigar from his mouth and shook his head.

"They went onto my website and entered their dead son's name as an interested party for a condo in the Widow Rock Towers." He walked to the bar and fixed himself another drink. "They entered that brat's name over and over."

That brat? Kate felt her face flush, and she clenched her fists.

Trace squeezed her arm tighter. He cleared his throat and asked, "How do you know it was the Tylers?"

"What makes you think it wasn't?" Forrest returned to his desk. Ice clinked in the drink in his hands.

"Did you threaten her?" Kate asked. She noticed the crushed model of the Widow Rock Towers. Pieces of it lay scattered across the floor.

"I politely asked her to stop and left when she demanded I leave," Forrest said. He set down the glass and opened the cigar box. "So to answer your question, no, I didn't threaten her."

"How'd you get the black eye?" Kate asked. "Did Redd hit you?"

He raised his head, grinning with a fresh cigar between his teeth, "No, it was some homeless man at the Tyler house. When I got back to my office, I found this." Forrest pointed at the smashed model.

"You didn't see Redd Tyler in your office?" Trace asked.

"He's on the security tape." Forrest sat back in his desk chair, holding his cigar in one hand and his drink in the other. "I turned over the footage to the deputies. Now, if you'll excuse me."

Trace motioned to Kate. It was time for them to leave, and he progressed to the door.

"Wait, Mr. Frazier," Kate stopped in the open doorway. "Did you recognize the homeless man?"

"Recognize him?" Forrest looked puzzled. "He was a homeless person. How the hell would I know who he is?"

"Maybe a neighbor?"

Forrest shook his head, clearly aggravated. "Look, if your sister wants to turn The Bluegill into a soup kitchen, that's her business—until my condo building goes up next to it. Then it's *my* business, and I'll bus them down to the Everglades."

Kate watched him a moment, then followed Trace out the door.

Outside the office, Trace turned to Kate. "So . . . where do you think Redd went?"

* * *

Redd's old pickup rolled into the cemetery and came to a stop. Jumping out, he gripped the baseball bat with both hands and weaved through the headstones. He looked for one in particular and halted when he found it. The name etched in the stone read:

NOAH TYLER
BELOVED SON
BEAUTIFUL CHILD

He screamed at the headstone. Kicked it. Raised the bat. Slammed it against the stone. Chipped the concrete. Cried. Hit the top. Hit it again. And again.

When he finally tired, he dropped the bat. It hit the ground, splintered and fractured. He fell to his knees and rubbed his fingers along the etched letters. The grey stone had chips around the edges. But the baseball bat lay in pieces. Broken himself, Redd fell onto his side in the dirt, curling up into the fetal position, and sobbed.

It was nearly an hour before he made it back to The Bluegill. He dropped what remained of the baseball bat on the porch—now three fragments of splintered wood. The front door was unlocked, and he stumbled into the parlor, staggered upstairs, and entered his bedroom. He expected to find Elise there, asleep, but the bed was empty. He turned on the light and went to the bathroom. Empty. He crossed the hall and looked in Noah's room. Empty. He returned downstairs, looked in the kitchen, the living room, the garage. The model trainset sat quiet and dark. He noticed the trees had been knocked over. Every single one. Again. He turned off the light and locked the door.

Finally, outside, he found Elise on the lanai, lying on a deck chair, arm dangling over the side. There was a broken wineglass shattered on the flagstones and an empty bottle beside her.

Gently lifting her into his arms, he carried her upstairs and put her to bed.

* * *

Thursday
September 4

Early the next morning, Kate parked in front of the Bear's Den in downtown Sienna Key. The meteorologist on the radio warned that Hurricane Sebastian was growing. The projected path predicted landfall to be north of Sarasota. She turned off the radio and entered the building.

The lobby was deserted, and she expected to find everyone in the breakroom watching the hurricane forecast. Instead, they were huddled in Jared's office, hovering over the laptop on his desk.

Jared looked up as she entered. "You gotta see this," he said.

"Are you tracking the storm?" Kate asked as she entered. Jared sat at the desk with Jensen on his right and Travel Agent and Intern Ernie on his left. "Sounds like it's going to make landfall further south than originally expected," she said.

Jared turned his laptop around. Photos of a car accident appeared on the screen. "Remember Jerry and Maxine Flagg?" he asked. "Authorities found them dead in their wrecked vehicle, although their injuries aren't entirely consistent with the crash."

"It looks like they were beaten to death and their bodies placed into the car afterward," Jensen added. "But get this…"

Jared clicked on an image, and it enlarged on the screen.

Kate gasped as she saw a polaroid of a stuffed elephant. The Polaroid she lifted from the boat lay buried in her purse.

"And there's more," Jensen added. "The murders connect to another murder in Atlanta."

"It's just awful," Travel Agent said, still wearing her headset.

Jared opened another browser tab on the screen and pulled up a new series of new photographs. This one showed a man lying face down in a pool of blood, possibly on the street or in an alleyway. Other photos showed close-ups of his battered, bashed-in head. Another showed the Polaroid of the stuffed elephant. It looked identical: plush grey fur, a comically long trunk, huge floppy ears, and two round button eyes. The grey fur on the body had a discolored patch, just like Mr. Belvedere.

"That weird photo of the stuffed animal links the two murders," Travel Agent said.

"The victim's name is Howie Logan," Jared added.

Jensen chuckled. "Wouldn't it be crazy if that stuffed elephant was possessed or something and murdering people?"

Jared pushed him away. "Why you gotta say somethin' like that? This is serious."

"What?" Jensen pushed him back. "It could happen—like in the Chucky movies. Or Annabelle."

"This ain't a movie," Jared said.

Kate moved her face closer to the screen, studying the picture. "Howie Logan? Does he have a connection to the lawyers?" she asked.

"None, as fat as anyone knows," Travel Agent said. "We've requested a client list."

Kate thought of Redd again and wondered if she was going to learn that he knew this Howie Logan somehow. Maybe he'd been a guest at the Bluegill. Maybe he was involved in the accident somehow.

"Where's Trace," she asked Travel Agent, but Jared answered.

"Headed to The Bluegill," he said. "He's bringing Redd Tyler in for questioning."

* * *

Dr. Yvette Cross pulled in front of The Bluegill and saw Redd outside on a ladder nailing plywood over the windows. She got out of her Mercedes and approached him.

"It sounds like the storm is headed straight for us," she yelled up at him. He muttered something unintelligible down to her, and she noticed he held several nails between his teeth. "We have to evacuate," she added.

He came down from the ladder and spat out the nails. Sheets of plywood lay scattered on the ground. "Elise is still in bed," he said. "She got drunk last night and is sleeping it off."

"She shouldn't be drinking while she's taking sedatives," the doctor said.

"We probably spend a few hundred dollars a week on Jack and other liquor," he said, pulling a pack of cigarettes from his back pocket. "I can't stop her."

"I wanted to check on her," she said. "That and talk to you."

He knocked a cigarette out of the pack and slipped it in his mouth. "Yeah?" he asked. "About what?"

"About the offer from the Friends of Historic Restoration," she said, watching him light the cigarette. "I think you know Elise isn't going to get better until you get her out of this place."

He took a drag and exhaled smoke. "This isn't the time to talk about it. That storm is headed straight for us like we got a bullseye painted on our ass."

She reached for him and put her hands over his. "The money you make selling this place would change your lives."

"She'll never leave."

"You need to convince her." She watched him for several seconds, waiting for an answer. When none came, she looked over at his old pickup parked in the drive. Paint flecked on the hood, and the body was scratched and dented. "You could buy a new truck."

He turned and lifted a sheet of plywood from the ground. "Do you think I don't know that?"

"Then what are you going to do about it?"

"What can I do? She's not listening to me." He carried the plywood up the ladder.

"Then make her listen." She stood at the base of the ladder and yelled up to him. "Buy a cabin in Colorado and board horses. Start over. Heal. Help her get over—"

"No. Don't say his name!" He dropped the plywood, and it fell to the ground, nearly hitting her. He raced down the ladder. "Don't even say his name. Don't even say it!"

The doctor stepped back and watched him, saying nothing.

He dropped to the ground and sat. He took another drag on the cigarette. She stepped on the plywood and knelt beside him.

"You're both grieving and dealing with his death in very different but equally severe and destructive ways," she said. "This house, these memories, they're destroying you both."

"It already has." He spoke through his tears. His voice trembled. "I don't think we can recover from this."

"Yes, Redd, you can. You both can. But not if you stay here." She removed an envelope from her purse and put it in his free hand.

With the cigarette dangling from his lips, he opened it and slipped out the folded letter.

"My only interest in you and The Bluegill is how it affects Elise and her mental health," she said as two police squad cars pulled up the circular drive. They parked, and a couple of Manatee County Sheriff's Deputies got out of the first car. Chief Guerra stepped out the second.

"Mr. Tyler," Trace said, approaching them. "We need to discuss your whereabouts last night."

CHAPTER TWENTY-TWO

Kate arrived at the Manatee County Sheriff's Office and asked to see Chief Guerra. She waited over an hour before the receptionist took her to an office in the back, where Trace was speaking to a couple of detectives.

She entered the room and approached him. "How's Redd?"

"I was wondering what took you so long." He looked up and shook his head. "They won't let Redd go unless Forrest Frazier drops the charges."

The detective at the desk added, "We're holding him until formal charges can be filed."

"How's he doing?" she asked. "Can I see him?"

Trace looked over at the detective. The detective nodded and got up from the desk.

"Follow me," he said and led her through several hallways to the holding cells. Red paced in a crowded holding tank of men–drunkards, burglars, and general troublemakers. He approached the front bars when Kate entered.

"What happened?" she asked him.

"Whaddya think happened?" He let out a long sigh. "The Big Enchilada of Doom got me on camera wrecking two hundred dollars worth of damage to his office."

"We're arranging bail," she said. "But what were you thinking?"

"The man attacked my wife." He raised his arms and leaned them against the bars. "And I don't need a lecture from you about taking matters into my own hands."

"I'm not here to lecture you. I probably would've done the same thing," she said. "But..."

"Yes?" He shot her a curious look.

"I want to know how you're involved with the Wade and Flagg law firm?" she asked.

"This again?" He stepped and shook a hand at her. "Let me tell you, I had nothing to do with whatever is going on with those attorneys, and I have no clue who that other person is."

"Howie Logan of Atlanta," she said. "Maybe he stayed at The Bluegill?"

His face turned red. "Kate, look...I just spent the last two hours getting grilled by Chief Guerra and a couple of detectives. I admit it; I took a bat and had some fun in Frazier's office. I've waited a long time to do that, and I don't mind telling you, I feel better. But they're not pinning some murders on me, and you'd better sure as hell not be helping them."

Kate bit her lip. She thought of the Polaroid weighing down her purse.

"Now, if you don't mind," he continued. "Can you go check on Kate? There's a hurricane coming in case you haven't heard."

"Of course, but Redd…I'm the one who found Jasper Wade's corpse," she said.

He hesitated. "I'm sorry. I didn't know."

"Thank you, but there's more to it than that," she said. She thought about what to say next and chose her words carefully. "I found a polaroid of a stuffed animal at the crime scene. It was a photo of that giant plush elephant you bought for Noah when he stayed overnight in the hospital."

"Mr. Belvedere," Redd said.

"Exactly. A photograph of Mr. Belvedere was left at all three crime scenes," she said. "Whatever's going on has something to do with Noah."

"No. It doesn't," he said. "And it doesn't have anything to do with me. I only saw that twisted ambulance chaser in the courtroom, and I never even met his partner in the firm. And whoever the other guy is, well, that's not my problem."

"But the photograph of Mr. Belvedere," she said.

"There's got to be thousands of stuffed elephants out there just like it. God knows why you think it's Mr. Belvedere or why the hell you would tell the Chief that it belonged to Noah," he said. "Besides, I didn't buy that giant stuffed animal for Noah."

She paused. Elise specifically said he'd bought it. "Then where did it come from?" she asked.

"I don't know. I thought maybe you got it for him. I was preoccupied that night. My son was hurt and in the hospital. Tracking down exactly who gave him a stuffed animal wasn't the priority."

"None of this makes any sense," she said, watching the crowd of detainees in the cell behind him. Fifteen to twenty men leaned against the walls, sat on metal chairs, strode back and forth within the confined space. No one seemed to be speaking to each other. "Somethings going on, and that elephant seems to be at the center of it."

"I had nothing to do with those murders," he said. The words came out so fast, and with such force, they ran together. "You do believe me, Kate. Right? You do believe me?"

Kate thanked him and promised to check on Elise. When she returned to the parking lot, she took the photograph from her purse. Maybe there were thousands of stuffed elephants out there just like it—*just like he said*—but still, the stain on the furry body bothered her. This was Mr. Belvedere. She was certain of it.

When she made it back into Sienna Key, Kate sent Ian a text message asking if he wanted to have lunch at the Tiki Hut. Waitress Lenna greeted her and offered her any table. Kate took a stool at the bar.

"Heather drew another picture for you," Lenna said. "I'll get it for you. It's in my locker."

Kate opened her laptop and poured over every detail of the murders she could find. To be honest, it was a nice distraction. The TVs on the wall were turned to different news stations. Though muted, they broadcasted weather maps and projected paths and viewer concerns about the approaching hurricane. There wasn't anything else on, despite that there was no new information. Sebastian had turned slightly south and was on course to hit somewhere north of Sarasota and had picked up speed. Now all they could do was wait.

She shut her laptop and wondered about Ian. She hadn't seen or spoken to him since yesterday. And his lack of response to her text messages was grating her nerves. She knew he had his iPhone with him, and the battery was probably dead, which was frequently his excuse for not returning her calls.

She straightened to relieve the ache in her shoulder when Lenna set a chicken sandwich and a piece of paper on the bar in front of her.

"Heather drew this for you," she said. "I promised to give it to you next time you came in."

Kate picked up the drawing. Colorful stick figures were drawn in crayon with a gray box in the sky shooting bright yellow lines. "My refrigerator is becoming an art gallery," she said.

"Well, Heather loves you and appreciates everything you did," Lenna said. "We're just sorry you got injured so bad. The meals on me. And there's no mayo."

"You've got to stop comping my meals," Kate told her. "I was just doing my job." She started to ask how Heather was doing but got distracted by a familiar song on the jukebox.

"Nine to Five," she said under her breath and turned on the stool.

Darren Riggler stood in the corner by the jukebox, smiling at her.

CHAPTER TWENTY-THREE

"What're you doing here?" Kate waved at Darren, inviting him to join her at the bar.

He walked over and took a stool beside her. "How's Raw Meat?"

"She's better. She's still shaken up." She looked down at her drink then back at him. A strand of his disheveled brown hair fell lazily over his left eye. He shot her a smile with his crooked grin, flashing that chipped front tooth. She returned the smile and wanted to reach out with a finger and brush the hair from his face. When she caught herself staring too long, she diverted her eyes and mumbled, "Elise never really recovered from losing her son."

"Of course she hasn't." He moved closer to her. He put his hand on hers. "A parent never recovers from losing a child."

"She's just so lost," she said. His hand felt warm. He squeezed his fingers over hers.

"Death changes you." His head moved closer to her face, whispered in her ear.

She turned her head into his. "We lost Noah, but it's like we lost her too."

"You did," he said. Their noses brushed. "Maybe Elise didn't die in that car accident, not physically anyway. But she did die on the inside. Spiritually. Emotionally. Whatever. She died on the inside."

"I need to help her," Kate said. Their mouths were close, his breath hot on her face. She wanted to kiss him. Why was she still talking? "I mean, I'm trying, but I don't know what I can do."

"There's nothing that you can do." His lips brushed her lips.

She pulled back. His eyes widened. He looked so serious. So focused on her. Like he really cared. Like he was really listening. Of course, that was comforting. But it wasn't right.

"Darren…What are you doing here?" she asked. "I thought you were heading out to Fort Lauderdale ahead of the storm."

He took a breath as if trying to regain his composure. "I turned around," he said. "The radio said the storm had shift south. You're directly in the path now."

"I know," she said.

He opened his mouth as if he wanted to tell her something but didn't know exactly how to say it. Or ask a question he already knew the answer to. He took her hand. "You gotta get out of here. Come to Fort Lauderdale with me."

"I can't." She pulled her hand away.

"Pack your bags. Secure your place and get the hell out." He sounded more urgent now. Worried. And any comfort she felt suddenly evaporated.

"Darren, please---"

"Just hit the road with me. Let's get out of here while we still can."

"Darren..." She looked down at her drink. Now she had to ask a question she already knew the answer to. "Has anything changed? A groupie in every city. Every night's a party. Girls waiting in your hotel room. I don't want to be a part of that."

"That's not the way it is," he said defensively. "Not anymore."

"What about—what's her name?" She pretended not to remember, but she did. She remembered that girl, that phone call. That crazy psycho bitch who was obsessed with him and left those threatening messages in her voicemail and warned her to stay away from him. "You know. *That* girl. I think her name was...Samantha?"

A flash of alarm swept across his face. "Who?"

She could almost see the wheels spinning in his head. Was his brain running through some list of *hot babes*? Scrambling to recall names and remember faces?

"Samantha," she said. "I'm sure you remember her. You had a real thing for her."

"Oh yeah, her." He shot her a devilish grin. "But my attorney said I wasn't allowed to show it to her without her permission."

Kate laughed. "You have an attorney?" she asked, studying him. He looked older. More mature. Grown up. Maybe he had changed. Still, there was Samantha. And undoubtedly a list of other *hot babes.* "She told me to stay away from you."

"That was a long time ago," he said.

A year ago, she thought.

"Look, Darren. I have a boyfriend." She said it quickly, like ripping off a Band-Aid. If he had Samantha—*or even worse, a Samantha in every city*—then she had Ian. "You broke my heart, and I just don't think I can go away with you without feeling . . ." A flicker of apprehension coursed through her. "I have a boyfriend now."

"I see..." He looked as if he'd just been slapped, then grinned again. "Then take the boyfriend along. We can all go to Fort Lauderdale together. Hang with the band. Hit the beaches. If the weather is bad up here, you know it'll be blue skies and sunshine down south."

He looked into his glass, and she couldn't help but appraise him. His face had a definition, a sense of character formed and deepened by experience. Ian lacked that and, she suspected, always would.

As if on cue, a short, redheaded man wearing a vertically striped shirt appeared and sat at the bar beside her, interrupting them.

"Ian," Kate said. "What are you doing here?"

He threw his keys on the countertop. "Newsflash. I've tracked down the founder's great, great-grandson. He's living in Canada---" He didn't even seem to notice the man she was talking to.

"Ian, this Darren Riggler." Kate motioned toward Darren.

Ian held up his phone and brought up an article on the screen. "I don't have a phone number or an address yet, but I'm closing in. And here's an article about him."

"Darren," she continued. "This is Ian Biggs, my boyfriend." She cringed when she said it. It sounded so high school.

Darren got up from his stool and extended his hand. Ian didn't seem to notice.

"Fact," he said, as if completely oblivious to Darren's presence. "If I can get to Canada, I can find him. I can convince him to come back here and meet with the city council."

Darren set his empty beer mug on the bar. "Well . . . it looks like you're busy, and I better be heading out." He nodded toward Kate. "Think about Fort Lauderdale, okay?"

"I'll see you the next time you're in town," she said.

He smiled, but it looked forced. His face turned dark. "Nine to five."

"Nine to five," she said in return. For some reason, she had a hunch that this would be the last time she saw him. Something about his conversation saddened her, and she reminded herself that he was a musician, and despite the fun times, she needed a steady, dependable relationship, not a never-ending Saturday night. Yet…her heart swelled with a feeling she had thought long since lost.

"Fact," Ian said as he snapped at Kate and pointed to his phone. "As long as he's got proof that his great, great grandfather was born in the lighthouse, we'll be able to--" His ginger eyebrows slanted in a sudden frown and his head whipped toward the door. Darren had just left. "Wait… did that guy just ask you to go to Fort Lauderdale with him? Should I be worried?"

"He's an old friend in town for a couple of days and stopped by to autograph a CD."

"Explain." Ian turned in his seat and faced her. "He's a musician selling his CDs door to door?"

"He's an old friend. I ran into him at lunch, and he gave me a CD. No big deal."

"Good." He seemed to ponder the possible threat level and deemed it harmless. He turned back to his phone. "Check out this article. It even mentions Sienna Key and its founder being born in the lighthouse."

Kate glanced at the screen. "It's a blog."

"It's the blog by the great, great-grandson of the town founder." He handed her his phone. She wouldn't take it. He waved it in front of her. "Newsflash. This may be our last chance to save the lighthouse."

"I don't know." She took his phone and scanned the article. "The great, great grandson of an urban legend sounds like a longshot."

"Challenge," he said. "Find a way to contact him."

"That's not a challenge I'm interested in accepting." She dropped his phone on the counter. "Even if he exists, do you think he's going to fly out here and talk to the city council?"

"Yes." He picked up his phone and handed it to her again. She still didn't take it. He waved it in his hand. "We have to at least try."

"No."

"Yes," he said. "This is your town. You and your sister grew up playing in that old lighthouse, and you're about to lose it." He took a breath as if realizing he was lecturing. "Look, I'm gonna hit the head. Just see what you can find, okay?"

She looked down at her chicken sandwich, sans mayonnaise. It hadn't even been touched yet. "Ian, I'm eating."

"Great. Order me something too."

He took off for the men's room as Kate picked up his phone. She scanned the blog and swiped through the articles. Bored, she closed the browser and noticed the photo gallery icon. Taking a bite of her sandwich, she pulled up his camera roll.

The first photo was of Forrest Frazier. Then the second. And the third. Getting in his red Ferrari. Coming out of the Mayfield Building in Bradenton. Talking on his cellphone. She flipped through the images, then found another.

An older man, probably in his fifties, came up next. He looked familiar: driving a truck. Fishing. Steering a sleek bass boat. A Yellowfin 23.

The name "Olivia" was stamped on the hull.

Kate dropped the phone.

CHAPTER TWENTY-FOUR

Kate barged into the men's room with her head raised, Ian's phone in hand, and yelling, "Why are there photos of Jasper Wade on your phone?"

Standing at the urinal, Ian zipped up his pants. "Kate, you can't come in here."

Another man a couple of stalls down shouted at her. "This is the men's room, lady!"

She sized him up. "And you made the cut?"

The guy shook his head and marched past her, out the door, without even washing his hands.

Ignoring him, she looked over at Ian, brandishing his phone. "Why are there photos of Jasper Wade on your phone?"

Who?"

"Jasper Wade."

"The attorney?" He walked to the sink and turned on the water. She stepped beside him, watching him in the mirror. He ran his hands under the soap dispenser.

"The attorney who was just found murdered," she said. She waited for him to offer an explanation. He said nothing, and she tried again. "Ian, Jasper Wade was murdered."

"I know." He turned off the water, wiped his hands on a paper towel, and then streaked them through his short red hair. He checked his reflection in the mirror. "It's all over the news. The Kingpin is holding a press conference about him tomorrow."

"That's beside the point, and you didn't answer my question." She looked down at the phone in her hand. "Were you following him?"

"Yes." He turned to her. "I was following him . . . along with several other investors in the Widow Rock Towers. Self-serving contributors to destroying a landmark, our history, and the environment."

"Are you not listening to me? Jasper Wade was murdered." She said it slowly, emphasizing each word, hoping it would sink in through his thick head. "I'm the one who found his corpse."

Ian stared at her, mouth open, eyes wide. "What?"

"I found Wade's corpse in the mangroves off the Bay."

His face turned grim, as if he heard her for the first time. "Oh, my God. Are you okay?"

"Why were you stalking him?"

"I wasn't *stalking* him, per se." He took his phone from her.

She grabbed it back. "What about Jerry and Maxine Flagg? Am I gonna find photos of them on your phone too?"

He snatched his phone from her hands again. "I was keeping tabs on anyone listed as an investor, looking for anything we could use against them."

"What about Howie Logan? Were you stalking him too?"

He cocked his head. "I don't know who that is."

"They're all dead, Ian. Dead," she said, making her point clear. "Do you know how that looks?"

He shook his head and reached for the bathroom door. "Irrelevant."

"No, this is extremely relevant." She moved ahead of him and stretched her arm across the doorway, blocking him. "It's the most relevant thing ever."

"You just don't get it, do you?" He sounded irritated now, standing in the doorway to the men's room, talking to her. "That's how I stopped the Kingpin in the past. I brought him to his knees and stopped that housing development. I saved the Florida panther and its habitat from becoming a new housing community and shopping mall, and God knows what else."

A man interrupted him, pushing past them, and entered the bathroom. Kate moved her arm. Ian walked into the bar.

"Where were you last Sunday?" she asked, following.

"Irrelevant." He walked faster, moving away from her. She kept up with him. They exited into the parking lot toward his Vespa scooter.

"Stop saying it's irrelevant. It's very relevant." She grasped his arm. "Tell me where you were."

He removed the helmet and fit it over his head. "Truth?"

"Truth," she said.

"I spent the day with the Mommy Warriors collecting dirty diapers for the protest. I wasn't anywhere near that attorney." He tightened the chin strap and mounted the scooter.

"I hope so." She watched him start the motor. "For your sake, I hope so."

"I was keeping tabs on those attorneys, but I didn't murder them…" He hesitated a moment, watching her. "Kate…I didn't murder anyone."

She stepped aside. Frowning, he rolled forward on the scooter and skirted past her out the parking lot.

Kate folded her arms, watching him disappear down the street. She didn't know what to believe. Redd's involvement was obvious. His motive was clear. Now she wondered if she'd been wrong.

***

Friday
September 5

Kate woke early at The Bluegill.

She'd gathered Tug, Doc, and Bert last night and carted them from the boathouse to the bed and breakfast. She wanted to stay with Elise while Redd was incarcerated.

"He hasn't been charged yet," she told Elise when she arrived.

"The night is still young," Elise said, as flippant as ever. That was all she said that evening before locking herself in Noah's room. She was still there when the sun came up.

Kate had slept in her childhood room, which had been converted into a spare bedroom for visiting friends and family. The animals followed her downstairs into the kitchen. She poured herself a cup of coffee and flipped on the television. Hurricane Sebastian's path veered farther south, just two days from land. Models showed it making landfall somewhere near Sarasota. This meant only one thing: in forty-eight hours, they'd be facing down the barrel of a loaded gun.

"The governor is issuing a mandatory evacuation of coastal and low-lying areas to begin early this afternoon," explained a weary-looking meteorologist with disheveled hair and a loosened tie.

The satellite shots of Sebastian were frightening, and Kate fully empathized with the weatherman's apprehension. As the storm strengthened, the mass of clouds circled a visible and well-defined eye. Churning over the warm Gulf waters, it absorbed more energy to become angrier and deadlier by the hour. Once it made landfall, forecasters predicted a 20-foot storm surge and catastrophic damage.

She knew she'd have to move her boathouse further upriver before it was too late. She couldn't take any more news and turned off the TV.

Tug barked, and the squirrel chirped when the doorbell rang. She glanced out the window and saw a yellow rental car parked out front. The animals raced ahead of her into the parlor, and Tug barked at the front door. Kate told him to hush before unlocking and opening the door.

An older man wearing a Hawaiian shirt, Bermuda shorts, and black dress-socks with leather sandals stood on the porch. He held a cellphone to his ear, saying, "Would you rather be forced to dance every time you heard music or be forced to sing along to any song you heard?"

"Mr. Vaughn," she said as he stepped inside.

The old man smiled at her and raised an index finger, signaling to give him a moment. "Just answer the question," he said into the phone. "Would you rather be forced to dance every time you heard music or be forced to sing along to any song you heard?"

"Mr. Vaughn," Kate said. Tug barked and ran circles around the man as Doc leaped onto an entryway table and raised up on his hind legs, investigating the strange face. Bert flew into the room and plowed into the vase of flowers on the table, knocking them over and upsetting the squirrel. Kate turned the vase and flowers upright as she asked, "What are you doing here?"

He held up a finger again, hushing her as he continued his call. "Sure, people will look at you funny, but either one you choose, own it...okay, I'll catch up with you at the airport. And son...I love you." He ended the call and stuffed his phone in his pocket. "I remember meeting you and your puppy dog when I was checking out, but I apologize. I forgot your name."

"It's Kate Parks," she said as she closed the door. "Mr. Vaughn, right? I'm surprised to see you. I thought you'd be past the Florida-Georgia line by now."

"Please, call me Linus," he said. He leaned down to pat Tug on the head and then glanced at the one-armed squirrel and the one-eyed owl. "You've got quite the menagerie."

Kate grabbed Tug by the collar as Doc jumped onto her shoulder. "What can I do for you, Linus?"

"I think I left my watch in the room." He stepped to the stairway and glanced up it, then turned back to Kate. "Do you mind if I run upstairs and look for it?'

She nodded. "That's fine. But hurry. We're closing up for the storm."

Linus shook his head. "We tried to leave town, but the Interstate is jammed, and the airport is packed. It's like Armageddon out there."

"Your best bet will be to go to a shelter. They'll start setting them up further inland." She knew it was coming, and the next few days, if not weeks, were going to be difficult.

Linus headed up the staircase. "We stopped at the grocery store, and the shelves were empty. Armageddon, I tell you. It's Armageddon out there."

"Do you remember which room you and your son were staying in?" she called to him. Tug tried to follow, but she held him back by his collar.

"I remember," he said, disappearing upstairs. "Like Armageddon, I tell you. Like Armageddon."

* * *

Forrest Frazier stood outside the Mayfair Plaza Building, behind a podium, and addressed the crowd. The Manatee County Sheriff's Department barricaded the north and south ends of the street. On the northern side, the nudists held picket signs behind the barricades and screamed for Frazier to leave the lighthouse alone. The Mommy Warriors yelled and screamed behind the southern barrier. In between, dozens of reporters and camera crews filled seats or stood within filming distance of the podium. Business leaders and local politicians were also in attendance. Jasper's wife, Liz, and his grieving family sat in the front row. Forrest winked at them as he thanked everyone for attending his press conference, despite the approaching storm.

"In light of the horrific tragedy, I'm renaming my proposed Widow Rock Towers to The Luxury Wade Towers in honor of attorney Jasper Wade," he said into the mic. His projected voice echoed across the block. The Ginger Dingus was standing with the Mommy Warriors, shaking a hand-painted sign, and Forrest made a mental note of that troublemaker's position. He paused for dramatic effect, then continued. "In honor of his hard work, achievements, and humanitarian contributions to our lives, I want my affordable, modernized condos with amazing beach-views and unique amenities to stand as a monument for not only him, my dear friend, but for everything right about our community."

The crowd applauded as Forrest raised a framed professional photo of Jasper and posed for photographs.

"We'll begin construction as soon as the skies clear," he announced into the mic. He waited for the cheering to die down, then finished. "Speaking of which, go secure your homes and please stay safe, follow all law enforcement guidelines, and I will see you after the storm passes."

Afterward, he answered questions from the press and thanked the Sheriff's Department for their tireless work. He shook hands with the politicians. Of course, in the most public way possible, he spoke privately to Japer's widow and family. "I'm giving you a special discount on not only one of the condos," he said, "but forty percent off design upgrades and SMART Home enhancements."

Amid the hoopla and cheers, he motioned for one of his security guards to come closer. He whispered in the guy's ear. "Find Ian Biggs' scooter and slash the tires. I want that Leprechaun walking home."

The security guard nodded and slipped into the crowd.

When the press conference was over, Forrest retreated to his corner office on the twelfth floor. Employees were busy boxing files and securing computers and equipment in preparation for the storm. He shut the door to block out the noise.

The pictures on the wall had been straightened, the floor swept, and the jagged pieces of the tower model lay stacked on the table. He ignored it and noticed a drink waiting on his desk. The flatscreen was already turned-on to news coverage of his press conference. He had the best assistant in the world.

Thinking of Shelley and watching himself speak on screen, he sat back in his chair and chewed on a fresh cigar. Not only did he have a little surprise waiting for that little bog-trodder—*a couple of slashed tires on his Vespa*—but he couldn't have paid for publicity like this. The condo project was going to explode with all this hype. He guessed that old cliché was right: there's no such thing as bad publicity.

Or was it every dark cloud has a silver lining?

His office door opened, and he expected to see Shelley bounce in wearing another tight blouse and short skirt. Dr. Yvette Cross stepped in instead.

"A hurricane is barreling down on the city, and you're holding a press conference for The Widow Rock Condo Project," she said after she shut the door.

Forrest turned his head, and the cigar between his lips drooped.

"It's The Luxury Wade Towers now." He held up his drink, offering her one. She shook her head, and he laughed. "Or were you lot listening to my press conference."

"While you were entertaining the press, authorities found another body." The doctor crossed her arms, standing at the door. "Your attorney's partner in the firm, he's dead too."

"Wade was my attorney. Let the other guy's clients dedicate their own building to him." He laughed at his joke. He sat at his desk and aimed the remote, cranking up the volume. His voice blared from the speakers, telling the crowd he would be renaming the condos. He smiled, and the cigar between his lips rose tall.

The doctor took the remote from him and turned off the TV. "You need to drop the charges against Redd Tyler," she said.

"Now, why should I do that? That pinheaded imbecile broke into my office and smashed my toys." He motioned to the broken model pieces stacked on the table against the wall. She walked over to it and picked up a cracked plastic wall.

"Because," she said, "if he's going to sell that old bed and breakfast, he can't be sitting in jail." She tossed the cracked piece on top of the heap.

"I've been meaning to talk to you about him." He removed the cigar from his mouth and held it between two fingers. "I want them to sign before the end of the day tomorrow."

"That's not going to happen. With Redd's arrest and Elise's depression and now that hurricane headed our way, their whole world is on hold."

"Then crank up the pressure." He spat as he spoke, nearly spilling his drink. "I expect you to talk them into it. Play them against each other. Sign Morticia's name and tell Gomer she acquiesced. He'll fall in line."

"I can't do that."

"Why?"

She let out an irritated laugh. "Legally? Morally? Ethically? Take your pick."

"Don't get all righteous on me now. Heaven closed its gates to you long before you got involved with the Tylers." He returned the cigar to his mouth and chewed on it as he spoke. "What's Nimrod going to say if he learns his trusted psychiatrist is pushing him to sell his home to an organization in which she's a secret trustee? There isn't enough malpractice insurance on the planet to pull you out of the fire."

Her eyes narrowed. "Are you blackmailing me?"

"Let's say," he said, smiling and chewing on the cigar. "I'm motivating you."

She threw the remote at him. "I'm outta here."

"What?" He laughed, spilling his drink as the remote bounced off his arm and hit the desktop.

"I'm done. I'm out." She threw her hands in the air and headed for the door. "I will deal with this—with the Tylers—when I get back."

"Don't go away mad." He rose from his desk. "This is just business. It has nothing to do with the way I feel about you, you know, personally. Or romantically…"

Opening the office door, she stopped in the doorway and looked back at him. "I'm getting out of town," she said. "That storm is going to be bad, and I'm leaving. I'll deal with the Tylers after it passes."

He crowded her at the door, extending his arms on either side of her. He pushed the door shut with his left hand and nuzzled her ear. "For a second, I thought you were leaving me."

She pulled the cigar from his mouth and flicked it to the floor. "There are days I'd like to rip your tonsils out and feed them to you."

He shot her a roguish grin. "Sounds kinky."

"Just drop the charges against Redd Tyler, or we'll never get them to sell," she said. Pulling the door back open, she ducked under his arm and left his office.

He watched her pass the empty cubicles and head for the elevator. The floor was nearly empty now, as most of his employees had left ahead of the storm.

Disappointed in his wussy office staff, he slammed his office door shut.

CHAPTER TWENTY-FIVE

Inside The Bluegill, Kate stepped up to the third floor and entered the dark master bedroom. The animals followed, and Doc leaped from her shoulder onto the bed and nudged Elise's cheek as she slept.

"C'mon, Sleeping Beauty," Kate said, jostling her shoulder to wake her. "Rise and shine."

Elise groaned and rolled over. Doc chattered beside her, and Tug barked from the floor.

"You need to wake up." Kate shook Elise's a little harder.

Elise slapped Kate's hand away. "Touch me again, and I'll tell people you're my mother."

Kate backed away and looked around. A turned-over pill bottle lay on the nightstand. An empty bottle of Jack stood beside it. Elise groaned. Kate watched her a moment, then stepped to the window and opened the shades. Sunlight brightened the room.

Elise cried out. "Stop it! Sunshine and fresh air! I can't breathe! It's burning my eyes!"

Kate ignored her hysterics and stared out the window. Below, on the drive, her Tahoe sat parked under a palm tree. Linus Vaughn's rental car sat parked beside it.

She looked back at her sister. Elise held a pillow over her head, covering her ears, and muttered, "I can hear the waves outside! SHUT UP WAVES!"

Doc scampered across the pillow and chirped in her face.

"Get this rabbit away from me before I cut its feet off and make key-chains out them." She scrunched the pillow over her head.

Calling the animals, Kate left the bedroom. Doc leaped off the bed and hopped into the hallway. Tug chased after him. She shut the door and heard something fall in Noah's room.

She entered his bedroom with Tug and Doc at her heels and found Linus standing beside the bed. He was holding a framed picture in his hands.

"What are you doing in here?" she asked. Tug growled.

Linus put down the picture. "I'm sorry. I was curious about what was in this room?"

"It's off-limits," she said sternly. "The whole third floor is off-limits to guests."

"It's a little boy's room. Where is he?"

Kate took a breath. The answer still stung. "He's no longer with us."

“I’m sorry. I didn’t mean to pry.” He looked away uncomfortably. An uncomfortable quiet surrounded them, and he moved past her out the room, into the hallway. Tug growled at him, and he bent down to hold out his palm. Tug sniffed it and gave his hand a slurp.

Kate shut the bedroom door. “Did you find your watch?”

Linus stood, looking puzzled. “I’m sorry?”

“Your watch? You thought you left it behind in your room.”

“Oh, yes. That,” he said, walking downstairs. Kate and the animals followed behind him, and he continued rambling. “No, I didn't find it.”

Downstairs, they stopped in the parlor. The owl sat on the entry table and watched them with one large eye. Doc hopped onto the table too, as Tug wagged his butt, inviting Linus to scratch it.

"I hope you and your son stay safe," she said and started to give him directions to the shelter when her iPhone buzzed. She looked down to see Trace's bearded face on her screen. “How’s Nellie?” she asked, answering the call. “Is she getting outta Dodge?”

She raised an index finger to Linus, indicating she needed a second.

“Yeah, she’s on her way to her Mom’s.” Trace’s voice came through loud across her phone’s speakers. “I’m getting her as far away from here as I can.”

“She’d better not be flying,” Kate said. “Pregnant women shouldn’t fly.” She mouthed “she’s pregnant” to Linus, and he nodded his understanding.

“I don’t think anyone is flying outta here now,” Trace said. “The airport is packed. Every flight is delayed. We’re setting up the shelter at Manatee High School. It’s far enough inland that we should be protected from the worst of it.”

“I’ll meet you there.” Kate ended the call and turned to Linus. “We’d better get you to the shelter,” she said. “Can you get hold of your son?”

* * *

Forrest Frazier sat comfortably at his desk with his feet propped up, chewing on a new cigar. He played and replayed his favorite moments from the press conference, quite pleased with himself. When Shelley entered, he froze the frame at the exact moment he'd taken Liz Wade's hand and told her, in the sincerest voice he could muster, about how sorry he was for her loss.

“See right there,” he said to Shelley and pointed to the TV screen with the remote. “I’m consoling the widow.”

She glanced at the image.

He continued. "That moment right there is perfect. It's priceless and shows I'm emotional and empathetic, blah blah blah. The media will eat it up."

She nodded but seemed bored by the whole conversation.

Forrest didn't notice. "I want you to take a screenshot of that precise moment and send it to PR. Tell 'em I'm going to donate ten thousand dollars to the Wade family."

She yawned.

He didn't notice. "Hell, Wade was loaded," he said, slapping his desk. "The gesture's the money shot … Make it five thousand."

When she still didn't reply, he removed the cigar and sat up straight in his chair. "Did you hear what I said? Shelley?"

"I'm not speaking to you." She turned her head away from him with her arms folded.

"C'mon, Shelley. Stop pouting." He stood, holding out his arms to embrace her.

"I'm not pouting." She turned away from him.

"What are you doing then?"

"I'm posting my resume on some employment sites."

"Why?" He flipped a tendril of hair out of her face. "Because you saw me meeting with Dr. Cross?"

"You mean, Yvette?" She slapped his hand away from her face.

"I told you, it's not like that," he said. "We're business partners. That's all."

She frowned. "Monkey business, maybe."

"Look…" He touched her chin, lifting her head. "She was here to get me to drop the charges against her client."

"I'm not listening." She tried to break free of his embrace, but he held her tight.

"That's all it was. That bullheaded numbskull is sitting in jail, and she wanted me to let him out."

"Redd Tyler?" She looked up at him, wide-eyed. "Did you drop the charges against him?"

"I'll probably live to regret it, but… yes." He flipped off the lights, letting the bluish light from the TV set the mood. He took her hand and brought her closer. "Now, let's drop it and make up."

She resisted and broke free of his grip. "I'm not fooling around in your office again," she said.

He gave her a little smirk. Snaking an arm around her shoulder, he led her out of his office and shut the door behind them. The entire floor was unnervingly dark. Quiet. As they walked, his fingers toyed with the bra strap on her shoulder.

"What'd you have in mind?" she asked as they strolled alone past empty cubicles with computers covered in plastic wrap. They made their way to the elevators.

"I have a big hotel suite." He pushed the down arrow. "Just sitting empty," he continued, stroking her cheek. "Waiting."

"I guess I could take my resume down off those employment sites."

"Good girl."

He kissed her as the elevator arrived. They stumbled into the carriage, locked in each other's arms.

A shadow stepped out from behind a cubicle, surprising them.

Shelley screamed.

Forrest couldn't quite comprehend the image a few feet away. Standing at the end of the aisle, the figure wore some kind of mask. It looked like an elephant's head. And he gripped something in his hands---a baseball bat.

Shelley screamed again as Forrest pressed the close door button in the carriage. The figure stepped forward.

Forrest panicked, mashing the button. The elephant man lunged toward them. Forrest pushed Shelley out of the elevator. She tumbled into the masked man, knocking him down. A violent cry ripped from her throat.

The elevator doors closed. The carriage dropped. Forrest leaned against the wall, sucking in air. His heart raced. A bell dinged with each passing floor. A moment later, the elevator stopped, and the doors opened.

He stumbled forward into the garage. Few cars were left, and he had a clear view of his Ferrari straight ahead. He scrambled to it. Tripped. Picked himself up. Several cigars fell out of the pocket in his jacket, but he didn't care. He left them behind as his feet pounded loudly on the concrete.

Tension gripped his entrails, making him feel sick and dizzy. His head throbbed, and his legs grew weak. With split-second decisiveness, he grabbed the door handle and slid into the front seat, panting.

Somewhere in the garage, the stairwell door banged shut with a loud echo.

His head whipped in the direction of the sound. Then the other. He listened.

Something hit the back bumper. Hard. The car rocked.

His mind reeled. He gripped the steering wheel then checked his pockets for his keys.

Metal on metal scraped loudly along the outside door, followed by a thump.

Forrest caught the figure just outside the passenger window. It wore the weird plush elephant mask. Gripped a baseball bat in gloved hands. Forrest pressed the horn. He screamed until his lungs ached.

The elephant man circled the front of the car and approached the driver's door. He stepped back, grey trunk swinging. He raised the bat and brought it crashing against the window. The glass cracked but didn't break.

A chill swept down Forrest's spine. He'd forgotten to lock the driver's door, and he reached for the lock button. Too late. The door opened.

Forrest shrieked. He lunged across the seat for the passenger door. A hand grasped his left ankle. Pulled him across the driver's seat and out of the car. His head hit the bottom of the door frame then the concrete. He spun and thrashed his arms to protect his face.

A muffled voice came from the mask, saying, "His little body looked battered and bloody as if someone picked up a baseball bat and beat the life out of him." In one swift motion, the elephant man raised the bat and brought it down with a crushing blow, splitting Forrest Frazier's skull wide open.

CHAPTER TWENTY-SIX

Kate drove through Bradenton as Linus followed in his rental car. Pulling onto 33rd Street, she headed for the old high school, a brick building with large white columns. The parking lot bustled with people carrying overnight bags and boxes of valuables from their cars. Pulling into a tight parking slot, she noted the large sign that boasted "Manatee High School: Home of the Hurricanes."

"You think Zach is here?" Linus asked as they entered through the glass doors into the gymnasium lobby. Wearing the bright Bermuda shirt and socks with sandals, he held up his camera and snapped a succession of photos.

Inside, teachers and several parents prepared sandwiches in a concession stand to the right. Students removed trophies from glass cases lining the walls. On either side of the trophy case stood thick metal doors leading into the gymnasium.

Kate held open the door for Linus, and they stepped into the gym. He took more pictures. Emergency teams were setting up cots on the basketball court. People around them played games on their phones and watched movies on their tablets. Several small TVs were set to The Weather Channel.

Kate put a reassuring hand on Linus' arm. "You left him a message that you'd meet him here, right? I'm sure you'll find him."

His body visibly shook as he cringed at the crowded gymnasium. "Like Armageddon," he said. "The people back home will never believe any of this."

She watched him push through the crowd, snapping more pictures and calling out Zach's name, just as she heard a male voice calling hers. She turned to see Trace approaching, all tan uniform and scruffy black beard beneath a black felt cowboy hat.

"How's Nellie?" she asked.

"Same as when you asked me an hour ago," he said. "She's on her way out of town and out of harm's way."

"I'm glad," she said. "But you should be with her."

An expression of restrained patience crossed his face. "You're right. I know, but we've got to go knocking on doors in the morning. Everyone's gotta evacuate the island tomorrow."

"Fun times," she said, looking at the crush of bodies surrounding them. Linus still wove between families, asking if anyone had seen his son. A group of high school students huddled around a TV set. Kate was tired of watching the same images and interviews repeated on TV. She couldn't bear the thought of being cooped up in here for the next forty-eight hours until the storm passed. If she moved her boathouse upriver into safer waters, she could ride it out at home. She looked back at Trace.

"What do we need to do tonight?" she asked.

He glanced at a clipboard in his hand. "We've got volunteers assigning cots and some university med students and a few nurses from Blake Medical setting up a station along the west wall."

His radio crackled, interrupting him. Travel Agent's panicked voice rang out. "Chief, a 911 call came in over at the Mayfair Building in Bradenton. Over."

He picked up the receiver. "I'm sure the Sheriff's Department has it covered. Over."

"It's Forrest Frazier's offices—again." Travel Agent's voice sounded concerned. "His secretary called it in. Over."

"Forrest Frazier?" Trace acknowledged Kate as she came up beside him. He forgot to say 'over,' but Travel Agent continued anyway.

"Yeah, with everything going on with him lately, I thought you'd want to know." Her voice cracked with static. "Over."

Trace waved at Kate. "C'mon."

They left the gymnasium and crossed the parking lot for his squad car.

Twenty minutes later, they pulled into the Mayfield Plaza parking garage. Deputies with the Manatee County Sheriff's Department collected evidence in Forrest Frazier's empty parking space and photographed the blood spatters. Frazier's name was printed on a plaque over the spot. Above it, a sign warned that violators would be towed at their own expense. However, there was no sign of his vehicle. Trace approached the group.

Kate hung back. She watched him talk to the deputies, then noticed several cigars scattered on the concrete by the elevators. She bent down for a closer look. Trace called to her, and she stood.

"They've got some broken glass and blood spatters. Something happened," he said. "They're talking to his secretary now."

"Assistant." She corrected him. He pointed up, and she clicked the elevator button. "She's his executive assistant."

By the time they reached the twelfth-floor office suites, they found more deputies searching the cubicles. Light emitted from Forrest's corner office, and when she entered, she found Shelley sitting alone at his desk.

Kate grabbed a bottle of cold water from the mini-fridge under the bar and brought it to the young woman. "Are you okay?" Kate asked. Shelley took the bottle but didn't answer.

Trace asked, "Can you tell us what happened?"

"I've called and called his cellphone, but he isn't answering," she said, her voice quivering.

Kate touched her shoulder, comforting her. "You want to tell us what happened?"

"I'll tell you what happened." Her voice trembled with both fear and anger. "Some crazy guy wearing an elephant mask happened. He came after us with a baseball bat as we were waiting for the elevator."

"Did you recognize him?"

Shelley looked up. "Did I recognize the psycho wearing an elephant head?"

"Point taken." Kate swallowed. "So…you escaped."

"Forrest pushed me out of the elevator right into that…that man…and took off."

"Forrest left you?" Kate asked. When Shelley didn't answer, Kate softened her voice. "Were you hurt?"

"No. The guy stood over me for a few seconds, then picked up his bat and ran for the stairwell. I think we scared him away."

Trace hung back by the doorway, listening. Kate looked over at him, then back at Shelley. "I get he was wearing a mask, but did you get any sense of who it could've been? Has your boss had any issues with anybody lately?"

She thought about it a moment. "There's the Leprechaun."

"The Leprechaun?" Trace suddenly spoke up, leaning forward. Shelley looked over at him as if she just realized he'd joined them.

"Yeah," Shelley said. "That short, redheaded protester that's been harassing us. He was on the news the other day."

Kate didn't want to say it. She didn't even want to think it. But Trace beat her to it.

"Ian Biggs?" he asked.

"I think that was his name," Shelley said. "He showed up here on Wednesday morning with a bunch of nudists and got into Forrest's, I mean, Mr. Frazier's face. He threatened Mr. Frazier that if he didn't stop the development plans, he'd be sorry."

Trace moved closer to them. "What exactly did he say?"

"That Mr. Frazier would be sorry," she said. She looked over at Kate as if she had said too much, then added, "That was about it."

Kate asked, "Do you know of anyone else who may have had issues with your boss?"

Shelley laughed at that. "Well, there was that whole group of nudists. And the Mommy Warriors. They were throwing dirty diapers at the crews on the job site."

Trace nodded. "But again, Ian Biggs was involved with both groups."

Kate glanced at him. She didn't like the direction this was headed. But could she really defend him? Fun Size had photos of both attorneys on his phone, and now they were dead. He'd been surveying Forrest Frazier too.

Now he was missing. She turned back to Shelley. "And where were you last night around 9 PM?"

Shelley's eyes narrowed as if she knew exactly where this was going. "I was at Forrest's hotel room… we were working late."

"Okay," Trace said. "Thank you for your time. A deputy is waiting in the hallway to take you home."

Shelley got up carrying her water bottle, and Kate escorted her to the office door.

"He may have gone home," Kate said, though she didn't believe it herself. "We're going to follow-up with the hotel to see if he's checked in, and we'll contact his wife too."

"I doubt you'll find him there," Shelley said at the doorway. "But maybe, I guess."

When she was gone, Kate turned to Trace. "I got something to tell you…" she started.

Trace interrupted her. "Look at this," he said, facing the TV.

She stared at the frozen image on the screen of Forrest Frazier talking to Liz Wade. The Wade family was there. Kate picked up the remote and clicked play. The video came to life. "That's from his press conference earlier today," she said.

Trace nodded. "Looks like he was watching himself give his speech."

Kate replayed the scene. "Somethings wrong," she said.

"What is it?"

"I'm not sure." She stepped closer to the TV and pointed to the woman Forrest was addressing on the screen. "That's Mrs. Wade, Jasper's wife."

Trace nodded. "Yeah."

"And who is the young woman next to her?" Kate pointed to a teenage girl, tall and stick-thin with jet-black straight hair and severe bangs.

"Their daughter, I'd imagine."

"That's not Olivia," she said.

Trace took the remote from her and zoomed in on the teenager's face, then glanced at Kate. "Maybe that's her sister," he said. "Do you know how many kids Jasper Wade had?"

"It wouldn't take long to find out." Kate chewed her bottom lip, thinking. "But if that is Olivia's sister, then where's Olivia?"

"We'll figure it out," he said, shutting off the TV. He rose from the desk and waved for her to follow. They left the office and returned to the elevators. "Your boyfriend's name came up again," he said as the elevator doors opened. "Shelley identified Ian as harassing Frazier."

"There's more," she said. She didn't want to say it, but she had to. "Ian had been tailing Frazier," she said. The doors closed, and the elevator started down. "Along with the two attorneys."

His jaw dropped. "Wade and Flagg?"

"I found pics on his phone of all three men. He'd been tailing them to find something incriminating. They were investors in Frazier's condo project, and he wanted something to use against them."

He seemed to think about it a moment. "We need to talk to him."

Kate shook her head. "I don't think Ian was behind this attack, or whatever you want to call it at this point."

"Two men were murdered, three if you count the guy in Atlanta," he said. "And things don't look good for Frazier. Your boyfriend has a history there."

"But this seems more personal. Ian's harassment has been limited to public events, stopping the condo development or halting a housing development," she said. There was a long stretch of silence between them before Kate added, "There's something else going on."

"You mean Redd?"

"I mean with my nephew's death," she said.

"Redd's in custody," he said. "He didn't attack Frazier and his secretary."

"Executive Assistant," she said.

"Either way, we need to talk to him," Trace said. "Where is he?"

"At his mother's house, I'm guessing."

The doors opened, and they returned to the lobby. The Sheriff's Deputies were still in the parking garage, and they approached them with the information about Ian. Kate gave them his mother's address and tried to explain that Ian wasn't capable of murder.

"I honestly believe there's something else going on here that has nothing to do with Mr. Biggs' surveillance and protests," she said.

Again, their answer was, "Thank you. We'll take it from here."

When Trace and Kate returned to his squad car, he told her to stay out of it. "The Manatee County Sheriff's Department has it under control," he said. "And besides, if Ian is involved, he could be dangerous."

His cellphone rang, ending the lecture. He answered the call and listened for a moment, then his eyes grew wide.

"It's Nellie," he said to Kate. "Traffic is at a standstill, and they had to turn back."

CHAPTER TWENTY-SEVEN

Kate thought about Ian as Trace drove through Bradenton. Murdering someone was a long way from taking a few photos. Still, she needed to talk to him. She called his cell, but it went to voicemail. She tried his mother's house, but there was no answer. Trace told her again to stay out of it. "Ian could be dangerous, and I want you to terminate all contact with him," he said, and she agreed. Still, she wondered where he could be? Could he have actually attacked Forrest Frazier at his office? Could tensions have escalated to murder? She rang his number again. Trace took the phone away from her.

The "Manatee High School: Home of the Hurricanes" sign appeared in the distance. Trace pulled into the crowded parking lot. The tires screeched as he paralleled parked along the front curb. Within a second, he was out of his squad car and darting between families carrying suitcases and boxes. Kate ran after him.

Inside, Nellie was among the volunteers at the concession stand. She stood behind the counter, making sandwiches. She waved as they approached then ran her hands down the curve of her belly. Trace ran to her.

"What are you doing?" he asked, hugging her.

"The highways are jammed, and the airports closed," she said. "I'm not going anywhere."

Kate approached and greeted her with a hug as well. The Mommy Warriors worked in the concession stand beside her, distributing sandwiches.

"Wonder Woman," she said, greeting Diana.

"If the tiara fits!" Diana smiled and held up her arm as if deflecting bullets with an invisible bracelet. She returned to distributing sandwiches as Trace pulled his wife close.

"You're not staying here," he said to Nellie. "You're not staying in a shelter."

"I can't stay at home," Nellie said as she handed a sandwich to a man in the line. She lifted another from a box on the counter. "This is the safest place to ride out the storm. Besides, I don't want to be away from you."

"No," Trace said, his voice firm. "You're not staying here."

Kate touched his arm. "Where's she gonna go? You're not going to drive her out of here; the Interstate is clogged. And she can't fly in her condition. What other choice does she have?"

"I don't care. She's not staying here," he said. "I'll take her to Blake Medical."

Nellie laughed as she handed sandwiches to a couple of kids in the line.

"And what? Check into a room?" Nellie shot him a patronizing smile. The kids' mother thanked her and moved on. "Kate's right, Honey. This is the safest place for me."

Another family stepped up to the concession stand. Now Trace took over and handed them sandwiches and Cokes. "I don't like it," he said to Nellie and Kate. "I don't like it one bit. If something happens, at least you'd be near doctors and---"

Nellie interrupted him. "You're over-reacting. The baby's not due for another month, and Hurricane Sebastian will be long gone by then."

Trace objected, but she put her fingers to his lips, shushing him. She smiled at Kate. "Have you eaten yet? You want a sandwich?"

Kate checked her watch. "Yeah, that'd hit the spot. What'cha got?"

"Ham or bologna."

"Anything without mayonnaise," Kate said. She watched Nellie grab a sandwich from the box. "Trace is right," she added. "You shouldn't be working so hard. Not in your condition."

Nellie laughed. "I'm fine," she insisted. "Want to feel the baby?" She guided Kate's hand to her belly, then laid it flat against the mound of her navel. "Feel that?"

Kate felt the motion inside Nellie's stomach. "She's kicking,"

"*He's* kicking," Nellie corrected her.

"I think you're in for a surprise," Kate said, shaking her head. "So, did you look at the baby book I gave Trace? I highlighted names with consonance."

"Consonance?" Nellie shot Trace a questionable look.

"Don't ask." He shrugged, then grabbed a Sprite from the cooler.

They left Nellie and the Mommy Warriors at the concession stand and joined the crowd entering the gymnasium. Passing through the metal doors, they stepped onto the poured urethane floor of the basketball court. Tables had been set up in front of the stacked bleachers, and they found an empty spot to sit. Trace unwrapped his sandwich and took a bite.

Kate sat beside him and took out her iPhone. Ian still hadn't returned her calls or text messages, and she considered calling him.

"Do you want me to take that phone away from you again?" He chewed as he spoke.

"I was checking to see if he responded. That's all." She unwrapped her sandwich, saw mayo dripping from the sides, and cringed. She tossed it on the table.

"Don't respond. Don't speak to him," he said. "Just leave him alone."

"We need to talk to him," she said. "I need to talk to him."

He took a bite of his sandwich. "It's out of our hands. The Sheriff's Department is taking it from here."

Kate had so many questions. Where is he? Why has he disappeared? Have you abducted any real estate moguls lately? But she knew Trace was right. She watched him finish his sandwich, then pick hers up from the middle of the table.

"You mind?" he asked.

"Knock yourself out," she said, standing. "I've got to head home anyway and move my boathouse further inland before it gets any later."

"Hey," he said with his mouth full. "I'm serious now. Stay away from Ian. He may be dangerous."

"I will," she said, sounding irritated. "Stop telling me that." She walked away, hoping Ian would be at her boathouse, waiting.

Heading for her Tahoe in the parking lot, Kate looked up at the sky. The night was still. No wind. Not even a breeze. It seemed almost eerie. Tomorrow, the outer bands of Hurricane Sebastian would reach the bay area, but tonight there was no sign of it.

Twenty minutes later, Kate crossed the Causeway into Sienna Key and returned to The Bluegill. The entire home looked dark and empty, with plywood covering some of the windows. More sheets of plywood lay scattered on the lawn. Thinking little of it, she headed up to the front porch and entered the home.

In the parlor, Tug jumped up on her legs, wagging his stubby tail. Doc chirped and hopped across the tile to greet her. Bert hooted and flapped his wings. Redd appeared on the staircase, surprising her.

"You're back," she said. "What are you doing here?"

"Frazier dropped the charges, and they released me," he said.

"I didn't know." She patted Tug on top of his head and greeted Doc and Bert. She wondered if she should mention that Frazier was missing but decided against it. Sleeping dogs and can of worms came to mind, so instead, she asked, "How long have you been out?"

"For a while," he said. "They let me out ahead of the evacuations. Tomorrow morning, I've got to finish boarding up the house and then get Elise to the shelter."

"How is she?"

He nodded toward the staircase. "She hasn't left Noah's room. I don't know how I'm going to get her out of there tomorrow."

She didn't know either. But all she could do was address one problem at a time.

Kate loaded the animals into her Tahoe and crossed the Causeway out of Sienna Key. She headed north of Bradenton. Tug stood in the passenger seat and placed his front paws on the window. He barked as she neared Palmetto Gardens, the mobile home park on the Manatee River.

When she parked, she looked for Ian's Vespa. It wasn't there. She couldn't dwell on that now, though. She had a job to do, and she was running out of time.

The animals followed her into the houseboat and watched curiously as she double-checked the lines, ensuring they weren't frayed, then tightened the cleats. It was an old vessel, and the cleats tended to wiggle loose in high winds. She secured what she could and put everything else into storage. An hour later, she navigated the houseboat up the Manatee River, tugging *The Kendell* behind it. A marina near Fort Hamer provided better protection, and she prayed it would be enough.

Just after one in the morning, she docked and tied down, checked and doubled-checked everything she could. Exhausted, she sat on the deck, surrounded by her animals. Ian hadn't returned a single call, and she sent him another text, letting him know that she'd moved the boathouse. No reply came.

Again, she noticed the sky, clear and starry. No wind. No breeze. No hint of what was coming.

CHAPTER TWENTY-EIGHT

Saturday
September 6

At sunrise, as Hurricane Sebastian inched closer, Kate knocked on doors, urging residents to evacuate. The Sienna Key Police Department had divided the island up into quadrants, and she took the north-eastern section while Officers Jared and Jensen took the southwest. At the same time, Trace cruised slowly through every neighborhood street, his voice blaring through the loudspeaker, "Attention. Attention. You are in a mandatory evacuation zone. Please leave immediately."

Kate moved from house to house as quickly as possible, explaining, "We need everybody off the island today before the Causeway closes ahead of the storm." Most people listened and were already packed and ready to flee.

Around her, nervous homeowners piled up sandbags along their property lines, and she noticed Jared and Jensen both parked their police boats in the street so, as the storm surge came flooding in, their equipment would be accessible and ready to use.

By mid-morning, she knocked on a familiar small house. A woman answered the door, wearing a Tiki Hut waitress uniform.

"Lenna," Kate said. "The mayor has called for a complete evacuation of Sienna Key."

"We're getting ready to leave." Lenna opened the door wider. She held both hands extended with her index fingers pointing forward, then brought her fingers in toward her body as if gesturing to a group of people to join her. "Come in."

Kate glanced at her watch. She didn't have time for a social visit but took a few minutes anyway; she wanted to check on Heather. She followed Lenna inside and raised her hand in front of her right ear and extend it outward and away from her body. "Everyone's leaving the island," she said. "And they'll be shutting the power off before lunch."

Lenna shivered. "We've got a hotel room reserved on the mainland."

"That's good," Kate said. "But you need to leave now. The roads and airports are choked."

Lenna turned and headed for the bedrooms, saying, "I'll get Heather."

As if on cue, a small girl peeked around the corner, wearing a pink Power Ranger costume. She held a teddy bear in her arms. A bony, older woman with grey swept-back hair and no eyebrows stood protectively beside her.

"You remember my mother-in-law," Lenna said.

Kate extended her hand. "Pleased to see you again, Mrs. O'Dell."

Lenna continued, motioning to her daughter. "And of course, you know Heather," she added.

"The famous artist," Kate said. She thought of the drawings—*the stick figure woman with the gun, the stick figure girl she was protecting*—covering her refrigerator door. She approached Heather and knelt in front of her. She placed her fists together, thumbs up, and rolled her hands forward, so her palms faced up with her fingers slightly curled in. Then she pointed at Heather's heart. "How have you been?"

Heather stared at her with wide eyes but didn't answer.

"Have you been okay?" Kate asked, making the sign again with her hands.

Heather lifted the teddy bear to her ear as if the stuffed brown bear was telling her a secret. Then she lowered the bear and nodded at Kate.

Lenna walked over to Heather. She signed with her hands as she spoke. "We're going on a trip," she said. "Do you want to go on a trip with Mama and Nana?"

Heather didn't respond. She clutched her teddy bear.

Mrs. O'Dell said, "We're packed and ready to go. How long do you think we'll be in the hotel?"

"It depends on how bad the town is damaged and how long it takes to restore power," Kate said. "It may be a few days."

Heather hid behind Lenna's legs and clutched her teddy bear. Kate motioned with her hands as she spoke. "Your mama is taking you to a safe place."

Heather watched her, trembling but saying nothing.

That was how Kate remembered seeing her nine months ago. The injury to her shoulder was worth having this little girl stand here safe today. She raised her hand, holding up her thumb, index finger, and pinkie finger, while keeping her ring finger and middle finger down. She held her hand out, palm facing Heather, and moved it back and forth slightly.

Heather repeated the motion.

A loud knock interrupted them, and Kate turned to see they'd left the front door open. Officers Jared and Jensen stood at the threshold.

"It's time to go," Jared said.

Mrs. O'Dell went to the door and opened it wider for them, inviting them in. "We'll be leaving soon," she said.

"Is it going to be that bad?" Lenna asked. "We've been through hurricanes before."

"I can guarantee you that you haven't seen anything like Sebastian," Jensen said as he stepped inside. "It's gonna be like Hurricane Andrew and Hurricane Katrina combined with something right out of a Stephen King novel."

Jared swatted him on the arm. "Why you gotta say that? You're just scaring everybody."

Jensen pushed him back. "They need to be scared."

When they returned outside, Kate looked up at the sky. Storm clouds gathered in the west. She turned to Jared and Jensen.

"Did you go to The Bluegill?" she asked. "Do you know if Redd and Elise left yet?"

Jared shrugged. "Redd was still hanging plywood over the windows."

"I'd better go check on them," she said, looking north toward the lighthouse. She wasn't too far away and could get there in ten or fifteen minutes at the most.

"We're heading to the high school," Jensen said. "We'll meet you there."

"I'm not going to the shelter." Kate shook her head. "I moved my boathouse upriver to Fort Hamer. I'm going to ride out the storm up there."

A cold breeze tousled her hair. Thunder rumbled somewhere in the distance.

"Okay," Jared said. "Hurry."

"And be careful," Jensen added.

Kate turned and rushed to her Tahoe, waiting a couple of streets away. When she reached The Bluegill, she found Redd standing atop a ladder, affixing plywood over a third-story window. The whole house looked boarded-up, tight and secure.

"It's time to leave," she yelled at him, getting out of her car. The wooden "Welcome to The Bluegill Beach Hideaway" sign rocked back and forth, squeaking in the wind.

"I'm just about done here." He climbed down from the ladder as she approached. "Looks like the hurricane should make landfall late tonight."

"You and Elise need to leave," she said. "They're shutting power off to the island in a few hours."

"Great." Redd shook his head, aggravated. "How can I leave if I can't get Elise out of Noah's room? She won't budge."

"You've got to do something…now," she said. "The Causeway will be closed soon."

"Well," he said, shrugging his shoulders. "What do you suggest?"

Kate shook her head and sighed. "I'll get her out of that room if I have to use a crowbar to do it," she yelled back to Redd as she sprinted up the steps to the front porch.

She entered the foyer, now ominously dark with every window covered by plywood. She made her way upstairs, flipping on lights along the way. Noah's bedroom door was shut, and she gave it a series of hard, impatient knocks.

"Hey, Ki--" Kate stopped and corrected herself. "Elise…It's your big sister."

"Go away!" Elise's muffled voice responded from the other side of the door.

"They're evacuating the island," Kate continued.

"I don't care. Go away!"

Kate pounded on the door and wrestled with the knob. "Damn it, Elise! We're running out of time!"

A siren wailed outside, along with Trace's tinny voice coming through the loudspeaker on his squad car. "Attention. Attention. You are in a mandatory evacuation zone." Kate pounded on the door again.

Finally, the lock clicked, and the door opened.

Kate entered the dark bedroom.

Elise returned to the rocking chair and wrapped an afghan around her.

"It's time to go," Kate said. "Everyone's evacuating the island."

Elise opened the children's book in her lap. "I can't," she said without looking up.

"Why not?"

"I don't want to leave him."

Kate looked around the room. "Noah isn't here, in this room. He's in here." She tapped her chest, indicating her heart. "If you leave, he'll go with you."

"I'm not talking about Noah. I'm talking about Doogie." Elise pointed toward the baby monitor on the bookshelf. "He's still out there."

Kate stepped to the bookcase by the window. Plywood was visible on the other side of the pane. She picked up the monitor. It crackled in her hand, but no voices were coming from it. She turned back to Elise.

"What can I do to convince you to leave?" she asked.

Elise ignored her and remained fixated on the book.

Kate knelt beside the rocking chair. "The whole town is evacuating to the high school," she said. "It'll be like a giant hurricane party."

"A party?" Elise looked up. "If it gets out of control, can we murder a stripper and hide the body by moving it from room to room?"

Kate let out a slight laugh and shook her head no.

Fifteen minutes later, she returned outside. She noticed Trace had arrived and was helping Redd shove the folded ladder and wicker deck furniture in the crawl space under the porch.

"Elise is packing a bag," she said to Redd. "She'll be ready to leave in a few minutes."

"About time." Trace rose and walked to a concrete birdbath on the lawn. He removed the large bowl and dumped the water.

"How'd you do it?" Redd asked, returning the latticework to cover the crawlspace and latching it in place.

"I told her that if the party gets out of control and a stripper is murdered, she could be the one to move the body from room to room," Kate said with a little smirk.

Redd looked puzzled. "There's going to be a stripper?"

Trace returned to the porch, wiping his hands on the front of his shirt. "Your sister has issues," he said.

"Tell us something we don't know," Redd said, giving Kate an unexpected hug. "You're meeting us at the shelter, right?"

Kate broke free of his embrace. "I moved my boathouse pretty far upriver, by Fort Hamer," she said. "I should be safe there. Besides, my animals are at home waiting for me."

"You're as stubborn as your sister," he said.

Leaving the two men at the porch, Kate climbed into her Tahoe and started the engine. The radio blasted with a newscaster's warning. "Once Hurricane Sebastian comes ashore, currently projected to be between ten and midnight Saturday, there will be no emergency services. Do not call 911. It will not be safe for rescue and emergency personnel to travel during the storm and have been ordered not to respond until after the hurricane passes through our area."

She flipped off the radio and turned on the headlights. By the time she reached the Causeway, a gridlock of red brake lights loomed in front of her. Horns blared. Drivers screamed. Fortunately, the islanders were evacuating—unfortunately, it was all at the same time. Forty-five minutes later, she finally reached the mainland and then to the highway, but I-75 was at a standstill. A wall of vehicles inched forward, honking in a constant chorus.

Kate turned off the Interstate, where the roads were almost navigable. As she forged ahead to Fort Hamer, along the Manatee River, a light rain came down, and a hard wind scattered drops against the windshield.

* * *

Redd entered The Bluegill noticing the lights were on in the parlor. He switched them off and headed upstairs, flipping off lights along the way. On the third floor, he called out for his wife, then noticed the door to Noah's bedroom was shut.

"You packed?" he asked, knocking on the door. "You ready to leave?"

"I'm not leaving." Elise sounded as obstinate as ever from behind the door.

"We need to leave," he said, jiggling the handle. "We're running out of time."

"Go without me."

"We're outta time, Elise." He pounded on the door. "They're going to shut the power off to the island."

"Go away!"

"Damn it, Elise!" He kicked the door. It flew open with a loud bang and hit the interior wall. He entered the room. "I'm done playing games. We're leaving."

She defiantly sat in the rocking chair with her legs up and her arms wrapped around her knees. "I'm not leaving."

"You told your sister you were." He stood over her with his hands at his hips. "She said you were packing a bag."

"I told her what I had to tell her." She hugged her knees tighter and turned her head. "To get her to leave me alone."

The power went off, plunging the room into darkness.

"We need to go. Now," he said. "They'll be closing the Causeway next."

"Then go," she yelled. "Just leave already!"

A heavy silence stretched between them as his eyes adjusted to the black.

"Fine. Suit yourself," he said, leaving Noah's room and fumbling in the dark to the staircase. He descended the steps slowly, running a hand along the walls for support. When he made it to the ground floor, he groped his way from the parlor into the kitchen. The box of hurricane supplies still sat on the counter, right where he'd left it. He pulled out the flashlight and flipped the ON/OFF switch several times. Nothing.

Frustrated, he stumbled to the locked garage door and dug his keys from his pocket. The door opened, and he stumbled into the garage. The shelves were directly to his right. His hand swept across tools and paint cans until stopping at a battery-operated lantern that he'd bought at the hardware store downtown. It lit up, casting shadows up the walls and illuminating the elaborate train set on the table in the center of the floor.

He stared at the model cars and plastic houses and prayed the hurricane wouldn't demolish it.

After a moment, he returned upstairs. The lantern cast a circle of light on the floor ahead of him and tossed moving shadows along the narrow hallway. Noah's broken door swung ajar, dangling from the hinges. He shined the lantern in the bedroom, lighting-up the bookshelves and toybox. Elise was on the bed among the stuffed animals, curled in a fetal position, facing the wall. He walked over to her and set the lantern on the nightstand.

"C'mon, Elise," he said. "We've got to leave. Now."

She murmured something that he couldn't understand.

"I'm not joking." He touched her arm. She pulled away. He grabbed her. Pulled her toward him. Hugged her. "I'm serious, Elise. We can't stay here."

She fought him, thrashing her arms and legs, screaming, "No. I'm not leaving him."

He released her and fell back. Sitting on the floor, he watched her in stunned silence, then jumped to his feet. He stomped to the bookcase. With a single sweep of his arm, he knocked everything off the top shelf. The framed photograph, the lamp, the baby monitor crashed to the floor. "He's not here," he shouted. "He's not here."

He shoved the books from the lower shelves onto the floor then turned to the dresser. He grabbed the shorts and red Spider-man T-shirt and wadded them into a ball.

Elise screamed and sprang from the bed. The stuffed animals tumbled as she launched herself at him. She struck him with her fists, shrieking. He gripped her wrists, restraining her, then lifted her into his arms. She kicked and spat. He grasped the lantern with his free hand and held tight to Elise with the other, carrying both out the room. She struggled as they descended the stairs and into the parlor, and she grasped the door casing and wouldn't let go as he fought to leave the house. With the wind whipping loudly around them, he wrestled her to his truck. He dropped the lantern and managed to open the passenger door. Then with one final huff, he tossed her onto the front seat.

She kicked and flailed her arms against him, struggling to climb out of the truck. The wind screamed along with her.

"The storm is headed directly for us," he yelled. "We can't stay here."

She planted her hands against his chest and pushed him away. "No, I don't care! I'm not leaving him!"

"Noah isn't here. He's not with us any longer."

"No," she cried. She forced her way past him, out of the truck, and ran to the porch. "I'm not leaving. I won't!" she cried. She entered the house, leaving the front door open and swinging in the wind.

Redd followed, carrying the lantern, and bolted into the dark parlor. She wasn't there.

"They're closing the Causeway. We'll be trapped," he yelled. His voice choked, and his eyes teared up. "Trapped," he said again, under his breath.

The wind whistled in through the open door. A bang in the darkness on his right startled him, and his head turned in that direction. He rushed into the kitchen, the lantern lighting his way. "Elise? Where are you?"

The door to the garage swayed open; its handle tapping against the wall.

"Elise," he said, entering the dark garage. He raised the lantern. Searched for his wife. He could hear her breathing but couldn't find her in the narrow swath of the lantern beam. He pressed the clicker on the wall.

The exterior doors rumbled and rose up into the ceiling, letting in the sunlight and the wind.

Elise stood over the model train set. Her black hair twisted in the strengthening breeze. "We can't just let Noah's things get destroyed in the storm," she said, her voice trembling.

"The house is locked up tight. It'll be okay."

"No, it's all we have left," she said and wiped the tears on her cheeks. "His room. His toys. This train set. It's all we have left."

"We can't stay here." Redd was crying now too, and it killed him to say that.

Her hands twisted nervously over a small model house, and she knocked over several plastic trees. Her eyes locked with his. "What about Doogie?" she asked. "We can't leave him here. Alone."

"Doogie?" He couldn't believe they were having this conversation again. He reached across the table and set the trees upright. The warm breeze coming into the garage blew them down again. He left them where they lay. "Forget about Doogie," he said. "He'll be fine. We just need to leave."

"I-I can't," she said. "He's my friend."

"Doogie is in your head. He doesn't exist. But I do. I'm real, and I'm still here."

"Doogie *is* real," she said. "He's real, and he talks to me."

"No, Elise. He's not. He's not real." He reached for her.

She pulled away. "Stop saying that."

"It's true. He's not real. He's just in your head."

"Don't say that."

"Yes—Elise, he's just in your head."

She slapped him. Hard.

He stepped back, away from her.

She turned to the model buildings and train tracks. "I hate you," she said through clenched teeth. "You shouldn't have called me that night. You distracted me, and I didn't see that car. You distracted me and got him killed, and I hate you for that!"

Screaming, she swept her arms across the model train set, pushing the plastic houses and buildings onto the floor. They crashed loudly at her feet as she grasped two train cars and threw them at the wall. They shattered into pieces. She stomped on the model buildings that had fallen to the floor, crushing them.

"You killed him," she screamed. "You killed him!"

Redd watched in horror.

She sobbed as she spat the words at him. "You killed him, and I hate you for that. I hate you!"

He stumbled backward, turned, and ambled out the garage. Pausing in the doorway, he spoke with his back to her. "I'm going to the shelter. Your Suburban is gassed up behind the house. You can take it when you decide to leave."

He left, closing the door and letting the wind cry behind him.

CHAPTER TWENTY-NINE

Kate drove for over an hour before making it back to Fort Hamer along the Manatee River. She'd avoided the Interstate, where a stream of red brake lights remained gridlocked like a strand of Christmas lights. Newscasters warned the Interstates were bottlenecked, even though all lanes were reassigned to northbound traffic only. Tolls were temporarily suspended. With the storm's arrival estimated at fifteen hours and counting, and more than a million locals ordered to evacuate, time was running out.

She reached the river marina and sat in her Tahoe parked by the guardrail, listening to the windshield wipers' monotonous swish. The lot was packed with vehicles, and the river crowded with boats, all hoping to have come far enough inland to escape Sebastian's wrath.

She looked back at her own houseboat with *The Kendell* attached to the aft, bobbing up and down in the waves. Curtains fluttered in the bedroom window, and a warm glow of light indicated someone was inside. Then she noticed Ian's Vespa parked under a large cypress tree with sparkling new tires.

She sprinted through the light rain across the dock toward the boats and reached hers as fast as she could. The door was open. Stepping inside, she called for Tug, Doc, and Bert. The owl flapped its wings as she approached the perch, and it let out a perturbed "Hoo Hooo" of warning. Ian stood in the living room with a box in his arms. Tug barked at his feet.

"I got all your voicemail messages and texts," he said, setting the box on the sofa.

Kate nodded. She looked over at it. Several of his vertical striped shirts lay atop books, some vinyl record albums, and a framed photograph. She knew what it meant.

"Where have you been?" Her voice choked with the question.

"At my Smother's," he said.

"The whole time?"

He didn't answer.

"The Chief thinks you may be dangerous," she said.

"What do you think?" He stood there, unblinking. The wind whistled outside and rocked the boathouse.

She placed a hand on the back of the sofa to maintain her balance. Tug barked and tumbled over with the heaving boat. She helped him to his feet and then looked up at Ian. "I don't think I ever told you how much I appreciated you being there for me when I got hurt," she said.

"And I appreciated you taking me in when I first moved here." He stepped toward her.

She embraced him. When they parted, she looked down at his box. "Are you evacuating? Or leaving?"

She already knew the answer.

The boat jolted again as the wind howled louder. They reached for the walls for support. Tug fell on his side again.

When the rocking stopped, Ian straightened and looked her square in the eyes. "It's gonna get bad," he said. "And we need to leave."

* * *

Elise listened to Redd's old truck pull away and fell to the garage floor. She lay there for several minutes in a ray of sunlight, sobbing. A cloud passed overhead and the sunbeam vanished. She rose then and pressed the clicker on the wall. The exterior doors rumbled shut, leaving her standing in a circle of light emitting from the lantern. She picked it up. Pieces of the plastic model buildings crushed under her feet as she stumbled into the kitchen.

Jack Daniels waited for her on the counter. She dropped the lantern and grasped the bottle. Whiskey spilled on her shirt as she gulped.

Leaving the lantern behind on the floor, she carried the bottle through the dark house, upstairs into Noah's room. Despite the inky blackness surrounding her, she could still make out the rocking chair, the bed, the bookcase. All his books lay scattered on the floor.

"No. No. No." She cried and dropped the bottle and sank to her knees. *Green Eggs and Ham. Charlotte's Web. Where The Darkness Hides.* She returned them to the bookshelf.

"This is not how it was," she said out loud, scolding herself. "How was it? How did he have his books?" She frantically moved them around on the shelf, rearranging their order. She noticed the picture on the floor, the frame broken, the glass cracked. She brought her hand to her mouth and shuddered. "No! No! No!"

She reached for the photo and picked it up. Little Noah smiled back at her, holding his stuffed elephant. She ran her thumb over the glass as if trying to wipe away the cracks. It cut her skin and smeared blood across Noah's face. She kissed him and carried the picture to the bed.

Static crackled from the baby monitor, and she jumped.

"Elise? Are you there?" Doogie's voice came through the speaker.

Elise shuffled her way through the dark and found the monitor lying on the floor. She listened but didn't respond.

His voice came through again. "Are you there?"

"Yes," she answered and placed her head against the wall, listening to the wind intensify outside.

* * *

Kate packed a duffle bag with enough clothes for a few days, toothbrush, first-aid kit, and some extra cash. Next, she herded the animals together. Bert sat perched in a large birdcage, feathers fluffed and his single eye watching her every move. Doc squeaked and chattered, running in circles inside his crate. Tug whined at her feet. She gave him a comforting pat and found Ian in the kitchenette.

"I unplugged all the appliances and turned off the fridge," he said. "And I bagged your laptop to protect it from any water damage."

She thanked him and set the duffle bag on the counter next to her laptop, wrapped tightly in layers of Saran wrap. "Why don't you bring your scooter into the boat?"

"I'll be all right," he said. "I just got new tires. Someone slashed the old ones."

"You can't drive back on a scooter." She placed the laptop in a box along with food for the animals. "Leave it here and ride with me to the shelter."

He didn't seem to be listening. "I'll be fine."

A wind gust howled outside that rocked the houseboat. Tug barked, and Bert screeched in an uproar. The artwork fell from the refrigerator and scattered on the floor. Kate grasped Ian's arm to keep her balance.

"It isn't safe," she said, releasing him as the shaking calmed.

"Acknowledge that." He rushed over to the window and looked outside.

She knelt and calmed Tug, then picked up the magnets and drawings. Her iPhone buzzed, and she answered it. "This Kate."

A panicked voice rang through the speaker. "Heather is missing."

"Lenna?" Kate stood with the artwork in hand. "Slow down and tell me what's going on."

"I can't find her. I don't know what to do." Lenna spoke so fast she could barely get the words out. "She was here one minute and gone the next."

"Slow down." Kate watched Ian as he leaned closer to the windowpane, looking up at the sky. She set the drawings on the counter. "Where are you?"

"At the house. I was packing suitcases and putting them in the car. When I turned around, she was gone."

"She's probably scared. Hiding in her safe place." Kate stared at the artwork. Stick figure woman holding a gun and protecting a stick-figure child. A stick figure man in black spewing scribbles of dark red. A gray box in the sky with bright streaks of yellow. Bright streaks of yellow—like light. *Like a lighthouse.* "I know where she is," Kate said to Lenna, then turned to Ian. "I have to head back to Sienna Key."

He turned from the window. "Is everything okay? What's going on?"

"Just take my animals to the shelter with you." She told Lenna she was on her way as she tossed Ian the keys to her Tahoe. "Here. Take my ride and head for the shelter."

He caught the keys. "Where are you going?"

Ending the call, she rushed outside and pounded down the dock. Wind shrieked in her ears and twisted her hair. Ian followed her outside.

"Where are you going?" he yelled again.

"To Widow Rock," she yelled back, heading for *The Kendell* fastened to the aft of her houseboat. She released the ties. "I've got to get to the lighthouse."

A second later, the motorboat roared to life.

CHAPTER THIRTY

Kate steered *The Kendell* south down the Manatee River into the choppy Bay waters. She could already tell the currents were picking up, and as she headed for the Gulf, the waves turned angry. Teenage boys surfed the immense whitecaps. She had half a mind to tell them to get out of there, but she couldn't waste time. She had to find Heather.

Pressing on, she fought the currents and the waves, praying her boat didn't capsize. The blowing rain slapped her face. Stung her eyes. She turned her head and squinted.

When the northern tip of Sienna Key came into view, the old Widow Rock lighthouse rose from the horizon just beyond it, whipped and beaten in the fierce winds and waves. She could almost hear the glass panes rattling in the distance.

She steered toward the northwestern tip of the island, coming to the rocky, off-limits area, and grounded the boat. Waves splashed against the rocks as she crossed over them and up onto the plateau where the lighthouse stood, overlooking the pilings. The billboard with Forrest Frazier's toothy smile welcomed her to the future site of his condos. The plywood rattled in the wind. She made her way past it to the wrought-iron fence that bordered the property and approached the entrance. The door creaked opened.

Her eyes adjusted to the dim light, and she stepped into a circular room. A single light bulb hung from a 30-foot cord that stretched up into the ceiling. Rotting furniture lay strewn across the floor: a deteriorating couch, a threadbare chair, the corpse of an old TV set.

"Heather?" she called out. No one answered. Of course, the little girl didn't respond. What was she thinking?

The door slammed shut in the wind, followed by a loud thump upstairs. She jumped. A spiral staircase wound up to the levels above. She placed her foot on the first step when something caught her attention. A sleeping bag lay crumbled by the couch. Several empty cans of beans were discarded around it.

A baby monitor lay on the sleeping bag.

She stepped to it and picked it up. Elise's mysterious friend crossed her mind, and she tried to remember what her sister called him. Another knock came from the landing above, and she looked up.

"Heather?" She called out but thought better of it. What if that man was here? Another thump. *Someone* was in the lantern room.

She climbed the spiral staircase. Slowly, cautiously, she made her way up, coming to a landing. She entered the lantern chamber.

Hazy light filtered in through the windows overlooking the Gulf. An enormous lamp dominated the center of the chamber; its rotating mirror encased in grimy glass. That mirror once focused the light from the beacon into a beam. Now it slept quietly in decay.

Behind it, cowering in the shadows, a little girl watched her.

"Heather," Kate said, kneeling. She motioned with her hands as she spoke. "What are you doing here?"

Heather stepped out of the shadows, clutching her bear. She still wore her pink Power Ranger costume. She lifted the teddy bear to her ear as if he was telling her a secret. After a moment, she lowered the bear.

"Teddy is scared?" Kate asked, signing with her hands. "There's a storm coming, and we have to take Teddy someplace safe."

Heather shook her head. She stepped defiantly back into the shadows.

"Why?" Kate signed.

Heather looked puzzled by the question. She lifted Teddy to her ear. After listening, she brought her free hand up in front of her body, palm facing inward, fingers spread.

"I'm scared too," Kate said. Her hands formed the words. "But you know what? If we go together, we can be strong."

Heather shrank back.

Kate inched closer. She raised her right hand, putting up her thumb, index finger, and pinkie finger while keeping her ring finger and middle finger down. She held her hand out, palm facing away from her, and moved it back and forth.

Heather smiled and responded.

Kate took her hand and led her out of the shadows. Heather clutched her bear. Together, they descended the spiral staircase and headed outside.

The wind pushed against them as Kate carried her over the slippery rocks, back to *The Kendell.* She pushed off into the churning water and cranked-up the motor. Waves rocked the boat as she rounded the northern tip then steered south along the Intracoastal waterway. She prayed they didn't capsize and told Heather to lie down in the center of the boat. Somehow, they made it to the turn. The waters between the island and the mainland were relatively calmer, and she passed under the Causeway bridge. A canal opened up and ran along the backyards of wealthy houses, each dark and empty. She passed several docks and a couple of boats that had been left behind. Mrs. O'Dell's home was straight ahead, and Kate beached the boat behind it. She jumped out and lifted Heather and her teddy bear onto the shore.

Lenna came running out of their back door. Her mother-in-law followed.

"You found her," Lenna yelled over the wind, her hair blowing wildly. She took Heather from Kate's arms and embraced her.

"The water's too choppy to take my boat back into Bradenton," Kate said. "We need to get to the shelter."

"We can take my car," Mrs. O'Dell said, keys in hand.

Lenna turned, still holding Heather. Kate followed them to the front of the house. A brown and mustard yellow station wagon waited for them in the driveway. Mrs. O'Dell unlocked it and helped Heather into the backseat.

"I'll drive," Kate said, taking the keys from the old woman and opening the driver's side door. The wind yanked the door from her hand, and she struggled to close it as she got behind the wheel. With Heather and Mrs. O'Dell in the back and Lenna climbing into the passenger seat, Kate flipped on the headlights and windshield wipers, then reversed out of the driveway.

"What if the Causeway is closed?" Lenna asked, stretching her arms forward and planting her palms firmly on the dashboard.

"We'll deal with that when we get there," Kate said. She checked the rearview mirror to make sure Heather was buckled into her seat.

Downtown loomed dark and deserted, more of a ghost town than she'd ever seen. The buildings stood hauntingly still, like waiting tombs. Empty shells. No noise. No movement. No people.

Racing across Main Street, she fought to keep the steering wheel steady and could feel the vehicle slide. Rain fell, but it wasn't a deluge yet. She prayed they'd make it to the shelter long before the weather got any worse.

Speeding along the empty road leading out of town, they approached the Causeway. The entrance ramp had slickened, and the station wagon hydroplaned more than once. Out of nowhere, she slammed the breaks. Lenna lurched forward.

"What's wrong?" she asked.

Kate didn't answer. She stared out the windshield. The wipers squeaked, scraping the glass. Something was out there, leaning against the barricades on the exit ramp. A coat? A dummy? A homeless man?

"What is it?" Lenna asked louder, panic rising in her voice. "The bridge is barricaded, isn't it? We're not going to be able to cross it."

"Wait here," Kate said. She got out of the station wagon into the rain and stood in the headlight beams. She squinted at the object ahead. Orange and white roadblocks stretched across the lanes on both ramps. Right smack in the middle of the exit ramp, a figure leaned against the center barricade.

She blinked, focusing her eyes through the rain.

It was a man; she was sure of it.

His arms stretched out across the top board of the barrier, hanging like a scarecrow. His head slung down, chin to chest, bowing. Jacket flaps blowing in the wind.

"Oh, dear God," Kate said, staring at the corpse of Forrest Frazier.

CHAPTER THIRTY-ONE

"It's Forrest Frazier," Kate said to Trace. The wind screaming into her phone made it nearly impossible for her to hear him. She couldn't take her eyes off the body. His corpse was tied to the barricade in the center of the exit ramp from the Causeway. His jacket whipped wildly with the lifeless limbs. The sight of it made her want to vomit. "His body…it's on display here, on the off-ramp."

"I'll be right there."

She ended the call.

Something pinned to the dead man's shirt rippled in the wind. She stepped closer. It was another polaroid, dangling like a sign. Another photo of the giant stuffed elephant.

Mr. Belvedere.

She brought her hand to her mouth. There was no denying it. These deaths—*these murders*—centered around Noah. And Redd was involved.

She didn't know how, but there was no doubt now. He was out of control. Lashing out from grief. Seeking revenge.

Lenna screamed behind her, standing in the headlight beams. Kate told her to get back in the car.

"What happened to him?" Lenna's voice was barely audible over the rain.

"Get back in the car," Kate yelled over her shoulder, louder. "Don't let Heather see this."

Lenna got back into the station wagon as Kate stood watch over the body, watching in horror as its arms waved in the wind. Its head turned toward her, dull eyes open as if he was watching her watch him. She turned away.

The attorneys. A man in Atlanta. Now, Forrest Frazier. How could Redd have done all this? Then a darker thought crossed her mind.

She brought up Elise's number on her phone. No answer. She tried again, then called Redd. Still no answer.

She was about to try again when Trace's squad car came over the Causeway. He parked on the other side of the barricades and got out of his car. Kate had never been so thankful to see that black cowboy hat shading his scruffy black beard. She ran to meet him at his car.

"It's Forrest Frazier," she said, her hair whipping in the wind.

Trace nodded but said nothing. He placed a hand on his hat to keep it from blowing away. They walked across the median to the barricades along the exit ramp and stopped in front of the corpse.

"There's the photograph again," she said, motioning to the fluttering polaroid pinned to the shirt. "It's Noah's elephant."

"You don't know that." He leaned forward as if getting a better look. "You don't know that this has anything to do with Noah."

"It's Redd," she said but pushed thoughts of Elise from her mind. She didn't even want to think it.

Trace wasn't buying it. "He's locked up."

"No." She watched the shock on his face and realized he didn't know. And it only confirmed her suspicions. "He's out," she said. "The charges were dropped, and he was released."

Thunder boomed, and Trace looked up at the sky.

"We're not going to solve anything now," he said. Together, they staggered, fighting the rain to the oncoming lane, where his squad car idled with its high beams lighting the pavement. "We need to clear a path for the crime scene unit. I've already called it in."

As they moved the slick barricades, a black and white van pulled up along with two more cop cars, lights flashing. The vehicles swerved through the opening they'd made and parked on the entrance ramp next to the station wagon. A forensic team jumped out.

Trace addressed the men, but Kate couldn't hear him with the wind strengthening in her ears. Lightning crackled, and she ducked and covered her head. They were running out of time.

Trace waved and yelled to her. "You need to get them out of here," he said, motioning to the station wagon. "Get them to the shelter."

He was right. Get to the shelter.

She sloshed back to the station wagon and fought the wind to open the door. Drenched, she slipped in behind the wheel. Lenna asked her what was going on, but she didn't respond and just watched the forensic team remove the body from the barricade.

Trace's bearded face appeared in her window, illumined by a lightning strike. She jumped, startled.

"You need to leave. Now," he said, tapping the glass.

She stared at him a moment, biting her lip. Rolling forward, she maneuvered the station wagon through the opening they'd created in the barricades as Trace returned to the forensic team. Passing him, she headed over the Causeway, and she drove as fast as she could through the torrential rain.

Half an hour later, Kate found a spot in the crowded parking lot at the high school and climbed out of the station wagon, battling the wind. She helped Mrs. O'Dell and Heather out as Lenna pulled suitcases from the back.

The four huddled against the rain and splashed across the blacktop into the deserted lobby. Kate shivered and wiped her face. The large metal doors on either side of the empty trophy case were shut, and she opened a door. Lenna, Heather, and Mrs. O'Dell stepped into the gymnasium. Kate came in behind them and squeezed water from her shirt.

"I've got to find my sister," she said to them. She dripped rainwater from her hair and clothes into an ever-expanding puddle beneath her.

"I'm sure she's here," Lenna said as she helped Heather out of her wet jacket. They were all soaked and trembling.

Kate scanned the crowd. Thousands of people sat on cots and atop sleeping bags spanning the entire basketball court. People clutched bags filled with their possessions. Many looked as though they had dressed hastily. One woman held a birdcage with two parakeets in her lap. An elderly woman in a corner sat atop a stack of photo albums. Squealing kids ran between the aisles, horsing around with new friends as mothers rocked crying babies. The heat from all the bodies left the place stifling, and the odor of food and people hung heavy in the air.

A redheaded guy wearing a vertically striped shirt stood near the entrance, arguing with a volunteer at the check-in table. The wire squirrel crate, large birdcage, and the leashed bulldog sat on the floor at his feet.

Kate pushed through the crowd toward them as her water-logged shoes sloshed on the flooring.

"You can't bring those animals in here," the volunteer was saying, standing behind his table and pointing at the animals.

"They're tame." Ian pointed to the woman with the parakeets in her lap. "She's got pets in here too."

"I don't care." The volunteer sat and slapped the top of the table. "They can't stay here."

Kate interrupted. "I'm Kate Parks, Florida Fish and Wildlife Officer, on inactive duty status and currently temporarily working with the Sienna Key law enforcement," she said as Tug greeted her, wagging his tail. "Is there a problem?"

"These animals can't stay here," he said, looking to Ian then her. "Did you just come in out of the rain?" he asked as he moved his paperwork across the table, away from the pool forming beneath her.

She ignored his sarcasm.

"These are rescue animals," she said. Doc chattered excitedly and rattled his cage. She poked a finger through the wire and scratched his head. "They don't have anywhere else to go."

The volunteer wasn't listening. "I don't care. I don't make the rules, I just—"

Trace appeared next to Kate, wringing the water from his cowboy hat. "I'll handle this," he said to her. His wet hair matted to his head, and water ran down his face and dripped from his beard. He turned to the volunteer.

"What if we keep them in one of the empty classrooms?" he asked.

The volunteer looked up at the ceiling. "Is there a leak somewhere?"

"An empty classroom?" he asked again. "Is there somewhere we can take the animals?"

"Maybe you could put them in the art room." He handed Trace a ring of keys. "But the school isn't responsible for any damage."

"There you go," Trace said, holding up the key ring.

Kate thanked the volunteer, then asked him, "Has Redd and Elise Tyler checked in?"

The volunteer handed her a clipboard with registration information. "I'm not sure," he said. "But you're welcome to look through. Just try not to drip on the paper."

She took the clipboard and flipped through the pages. "Looks like Redd checked in a few hours ago," she said. "But what about Elise? Why's her name not listed?"

"If Redd is here, you know your sister is too," Trace said.

"I guess…" She returned the clipboard and picked up the squirrel crate. Ian grabbed the big birdcage as she asked him, "Have you seen them? Do you know where they're camping out?"

Trace spoke up before Ian could answer. "We'll find them," he said, taking Tug's leash. "You know they're here, somewhere. We'll run into them while we're looking for a classroom for your petting zoo."

"Good idea," Ian said, shifting his arms around the large birdcage to distribute the way. He looked like he was about to drop it. "I'll help."

Trace took the birdcage from him, gripping it in his right hand as his left held fast to Tug's leash. "No," he said firmly. "We've got it."

"Chief!" Ian looked at him, puzzled, then turned to Kate. "Is it my imagination, or did the temperature just drop thirty degrees?"

"It's not your imagination," Trace continued. "When this storm passes, we're going to have a conversation about your surveillance of three murder victims."

"My surveillance?" Ian let out an indignant laugh and turned to Kate. "You told him about the photos on my phone."

"Ian, Frazier was murdered," Kate said.

"Murdered?" His eyes widened, and he shook his head. "Wha—what happened?"

"Why don't you tell us," Trace said.

Ian sighed. "Look, Chief, I didn't like the Kingpin or his goons, but I didn't murder anybody."

Trace's eyes narrowed. "Where were you last night?"

"Are you accusing me of something?"

"Just answer the question."

"I was at my mother's house." Ian stammered. "Do I need her to confirm that?"

"That'd be a start," Trace said.

"Ian—" Kate added. "No one is accusing you of anything."

"Yes, you are," Ian shouted. "That's exactly what you're doing. And you're using some innocent photos on my phone to knot the noose."

"Just don't leave the building." Trace said.

"Where am I gonna go?" Ian waved toward the doors. "There's a hurricane out there."

"When the hurricane passes—don't leave the building," Trace continued. "I'll be looking for you."

"Whatever!" He turned and headed into the crowd.

"Ian—wait!" Kate yelled. Tug barked.

"Let him go," Trace said. "I told you to stay away from him."

She turned to him. "If those murders are some kind of vendetta for my nephew's death, then Ian would have no motive, and Elise could be in real danger."

"Trust me," he said. "Your sister is here, safe and sound. Now, let's find a room for your animals."

As he spoke, Kate noticed Lenna, Heather, and Mrs. O'Dell by the stacked bleachers. They looked liked they were getting dry clothes from a pregnant woman. "There's Nellie," she said and pointed her out to Trace.

They carried the squirrel crate and large birdcage through the multitude of evacuees. Tug followed, struggling against the leash to greet unfamiliar faces and sniff unusual odors. When they reached the bleachers, Nellie laughed and handed them a bundle of dry clothes.

"I'm so glad you made it back. I was getting worried," she said, hugging Trace after he set the birdcage on the floor. Bert hooted and fluffed his feathers. "Now, get out of those wet clothes before you catch the flu."

After they changed out of their wet clothes, Kate, Trace, and the others followed Nellie across the overflowing basketball court to the free throw zone under the hoop where a dozen rolled-up sleeping bags piled up against a partition. Trace set down the birdcage again, and Kate put down the squirrel crate. Tug sniffed Heather's leg as she patted his head. Nellie helped Mrs. O'Dell find a chair, and Lenna thanked her.

"I hope it's comfortable enough," Nellie said as she reached for a sleeping bag, then straightened and groaned. She gripped her lower back. Trace jumped to her side and placed his hands on her, rubbing the pain away.

Lenna came up to her other side. "When are you due?" she asked.

Nellie grimaced. "In about a month." She bent forward and motioned for them both to take a step back. "I'm okay. Really. I'm okay. I just need some air."

Trace gripped her shoulder. "Don't push yourself," he said.

She shot him a tired smile. "Really. I'm fine. I just need to pee. Again."

Lenna offered to help her to the bathroom and, taking Heather by the hand, guided Nellie through the wall of bodies around them.

When they were gone, Kate turned to Trace. "We've got to find my sister," she said, lifting the squirrel crate and wrapping Tug's leash around her wrist. "I have a bad feeling."

"We'll find her," he said. He picked up the large birdcage and headed into the crowd. "C'mon, let's find that empty art room before that volunteer comes back with animal control."

CHAPTER THIRTY-TWO

Kate carried the squirrel crate in one hand and held Tug's leash in the other. Trace walked beside her with his arms wrapped around the large birdcage. They pushed through the crowded gym to double doors in the back corner that opened into a breezeway. Rain belted the roof and rattled the windows, and Kate realized the storm sounded so much worse away from the thick gymnasium walls that buffered a lot of the noise. Crossing over the bridge, they entered the high school with the animals in tow. Emergency lights dimly lit the empty hallways, and their footsteps echoed as they moved through them.

"I was hoping we'd run into Elise," she said.

"There's a lot of people here," he said. "It may take some time to track her down. But I'm sure she's fine."

"I've got warning bells going off about Redd. I mean, they're both unstable, but you didn't see him smash their TV when Frazier's face popped up on the screen."

"Either way, I'm keeping an eye on your boyfriend."

"I don't think he's my boyfriend anymore."

They stepped down a dark hallway and stopped at the door labeled "Art Room."

"I can't say that I'm disappointed." He put down the birdcage and fished a set of keys from his pocket. "The guy's bad news."

The door opened into an art room, and Kate set the crate on a table. Doc squeaked in protest, and Bert turned his head away from her, signifying his disapproval. The squirrel chirped, rising on his haunches and reaching his single arm through the wire mesh toward her. She opened the crate door, and he hopped onto her shoulder.

Trace looked perplexed. "What are you doing?"

She whistled, and Doc scurried from her left shoulder to her right and back again, then sought shelter behind her neck. "They're anxious," she said and leaned down to pet the bulldog behind his ears. Then she stepped out of the room with Doc on her shoulder, peeking out from under her hair. Trace locked the door and handed her the keyring.

"Everyone's anxious," he said. They walked down the dark hallway. "I'm anxious about the storm. I'm anxious about Nellie. I'm anxious about the baby."

"Well, duh," Kate said. The keys jingled as she slipped them into her pocket. "It's a baby."

He stopped and ran his hands through his hair. "I'm forty-five, Kate. I'm too old to be starting a family."

"That's crazy talk."

"A baby. A little baby boy. How am I gonna have the energy to keep up with him?"

"For starters, *he's* going to be a *she*. And so you're forty—"

"Forty-five."

"Forty-five, who cares? It's fatherhood, not fortyhood. You're going to make a great father at fifty. Fifty-five. Sixty."

"You're not helping."

She shot him a warm smile. "How long have we known each other?"

He ran a hand across his chin, rubbing his beard. "I don't know. Twenty years."

"A long time. And you're patient. You're sensible. You know all the dad jokes." She put a hand on his shoulder. "I can't think of a better time in your life to welcome a baby into the world. She's going to be the luckiest kid ever."

"Thank you," he said.

They returned to breezeway without saying a word. Rain pounded the roof. Wind gusts wailed against the windows.

Finally, he added, "And we're having a boy."

She laughed. "Oh, the universe is about to slap you up the side of the head."

When they made it back into the crowded gymnasium, she noticed the eerie silence. People huddled together as the storm raged outside. Adults sat speechless, listening to the wind and thunder while their children played, blissfully unaware of what was going on outside.

A group clustered around a laptop was equally dumbstruck. The Vaughn father and son were with them, as was Nellie. Kate and Trace joined the table, and Nellie held out her arms to hug her husband. Trace wrapped his arms around her. Before them, on the laptop screen, shots of the cresting waves battered the shores of Florida's gulf coast. Kate stared speechless, mouth open, eyes wide and unblinking. A boardwalk disintegrated in the raging swell. The roof of a restaurant tore away from the building and shredded into hundreds of projectiles. A rush of water flooded a neighborhood street and swept away cars, trees, light posts, and anything else in its path.

"Dear Lord." Trace held Nellie tight as if he was trying to shield her from the images. "It's made landfall."

She pressed her head against his chest. "All we can do now is wait it out."

"I'd feel better if you stayed at Blake Medical," he said.

"The hospital is going to be overrun with people who need medical attention. I'd just be taking up space."

Kate listened to them argue and silently agreed with Trace but kept her mouth shut. She just stared at the laptop. She couldn't take her eyes from the screen and prayed her boathouse was safe in Fort Hamer, far up the Manatee River. Doc chirped and moved from her left shoulder to her right. She told him to hush up.

Linus Vaughn stood next to Kate. He'd changed into another bright Bermuda shirt but still wore black dress-socks with his sandals. Stepping away from the group, he wiped his eyes with a handkerchief that he slipped back into his pocket.

Kate noticed his concerned expression and stepped toward him, saying, "It's okay, Mr. Vaughn. We'll get through this."

"Please call me Linus," he said, patting her hand on his shoulder. He looked up at her. "I know you're right."

"Of course, I'm right," she said. "Did you find your son?"

"Zach's around here somewhere." He turned his head, then looked back at Kate. "He probably met some pretty girl and is off talking to her."

Kate nodded and smiled. "ell, if you'll excuse me," she said. "I've got to find someone too."

Linus took her hand. "Wait," he said. He looked panicked. "You wanna play a game? How about…would you rather be an amazing artist but not be able to see any of the art you created or be an amazing musician but cannot hear any of the music you create?"

Kate paused and looked around the crowded gymnasium. "Mr. Vaughn---"

"Linus---"

"Linus, I'm sure your son would make a much better opponent," she said, smiling politely. She noticed Redd a few cots away, fishing a sandwich out of a cooler, and she excused herself again. "I see someone I need to speak to," she said. "I hope you find Zach."

Pushing her way through the crowd, she called out to Redd. Doc poked his head out from the pouch of her hoodie, seemingly curious to see the familiar voice.

"Where have you been?" she asked, confronting him at his cot. "I've been looking for you for the last hour."

"I've been hanging out at my assigned spot," he said, unwrapping the cellophane from a sandwich and opening a can of Mountain Dew.

"Where's Elise?" She looked past him at the mass of people sitting on cots, staring at phones, munching on junk food. She didn't see her sister, though.

He shrugged, avoiding eye contact. "She didn't want to come with me. I couldn't budge her."

Kate couldn't believe what she was hearing. "What do you mean she didn't want to come? Where is she?"

"I gassed up her Suburban, and she coulda taken it here." He spoke louder but still wouldn't look her in the eyes.

She shoved him to force him to raise his head. "You left her at The Bluegill?"

Doc let out a high-pitched screech as if he was just surprised.

Redd raised his hands. "I did everything I could. I picked her up and carried her out of the house and got her in my truck. She hit me, spit on me, and ran back inside."

"You left her?"

"What did you expect me to do? Knock her out and carry her here?" His voice rose an octave. "She had the Suburban. She coulda gotten here when she was good and ready."

"You're a jackass; you know that? A class-A jackass." She turned toward the front of the gym. Ian still had the keys to her Tahoe, and there wasn't time to hunt him down. She felt the keys to Mrs. O'Dell's station wagon in her pocket and pushed forward through the crowd.

"Where are you going?" Redd asked, following in her wake.

"Someone's got to go get her." Kate paused and lifted Doc off her shoulder. She handed him the squirrel. Doc squeaked and jumped back onto her arm. "Bert and Tug are locked in the art room. Just stay with them till I get back...with your wife."

She handed him the keyring.

"You can't go out there." His palm closed around the keys. "It's getting worse."

"I know. And my kid sister's out there in it!" She looked out the doors. Maybe she could reach The Bluegill in time. God willing. Before...

Thunder boomed, punctuating her thought and violently vibrating the floor and walls.

"Kate, wait." Redd grabbed her hand. "I should go with you."

"You've done enough." She ripped her hand from his grasp. "Just watch over my animals."

Leaving him in the crowd, she pushed through the metal doors and stopped before the large windows in the lobby. The wind howled and whipped trash and branches across the parking lot. Thunder rumbled, rattling the walls again. For a moment, her breath caught in her throat. Could she do this? Did she have a choice? Elise needed her. She forced the double glass doors open and stepped into the rain. Doc clung tight to her shoulder.

Powerful wind gusts swirled around her, nearly knocking her down. Limbs on the thick oak trees swayed back and forth in every direction. Spindly Pines bent almost in half. Leaves and trash blew past. The howling in her ears grew louder, stronger as if powered by some enraged fury.

She grasped Doc and held him close to her chest. Squinting in the driving rain, she pushed forward. No longer did she have any delusions about reaching The Bluegill before the gale hit. Where she was going, she'd be driving directly into the full brunt of the storm.

She found the station wagon and fought to open the driver's side door. Redd yelled at her from the entrance doors, but his voice drowned out in the wind. Starting the engine and putting the gearshift into reverse, she pulled out of the parking spot.

CHAPTER THIRTY-THREE

Kate sped through the empty Bradenton streets. Rivers of rushing water reflected back at her through the high beams but didn't slow her down. She remained in the center of the road, avoiding the pools along the curbs, and raced through the shadowy city. Lightning flashes revealed the cloaked skyscrapers and electrified towering thunder clouds.

She tried calling Elise but got another round of fast busy signals. She tried again a few minutes later and got a crackly connection to her voicemail. "Kid, it's me, Kate," she shouted over the rain pummeling the roof. It was useless, though. The connection ended, and she tossed her phone onto the passenger seat.

Doc chirped when the phone landed beside him. She questioned the wisdom of bringing him, but it was too late now. He was along for the ride.

Heading west toward the coast, she pushed the speedometer past seventy, blowing through intersections and past stop signs. The Causeway lay ahead, and she gripped the steering wheel to fight the powerful winds onto the entrance ramp. The windshield wipers screeched back and forth.

As the station wagon accelerated upward, she felt Sebastian's brute strength. Gusts hit the side of the vehicle like blows from an invisible fist, and she fought the steering wheel, pulling to the left to keep from plummeting into the churning Bay waters below.

Lord, give me strength, she prayed as she wrestled with the wheel, forcing a gradual left. The rain intensified, hailing down on the car with such force that she knew it was denting the hood. The windshield wipers had no hope of keeping up, and she strained to see ahead.

Somehow, blind and tense, she made it across the bridge and onto the island. Doc chattered in the passenger seat, displaying his relief. She sped up again, sloshing through the flooded downtown streets in Sienna Key and into the familiar dark neighborhood.

When she arrived at The Bluegill, she left the station wagon running and bolted to the front porch. She pounded on the door and was shocked to find it open. She entered the dark parlor.

"Elise?" Her voice echoed. Barely able to see anything, she ran upstairs with a hand along the wall to help guide her.

She entered the master bedroom. Empty.

The bathroom. Empty.

Noah's room. Empty.

Elise wasn't there.

Kate wondered if she could've left for the shelter. Perhaps this whole trip had been a fool's errand. She noticed the framed photograph lying on the floor next to Noah's bed and picked it up. A bloody smear ran across the cracks in the glass. Beneath it, her sister looked so happy, all teeth and dimples next to Noah and his giant stuffed elephant.

She hoped Elise had come to her senses and made it to the high school. Now, Kate wondered, could she make it too?

* * *

At the crowded shelter, Redd lay on an uncomfortable cot wishing he had a cigarette. The clamor in the gymnasium was headache-inducing under the flickering lights and the crying children. The AC had shut-off, and people argued and complained in the stifling air. Between that and the rumbling wind and thunder outside, his blood pressure was rising.

Kate's obnoxious boyfriend didn't help matters either.

Ian called out to Redd as he led a middle-aged woman by the hand through the crowd. She was a thin woman with hair as red as his. Redd cringed when they approached.

"This is my mom," Ian said, introducing the woman.

Redd glanced at her. "Good for you."

"We're looking for Kate," Ian continued, oblivious to Redd's aggravation. "My mother can vouch for my whereabouts. I want her to talk to Kate and Chief Guerra."

Redd nodded toward the front doors. "She left."

"Left?" Ian's expression darkened, and he clutched his mother's hand. "Where'd she go?"

"She went back to find her sister?"

"Back? Back where?" Ian looked toward the front of the gym, then back at Redd. "Where is she?"

"She went to The Bluegill after Elise."

Ian shook his head. "She's out there in this hurricane? You let her go out there?"

"I didn't *let* her do anything. She's a grown woman."

"You've got to do something!" Ian yelled at him. "She'll die out there."

Thunder shook the walls and drowned out their voices

Redd could feel the vibrations in his teeth. He stared at Ian for several seconds. "What do you want me to do?"

"Nothing. Just sit here and do nothing." Ian took his mother by the arm. "There's such a thing as karma, you know."

Redd watched him leave, sorta feeling guilty. He did everything in his power to get Elise to leave. She had the Suburban, so it wasn't like he left her stranded. And he told Kate not to go after her. What did everyone expect him to do—give up his life just because Elise had a death wish?

He pulled the keyring from his pocket. They jingled in his hand, and he figured the least he could do was look after Kate's animals like she asked. Plus, it'd give him an opportunity to catch a smoke.

Getting up, he sauntered to the back of the gym. The doors there opened into a breezeway, and he crossed it, entering the high school. The dark hallways were empty, and he turned a corner searching for the art room. Pausing, he knocked a cigarette from the pack and lit it. Ahead, at the end of the hall, a figure appeared and seemed to be watching him.

He focused his eyes.

"Hey," he called out. "I just needed a smoke. I can put it out."

Thunder crashed, and a flash of lightning illuminated a man at the end of the hallway. Tall. Dressed in black. Wearing some kind of grey hat. *A mask? An elephant head?* He brandished a baseball bat in his hands.

Redd stumbled backward and dropped the pack of cigarettes. The keys fell to the floor. His mind struggled to process what he was seeing: a shadowy apparition coming toward him.

He turned to a classroom door. Struggled with the knob. Locked. He ran to another door. Pounded on it. Tried the handle. Turned his head. The figure was moving faster down the hallway, straight for him.

Redd spun in the opposite direction, bolting past locked classroom doors. He ran blindly, turning a corner, through another hallway, and then another—no idea where he was going.

He came to an abrupt halt, teetering on the edge of a stairwell. The steps dissolved into a pit of darkness. No lights. There had to be emergency lights in the stairwell. Who turned out the lights?

His brain fired off an explosion of commands and counter commands to his beleaguered limbs. Run. No. Stop. No. Go. No. Hide. It was hard to know what to do. His heart pounded. He inhaled and tried to get his bearings. He'd been here before. Had gone to this school as a kid. He just needed to remember . . .

The cafeteria was straight down at the foot of the stairs, to the right. Yes! That's where he was. And there was an exit door to the left.

He gripped the banister with his right hand, crouching slightly, and prepared for the rapid descent. Once he made it down, he'd have to make a dash for it. But what if that madman was lying in wait in the darkness? His legs buckled as he lunged forward, galloping two and three steps at a time, down into the abyss. What if the exit was locked? He'd have to break the glass.

He moved faster down the steps, into the darkness. He had another horrible thought. What if the exit was locked and that psycho was waiting? No, that wasn't possible. The madman was behind him. Somewhere. Redd slowed his pace to a single step at a time to avoid tripping. He moved off the last step. His foot planted on solid tile. Turning left, he slammed into a wall with a startling thud and bounced backward. He hit the floor, stunned.

A wall? He didn't remember a wall there.

He raised his eyes to meet the obstacle. Hovering over him was the silhouette of the figure with a raised baseball bat in his hands. Horrible wheezing sounds came through that hideous elephant mask.

Redd gasped. His legs trembled.

The elephant man stood there, unmoving.

Redd got to his feet, inhaled a deep, labored breath, and inched backward toward the stairs.

"Is this some kind of joke? Who are you?" he yelled at the unmoving figure, but his voice choked. Again, his brain shot out a series of conflicting orders. Fight. No. Run back up the stairs. No. Reason with him. No. Fight.

Redd tensed his limbs and hurled his body full speed ahead, crashing against the elephant man, throwing him off-balance. The bat dropped and hit the tile floor. Redd scrambled past him. The exit door was just ten feet away. Filtered light came through the glass. He could hear the rain outside. He ran toward it, a mass of flailing limbs and mindless terror.

Something gripped the back of his shirt. Redd turned his head. That hideous, surreal elephant face! Those black eyes! The madman had him!

Redd struggled forward. His shirt ripped. He rushed headlong toward the exit. Hit the push bar. The door swung open. The wind caught it and whipped it against the brick wall, shattering the glass.

Redd darted into the rain and wind, barely able to stand, and stumbled into the open courtyard. He was certain he heard the pounding of his attacker's footsteps close behind. Or maybe it was just the rain. He didn't want to look back. His eyes darted from a brick wall to his right, to the gymnasium on his left, to the chain-link fence ahead. Just beyond it, open roadway lay straight ahead. He swerved toward the gym.

A hand grabbed him by the throat and threw him to the wet pavement.

On his side, Redd squinted with his arms raised, shielding his face. Rain beat down so hard he could barely open his eyes. "Who are you?" he screamed.

The elephant man appeared in the lightning flashes, raised the baseball bat in the air, and swung it against Redd's thigh.

Redd wailed in agony. He got up onto his hands and knees. The second blow sent his head crashing against the pavement.

The elephant man stood motionless, looming over Redd with his twisted trunk swaying in the wind. A muffled voice came from the mask, saying, "His little body looked battered and bloody as if someone picked up a baseball bat and beat the life out of him."

A gloved hand reached out and wrapped thick fingers around Redd's throat again, but Redd caught him off guard with a sudden burst of stamina. He rolled onto his side and scrambled to his feet with a yelp, limping toward a cluster of bushes along the fence.

The elephant man pursued.

Stumbling toward the fence in the downpour, Redd called for help. Thunder boomed in the sky, rattling his teeth. He grasped the chain link. Fell to his knees.

The elephant man splashed toward him. The swinging bat cut the air.

Retching, Redd gripped the chain link with slack white fingers and lifted himself up. He tried to climb. Clawing his way up, he barely made it afoot when the muffled voice behind him repeated, "His little body looked battered and bloody as if someone picked up a baseball bat and beat the life out of him."

With one swift, savage thrust, the psycho cracked the bat against Redd's back.

It knocked the air out of Redd's lungs. He dropped to the ground, writhing in pain. Rain battered his face, drowning him. He looked up. The bat lifted high above him.

A scream rang out in the storm.

The elephant man lowered the bat. Redd squinted in the rain, barely making out people a few feet away.

Standing against the gym's side wall, a bleached-blonde woman wearing a Tiki Hut uniform clutched a little girl. "What're you doing?" she yelled. "You people need to get back inside."

Redd cried out and stretched an arm toward her. "Help me," he moaned.

The little girl darted into the rain, rushing toward him.

The woman screamed, "Heather!"

Heather took Redd's hand. He sat up, coughing blood, and looked behind him. The elephant man was gone.

CHAPTER THIRTY-FOUR

Kate sprinted from the front porch to the station wagon. Her clothing was soaked when she climbed in behind the wheel and fought the wind to close the door. She didn't have a choice. She had to make it back to the high school or at least get off the island.

She buckled her seat belt. Doc chattered in the passenger seat. She spoke to him, her voice soothing, and told him everything was going to be okay.

Rolling forward, she drove, splashing onto the saturated streets, and sped out of the neighborhood. The wheels threw towering waves behind the vehicle, and rain gushed waterfalls across the windshield. The wiper blades squealed, struggling to keep up. Passing through downtown, she moved along the road to the Causeway ramp. She didn't know how she was going to cross now.

A powerful gust slammed the station wagon, a force unlike anything she'd experienced so far. It lifted the left-side wheels off the ground, sending her hydroplaning to the right, out of control. She jerked the wheel in the opposite direction. The rear fishtailed to the left. She spun erratically. Suspended in midair, she smashed into a concrete barrier. The impact thrust her forward, and her seat belt constricted across her chest. The airbags deployed.

She opened her eyes.

Doc poked up from the passenger floorboard. He hopped onto the seat, shaking his head as if dizzy. He appeared unharmed, though.

Looking straight out the windshield, Kate assessed her situation. They'd landed on the median. The tattered fragments of Noah's memorial lay scattered around the vehicle. Wind whipped the white cross into the air, and it took flight, striking her windshield. She ducked as it hit the glass.

Something told her to get out of the car. As if something was calling to her. Yelling her name. Screaming.

She opened the door. Stepped into the rain.

The windshield wipers scraped the glass with a monotonous screech. The headlights cast two yellow-white beams into the downpour. And she could barely make out the silhouette of a woman sitting in the middle of the exit ramp in the rain. Two rivers of water rushed by either side of her and down the concrete slope.

Elise!

Kate ran to her.

"Are you crazy?" she yelled. "What are you doing here?"

Elise didn't up. "Go away, Kate."

Kate grasped her hand and tried to pull her to her feet. "We need to leave. Now."

"Then leave." Elise resisted Kate and stared straight ahead. Rain streaked her face, matted her hair.

Kate squeezed her hand tighter.

Elise yanked her arm away. "I swear to God, if you touch me, I'll—" She stopped and buried her face in her hands. "I'll … I'll never see him again. He's gone. He's really gone."

She sobbed.

"I know." Kate knelt beside her sister and wrapped her arms around her. This time Elise didn't recoil from her embrace. They held each other in the running water, the rain soaking them.

"I know," Kate said again, holding her sister tight against the wind.

"He died here." Elise cried into Kate's shoulder.

Kate grasped Elise by the shoulders and looked her in the eyes. "We can't stay out here. We've gotta get to safety."

"I want to die." Elise's body went slack, and she slipped to the ground, rolling in the mud. Another running torrent of water washed over her.

Kate grabbed her arms, forced her to sit up. "No, you don't."

"I do. I can't go on without him." Elise fought Kate.

Kate pulled Elise to her feet. "Come on. Let's get out of here."

Arm in arm, they fought the wind and stumbled back to the station wagon. Another powerful gust pushed against them, nearly knocking them off their feet. It moved the whole car as they approached. The vehicle skidded across the ramp before them and slammed into a light pole. The sisters turned their backs to the wind, hanging tight to each other.

"Where's your Suburban?" Kate asked.

"In a ditch." Elise pointed toward town.

Kate held her palm over her brow to shield her eyes and look around. No cars would be coming along. They couldn't call AAA or even 911. They'd have to make it back to the station wagon. She prayed it would start.

From the beach beyond the ramp, the form of a man emerged from the swaying palm trees. He was a black shadow in a raincoat, blowing in the wind. Faceless beneath a hat. They stopped as he approached.

"Who is that?" Kate called out. She wiped the water from her eyes.

"It's him," Elise said. "It's Doogie."

Kate watched the man step toward them. Through the wind and rain, his face came into view. She couldn't believe what she was seeing—*who* she was seeing. Her mouth opened, and she whispered, "Dad."

* * *

Trace stood alone amid a crush of people in the high school gymnasium. Rain pounded the roof. The lights flickered. Tensions rose, and he held up his arms, addressing the crowd. "Everything's all right," he said.

Ian emerged from the mass of bodies, out of breath. "Chief!"

Trace turned his head as he approached. "This isn't the time, Mr. Biggs. We'll talk after the storm passes."

"She's gone, Chief. She's gone," Ian said. He gasped as he spoke. "Redd says she left."

Trace stepped toward him. "Who's gone?"

"Kate. She went out there." Ian pointed to the front of the gymnasium. As if on cue, thunder rattled the walls. When it died, Ian continued. "Kate went after her sister."

"No—she didn't." Trace pressed through the crowd toward the front doors of the gym.

Ian caught up to him. "We need to go after her."

Trace pushed open the metal double doors into the lobby. He halted before the windows, paused before the massive wall of swirling blackness just beyond the panes. The wind howled with the beating rain. A tree limb hit the glass with such force that the two men jumped. The shrieking intensified, like the sound of a freight train. Or a tornado.

"She's out there in this!" Ian yelled over the roar.

Trace shook his head. "Dear God, help her."

Ian said, "We gotta move away from the windows!" He pulled Trace's arm, tugging him back toward the gym doors.

Trace couldn't take his eyes off the rattling windows. The glass vibrated like it would explode at any second.

"C'mon!" Ian yelled. He pulled Trace backward through the doorway and into the gym. He shut the metal doors, slightly muffling the roaring wind.

"Dear God, help her," Trace muttered again, placing a hand flat on the door.

Jared and Jensen approached, coming through the crowd, shouting. Trace turned to them. He could still hear the glass rattling in the lobby, and the roof creaked like it was about to come apart.

"Yeah, what is?" he asked, trying his best to sound calm.

"Chief, it's your wife," Jared said. "She needs you."

* * *

"Dad?" Kate said, her weak voice lodging in her throat. She stared at the man standing before them. "Is it really you?"

"Hello, Kate," he said.

Elise ran to him and hugged him. "Doogie," she said.

Kate stared in disbelief. Had she forgotten? All those years ago ... when Elise was a toddler. She called their daddy "*Doogie*." Why didn't she remember that earlier?

Doogie released Elise from his embrace and held his arms out to Kate. She backed away from him.

"What are you doing here?" She struggled to be heard over the rain.

The wind intensified, howling around them. It whipped the hat off Doogie's head, and the chin strap stretched taut across his neck.

"We need to get out of this storm," he said, returning the yellow hat to his head. Thunder boomed, shaking the ground.

Kate shook her head, still trying to grasp what was happening. "No. Wait. What are you doing here? Where have you been?"

"I got Elise's car outta a ditch," he said. He pointed to the Suburban parked on a sidewalk running along the beach. "Then we can talk."

Doogie and Elise ran through the rain to the vehicle. Kate returned to the battered station wagon and pulled Doc from the passenger seat.

Inside the Suburban, Elise scooted to the center of the bench seat. Kate climbed in next to her, sitting on the edge by the door, cradling the squirrel. Doogie got in behind the wheel.

His head turned to Kate and the wet squirrel in her arms. "What's that?" he asked.

"It's Doc," she said. "We need to go to the high school in Bradenton. We've set up a shelter there."

"Too dangerous," he said, starting the engine. "We'll never make it across the Causeway."

He pulled off the sidewalk and drove off the curb to make a U-turn across the entrance ramp. They rode in silence, passing the empty downtown buildings. Ten minutes later, he parked in front of The Bluegill.

The palm trees swayed. A tall pine tree bent unnaturally toward the ground. Leaves and trash were airborne.

They hurried out of the Suburban. Kate could barely move against the roaring wind, and Elise was knocked to the ground. Kate tried to help her up, but the gale force was too strong. She stumbled. Doogie ran to their side of the truck and reached for them. Holding to each other for support, they moved together across the yard and struggled into the house. Once inside, they forced the front door shut. With the power out and the windows boarded, the darkness was impenetrable.

Blind, Kate fumbled into the kitchen, where the box of hurricane supplies remained on the counter. She felt inside it—batteries, charcoal, peanut butter, jelly, paper plates, plastic utensils, baby wipes. A flashlight lay discarded by the box. She flipped the ON/OFF switch several times, but it remained dark. She threw it down and found three candles in a drawer. She lit them and returned to the living room. Elise had changed clothes and was holding a towel around Doc, drying him off. Doogie stood in a dark corner, wiping his face.

Kate stared at her father. “You were hiding out in the lighthouse, weren’t you?”

“Yes.” He put down the towel.

Elise set down the dry clothes and tilted her head. “You were in the lighthouse this whole time?”

Kate said, “How long?”

“About ten months.” He shook his head, flinging water from his hair. “I came back to Sienna Key when I heard about Noah.”

“Why?” Kate only half-listened as she struggled to comprehend. “Why didn’t you tell us? Why all the--all the—”

“Secrecy.” Elise finished the sentence.

Doogie looked at his boots. “I didn’t know what to say. I didn’t know how you’d react.”

Kate’s annoyance increased when a painful throb rippled through her shoulder. She massaged the ache away as she spoke. “Why …? How …? I’m not even sure where to begin.”

“Well … I disappeared.” A hint of nervousness flittered across his face. “I’m sure you want to know why.”

“For starters, yes.” Kate set the candles on the floor. Elise sat across from her. The flickering light cast shadows across their faces as they stared up at their father.

“The situation with your mother was bad. Volatile,” he said. He remained in the corner, in the dark, away from them. “I was angry and drinking. I was worried I'd do something to hurt your mother—or worse, something to you girls.”

Kate narrowed her eyes, her voice harsh, and said, “What does that mean?”

“Kate, stop it, will you?” Elise scolded her. “It doesn’t matter why he left, just that he’s back now.”

“It’s all right,” Doogie said. “It’s a fair question.” He looked Kate directly eye to eye. “You have every right to be angry. I was a horrible father back then and an even worse man.”

Kate didn’t want to hear any more. His little speech sounded rehearsed. “You were our daddy,” she stated. “We needed you.”

“I was drinking. Heavily,” Doogie said, raising his voice. “I would’ve hurt you. I had already hurt your mother.”

“I don’t believe it.” Kate turned away, folding her arms. “Mother died after you left us. We waited for you to come back, but you never did.”

“I wanted to.” He closed his eyes as if it hurt too much to look at them. "I honestly did."

"You see. He wanted to," Elise said. She cradled Doc in her arms like a baby. "Now, let's change the subject. Why don't you tell us where you found this gimpy rabbit?"

Kate took the one-armed squirrel from Elise and set him on the floor. He sniffed at the candle and then jumped into Kate's lap.

"You should've come to Mother's funeral." Kate pet the squirrel a little too hard as she spoke. He made a clicking noise and scurried off her lap. She watched him scramble across the floor.

"I didn't know she'd passed," he said. "I found out about her passing a few years after she was gone." He faltered as if trying to come up with better words. Taking another approach, his voice changed again, and this time it sounded almost hopeful. "I came by and watched you from afar. But I didn't want to disrupt your lives. You were getting along fine without me."

"No." Kate wasn't ready to let him off that easy. "We needed you."

"You needed a father, and that wasn't me." He stepped out of the shadows and paced the room. "You know, you create this script of what an ideal father is supposed to be, and then you try to live up to it, but that's not reality. And when you don't—you can't—you feel you're not worthy, and you pull away."

"Were you even thinking about us?" Kate watched him move about the room, her eyes watering. "Did you ever miss us or regret leaving?"

"Yes." He seemed to think about that a moment. Finally, he stepped forward and joined them around the candles on the floor. "Every day. Every hour. Every minute. Just because I wasn't there, didn't mean I didn't love you. I loved you terribly. Don't you get it? I had to fix what was broken inside me before I hurt one of you."

Elise took his hand. "We're glad you're back now—just when we need you most."

Kate chewed her lower lip, listening to the storm rage outside. The whole house creaked and groaned with it. The roof rasped with the sound of shingles breaking away and scraping the eaves, which frightened her.

She stiffened, bracing for the worst.

CHAPTER THIRTY-FIVE

Trace rushed across the crowded gymnasium to his wife.

Nellie sat on the edge of a cot in the center of the free-throw lane, under the basketball hoop. She twisted and squirmed, clearly trying to relieve the pain pressing against her pelvis.

"I'm alright," she told him, raising a hand to stop him from coming any closer. "Really. It's okay." Thunder drowned out her voice and reverberated through the walls. She clutched her stomach.

Trace knelt beside her. "Are you sure?" he asked.

"Yes." She gulped a breath and straightened up. "It's over," she added. "Just a cramp or something. Nothing serious."

"You know, Chief," Jensen said, leaning over Trace's shoulder. "I read somewhere that a sudden change in the barometric pressure can induce labor."

Jared punched him in the arm. "Why would you say that?"

Jensen cringed and rubbed his bicep. "What?"

"Why say that about inducing labor?" Jared asked. "Can't you see that this whole situation is stressful enough without you adding to it?"

Trace ignored them and placed his hands firmly on his wife's back, massaging the pain away. Despite her smile, which he was sure was forced, he could sense it was something more. A contraction.

"The doctor said there would be some false labor pains," she said, gulping a breath. "That's all it was. False labor pains."

That's all it was, Trace thought. A false labor pain that didn't last. He prayed that Jensen wasn't right about the barometric pressure. He couldn't be. The due date was still a month away. There was no way Little Thomas would come early. They were scaring themselves.

But still ….

He'd heard horror stories from other officers who had assisted expectant mothers en route to the hospital. Stories about mothers who, for one reason or another, couldn't make it and delivered on the side of a road or in the back of a squad car, without doctors or drugs or epidurals. Stories about the blood. The ripping flesh. The pain. A pain so intense, so penetrating, the screaming mother sounded like a wounded animal. One woman bit through her tongue before the baby finally pushed out of her. Another pulled out large wads of her own hair. Ripped it right out of her head.

He feared for Nellie and didn't want her to suffer through anything like that.

She looked into his face but didn't speak. She clutched her stomach and shuddered with another contraction.

Trace stood, keeping a hand on her shoulder. Where could they go in the jam-packed gymnasium? People surrounded them, watching, blocking every path. He waved his free hand at Jared and Jensen. "We need to get her out of here."

Thunder rumbled, and the lights flickered.

Jensen looked up. "I don't think we're going anywhere in this weather."

"He means, out of the crowd," Jared said, pushing him.

Jensen pushed back. "He didn't say that. He said we need to get her out of here."

"It was implied." Jared pushed Jensen again, harder.

"Guys, stop it," Trace said. "We need to get Nellie out of this crowd. Someplace quiet."

Jared pointed toward the locker rooms. "We can take her in there."

Nellie reached for Trace's hand. He grasped it and looked down at her.

She took deep breaths. "It's passing," she said between gasps.

"Let's get you somewhere more comfortable," Trace said. Placing a hand firmly on her back, he helped her to her feet. "Someplace private."

As soon as she stood, her water broke. He stared at the fluid trickling down her legs and puddling at her feet. He thought of those stories again, of cops delivering babies on the side of the road and in the back of squad cars.

"No," Nellie said, looking down. "We're not ready."

Jensen hit Jared square on the shoulder. "See? I told you. It's the barometric pressure."

Thunder roared.

"Come on," Trace said firmly, leading her away from the cot. He helped her from the free throw zone and into the mass of onlookers.

"Coming through," Jared said, a couple of steps ahead of Trace and Nellie, moving folks out of the way. "Make way. Coming through."

"Move it, people!" Jensen yelled and blew his whistle. The crowd separated, making a pathway.

Nellie stopped. She gripped her stomach. Another contraction rippled through her body.

Thunder shook the gymnasium. The lights went out. Screams erupted in the dark. Nellie fell to her knees, clutching her stomach. Blind, Trace reached for her, held her. Emergency lights came on. He could see her again, barely, and helped her to her feet.

Turning to Jared, he said, "Get the nurses from the medical station."

"I think they're just med students," Jensen said.

"It doesn't matter." Jared snapped at him. He took off into the crowd.

"Hurry!" Trace yelled, leading his wife to the locker rooms.

Jensen followed. "Don't worry about noth'n, Chief. Okay?" he said. "I'm still here." People approached Trace and Nellie, and he told them to back off. He looked over at Nellie. "I'm not goin' nowhere."

Rain beat hard above them. The wind howled, tearing at the roof. Thunder boomed again, shaking the building like an earthquake.

The emergency lights went out. Darkness enveloped them.

The sound of shuffling and movement echoed in every direction. People yelled. Prayed. Cried. Nellie dropped to the floor and screamed.

Trace took the flashlight from his belt and switched it on. Jensen did the same.

Nellie trembled at Trace's boots, clutching her stomach. He bent down to her, shined the light on her. This pain seemed sharper than the last, caused her to suck in her breath and grit her teeth.

"It's going to be okay," he said, taking her hand. She clutched it, squeezed it tightly through the pain. He held her close. "We'll get through this."

Arm in arm, he helped her back onto her feet and, using his flashlight to guide them, led her into the locker room.

"Brush your … teeth and comb … your … hair," she said through her teeth, leaning her head against Trace's shoulder. "The baby's coming."

Trace squeezed her hand and cursed under his breath, "Mother cruncher."

* * *

Kate found a battery-operated Coleman lantern discarded on the kitchen floor and flipped it on. It lit up the room, and she carried it upstairs, where Elise sat alone in Noah's bedroom.

"I want to be alone," Elise said, sitting in the rocker.

Kate didn't respond, listening to the rain and wind pummel the house. The walls creaked so eerily in the gale-force winds that she wondered if they could collapse around them. Stuffed animals above the bed trembled. Doc raised up on her shoulder, swishing his bushy tail. The lantern cast a pale glow around the bedroom. With the windows boarded up, any area outside the lantern light was lost in thick, inky blackness. Though she couldn't see the lightning, she could hear the angry thunder compete with the rain beating the roof.

The bookcase rattled, keeping her on edge. She glanced at Elise, huddled in the rocking chair. Her sister wrapped the afghan tighter over her shoulders and locked her arms around her knees.

The walls trembled with another thunderclap, shaking the bookcase, and knocked the worn copy of *Where the Darkness Hides* to the floor. Kate jumped at the loud thump. Doc jumped too and leaped to the floor to investigate. She raised the lantern and looked around the room. Many of the stuffed animals had fallen onto the small bed. A model airplane dangled from the ceiling, swaying violently from the turbulence. A toy box sat positioned under the window.

Letting out a breath, she shut her eyes and focused on the rain thumping the roof. It intensified, then quieted. The sound was hypnotic, and she didn't even hear Doogie enter the bedroom. He shined a flashlight in her direction and paused in the doorway.

"Sebastian made landfall"—his voice rose above another loud boom of thunder—"south of Sarasota."

Kate couldn't see him behind the blinding light in his hands, and when he lowered the flashlight, it still took a moment for her eyes to adjust. She sensed him stepping beside her. Out of the corner of her eye, she saw Doc dash across the floor toward him.

"We've just got to make it through the night." He walked over to the rocking chair and put a hand on Elise's shoulder.

Doc followed, cautiously investigating the cuff of his right pant leg.

"It's about to get worse," Kate said.

A corner of Elise's mouth turned upward, but her smile was without humor. She turned to Doogie. "Why didn't you sell her to gypsies or leave her in the woods somewhere?"

The wind howled at the window, and a sudden gust ripped the plywood from the casing. The glass shattered. Wind and rain blew into the room.

Elise screamed. The rocker overturned, spilling her to the floor. Kate and Doogie rushed to the bed, flipped the mattress off it, and forced it to the open window. They fought the incoming wind. The force bent the mattress, folded it like a sheet of paper, and pushed them back. Doogie shoved the mattress against the window and held it there. He yelled at Kate to move the bookcase. She got to one side of it and scooted it across the carpet to the front of the mattress.

The mattress shuddered in front of the broken window. The wind squealed and screamed like a dying thing. Kate and Doogie were silent for a couple of minutes, staring at each other.

"It's not going to hold," Kate yelled to him over the wind.

"We need to go downstairs." He pointed toward the bedroom door. "It's not safe in here."

Elise turned the rocker right side up and sat down. "I'm not leaving Noah's room."

Doogie stepped to her, knelt beside the rocker. "C'mon, kid. It's not safe."

Kate watched her sister look up at him.

"I'm not leaving." Gripping the edges of the afghan and pulling it taut against her back, she sank deeper into the cradle of the rocking chair. Her voice sounded raspy and tired, and a clap of thunder tapped her willpower.

The wind grew louder. It sounded like a howling wolf for a second and then a train. The roar became deafening. Debris hit the house. The roof rattled and banged.

Kate looked up.

Doogie moved the box spring and bedframe to the window, struggling to position them against the mattress. He looked back at Kate.

Elise picked up the weathered copy of *Where the Darkness Hides* from the floor. With the soft lantern light illuminating her face, she set the book in her lap and opened the cover.

Doogie looked puzzled. "We don't have time for this."

Elise read out loud, raising her voice over the shrieking wind.

"We don't have time for this," Doogie yelled. He turned to Kate. "Do something."

Kate listened to the roar of the wind. Something massive hit the side of the house. The impact was loud and shook the walls. What could she do? If their number was up, she couldn't possibly do anything to prevent it. And at least they'd be going as a family, together. She dropped to the floor, next to Elise. Doc scurried to her, his tail raised high, and hopped onto her thigh. He stood on his hind legs and pawed at Kate with his single arm.

Thunder rocked the house, and Elise stopped reading. She turned toward the bedroom door. Doc let out a series of warning chirps and clicks. Kate heard it too. A pounding that seemed separate from the rain beating the exterior of the house. *BAM! BAM! BAM!* Intense. Determined. It sounded different from the wind.

It was coming from downstairs.

The hairs on the back of Kate's neck rose. Another *BAM! BAM! BAM!* She definitely didn't imagine it. She turned to Doogie. His eyes widened.

"That's the front door," he said. "Someone's at the door."

CHAPTER THIRTY-SIX

Trace clutched Nellie in his arms as they huddled in the locker room shower. The only light came from their flashlights, narrow beams that cast shadows up the tiled walls. She kept yelling to him, "The baby's coming," as he kept telling her, "Don't push! Don't push!"

She screamed through another contraction.

Jared returned with a couple of med students. "We couldn't find any nurses," he said.

"How's she doing, Chief?" the first student asked. "We could hear her screaming all the way out there."

"This is kinda above our paygrade," said the second.

Behind them, a man wearing a brightly colored Bermuda shirt and black dress-socks with sandals pushed to the front of the crowd. He approached Trace and kneeled beside Nellie. "How far along is she?" he asked.

Trace pushed him back. "And you are?"

"Linus Vaughn," he said.

A younger man rushed to them. "Leave them alone, Dad," he said. "They don't need you getting in the way."

Linus ignored his son and motioned to Jared. "Get some towels, rubbing alcohol, blankets, anything you can find."

Jensen pointed to a towel rack in the corner. "There's towels right there."

Jared swatted him upside the head. "Those are dirty!"

Jensen rubbed the side of his head. He looked back at Nellie. "Look at the mess she's making. You think it's gonna make a difference?"

Jared swatted him. "Now, why you gotta go and say somethin' like that? What's the matter with you?" He signaled for Jensen to follow him.

Their boots pounded through the locker room, and their lights disappeared around the corner, followed by the slam of the heavy swinging door.

"Dad, stop this," Zach said again. "You're just getting in the way."

Linus looked at Trace. "My wife went into labor during a winter storm in Atlanta. The whole city shut down, and I delivered my son in the plumbing aisle at The Home Depot."

Trace didn't comment. He remained focused on his wife. Linus stooped beside Nellie and looked at his wristwatch.

"Contractions are regular, three to five minutes apart and lasting over a minute," he said, then added. "Now there's nothing to worry about. Women deliver babies every day."

Trace glanced at him then turned to Nellie again when she grabbed hold of his arm.

"I can't do this. I can't do this." Her voice quivered with pain and fear.

"You can," Trace said. "I'm right here with you. We'll get through this."

Nellie screamed again, throwing her head back. She clutched her back and rolled onto her side. She bunched her legs, straightened them again, and turned to her other side. Travel Agent then motioned to the gawking crowd in the locker room and shooed everyone out.

Trace rubbed his wife's shoulders and followed a line down her spine. "Remember what we learned in the classes? The birthing ball. Hands and knees. Breathing."

She screamed, an agonizing, guttural release. She gulped a deep breath and held it, squeezing her face through the pain.

Trace could see spasms tear into her pelvis, shoot through her hips, and into her spine. He felt it, too, and dug his fingers into the pressure points along her back. "Hang in there," he whispered, over and over in her ear. She let out a breath and panted. He gave her some water from a Dixie cup, and she sipped it.

"It'll all be over soon," Linus said. "And you'll have a beautiful baby in your arms."

The clamor of people gathered outside the locker room door competed with the rain, and Trace knew they were listening. Nellie looked exhausted. Her sweaty face turned pale. Blood streamed between her legs and pooled around her on the floor.

He squeezed her hand, wishing there was something more he could do.

* * *

Grabbing the lantern, Kate rose and left Noah's bedroom. Doc rushed out from under the bed and chased after her into the hallway. The light tossed shrinking shadows across the walls and the closed bedroom doors. Doogie and Elise followed. Three more loud knocks echoed up the stairs. They descended the staircase two steps at a time, and Kate nearly stepped on Doc as he bound down the steps ahead of them.

"I hope it's the Zodiac Killer," Elise said. "You know, they never caught him … or her."

Doogie came to the last step and placed a hand on Kate's shoulder. Around them, pictures wobbled on the wall. They reached the parlor. Kate's hand automatically brushed the light switch, but nothing happened. She reminded herself the power was out as Doogie reached the front door, ready to turn the deadbolt.

"Wait." She gripped his arm. "We don't know who it is."

He said, "There's only one way to find out." He twisted the deadbolt and turned the doorknob.

The door whipped open with the force of the wind, nearly knocking them down. Muddy leaves blew into the house and churned around the outline of a young woman on the porch. Her blonde hair was soaked and matted to her head, and her floral-print blouse clung to her body. She rushed in with a torrent of rain.

Elise stepped aside, giving the drenched woman some room. Doogie forced the door shut and locked it. Doc reared up on his hind legs, inspecting the visitor.

"I'm sorry." The woman broke down sobbing. A cut above her left eye bled, streaking red down the left side of her face.

Kate removed the afghan from Elise's shoulders and covered the trembling woman. Elise took the afghan back. Kate grabbed it and offered it to her again.

"It's alright." The trembling woman waved a hand, declining the blanket. Her words came out so fast they almost sounded like one long syllable. "I need your help."

"No," Elise said. "Now go away."

"Please." The woman sounded like she was about to break down. "I've been knocking on doors. You're the only one that answered."

"What were you even doing out there?" Elise wrapped her afghan tighter around her shoulders and glared at the stranger. "What kind of moron are you? Don't you know there's a hurricane out there?"

Kate stared at the woman, at the stringy blonde hair, the drenched flowery blouse, the mascara running down her cheeks. She was almost unrecognizable.

Almost.

"Olivia?" Kate stepped closer, raising the lantern for a better look. "You're Olivia Wade."

Standing there dripping on the floor, the woman didn't answer. She turned to Doogie, crying. "My son is trapped in the car. We were run off the road."

"Your son?" Kate said over her. "I didn't know you had a son."

"Yes, he's six years old." The woman gasped, on the verge of hyperventilating. Kate put a hand on her back, trying to calm her.

"Six …" Elise said. The afghan fell from her shoulders. "My little boy would've been six years old."

The woman pleaded. "Can you help me? Please!"

"Slow down and breathe." Kate took a step back. "Tell me what happened."

"My little boy—he's hurt," she said. She broke down and sobbed as she got the words out. "We ran off the road. Hit a tree. My little boy—"

"Elise is right. Why were you even out there?" Doogie yelled at her.

"Where is he?" Kate's narrow gaze sharpened on Olivia's face. The gash above her eye looked bad, and she suspected the woman wasn't suffering from a concussion. Kate touched her shoulder. "Slow down and breathe. Where's your car?"

"Out there." She motioned toward the door. "He didn't wake up. Blood … his head was bleeding."

Doogie leaned toward her. "Where out there? Where's your car?"

"Off the road, about a mile or so." The woman pointed west. "I'm sorry to bother you, but we crashed our car. He's hurt. I didn't know what to do."

"I'm going after him," Doogie said.

Elise said, "You put your little boy in danger then left him out there alone . . . in a hurricane? Someone should give you an award or something." She turned and entered the dark living room. Doc scampered after her, waving his bushy tail. He jumped onto the couch as she sat down. She looked at the furry, one-armed squirrel with surprise, then back at the soaked woman in the foyer. "You might as well sit down and wait and stay out of everyone's way. Doogie will find your car and get your little boy."

The woman stepped into the living room as Doogie started for the stairs with his flashlight shining.

Elise called up to him, "Where are you going?"

"I'm seeing if your husband—what's his name?" he yelled back.

"Redd."

"If Redd has any boots I can wear." Doogie stomped up the stairs.

"Get something dry out of my closet that the Mother of the Year here can wear," Elise called out after him. "I don't want her dripping all over my couch."

Kate picked up her iPhone. She swiped the screen when she realized there was no signal. She held it against her ear, waiting, but it remained dead and useless. She turned back to their guest standing by the couch. "Let's take care of the cut above your eye."

Carrying the lantern, she led Olivia into the kitchen. Elise and Doc ran after them.

Kate went to the sink to soak a dishtowel under the tap. "Sit down and let me see about cleaning that wound."

"Thank you," Olivia said, sitting at the kitchen table.

Doc hopped onto a chair and then the table. He rose on his hind legs again, curious about her.

She glanced at the squirrel and then over at Elise. "Is he allowed on the furniture?"

"No. Are you?" Elise said as Kate handed Olivia the wet cloth.

She took it and held it to her forehead.

Kate moved to the entryway, almost blocking it. She held the lantern, allowing it to illuminate the kitchen and highlight their visitor. "You didn't answer my question earlier. Are you Olivia Wade?"

"Yes." She held the cloth to her forehead and wiped away the blood. "Yes, I am."

Doogie pushed past Kate into the kitchen, slipping his arms into his raincoat. He wore a pair of Redd's boots. "I'm going out there. I'll be back with the kid as fast as I can."

"You can't go out into this storm," Kate said.

Doogie set down the flashlight and put his rainhat over his head. "We can't leave that kid out there."

"I'd better go with you." Olivia got up from the table.

"You've done enough." Elise waved a hand, dismissing her. "Now just sit, shut up, and stay out of everybody's way."

Doogie said, "I'll be back soon." Grabbing the flashlight, he rushed past Kate.

She watched him disappear down the hall. A moment later, wind howled through the parlor, and the front door slammed shut. An unwelcome chill stretched even tighter between them.

A knot formed in Kate's stomach.

Worry lines deepened in Elise's forehead. Her voice broke when she said, "Look, I'm sorry about your kid, okay?"

Olivia didn't respond. She sat with her thin fingers curled into tense fists in her lap.

"Doogie—that's my daddy," Elise said, walking to the cupboard. "He'll find your car and bring your son back."

"I should've never given him up," Olivia said quietly.

"He'll be fine. Doogie will find him." Elise removed a first-aid kit from the cupboard and returned to the table. She set it down, opened it, and held up a bottle of rubbing alcohol. "What's your son's name?"

Olivia looked up. She glanced at Kate a moment and turned to Elise.

"Noah," she said. "It's Noah."

CHAPTER THIRTY-SEVEN

"Noah?" Kate wasn't sure she heard Olivia correctly and stepped out of the doorway toward the kitchen table. In her hand, the lantern swung with her movement and threw shadows up the walls and across Olivia's face.

Elise dropped the bottle of rubbing alcohol. The liquid spilled on the floor.

Olivia lowered the cloth from her face. The cut above her eye had stopped bleeding, but a pinkish-red smear ran down her face. She glanced at Elise then over at Kate. "What's wrong?"

"Elise's son...his name was Noah," Kate said.

The corners of Olivia's mouth turned up in a devilish smile. "What do you mean?"

"I lost Noah—*my* Noah—last year," Elise said. She knelt and picked up the bottle. "It just surprised me, that's all."

"Oh, I'm sorry. I didn't know." Olivia returned the cloth to the wound above her eye. "It's a weird coincidence...I guess."

Elise took the bottle back to the counter. She pulled another candle from a drawer and lit it. "I guess," she said as she placed it on the table near Olivia.

"Coincidences only occur until a connection is made." Kate tossed a dishrag on the floor over the puddle. She looked at Doc, who still sat on his haunches, seemingly curious about the flickering candle.

Olivia shook her head. "And sometimes coincidences are the universe's way of guiding you to your destiny." She turned back to Elise. "Tell me about your Noah."

Elise diverted her eyes. "I don't want to talk about him."

"Please." Olivia took her hand. "It might help me take my mind off my little boy and this hurricane and everything."

Elise pulled her hand free and knelt to pick the dish rag up from the floor. Doc watched with great interest as she rose and tossed the rag into the sink. "I wonder what's keeping Doogie."

"I'm sure he's fine," Kate said. "He hasn't been gone that long."

Olivia stood. "What was your Noah like? Do you have any pictures?"

"No," Elise snapped.

Olivia shrank back. "Okay, sorry I asked."

Elise stared at her for several seconds. She looked like she had something to say but wasn't sure how to form the words. Finally, she rubbed her hands together and said, "Doogie didn't bring you any dry clothes. Let me see if I can find you some."

She brushed past them and disappeared into the hall.

Now alone, Kate stepped toward Olivia. "I don't know what game you're playing," she said, "but it ends now. What are you doing here?"

Olivia sat at the table and seemed distracted by the squirrel chattering by the candle. "Cute little critter there. Where'd you get it?"

Kate chewed her lower lip, studying her. "Why are you avoiding my question?"

"Where's its other arm?" She pointed at the stub on Doc's arm.

"Answer my question. What are you doing here?"

"Trying to rescue my son," Olivia said. The flickering candlelight illuminated her eyes.

Kate knew she was lying, but why? What was she up to? She told Olivia to wait there in the kitchen. She called for Doc, and he leaped from the table onto her shoulder. She scratched his little head and picked up the lantern. "I'll be right back."

Kate left the kitchen, carrying both Doc and the lantern, and headed upstairs. Elise was in her bedroom, laying T-shirt and sweatpants on the bed.

"Something's wrong here," Kate said, entering.

"I like her." Elise looked up. "She's the creepy, indifferent sister I never had."

"She's Olivia Wade—the daughter of that attorney who was found dead," Kate said. "Forrest Frazier's attorney, who coincidentally was also just found dead."

Elise put down the T-shirt and turned to Kate. "Come again? Forrest Frazier is dead?"

"Murdered."

"What?" Elise gasped, bringing a hand to her mouth. "How? When?"

"That not important right now." Kate stepped next to her. Doc leaped out of her arms, onto the bed, and sniffed the clothing Elise was folding. Kate watched him as she spoke. "I think your husband is involved in both murders, and I think the attorney's daughter downstairs is thinking the same thing. She's up to something."

"You think Redd murdered those men?" She waved Doc away from the shirt and sweatpants and returned to folding them.

Kate took the T-shirt from her hands. "She's Jasper Wade's daughter," she said. "Her father was murdered. If I figured it out, if I put the pieces together, you know she did too."

Elise smiled and shook her head. "Redd and I don't blame Jasper Wade or Forrest Frazier. We blame ..." She mumbled and went back to folding. "Never mind."

Kate put her hands on her hips. "If you have something to say to me, say it."

Thunder rocked the house, rattling the walls.

Elise didn't seem to notice. "What's the point of saying anything. You only hear what you want to hear, and you do anything you want, no matter who it hurts."

"And here we are." Kate folded her arms. Doc jumped to the floor and scrambled under the bed.

Elise poked her sister. "You shouldn't have taken him out that night … and to a bar?"

"It was a brewhouse, and I woulda got him back safe and sound."

"He shoulda been home, safe and sound, in the first place." Elise leaned toward her sister, getting in her face.

Kate bent forward, inching closer to Elise. "I told you not to drive home mad. And do you remember the last thing you said to me before the crash?" Kate waited for her to answer. "Do you?"

"I'm not listening to this." Elise turned away.

Kate grabbed her arm and swung her back around. "You told me I could've gotten him killed. But you know what, Elise, *you* got him killed."

"Shut up!" Elise screamed at her and covered her ears.

Kate continued. "*You* were driving. *You* were behind the wheel. *You* killed him, Elise. Not Redd. Not me. You, Elise. You killed him."

"Stop it!" Elise moved away from the bed, toward the corner of the room, her back turned.

"He's dead!" Kate stepped toward her. "And no matter how many hours you sit locked in his room or how many times you read that silly children's book, he's never coming—"

A crash rang out from the hallway, and Kate turned her head toward the door. Doc dashed out from under the bed to a chair. He rose on his haunches, nose twitching.

Elise said, "That came from Noah's room."

Together, they headed into the hallway. A light came from Noah's bedroom. They entered and found Olivia standing by the mattress over the window. Rain and wind blew in through the broken glass, but she seemed unaffected. She held the wet bed sheets in her hands.

"What are you doing in here?" Elise demanded.

Olivia locked eyes with her and smiled.

* * *

In the dark locker room, Trace held his wife's hand as she screamed through the contractions. Linus knelt by her side. Travel Agent kept a flashlight focused on them.

Nellie squeezed her eyes shut, her face clenching. When she relaxed, she reached for Trace's arm and tried to lift herself up.

"What are you doing?" Trace said. He tried to hold her back.

"Got to get up." She sounded winded and struggled to speak. "Help me. Please."

With Trace's help, she got to her feet. She took a couple of steps, her hands clutching her lower back. Leaving the shower, Trace and Linus walked with her on either side.

"I wish we had something for the pain," Trace said.

Jared and Jensen returned, their arms loaded with boxes. They set them down on a bench in front of a wall of lockers.

"I found hydrogen peroxide and towels," Jared said. He lifted a pair of scissors from the box. "I didn't know what else we might need."

Jensen nodded at the scissors in Jared's hand. "Whad'ya think he's gonna do with those? Cut the baby out?"

Jared shook his head. "Now, why you gotta go and say something like that?"

"Those are for arts and crafts." Jensen grabbed the scissors. "They can't perform a C-section with those."

"They're not gonna perform a C-section." Jared grabbed them back.

"Not with those scissors, they're not!" Jensen took the scissors and tossed them back in the box.

Trace focused solely on Nellie, who was moving side to side, clearly trying to find a position that would bring her any relief. She was near the towel rack when the next pain knocked her to the floor. She grasped the rack for support, bringing a pile of towels down with her. Trace fell to the floor beside her.

She let out a long, shrill scream.

Putting an arm around her, he folded himself against her and held her. He cradled her head in his lap. He didn't know what else to do. When her scream subsided, she curled her body and pressed her face into the curve of his arm. She gulped a breath, then stiffened as if holding in another agonizing cry from deep within her body. She pressed her arms across her abdomen, bracing for what was coming. It came anyway.

"Let it out," he whispered in her ear, and she screamed.

He felt as if his own body was splitting open alongside hers, and he clenched his jaw to meet the pain. He held tight to her, and when the latest contraction finally passed, she collapsed in his arms. Her head fell against his chest. Her hair was wet and matted, her pale face drenched in sweat.

"Chief," Linus said, kneeling beside Nellie's legs. "You better get over here."

Trace lifted Nellie's head and moved. Jared took his place, cradling her head in his lap. Trace moved to Nellie's legs as another contraction seized her. She screamed—an unbearable shriek that echoed through the locker room.

Trace positioned between her legs. He saw the head.

"Keep pushing," Linus said. "You're doing fine. Keep pushing."

Nellie strained her body and screamed. Her flesh ripped. Then out it came, a gangly thing covered in blood.

"I've got it," Trace said. "I've got it." He lifted the tiny body, shrunken and dark, and cradled it in his arms. "Why's it so blue?" he said, looking at Travel Agent and then down at the newborn. Panic rose in his voice. The baby didn't move. "Is it supposed to be blue? Is it okay?"

The baby's head turned toward Trace and faced him with the largest, most startled eyes he'd ever seen. Their eyes locked, and he immediately thought, I know you.

The baby let out a cry.

"Okay, he's crying," he said. "We're good. He's crying."

He rushed to Nellie's side.

"Open your eyes," he whispered to his wife. "Open your eyes, Nellie. You gotta see this."

Nellie squinted and stretched out her arms as Trace gently handed the baby to her. He cut the cord and then broke down, sobbing. He was suddenly, officially, a dad.

"It's a girl," Nellie said. "It's a girl."

Tears streamed down his face. "A girl?" He hadn't even noticed in all the excitement. "A baby girl?"

She nodded.

Trace turned to the crowd gathered in the locker room and yelled, "It's a girl!"

A loud cheer rang out that carried through the entire gymnasium. So loud, in fact, it drowned out the raging storm.

* * *

Kate raised the lantern and entered Noah's dark bedroom. "What are you doing in here?" she asked.

Olivia looked up from the mattress pressed against the window. It shuddered and flapped in the wind. She turned toward Elise, standing back in the doorway. "You have a little boy?"

"I did." Elise's voice choked.

Kate stepped in front of her sister, protecting her. "We already covered that," she said. "Now go back downstairs. Doogie will be back in a minute with your son."

"I should've never given him up." Olivia touched the framed pictures on the dresser. Her hair fluttered in the wind. "Is this your Noah?"

"Get out of this room." Kate clenched her fists and took a threatening step forward. She wished she still had her gun.

"He was a cute little boy." Olivia put down the photo and picked up the sheets again. She brought them to her face and inhaled.

Elise straightened and clenched her fists. "Get out of this room!"

Kate moved to the window, closer to Olivia. "We're not going to ask you again."

"What happened?" Olivia picked up a stuffed dinosaur from the discarded animals scattered on the floor. She turned toward Elise. "What did you do to him?"

"Excuse me?" Elise snatched the dino from her hands.

"I mean, it's just so awful," Olivia said. "He was so young. Same age as *my* Noah."

"Normally, I like insane people, especially the criminally insane." Elise set the dino on the dresser. "But you're starting to look like a woman who no longer wants her front teeth."

"Don't make me forcibly remove you," Kate said. "You know I'm in law enforcement."

Olivia stared at her for several seconds, unblinking, and then smiled. "I'm sorry. I didn't mean any harm."

"Doogie will be back any moment," Elise offered and then added, "with your son."

"No …." Olivia ran a hand through the wet curls cascading around her shoulders. The wind coming through the broken window howled and disturbed the mattress again. "No," she said, her eyes growing intense. "He won't."

CHAPTER THIRTY-EIGHT

Doogie drove the Suburban through the heavy downpour, leaving the neighborhood. He turned onto the road leading to downtown and came to a green hatchback on the side of the road with its hazards flashing. He pulled up next to it and hopped out of the vehicle. His flashlight cut through the dark. Sloshing from puddle to puddle, he raced to the ugly little car. Water spilled from the brim of his hat. He shined the flashlight through the glass. Peered inside. Nothing. He opened the driver's side door.

A blinding white burst of lightning lit the car interior for a second, leaving him cringing, blinded. His eyes adjusted to the blackness, then he jammed them shut as a second roaring explosion of thunder rocked the vehicle, violently rattling the car windows, making him think the glass might shatter. As he opened his eyes again, another, steadier, rumble assailed the empty interior. The child was gone.

A crumpled stuffed animal lay discarded in the passenger seat. He reached into the car and picked it up. It was a plush gray body, possibly a hefty hippo or maybe an elephant. Its innards, tufts of white stuffing, spilled from the neck.

He tossed the headless body on the seat and glanced out of the drenched windshield, down the street. A solid wall of rain came down vertically, no wind at the moment, but the most torrential rain he could remember. He slipped into the hatchback and shut the door.

No child should be out in this, he thought. Sitting behind the steering wheel, he listened to rain beat down on the roof and tried to think of where the kid might have gone. Wherever he was, he hoped he was all right.

* * *

Kate and Elise escorted Olivia out of Noah's bedroom and down the staircase. Kate held the lantern to lead the way. Doc darted out of the bedroom after them, leaning to the right as he hopped down the steps.

"What do you mean, he won't find your son?" Kate demanded as they reached the ground floor. "What's going on?"

Olivia moved past her through the parlor. "I didn't mean anything. We're just stressed, right?" she said as she entered the kitchen. "I mean, with the storm and everything."

"I don't trust you," Kate said.

Olivia came to the table where the candle still burned, paused, and flipped around toward Elise. "So why won't you tell me what happened to little Noah?"

Elise looked away. "I don't like to talk about it."

"Maybe it'll help," Olivia said. "Clear your conscience."

Kate stepped between Olivia and her sister. "Stop it," she said. "We'd ask you to leave, but there's a hurricane out there. As soon as it passes, as soon as the roads clear, I want you to leave."

Elise pushed Kate aside and placed her hands on her hips. Her eyes teared as she spoke. "My son died in a car crash."

"I see." Olivia seemed to think about it for several seconds. "Where'd it happen?"

Pain flashed across Elise's face, and she brought a hand to her mouth.

"Look." Kate pointed at Olivia. "Whatever you're fishing for, you're not gonna find it here. Game over."

Olivia brushed Kate's hand away and focused on Elise. "I asked you a question. Where was the accident that killed your son?"

Elise turned away. She didn't answer.

Olivia didn't back down. "I heard you and your sister talking in the bedroom. It sounds like you ki—"

"That's enough!" Kate yelled.

Olivia raised her voice at Elise. "Noah died, and I want to know what happened."

Kate grabbed Olivia's arms and whipped her around to face her. "You know as well as I do what happened. Your father represented the drunk who hit my sister, who killed my nephew."

Olivia broke free of Kate's grip and took a step back. She ran a hand through her hair as if composing herself. "Your nephew," she said calmly, quietly. "Are you sure he was your nephew?"

Kate couldn't take another second. "What is that supposed to mean?" She was done with this conversation. One more word, and she would kick that woman out the front door on her ass, storm or no storm.

"We were sideswiped coming off the Causeway," Elise replied in a low, tortured voice. Her eyes darkened with pain. "Forrest Frazier's car veered into our lane, struck us head-on."

Olivia seemed to think about it a second. "And Forrest Frazier, he'd been drinking?"

Kate swung around. "You already know the answer to that!"

Elise raised a hand, hushing her sister. Her face clouded with uneasiness. "Yes, he'd been drinking."

"I'm sorry," Olivia said. A chilled silence surrounded them. No rain. No wind. Just an unnatural hush. Finally, Olivia continued. "It's just—"

She stopped talking as the thumping rain returned.

"Just what?" Elise said, raising her voice.

Olivia's eyes glistened with tears. She glanced at Kate, then at Elise. She smiled and asked, "Did he know he was adopted?"

"What?" Elise's body shook as if she was suddenly stricken with nausea. "What'd you say?"

Olivia laughed. "Well, did he? Did your little Noah know he was adopted?"

"Okay, that's enough." Kate lunged forward and grabbed Olivia by the arm. Storm be damned, she'd had enough.

* * *

Hugging the headless stuffed animal close to his chest, Doogie exited the abandoned hatchback and braved the wind and rain. He shined his flashlight over the pavement and splashed through the puddles toward the Suburban.

A lightning strike highlighted a figure standing ahead of him in the street. A silhouette of a man wearing a large hat. Another lightning flash, and he saw it was a mask—an elephant head.

Doogie dropped the headless stuffed elephant body.

* * *

Kate bolted across the kitchen and grabbed Olivia's arm. Olivia resisted her.

Elise broke them up. "What'd you say?"

Olivia ran a hand through her blonde curls. Her hair was drying, and she flipped a strand from her face. Her eyes narrowed. "He was adopted, right? Did you tell him?"

"How--" Elise's mouth fell open. "How did you—what?"

Olivia said, "Did you ever tell him the truth? You weren't his mother. Did you tell him that?"

Kate yanked Olivia out of the kitchen. "You need to leave. Now."

Olivia turned her head to scream back to Elise. "Or did you lie to him?"

Kate pushed Olivia into the parlor. "I don't care if it's a category five out there; get out of this house."

Olivia resisted and screamed, "It's not good to lie to children, Elise. The truth always comes out."

Kate gripped Olivia's arm and struggled to open the front door. "Get out. Leave."

She forced Olivia through the doorway and pushed her outside.

Olivia fell onto the slick front porch into the rain. Elise joined Kate at the threshold of the front door. They watched Olivia stumble off the porch and stagger into the yard. She struggled to stand in the downpour. Shaking, she turned and looked back at them.

"It's not good to lie, Elise! It's not good to lie!" she cried out, her voice drowned by the wind and rain.

A powerful gust knocked her down. She screamed as it carried her away.

Elise slammed the door shut and locked it.

Kate ran to her iPhone lying on the end table in the living room. Still no service. She returned to the front door and looked through the peephole onto the porch. She didn't see Olivia anywhere. She wished the windows weren't covered so she could look outside.

"I'm worried about Doogie," Elise said. She sat on the couch and wrapped her arms around her legs.

"I know." Kate took a seat beside her. "Me too."

"What do you think that woman wanted?"

Something banged against the door. The sisters jumped, startled. Kate got up and rushed to the door, looked through the peephole. Nothing but sheets of rain. Debris blew all around, and she realized something heavy must've hit the side of the house. The wind intensified. She backed away and stood in the middle of the room, wondering how much more the roof could take. For two or three long minutes, the rain came down, the sound of it riveting her to the spot.

Elise stepped beside her and took her hand. "Doogie is out there."

Kate shook her head and returned to the kitchen. Elise followed. Kate grabbed the lantern from the table.

"And that woman is out there too," Elise said.

"I know," Kate answered. She raised the lantern, shrinking back the shadows. She returned to the parlor and opened the closet. She removed a raincoat. Elise stepped beside her, and Kate handed her one too.

She opened the door. The lantern swung wildly in her hand. The wind was so strong that it pulled the door away from her and slammed it against the exterior wall. She held her breath. Elise gripped her hand, and she let it out.

Doc scrambled out from under the couch and jumped up onto Kate's pant leg. He climbed up her body and snuggled under her thick raincoat. She could feel him clinging to her back.

She looked over at Elise and forced a smile.

Elise squeezed her hand. "Let's do this," she said. "But don't think this makes us friends."

Kate nodded her understanding.

Together, they left the house and stepped into the hurricane.

CHAPTER THIRTY-NINE

Kate and Elise stepped off the front porch, moving across the lawn through the driving rain, holding hands. Doc clung to Kate's back, beneath her raincoat. She tried to keep the lantern low as the wind whipped from side to side. They headed for the driveway.

Rain fell in sheets, and the wind slapped so hard that it left a burning sensation on Kate's skin. Brief flashes of lightning illuminated the flooded yard and the raging waters rushing down the driveway. Palm trees thrashed in the wind. The intensity frightened her. She didn't have a choice, though. Their father was out there, somewhere, in this storm.

Halfway down the driveway, Elise planted her feet and pushed against Kate's side. "It's getting worse!" The wind took her voice.

Kate tightened her grip on her sister's hand.

The lantern swayed violently, tossing streams of weak light ahead of them. For better balance, they let go of each other and sloshed to the center of the street, the highest point. It didn't help much. They still splashed through an ever-rising flow of water. In every direction, debris shattered the windows of surrounding houses. Glass breaking and blowing in the wind competed with the rolling thunder.

They waded down the street, past the Needermans' dolphin mailbox, which now leaned to the right. They turned onto another road and slogged to the edge of the neighborhood.

Doc huddled on Kate's right shoulder, under her coat. He remained unexpectedly calm.

Retaking Elise's hand, Kate followed the street. She led the way, staggering, aiming the lantern light on the deep puddles pooling along the curb. Dripping with sweat and rainwater, they wandered for half an hour. Wind and rain came in waves, intensifying, then letting up for a few minutes before raring up again. Puddles turned into angry rivers that washed over their waterlogged shoes.

Sloshing forward, Kate finally saw two blurry objects in the street ahead: the Suburban with its hazard lights flashing and an old green Chevy hatchback parked in front of it. She couldn't tell if there was anyone in the vehicles.

Letting go of Elise, Kate rushed to the Suburban. Doc poked his head out from under her coat, and she could feel his warm furry face on her neck. A second in the weather, and he ducked back under the collar for cover. She told him to be still and peered through the windows, cupping her hands above her brows to shield her eyes from the rain. The Suburban was empty. No keys in the ignition. She waded over to the hatchback. No one there either. Turning, she raised the lantern to scan the street and surrounding houses. She yelled for Doogie. He didn't answer.

Elise sloshed into the middle of the street between the two vehicles, where a soggy stuffed animal lay in a puddle on the pavement. She grasped a saturated leg and held the headless body for Kate to see. It looked like an elephant body.

"What have they done to Mr. Belvedere?" Elise screamed. She shook the headless elephant.

Kate's eyes widened. Behind her sister, a figure moved down the street, closing in on them. She could barely make him out through the rain. At first, she thought it was Doogie and waved to him. He was twenty yards away. And approaching. Fast.

A flash of lightning revealed something else.

Mr. Belvedere.

The man coming toward them wore Mr. Belvedere's head.

Kate gasped. She screamed, "Elise!"

Elise's head turned, and she dropped the headless stuffed animal.

The elephant man ran toward them. Fifteen yards. Fourteen. Thirteen.

Elise didn't move. She seemed frozen.

Kate ran to her, grabbed her arm, and pulled her out of the street. They scrambled toward a large house. Doc's one claw dug into her shoulder. She ignored the pain.

They made it to the house. Boards covered the windows and doors. The sisters rounded the corner. Headed to an expansive backyard that ended into the raging Gulf waters. Elise seemed mesmerized by the crashing waves, and she hesitated. Kate yanked her arm, telling her to move.

They made it to the beach. Angry swells splashed them as they sprinted as fast as they could in the wet sand, passing empty houses and flooded yards. Kate pointed toward a black structure in the distance. It looked like a beached whale lying on its side. When they got closer, she saw it was an overturned sailboat.

They ran to it and scrambled inside the hull. Kate turned off the lantern. Darkness hid them.

"See if there's anything we can use to defend ourselves," Kate said, finding a dry spot. She pulled Doc from her shoulder and checked to make sure he was alright. He looked wet but no worse for the wear. She set him down and felt her shoulder to see if it was bleeding. His little claw had dug into her pretty tight.

"Anything we can use for a weapon?" she asked, finding no sign of blood. Elise opened a tackle box and pulled out a fishing knife. Kate found a fire extinguisher next to her leg, but it was unexpectedly light, and she discarded it. The metal container banged against the deck, and the sisters froze.

"You think he heard that?" Elise whispered.

Kate peeked over the edge. The rain seemed to let up a little, and she could see the elephant man in the distance. He trudged along the beach, heading in their direction. She waited for him to pass and then sat down again in the hull.

Thunder boomed, rocking the boat.

Elise trembled, and it reflected in her voice. "Who is that?"

"I don't know," Kate whispered.

Elise rubbed her shoulders and sat beside Kate. "What do you think happened to Doogie?" she asked.

Kate didn't answer.

For the moment, they stayed where they were, hugging their knees inside the dark hull of the boat. Not able to wait any longer, Kate glanced over the side. She didn't see him. Ducking back inside, she whistled for Doc. The squirrel jumped onto her shoulder, and she picked him up. She placed him carefully into the inner pocket of the raincoat. He fit in snuggly, and she closed the flap.

Elise stood. "Are we leaving?"

"We can't stay here," Kate answered. "He'll figure it out sooner or later." She grabbed the lantern. With a splash, she was in the shallow water and back on the beach. She looked at Elise. "I think he's gone."

Elise joined her and handed her the knife.

Kate held it in her hand. "If we can make it into town, we can get a weapon from the Bear's Den."

Elise shook her head. "We can't walk to town in this storm."

"I don't think we have a choice. We can't go back to The Bluegill," Kate said. She slipped the knife between her belt and the waist of her jeans. The rain fell harder now, and the wind returned. A wave of apprehension swept through her as the churning blackness stretched ahead. In lightning flashes, she could make out the downtown skyline.

With a loud clap of thunder, the rain intensified.

"Okay . . ." Elise squinted her eyes. Water collected on her lashes. "I guess it's now or never."

"C'mon. It's not that far," Kate said, raising the lantern to lead the way.

Rain pelted them as they ran in the opposite direction along the beach.

The rain came in waves, falling heavy, then letting up, then dumping on them again. After what seemed like an hour of slogging across the dunes, Kate saw something ahead: a framework of bleached wood rising from the beach.

"It's the boardwalk," Elise said, pointing. "We're almost in town."

A lightning flash in the distance lit the walkway, and Kate scrambled to it. She climbed onto the boardwalk then turned to give Elise a hand. They were too exhausted to run. Instead, they walked in silence. The downtown buildings loomed larger, closer.

They came to the end of the boardwalk, where the dark bait shops and beach supply stores were located. Of course, the windows and doors were boarded over. A sidewalk wound along the street, and they followed it, hand in hand, into downtown.

The Bear's Den on Main Street looked as foreboding as the buildings around it but without storm shutters. The wind had ripped the plywood away and shattered a window. They climbed through it, careful not to cut themselves on the jagged shards of glass, and entered the building, shivering in the dark. Drenched but safe.

Kate set the lantern down and stripped off her raincoat. Doc scrambled out of her pocket and stood on top of the counter. Broken glass crunched beneath her shoes with every step.

"Now what?" Elise asked.

Kate grabbed the lantern and led Elise through the narrow hallway to the back. She shined the light on the gun rack. Empty.

Elise's brows drew together in an agonized expression. "We need something more than a fishing knife."

Kate didn't answer. She removed the knife from the waistband of her jeans. "Well, it's all we have."

She placed the knife on the floor. Within the glow of the lantern light, they sat for an hour and listened to the rain and wind. Doc joined them and curled up in Kate's lap. She scratched his head, and it calmed her. For the moment, it felt like the immediate danger was over.

Elise interrupted the quiet. "I need to know something," she said. "Why'd you come to get me?"

Kate glanced at her. Old feelings and memories flooded back, catching her off guard. "Are you kidding?" she asked with a smirk. "I'm your big sister."

"But you disappeared for a whole year on me. You were my big sister then, too."

"At Noah's funeral, you told me to leave," Kate said. "You said you never wanted to see me again."

"I was mad and hurt. But I didn't mean it."

"I know." Kate swallowed a couple of times before she could speak. "And then you didn't even visit me in the hospital or come check on me when I got out."

"That was wrong. I should've gone to visit you when you got shot. I wanted to." Her voice dopped and sounded tinged with guilt. "I'm just surprised after all that; you still came to see me."

Kate cleared her throat. "Redd kept pestering me. Then your psychiatrist called."

"So that's why you showed up?" Elise sounded insulted. "Because my head shrink asked you to?"

"I didn't think you wanted anything to do with me," Kate said. "I thought you hated me."

"What you're saying is, you didn't want to see me?" Elise stood and placed her hands on her hips.

Kate looked up at her. "I'm not saying that at all."

"Yes. You are," Elise said. "That's exactly what you're saying."

Kate got to her feet, and Doc jumped to the floor. She leaned toward Elsie and poked her in the chest. "You know, your whole life, you swing from one mood to the next. You're a psychopath; you know that? You're certifiably psychotic."

"And my whole life, you've tried to hold me back. You're jealous of me."

"Jealous?" Kate couldn't believe what she was hearing.

"Yes, jealous," Elise said. She walked out of the back room. Kate followed her through the dark hallway as Elise continued her rant. "You were jealous that Mother left me The Bluegill, and you were jealous that I got married, and you were jealous when we were approved for the adoption."

"Jealous?" Kate let out a sarcastic laugh. They stopped in the lobby, facing each other in the dark. The wind coming through the broken window blew their hair, and Kate raised her voice over it. "I knew coming to see you was a mistake," she said. "I knew there was no point in trying to rebuild our relationship."

"Then your instincts were right. I *do* hate you." Elise waved her arms as she spoke. "I told you I never wanted to see you again. Did you think I didn't mean it?"

"Of course you meant it. That's why I stayed away from you for the last year. And I should've never come back."

"Right. You shouldn't have. We've been bad for each other our entire lives." Elise turned and headed for the front door. Glass shards crunched under her feet.

Kate ran to her and grabbed her arm, stopping her. "Where are you going?"

"As far away from you as I can get." Elise swung her arm to break Kate's grip.

"We need to stay together," Kate said. "That psycho's still out there, and as psychotic as you can be, he's got you beat by a bloody mile."

"No," Elise said. "This is it. Our relationship ends here. From this moment on, we are no longer sisters." She turned back toward the door.

Kate called after her.

"I'm not listening," Elise yelled. She turned the deadbolt on the front door.

"Okay, you're right." Kate stopped her, saying, "Noah's death was my fault. He's dead because of me. And I guess, maybe, that's why I stayed away too."

A cold, congested expression settled on Elise's face. "Go on."

"I knew it was my fault. I've always known," Kate said. "Maybe you were driving. Maybe Redd's call distracted you. Maybe Forrest Frazier, the bastard that he was, was drunk and should never have been on the road in the first place, but I'm the one who put that terrible night in motion."

Elise pressed her head against the glass door.

Kate continued. "I shouldn't have taken Noah out of the house that night. If I hadn't done that, he'd still be here."

Elise closed her eyes and said nothing.

"So, you're right." Kate turned away. "You have every right to hate me. It was my fault, and I have to live with that."

"You're damn right; it was your fault," Elise said, turning from the door. "And I will never forgiv—"

Something hit the door with a loud bang. Elise jumped back.

Lightning flashed again, highlighting a silhouetted figure on the other side of the glass.

Kate froze and grabbed Elise's arm. "He's here," she said.

CHAPTER FORTY

Kate couldn't believe her eyes. The masked psycho stood there on the other side of the glass door, staring in. The plush elephant head looked soaked and grotesque. He gripped a baseball bat with both hands.

"No." Elise wiped her cheeks. She stuttered under her breath, "N-no, p-please… No."

Kate sprang forward to the door and turned the deadbolt just as the masked man hit the glass again with the bat, cracking it. The sound reverberated through the room. Kate grabbed Elise and pulled her away from the door. They stepped backward toward the reception desk. Elise seemed transfixed, her eyes wide, her hand to her mouth.

The elephant man moved to the broken window. Kate pulled Elise backward into the narrow hallway. They fled, rounding the corner into the back room as she heard the crunch of glass behind her. He had entered the building was coming after them. She made it to the back room and killed the lantern, plunging them into darkness.

Her hand searched the floor for the knife. She couldn't find it. It was too dark to see. They were out of time. She grabbed Elise's arm. Yanked her forward across the room. They returned to the dark hallway and slipped into Trace's office, among the clutter of baby gifts and boxes. Kate bumped into the rocking horse. She wanted to shout in pain but shook it off and pulled Elise to the desk. A hiding place. They slipped behind it. Kate held her breath as she stopped the rocking horse from moving and eased a box of files over to further hide them.

She suddenly thought about Doc. He wasn't there, and she didn't know where he'd scampered off to.

"Did he see us?" Elise whispered, trembling.

"Shhhhh." Kate squeezed Elise's arm to hush her. The space beneath the desk was cramped. They huddled together, wedged between the rolling chair and the wall.

Kate listened.

Heavy boots thumped on the tile floor in the hallway. She wished she'd shut the office door. He entered the room. She prayed he didn't have a flashlight.

His voice pierced the quiet darkness. "I know you're in here."

The floor creaked under his boots.

They slipped deeper into the void under the desk.

The footsteps grew louder. Moved closer. If he didn't have a flashlight, he might not see them. That would be their only hope.

"Elise?" The voice sounded muffled under the mask. "I know you're here. Don't make me look for you." He put the next words into the silence carefully, one syllable at a time. "You're only making it worse . . . when I find you."

The rocking horse moved.

Kate sensed it more than saw it.

She looked around. Boxes surrounded them. Maybe she could hit him with a file folder. She wished she knew where Doc was. She wished she had the knife. She needed something. Anything. Her fingertips brushed the frilly lace of a baby dress. Nothing she could use to defend them, if it came to that—*when* it came to that.

Elise crouched beside her, breathing heavily. Breathing loud.

The footsteps halted.

Elise bumped the edge of the desk.

The man's boots scraped the tile as if he'd whirled around. He stood directly on the other side of the desk.

"There you are!"

His voice came out of a hush so clear that it struck Kate cold. She wondered if he'd removed the elephant mask.

A strange clicking followed. A wild tapping, as if little paws were scuttling across the floor. The man screamed with pain.

Doc?

Unseen, yet heard, the squirrel screeched loudly. A crash shattered the stillness. Boxes fell, their contents spilling. The rocking horse hit the floor. A sharp clang lingered in the dark, and Kate realized he'd kicked the stroller. It rolled across the tile, clattering.

Kate rose from under the desk. Elise slid out behind her. Her eyes had adjusted to the darkness enough to see the man scream and flail his arms.

She stopped moving, and Elise bumped into her. Kate jumped at a thud as Doc's furry body hit her square in the chest. He bounced off her and disappeared into the dark.

The man moved in front of them, pinning them.

"There you are," he said. He flipped on a flashlight.

She couldn't see his face for the glare.

He shifted the beam onto Elise. Highlighted her torn white shirt. Traveled up and fixed on her face.

Kate watched as Elise froze. She shuddered, shaking, asking, "Who are you?"

The plush elephant head covered his face again and muffled his voice. "His little body looked battered and bloody," he said. "As if someone picked up a baseball bat and beat the life out of him."

If he was aware of Kate, he gave no sign. Instead, he focused solely on Elise and said again, "His little body looked battered and bloody as if someone picked up a baseball bat and beat the life out of him."

Elise shook her head. "Please …."

He repeated, "His little body looked battered and bloody as if someone picked up a baseball bat and beat the life out of him."

Elise cried, "Please!" Sobbing, she bunched her hands into fists. He dropped the flashlight and gripped the bat with both hands.

Kate's back pressed against the wall. The top of her head hit something cold. Metallic. She lifted a hand and felt the cold steel shaft of White Fang. She grabbed the putter. Tore it from the wall. Gripped it with both hands and swung. The blunt blade struck him in the face.

For a second, nothing happened.

She wondered if the plush mask had absorbed the blow.

She stood frozen, trapped in an accidental freeze-frame, thinking, God, oh God! She could hear Elise breathing.

The bat hit the floor. A piercing shriek ripped from his throat, and he dropped to his knees. Ripped off the mask. Clutched his face. His foot kicked the flashlight and spun it across the room.

Kate threw down the club and picked up the flashlight. Now she saw the man curled up on the floor, quivering, crying, with his hands covering his bloody face.

She'd broken his nose.

No time to gloat, she grabbed her sister's arm. "We need to go."

"I want to see who it is," Elise said, fighting Kate's grip.

"We need to go," Kate repeated, "Now."

"Not yet." Elise moved closer to the man hunched over on the floor. "I need to know," she said.

Kate pulled her away. They backed out of the office and into the hallway. She swept the light across the floor. Where was Doc? She couldn't find Doc.

"C'mon," Elise said. "What are you looking for?"

Kate shined the light from wall to wall. The back exit door came into view. She turned again and shined the light behind them, down the hallway.

"C'mon," Elise said again.

Kate lowered the light. They headed for the exit. Doc scrambled after them. He leaped onto Kate's leg as she flung open the door. She picked him up and set him on her shoulder. Outside, she saw the dock, but the police boats weren't there. She remembered Jared and Jensen tied them off in the neighborhoods where they would be accessible after the storm passed.

In the rain and wind again, Kate turned off the telltale flashlight and threw the batteries on the plank. They vanished in a rush of water. From that point forward, as much as it was an enemy, the darkness was a friend. Paralleling the flooded alleyway along the back of the buildings, Kate and Elise ran north until rounding a corner that opened onto Main Street.

They maneuvered between broken tree limbs, climbed over downed light poles, and avoided blowing trash and unidentifiable wreckage. The storefronts were boarded up. Windows that were exposed were now gaping mouths of jagged glass. Roofs were gone. Flying debris crashed everywhere around them.

Elise stopped and spun slowly, her eyes squinting against the rain. "There's got to be somewhere we can hide," she yelled over the wind.

Kate ran ahead of her, Doc clinging to her shoulder. "Keep moving! We can't stay here."

Elise caught up to her. "We've gotta get out of the weather. We've gotta hide."

Kate paused, looked around, then started running again. "We can't stay in town. He'll find us here."

Sighing, Elise followed.

Continuing along the sidewalk, Kate leaned against a brick building to catch her breath. Shivering, Elise came up next to her. Doc moved from her left shoulder to her right. Even beyond exhaustion, they plunged away from the sidewalk without any idea where they were going--no plan except to try and make it to morning.

All the while, the heavy rains blinded them. It reminded Kate the floodwaters were coming. And she and her sister were trapped there. No matter where they ran, no matter where they hid, they wouldn't escape the coming flood.

Then she noticed it: a brilliant beam of light.

In the distance, the Widow Rock Lighthouse, a beacon meant to guide boats entering the bay through darkness and fog, came to life.

CHAPTER FORTY-ONE

The winds roared as Kate ran across the beach toward the rocky shore beneath the lighthouse. Elise followed, struggling to keep up. Doc chirped, hanging on to her shoulder, and she could feel his single little hand gripping her shirt.

Scattered wood and seaweed strewn along the beach became visible in the lightning flashes, like wispy carcasses along the ground. When the sisters came to the rocks, they slowed and climbed over them. Furious waves broke against the large stones, and Kate slipped but regained her balance.

"Are you okay?" Elise called back to her.

Kate motioned for her to keep moving.

With the next lightning strike, Kate saw a beached sailboat ahead, its hull eviscerated against the rocks. They scaled the ripped fiberglass fragments and waited. Another bolt of lightning, and this time Kate had a better vantage point to thoroughly search the rocks that led up from the beach.

They continued to climb. Hand over fist, they surmounted the large, slippery boulders toward the top. When they reached flat ground, Kate saw the remains of Forrest Frazier's billboard. The poster had shredded, and strips of his face flapped in the wind like a dozen skinny flags. She scrambled for the lighthouse yard, weaving through an opening in the wrought-iron perimeter fence. Elise kept pace one step behind.

They walked forward wearily, together, and once they reached the lighthouse, they stood at the base, looking up. The light shined brilliant above them, casting a beam against the black clouds. Kate opened the entry door and waited for the next burst of lightning to illuminate the interior. Together, they entered.

Once out of the wind and rain, Doc jumped from Kate's shoulder to the floor. He raised up on his hind legs, nose twitching, checking out the dark surroundings.

Nothing had changed. Nothing looked out of place. The modest efficiency was as filthy as ever. A ratty couch sat against the far wall, in front of an old television set. Elise walked to the sleeping bag in the corner. She picked up an empty can of beans and then the baby monitor. Kate stepped beside her.

"Do you think Doogie's here?" Elise whispered.

"If he is, then he's up there." Kate pointed upward, where the staircase corkscrewed into the lantern chamber. Light came from that upstairs landing. She started toward the stairs when Elise grabbed her hand, stopping her.

"I need to say something," Elise said.

"Save it." Kate ascended a couple of steps. Elise stopped her.

"No, it can't wait," Elise said. "I shouldn't have blamed you. It wasn't your fault, and I know that. It was my fault."

"We don't have time—"

Elise didn't let her finish. "We may be out of time," she said. "If this is my last opportunity to say this, then I need to tell you. I directed my anger at you, and that was wrong. It was my job to protect Noah, and I failed. I failed him. Not you."

Kate came back down the steps and embraced her sister. "You were a good mother, and he loved you and knew that you loved him. You made him happy," she whispered. "Forrest Frazier took him away from us. Don't you ever forget that. Forrest Fraser did. And now he's dead."

"He's dead. He's really dead." Elise tightened her embrace on Kate. "And Noah is really gone."

Kate let her go.

Around them, the whole structure creaked, and Doc jumped up to Kate's shoulder. He chirped several times as if telling them something. A warning voice whispered in her head.

"Hello?" Kate called up the circular staircase. Her voice echoed.

The wind howled and whistled through the interior, and they heard a soft roar like a nearby train passing. Kate knew instantly.

The floodwater.

The soft roar turned violent. They looked out the open doorway and saw the entire beach disappear beneath a cloak of rippling blackness. With an earsplitting crash, seawater rushed in. It swamped the ground floor, and they stood in cold water rising to their knees.

Kate escaped up the staircase. Elise ran a step behind her.

Halfway up, Kate looked back. The water steadily rose. Furniture disappeared underwater as trash swirled on the surface. She hurried up the spiral staircase.

Olivia stood there at the top, waiting.

Elise screamed as the woman cracked Kate over the head, knocking her out.

* * *

Kate moaned and flinched, still immersed in the desolate haze of semiconsciousness. She tried to remember where she'd been, what she'd been doing before her body succumbed to this dreadful state of fatigue and confusion.

If she could just open her eyes … if she could manage to raise her head and get her bearings. But her motor system bluntly refused to obey, causing her to focus on the dull, throbbing ache that penetrated the entire length of her head, neck, and shoulders.

I must be asleep, she thought, reaching down instinctively for the blankets at her feet. She discovered, instead, thin, coarse rope wrapped around her wrists.

As her mind began the slow, tenuous journey back to reality, she realized that she was inside and suddenly found it necessary to distinguish between the crack of the wind in her ears and the flutter of her heartbeat.

Somewhere—far away—a voice called her name.

She couldn't comprehend the words, only the tone. It invaded her sleep so stealthily that it seemed perfectly natural within the dreamscape. The voice seemed so familiar, almost friendly. Then recognition hurdled her into consciousness.

Kate opened her eyes. A blurry figure stood over her, touching her face. Gradually, it came into view. The voice grew louder.

"It looks like she's waking up."

A male was speaking.

"What are we going to do with them?"

Now a female spoke.

The room came into focus. She was sitting on the floor, hands tied. Her sister beside her. The Elephant Man stood in the corner. The mask looked tattered and frayed. The gray fur clumped in patches. Other parts were matted with dried blood. He held the baseball bat in one hand and a small card in the other. He waved it.

A photograph.

The one of Elise and Noah with Mr. Belvedere.

He tossed the picture onto Elise's lap.

Olivia stood next to Elise. She ran a hand through her blonde curls and laughed. "Do you recognize it?" she asked.

"D-do I—recognize—w-what?" Elise asked, stuttering from fear.

Kate turned her head toward her sister and said, "She's talking about the stuffed animal in the picture. Mr. Belvedere."

"It was my gift to my son when he was in the hospital," said the man, thumping the top of the bat in his free hand, then he raised it to remove the mask. The elephant head drooped in his hands. He smiled.

For the first time, Kate had a clear view of him, of his face. And she hated what she saw.

Darren Riggler.

He stood there in front of them, by the large, mirrored lantern in the center of the room, holding the sagging, bloody elephant head in one hand the bat in the other. Both his eyes looked blackened, and his nose was swollen and bent.

"You!" Elise said. "I knew you weren't as dumb as you look."

Darren stared at her for several seconds in silence and then spoke slowly. "His little body looked battered and bloody." His voice grew stronger, louder, no longer inhibited by the mask, as he continued, saying, "As if someone picked up a baseball bat and beat the life out of him."

"*Your* son?" A soft gasp escaped Kate's throat. As the truth of his words sank in, she recited a line from his song. "We shoulda run away; we coulda been happy. If we got away, I coulda made you love me." She bit her lower lip, putting the pieces together. "You weren't singing about me, were you?"

Darren shook his head. He raised a hand to touch his swollen nose and flinched. "I almost had him out of the bar that night. Do you realize if I'd succeeded in taking him, he'd still be alive right now?"

Kate struggled with the ropes around her wrists. "You're talking about kidnapping."

"I'm talking about taking my son back." He smiled, flashing his crooked grin. His chipped front tooth looked more like a fang. "Oh, Katie, you just don't get it. I knew you wouldn't understand. That's why I didn't want to involve you. I asked you to leave. I begged you to leave, didn't I? Didn't I ask you to meet me in Fort Lauderdale? I tried to get you out of here, but you wouldn't listen."

Kate leaned forward. "You don't have to do this."

As she said that, the tapping of claws on the metal spiral steps caught her attention, and she turned her head just in time to see Doc scamper onto the landing and launch himself at Darren, screeching.

Darren swung the bat and knocked the squirrel out of the air.

Doc struck the wall and tumbled to the floor. He didn't move.

Kate yelled, and Darren laughed. He thumped the top of the bat into his hand again and said, "We aren't playing that game again."

Kate looked over at Doc's limp body, then took a deep breath to collect herself. Her mind raced. She turned to Darren." W-What have you done?"

"Justice," he said. He leaned the bat against the wall. "I delivered justice."

Kate paused, trying to comprehend his words. "You murdered Forrest Frazier," she said.

"He had to die. For what he did, he had to die."

"Why?"

"He murdered my son, Katie," he said. "He murdered my son. His little body looked battered and bloody as if someone had picked up a baseball bat and beat the life out of him."

"The accident?" Elise's voice trembled. "You were there that night. You saw him."

"Look who joined the party." Olivia chuckled at her joke. "Darren and me, we were Noah's birth parents."

"He was *my* little boy," Elise screamed, sobbing. "Mine."

"You stole him from us," Olivia said. "I shoulda beat your ass till hell wouldn't have it."

"You," Kate said, staring wide-eyed at the young blonde in the flower print dress, now dirty and tattered from the weather. "You're Samantha. The crazy girl who left me those threatening messages and warned me to stay out of Darren's life."

"You should've heeded my warnings," Olivia, no—*Samantha*—said. "But you guys came right back in and messed with our lives all over again, didn't you?"

"I don't know what you're talking about," Kate said.

"I'm talking about our baby." Samantha spat as she spoke. "I'm talking about Noah. Elise and Redd stole him away from us."

"We adopted him." Elise could barely get the words out through her tears.

"You killed him." Darren leaned into her face; screamed at her now. "His little body looked battered and bloody as if someone picked up a baseball bat and beat the life out of him."

Elise looked away.

Darren stepped back and stood straight again. He wiped his mouth with the back of his forearm and winced when he brushed the tip of his nose. He shook it off, seeming to refocus his anger. "You and your husband—careless, irresponsible parents—killed my son," he said, a little calmer now but no less threatening. "I tried to save him. But I didn't act quickly enough."

Kate watched him. If she could keep him talking, maybe she could figure a way out of this. Keep him from swinging that bat. Keep him from .... "That night at Brewsky Bill's," she said, the pieces falling in place. "That night when Noah disappeared, you knew then that he was your son."

"Oh, Katie, we didn't meet by accident," he said. 'When I learned the Tylers adopted my son, I tracked them down. I knew if I got close to you, the lonely, single workaholic, I could keep tabs on the couple who snatched my son and wait for my chance to get him back."

"You were stalking us?" Elise asked.

"I was accessing you, like when we had dinner at your house, Raw Meat," he said. "I was going to take my son that night at the Brewsky Bills. He could have escaped with me, and none of this would've had to happen. No pain. No sadness. No deaths." Darren spoke with a malevolence that turned Kate's blood to ice water. "But you stopped that when you found us in the alley."

"You used me," Kate said.

"I had to stay close to my son. Keep tabs on Elise and Redd." He actually looked sincere. "I never wanted to hurt you, Katie. I loved you. I really did."

"You loved her?" Samantha asked, her shrill voice rising two octaves.

"If you loved me, if you still do," Kate said, "then take this up with me. Let Elise go."

"Elise has blood on her hands." He pointed at her as he shouted. "She was supposed to protect my son, but her incompetence led to his murder."

"Noah's death was our fault, Darren," Kate said. "Yours and mine. He's dead because of us. We set that whole night in motion."

"He was taken from me," he shouted at her. She was getting to him, and he couldn't control his teetering emotions, adding, "If he'd been with me, I would've protected him."

Fear and anger knotted inside her, and Kate spoke deliberately to hide it. "Maybe Elise was driving. Maybe Redd's call distracted her. Maybe Forrest Frazier was drunk and should not have been on the road in the first place, but you and I were the ones who took Noah out of his home that night."

"No!" Darren screamed.

Kate continued. "If we hadn't done that, he would've been safe in his bed instead of on the road in the middle of the night and struck by that drunk driver."

"I should've taken him that night." Darren's eyes intensified. "We were almost away when you found us in the alley. You took him out of my arms and gave him to that bitch, who got him killed." He screamed in Elise's face again. "You were not his mother."

He spit on her.

Elise struggled and moved her head back. "Don't you think that hurt me as much as it hurt you? That killed me inside."

"No, it didn't kill you!" He waved his hands as if he could reach out and wrap them around her throat. "You and your sister are still here. My son is not. My son is dead."

"You can't bring him back by killing us," Kate said.

"No, I can't bring him back. But I could do the next best thing … take down everyone involved in his death."

Kate shook her head. "Forrest Frazier deserved to be locked up in jail for the rest of his life, but he didn't deserve to die."

"Yes, Kate, he did," Elise said. Her voice trembled. "He murdered my son and deserved to die for it… And so do I, for allowing it to happen."

Kate whipped her head toward her sister, not believing what she just heard.

Darren smiled at Elise. "Good girl. Wise girl. Your turn is coming."

"Okay, you murdered Forrest Frazier," Kate said as her eyes met his. She felt a shock run through her. "And Jasper Wade? The attorney who kept him out of jail?"

"And his business partner," Samantha said with a laugh.

"And what's in it for you?" Kate watched Samantha as she strolled over to Darren and draped an arm around his shoulder. "Why pretend to be his daughter?" Kate asked.

Samantha smiled. "Oh, I don't know. For the fun of it. Because Darren asked me to."

"I needed her here, in Sienna Key," he said.

"But why?" Sick fear coiled in the pit of Kate's stomach. She studied Darren, his fierce eyes bright with hysteria. How could she have so completely misjudged him? Been so heinously fooled by him? Samantha … Kate understood. Samantha, all wild-eyed and frenetic, oozed batshit crazy from her pores. But Darren? He left her reeling. She turned to Samantha. "Why pretend to be Olivia Wade?"

Darren turned to Samantha and wrapped her in his arms, kissed her, then looked back at Kate. "Because," he said. "It kept her distracted. Kept her occupied."

Kate still couldn't get her head wrapped around it. "To what end?"

"I needed her out of her home and keeping tabs on you and your family while I completed the next phase." Darren grinned. "I had to handle something … something that would be difficult for her to accept."

"What?" Samantha stopped smiling. A swift shadow of comprehension swept across her face.

He shrugged. "I had to, babe."

His swollen nose appeared to grow larger.

"No!" Samantha broke from his arms and took a step back.

"That old man separated us." He reached for her, but she moved further away from him. Taking a deep breath, he seemed to collect his patience and spoke to her like he was scolding a puppy. "Your old man tried to break us up. He forced you to give our child up for adoption. And I needed your attention focused elsewhere while I righted that wrong."

"The old man?" Kate asked. "You're talking about Howie Logan, the victim in Atlanta."

"My daddy…" Samantha backed up against the wall. She raised a hand to her cover her mouth,

"He was a monster. You know that," Darren said to her. "He forced you to give your baby away."

She screamed at him. "You killed my daddy?"

"He deserved to die. He was just as guilty as Forrest Frazier or Jasper Wade or Redd Tyler."

Kate stiffened. "Redd?"

Elise cried out too and exploded into a sudden burst of fury and restrained energy, desperately trying to break free of the ropes binding her to the chair.

Darren and Samantha were too preoccupied to notice.

"My daddy? Not my daddy!" Samantha raised her fists and pounded them against his chest, screaming without words, spit trailing behind her.

Startled, Darren retreated toward the stairwell. His last cry split the air: "Don't!"

She continued hitting him, pushing him. "You killed my daddy?"

He fell, somersaulting backward from one step to the next. Samantha lunged down the staircase after him.

Kate looked at Elise. It was now or never.

CHAPTER FORTY-TWO

Kate wiggled her wrists and squeezed one hand free of the rope. She untied her hands and rose to her feet. Shouting echoed from the stairwell, but she ignored it and focused on freeing Elise. When they were both standing, Kate looked over the railing.

Samantha and Darren splashed into the edge of the water, rising on the staircase. She slapped him from an upper step as he raised his arms and grasped hold of either side of her face. He threw her down and held her head under. Her blonde hair floated on top of the water as her arms and legs flailed about.

Kate took a step toward the spiral staircase. Elise clutched her arm and shook her head, giving Kate a silent warning. She pulled Kate away from the stairwell.

"We need to get out of here," Elise said, going to the window. Curved windowpanes wrapped around the entire room, looking out in every direction.

Kate looked down. Water rushed below. A small skiff tied to the perimeter fence bobbed in the raging current. They had to reach it, Kate thought as she helped Elise up onto the counter. Together, they kicked out a windowpane. Elise slipped through it and out onto the narrow ledge first. Kate started to follow when Darren appeared at the top of the stairwell. He held the baseball bat in his hands.

"Hey," he yelled. "Where do you think you're going?"

Kate turned toward him.

Without regard for his size or strength, she hurdled into him with the force of her whole body, baring teeth, and battering fists. She slammed into his chest. He staggered and fell. His hand flew open. The bat dropped and rolled behind the lantern.

Elise poked her head back through the window and yelled something.

Kate found the bat. Gripped it with both hands. Aimed for the lantern. Smashed the mirror. Glass shattered. Light exploded in every direction. Brilliant. Blinding. She averted her eyes. Blinked. Raised a hand. Flashes of color burst before her.

God willing, it blinded Darren as well.

"Come on," Elise yelled from the window.

Kate blinked. Gripped the bat with both hands. Blinked again. Tried to block out the light. She scanned the room. Nothing but white. Where was he?

Elise screamed again.

Kate dropped the bat and rushed to her. Doc scampered out of the glaring light and joined her as she climbed out the window. She held him and balanced onto the narrow ledge. The entire structure rumbled. The wind pushed her with a sudden angry force. She slipped. Elise grabbed her arm, kept her from falling.

"We need to get to his boat," Kate said. She pointed to the skiff bouncing on the waves.

In the darkness, she couldn't see the water, but she could hear it rushing below. A mass of something—*the remains of the billboard?*—swept past.

"Do you think we can?" Elise asked. "It's a long jump down, and God knows how deep the water is."

The lighthouse shook again.

Kate placed a hand on the wall. It sounded like a ship trying to break loose from its moorings. "We can't stay here," she said, looking down again.

The roaring current would be hard to fight, but if they could get to the skiff, they should be safe. Maybe they could wait it out. A rescue boat might find them when day broke. Maybe. If they were lucky.

"We've got to try," Kate said, pointing.

"The water sounds pretty violent," Elise said. "I don't think we'll be able to swim in it, much less make it to that boat."

Perched on Kate's shoulder, Doc chattered as though he agreed.

"We're not going to be able to swim." Kate stared down at the swirling black waters. A large wood plank rushed by before the violent currents swept it away. "We'll have to let the current take us to it."

Elise lowered her head and cringed. "We're going to get so pummeled they won't even be able to use us for spare parts," she said.

The wind picked up again, and glass exploded behind them. The other windows rattled.

"We can't stay here," Kate screamed, her hair whipping violently around her head.

Elise nodded as the groaning within the lighthouse grew louder.

"On the count of three, we'll jump," Kate said. She took hold of Doc and clutched him protectively in her right hand.

The sisters exchanged nervous smiles.

"Good luck, Kid." Kate raised her left hand and extended her pinky finger. Elise hooked her pinky over Kate's. Letting go, Kate moved to the brink of the ledge, took a deep breath, and jumped.

The dark floodwaters swallowed her. Her head rose above the waves and she gasped. Doc climbed on top her wet head. Swept away with the force of the current, she flapped her arms and legs to stay at the surface. She didn't have a chance to see Elise jump in behind her. Frantic, Doc dug his single claw into her scalp, hanging on for dear life.

She was already out of breath when she glimpsed the skiff raging toward her. She fought the current to it. Reached for it. Missed. Swept past it and grasped a wood fence post. Doc squealed. She used both hands to hang on, fighting the powerful forces that tried to tear her away.

Looking back, she screamed for Elise. The water churned around her. Every time she opened her mouth, saltwater rushed down her throat. She couldn't see her sister.

Darren appeared on the upper ledge of the lighthouse. He jumped. Splashed into the dark water. The current rushed him toward her.

He reached and grabbed her hair. "Nine to Five, bitch," he said.

"No!" she screamed and punched him square in the nose.

He cried out. Blood splattered like a popped cyst. He recoiled, then lunged for her again, baring his teeth.

Doc squealed, jumped from her head, and pounced on his face. He shrieked and released her. Doc shrieked again and bit into Darren's face. He let out a gurgled cry as his head disappeared under the swirling waves. He was gone, and so was Doc.

Treading the water with one arm to keep her head from going under, Kate wrapped her other around the post with all her strength. She screamed for Doc. Turned her head, spat out water. Waited. Neither Darren nor the squirrel emerged. She turned her head again and spit out sea water, then called out for Elise.

The skiff surprised her. Struck her. Hard. She lost the grip on the fence post and submerged deep in the churning waters. The current took her. Swept her away. She fought to raise her head above the waves. Swallowed more water. Plummeted deeper. Fought back to the surface.

The whirl of a boat engine rose over the roar of the rushing water. A light cut the darkness.

She blinked water from her eyes. A blurry police boat headed toward her. The light shined in her eyes. Jared? Jensen? Trace? A hand reached for her. Grasped her arm. Pulled her from the water.

Lying in the boat, she coughed up salt water and squinted to better see the man standing over her.

Doogie's face came into focus.

He put a blanket over her.

She sat up and coughed again. "Elise." She struggled to speak. Her throat burned. "She's in the water."

Doogie shined his flashlight across the waves. The boat rocked violently side to side, and he steadied himself as he held the flashlight.

Kate peered into the swirling waters. Nothing. They circled the lighthouse, calling for Elise. But there was no sign of her … of anyone.

Kate laid back down, shivering. Without a word, Doogie revved up the motor just as she passed out.

CHAPTER FORTY-THREE

Kate opened her eyes and threw up saltwater. She got her bearings and looked around the motorboat. "Elise," she cried. "Where's Elise?"

"I'll find her," Doogie said. He pulled up to a crude dock that had been constructed on the mainland for volunteers rescuing stranded people. "I'm not giving up," he added.

Two men lifted Kate out of the police boat. Another waved for an ambulance. She raised her arms, stopping them as they tried to lift her onto a gurney.

"My sister's still out there, by the lighthouse," she said.

The two men tending to her glanced at each other, and one of them shook his head.

"I'm going back out there," Doogie said to them. He pushed the boat from the dock. "I'll find her," he called out as he cranked the motor and sped away.

Kate let her head rest on the gurney. She trembled, and her lips felt numb. Her fingers were blue and aching. As they lifted her into the waiting ambulance, she lost consciousness again.

When she woke, paramedics were rolling her down a hospital corridor. They left her beside the wall, among other patients lying on stretchers. People around her moaned and sobbed. She turned on her side to face the wall, trying to block out the misery. She could only think of Elise. Did she make it to the skiff? Did the dark waters carry her away? Did she even jump? The current had been more powerful than Kate had predicted, and she almost didn't make it. What chances did Elise have?

A nurse finally came up beside her and took her vitals. "Name?" she asked.

Kate answered the questions as the nurse examined a deep cut on her forearm. It must've happened when the skiff hit her. She wasn't even aware her arm had been sliced open.

"This'll need stitches," the nurse said. "I have to clean it first."

"My sister…" Kate flinched. She couldn't stop shivering, and her voice sounded scratchy. "Elise Tyler. Is she here?"

"I'll check. For now, you need to rest," the nurse said, placing a heated blanket over her.

Kate let the warmth seep into her core as she closed her eyes. She listened to the nurses' talk.

"She has a laceration on her arm that requires stitches. And she has a contusion on her head. She may have a concussion."

Another voice answered, and Kate tried to hang on. She wanted to ask if they'd heard anything about her sister, but her mouth wouldn't respond, and she couldn't open her eyes. For the first time in hours, she felt comfortable and relaxed. And the voices drifted away.

When she woke again, daylight streamed through the crowded hallway. She still lay on the stretcher beside dozens of other people lined up against the walls. A bandage covered her forearm.

Trace surprised her when he spoke, and she found him standing beside her. "How you hold'n up?" he asked.

She gazed at him and at Nellie seated in a wheelchair by his side, holding the baby.

Kate struggled to sit. "You had the—"

"She came last night at the shelter," Nellie said.

"She?" Kate stared at the newborn wrapped securely in a blanket. Her face was barely visible. Still, she was simply the cutest baby Kate had ever seen.

Trace nodded. "You called it. Little Thomas turned out to be a girl."

"I told you." Kate's eyes teared up. "Oh my God, she's beautiful. What'd you decide for her name?"

"Sebastian."

Kate scrunched her face and jerked back on the cot. "No. You can't."

"He's joking," Nellie said. "It's Dakota Rose. Dakota Rose Guerra."

Trace said, "And baby Dakota Rose wasn't going to let a historic storm wash out her big debut. She didn't exactly make it easy, though."

Kate laughed through her tears and waved at the bright-eyed baby. "Of course, she didn't. She's beautiful. Hi, Dakota. I'm your Aunt Kate."

A nurse interrupted them and wheeled Nellie away.

Trace leaned down to whisper in Kate's ear. "We haven't found Elise yet," he said, moving a tendril of hair from her face, "but we're still looking. We haven't given up."

Kate grasped his hand and said, "She was right behind me when we jumped out of the lighthouse."

Fear gripped her. Jumping from the lighthouse into the floodwaters was the hardest thing she'd ever done, and she didn't want to think about how close she came to drowning. Could Elise have been as fortunate? Was she as strong?

"We're checking other hospitals," Trace said to comfort her. "Redd is here. He was attacked and severely beaten, but he's stable."

Kate heard him but could only think of her sister. Trace hugged her and promised to check on her later.

She remained in the hospital for the rest of the day, but the rooms were full, so she stayed in the corridor with numerous other patients. Her head ached, and she floated between groggy consciousness and nightmares about Darren, the lighthouse, and the storm. Nurses woke her almost every hour.

"What about my sister?" Kate asked every time they took her vitals.

"We have no record of her here," each nurse said. "Lots of people are out looking for family and loved ones, including your sister."

She knew what that meant. Eventually, Elise would stumble into the hospital, or someone would find her body. Until then, all Kate could do was wait.

"How's Redd?" she finally asked late in the day. "Can I see him?"

"Not yet," the nurse said. "He's stable, and you need to rest right now."

She drifted to sleep, wondering if he knew Elise was missing.

When Kate woke again, night had fallen. She wasn't sure how late it was or how long she'd been out, and her eyes were blurry. As they cleared, she peered down the corridor. Something was going on at the emergency entrance. Someone was coming in.

Doogie.

And he carried Elise in his arms.

Paramedics ran to them and placed Elise on a gurney.

Kate's heart stopped. She flipped off the stretcher and limped down the hallway. Reaching the entrance, she fell to her knees beside her sister. Her fingers brushed Elise's muddy face. Unconscious but breathing. Kate squeezed her hand.

"She'll be okay," the paramedic said before they wheeled her away.

Kate turned to Doogie and hugged him. "Thank you, Dad," she whispered. "Thank you."

* * *

In the end, Hurricane Sebastian had hit the city with lightning speed—much faster than predicted—and with greater force. There was no cell service, and most roads were either blocked by fallen trees and debris or completely flooded.

For a week, as the state returned to business as usual, police searched for Darren Riggler's body. Authorities assumed it had been swept out to sea when the floodwaters receded.

His van was found abandoned on a Louisiana country road, in the middle of an intersection—a crossroad—with no clue as to who left it there or where the driver went next.

* * *

Kate and Elise were discharged from the hospital together. Redd was still recovering, but Elise was well enough to leave, and Kate's arm was bandaged. Trace picked them up at the hospital, with Tug and Bert waiting excitedly in his patrol car.

He drove Kate up to Fort Hamer, but her houseboat was gone. It had blown away. Nothing remained of any of the boats on the Manatee River.

"You and the abandoned dog and the one-eyed owl can stay with Nellie and me," Trace told her. "We'll make room for you … despite the new baby. And the fact that the power is still out throughout much of Sienna Key."

"We need to check on The Bluegill," Kate said quietly and joined Elise, waiting in the squad car.

Downtown remained deserted. Rubbish and broken glass littered the streets and sidewalks. The shops looked battered, but their interiors remained intact.

Miraculously, The Bluegill had suffered no structural damage—just broken windows and missing shingles. And beyond it, the Widow Rock Lighthouse soared tall on the horizon. After all, it had been through—the crashing waves, the crumbling walls—Kate couldn't believe it still stood.

She turned back to Trace. "I have to stay here," she said, "with Elise at The Bluegill."

Trace parked among the debris and helped Kate, Elise, Tug, and Bert out of his car before saying goodbye. Broken limbs, split poles, and muddy trash lay strewn across the yard. They were careful not to step on the downed power lines; the power was still off, but just in case, one was still live somehow.

Doogie waited for them on the front porch, and Kate and Elise stepped up onto it with Tug and Bert. He hugged the girls and walked them inside and locked the door behind them.

"I've fixed the window in Noah's room," he said. "Tomorrow, I'll start making repairs to the roof and siding. We'll get this place cleaned up and looking like home again."

Without responding, Kate walked upstairs to the third floor. She entered the guest room that had once been her childhood bedroom and collapsed onto the bed, and she didn't leave. She stayed there with the curtains drawn, hiding in the dark.

Linus and Zach Vaughn stopped by to check on her. Elise led them up into Kate's room.

"We saw Dakota Rose," Linus said, sitting down on the bed beside her.

"My dad helped deliver her," Zach added. "He told me how he helped my mom deliver me in a Home Depot during a blizzard that shut the whole city down."

Linus laughed. "Well, we've got a plane to catch. The Tampa airport's reopened, and we're on the first flight home."

They headed for the door as Linus asked, "Where we going to vacation next?"

"I don't know," Zach said. "Would you rather be left behind in the bush on an African safari or in the middle of the ocean on a scuba trip?"

"Neither, Dad," Zach said and closing the door behind them.

With the power restored, life slowly got back to normal in Sienna Key. Kate, though, remained locked in the guest room, often sitting in the dark with curtains drawn. She hardly ate and lost fifteen pounds within a month. She wouldn't speak to anyone and kept her iPhone turned off.

Doogie came into her room and woke her one afternoon. At that point, she wasn't sure if she'd been there, three days or three weeks.

"I've been fixing the damage to the place," he said. "You and Elise should be able to open back up for business soon."

Kate turned toward the wall and thrust a pillow over her head.

Doogie said, "Redd will be coming home tomorrow, so I'm leaving The Bluegill."

She flipped the pillow away from her face and looked up at him. "You're leaving us?" she asked. "Again?"

"I'm joining a construction crew," he said. "I'm going to stay in one of the temporary housing trailers and start rebuilding my life while we rebuild downtown."

Kate wasn't sure what to say. "You're staying here? In Sienna Key?"

"I talked to Elise, and I want to stay near the both of you. I have a lot of time to make up for, if you'll have me."

Kate felt empty inside. She knew she should feel something—elation of having her father back, outrage that he thought he could just step back into their lives. She should feel *something*. However, she didn't feel anything at all, so she rolled over onto her side in the bed, faced the wall, and shut her eyes. She heard Doogie exit the room and the door shut behind him.

Redd came home the following day. His arm was in a cast, and he wore a neck and back brace. He wasn't able to walk upstairs yet, but Elise let Kate know that he wasn't happy about the hospital bills. She tried to coax Kate to come downstairs to see him, but she refused.

Trace and Nellie stopped by with the baby, but Kate didn't speak to them. She hadn't spoken to either since the day she left the hospital. He was gravely alarmed. Kate was in bad shape, worse than he feared.

Even Ian stopped by. She wanted nothing to do with him.

She didn't want to see anyone, not even Tug or Bert.

Elise finally barged into the room. Kate told her she wasn't ready to talk, so Elise sat beside her on the bed and opened *Where the Darkness Hides*. She flipped the pages and cleared her throat. Kate said nothing in response and just listened to Elise read.

When Elise finished, she got off the bed and left the room.

The next day, she barged into the room, and Kate still ignored her.

After listening to Elise read for a solid week, out of the blue, Kate asked about Bert.

"He's missing an eye," Elise said.

Kate chuckled a little at that. "And Tug?" she asked.

"He likes to eat," Elise said.

Four months after Hurricane Sebastian had ripped their lives apart, she stepped out of the dark bedroom. Elise and Redd were in the garage, rebuilding the trainset. Kate joined them and helped glue model houses back together. Then she put the leash on Tug and left the Bluegill.

She looked somewhat normal again, although she certainly didn't feel normal yet. She now had an ugly scar on her forearm to match the one on her shoulder, and her mind was equally scarred and needed time to fully heal, if it ever would.

Downtown Sienna Key had people bustling about. Shops held sidewalk sales. Families visited the beach. And the Widow Rock Lighthouse stood on the horizon. She stared at it and was surprised how little had changed.

Tug barked at a squirrel, and it scampered up an oak tree. Standing on its haunches, it chirped at her then disappeared into the foliage. She thought of Doc and gave him a silent thank you. Wherever he was, she hoped he felt loved. She knew she did.

Entering the Bear's Den, she found Travel Agent had hung a WELCOME BACK banner above the reception desk.

Trace, Jared, Jensen, and even Intern Ernie waited for her on the dock in the back of the building and yelled "Surprise!" when she approached. Tug greeted everyone, wagging his stubby tail. Travel Agent brought out a cake. Intern Ernie had unfolded several chairs for a safety class and handed Kate a stack of folders. Trace took them away from her.

"I told you not to touch my stuff," he said, stern as ever. "You bent the White Fang all to hell."

"Well, Chief, like you once told me, you have to play the ball wherever it lands." Kate nodded as people arrived on the dock, taking seats and flipping through the folders Intern Ernie had laid out on the chairs. Jared and Jensen cut the cake and shared it with their guests. A lanky teenage boy with sun-bleached shaggy hair and sunglasses, along with his group of friends, were among them.

Kate called for everyone's attention and welcomed them to her safety class. "Hello, boaters," she said, rubbing her shoulder. It was more out of habit than ache. "I'm Kate Parks, boat safety instructor for the Sienna Key law enforcement."

She smiled like she meant it.

ABOUT THE AUTHOR

JC Gatlin lives in Tampa, Florida, and writes mystery novels that include sunny Florida locales and quirky locals as characters. His last novel, *H_NGM_N: Murder is the Word*, won the coveted Florida Royal Palm Literary Award for Best Mystery in 2019. He is active in the Florida Writer's Association and is a board member on the Florida Writer's Foundation, a charity organization that fights illiteracy.

www.JCGatlin.com

Facebook: https://www.facebook.com/AuthorJcGatlin
Instagram: https://www.instagram.com/jcgatlinauthor/
YouTube: https://www.youtube.com/c/JCGatlin
Goodreads: https://www.goodreads.com/jc_gatlin

Made in the USA
Columbia, SC
10 May 2021

37073089R00150